"What if I'm not sensible?"

Nigel started. "What do you mean?"

"I mean just what I said. What if I'm not sensible? Or rather, what if I've tired of being sensible? I have never before believed in silly nonsense like magic or fate. You, Mr. Cavendish," Felicity met his gaze, "have persuaded me otherwise."

"I have?" he said slowly.

"Indeed you have."

She wasn't at all sure this was the right moment to tell him that she had decided his appearance in the night was fate. But she already knew, without question, without doubt, he was the man for her.

"Do you care to elaborate?"

She picked up her glass and took a long sip of champagne, then shook her head. "No."

He frowned. "No?"

"No."

He narrowed his eyes. "Will you ever?"

"My dear, Mr. Cavendish." She looked into his eyes and smiled in a slow, provocative manner that came from somewhere deep inside her she never knew existed. "You may count on it."

By Victoria Alexander

VICTORIA ALEXANDER

What A Lady Wants

AVON BOOKS
An Imprint of HarperCollins*Publishers*

AVON BOOKS
An Imprint of HarperCollins*Publishers*
10 East 53rd Street
New York, New York 10022-5299

This book is dedicated with thanks
to Brian and Karen Grogan,
for brilliance, wisdom,
and knowing how to have a good time
on land or sea.

Prologue

London
April 1854

"And now there are three," Oliver Leighton, the Earl of Norcroft, said under his breath.

"Three." The Honorable Nigel Cavendish, heir to Viscount Cavendish, echoed the single word with a distinct note of disgust in his voice.

"You both realize there is a positive aspect to this," said Daniel Sinclair, the one American among them, and no doubt the only American currently present in the gentlemen's club they favored in the heart of London. Two skeptical gazes turned toward him. "It could have been one of us."

"Hear, hear," Cavendish said and raised his glass.

The men had gathered to lament the passing of one of their own from the joys of bachelorhood to the bonds of holy matrimony. Although, if truth were told, the gentleman in question, Lord Warton, would have chuckled at the morose expressions on the faces of his three friends, especially as he was so blissfully happy. He was even now off somewhere in the south of Spain, no doubt enjoying the charms of the lovely new Lady Warton.

"He does forfeit his share of the tontine as well," Oliver pointed out.

Sinclair scoffed. "I very much doubt if he cares."

Together with Warton, who had originally proposed the idea, the four men had formed a tontine based entirely on their mutual aversion to marriage. The last man to remain unwed, the last man standing, as it were, would win the tontine.

"Ah yes." Cavendish swirled the brandy in his glass. "One shilling from each of us, including Warton, for a grand total of four shillings."

"And there is a bottle of Cognac at stake as well." Sinclair grinned. "That alone is worth the effort of remaining happily unwed if indeed any of us needed further encouragement."

"Let us not forget, gentlemen, the four shillings and the Cognac are merely a symbol," Oliver said. "The true prize is—"

"Freedom," Cavendish said firmly. "The right to do exactly as we please when we please without having to answer to anyone."

And who would value that more than Cavendish? Of the three remaining members of the tontine, Nigel Cavendish was the one among them most prone to scandalous behavior, particularly with members of the opposite sex. More specifically, with widows, or with wives of a certain persuasion who saw no need to remain faithful to husbands who, more often then not, were seeking their own entertainment outside the bonds of marriage. Such amorous adventures had landed Cavendish in the center of scandal on any number of occasions, and Oliver could name several instances when he had very nearly been shot as well.

Oliver had been friends with Cavendish since their school days and had to admit the man hadn't changed at all through the years. He remained the fun-loving scoundrel he'd been in his youth. Oliver had wondered now and again what would happen when Cavendish at last inherited his title and the responsibility for the Cavendish family, investments, and fortune. Still, Cavendish was a good sort and a good friend.

"And yet, Cavendish, one has to wonder if freedom of that nature is worth the trouble," Sinclair said thoughtfully. "I suspect Warton and Helmsley would both say the love of a good woman, the prospects of family, a trusted partner for the rest of your days, even companionship, are well worth the sacrifice of some liberties. You flit from woman to woman, and what have you to show for your troubles?"

Cavendish grinned. "Memories, old chap, some damn fine memories."

Oliver laughed. "He has you there."

"Indeed he does." Sinclair chuckled.

Daniel Sinclair had come into their circle when his father had arranged for him to marry Oliver's cousin. Neither Sinclair nor Oliver's cousin, Fiona, was in favor of that, which was fortunate, as Fiona had fallen in love with Lord Helmsley, an old friend of Oliver's. Still, Sinclair and Oliver had found, in spite of their cultural differences, common ground, and had become friends in the months since his arrival in England.

Sinclair was in London seeking investors for a railroad venture in America, and thus far all the members of the tontine, as well as Helmsley, had invested. The American expected it would take several more months to acquire the financing he needed, then he planned to return to America to develop his railroad. There wasn't a doubt in Oliver's mind that Sinclair would increase their fortunes substantially.

"What do you think, Norcroft?" Cavendish studied his friend. "Which is worth the trouble? Liberty or love?"

"It's entirely too early in the evening and I am far too sober for a question like that." Oliver took a sip of his brandy. "No, a question of that nature should only be discussed very late at night, after indulging in an excess of spirits. When one sees the world in an entirely different light and thinks one's own observations to be both insightful and brilliant."

"Still, you must admit, it is an intriguing question," Sinclair said mildly.

"And I for one would like to know what you think."

Cavendish eyed Oliver curiously. "Come now, Norcroft, what do you say? Freedom or love?"

"Very well then." Oliver considered the question for a moment. "I think it's all relative and very much dependent on one's position in life. You, for example." He met Cavendish's gaze. "You have yet to come into your title and the responsibilities that accompany it. You have the freedom, and the money I might add, to do precisely as you wish, and you do. You're charming and great fun to be with and a good friend, but your life to this point has consisted entirely of frivolity and nothing of substance whatsoever."

"That's rather harsh." Cavendish winced. "True, but harsh."

"Love, for you, would force you to change your entire existence," Oliver added.

Cavendish grinned. "And therefore definitely not worth the trouble."

Oliver turned his gaze toward Sinclair. "You have a father who has built a financial empire, yet you have not depended on that. You have seized the freedom you need to strive for success by your own hand and in the process have taken on a great many responsibilities. It's quite admirable and very American of you. For you, love would be most inconvenient."

Sinclair chuckled. "Yes, I suppose it would."

"As for myself." Oliver sipped his brandy and thought for a moment. "I think I fall somewhere between the two of you. I have inherited my position and my fortune. I am head of my family and have the responsibilities inherent in that. Therefore my freedoms are already limited. For me, love would neither change my life nor would it be at all awkward. Indeed, as I have said before"—he smiled ruefully—"I am not averse to marriage."

"Then you shall, no doubt, be the next to go." Cavendish smiled in a smug manner. "Which relieves my mind greatly."

Oliver laughed. "While I am not fleeing for my life at the mere mention of wedded bliss, I am not actively seeking a wife either. I fear, gentlemen, I am something of a romantic. I have no doubt that one day I shall meet a woman I cannot live without. As I have not done so thus far"—he shrugged—"I suspect it will be some time before I plunge into matrimony. Therefore." He raised his glass. "I fully intend on drinking a toast to the rest of you when I become the sole proprietor of the Cognac."

"What an amazing coincidence." Sinclair grinned. "I was planning the exact same thing."

"I would advise both of you to change your plans," Cavendish said firmly. "I fully intend to be the last man standing, and I do hate to lose a wager. Especially one that is as suited to me as this one. Why, I can practically taste the Cognac now."

"We can debate who will be the last to fall all we wish." Oliver considered the other men thoughtfully. "A much more interesting question is . . . who will be next?"

One

What a lady really wants is a man who will make every day an adventure.
Lady Felicity Melville

"You should know, before I go any further, that this is contrary to everything I have ever believed in, be that God or science or nature itself." Lady Felicity Melville braced her hands on the stone balustrade of the tiny balcony off her bedchamber and stared up into the night sky. "Still, desperate times and all that. Not that I am precisely desperate, mind you, although I will admit that when one reaches the age of three-and-twenty and is still unwed, desperation begins to nip at one's heels like an ill-mannered spaniel.

"I'm really quite sensible, you know. I don't believe in superstitious nonsense; I never have." She straightened and crossed her arms over her chest. "Fairies, elves, spells, those sorts of things. It's all absurd, and under other circumstances, I would never think of placing my future, my fate, on the ridiculous notion of wishing upon a star."

Felicity stared at the star she had selected for the aforementioned ridiculous notion. Certainly, if this had even the vaguest possibility of working, it would require the perfect star. Not one that was overly bright. Obviously a too bright star would attract no end of attention and, therefore, no end of wishes, and would be—Felicity cringed at the absurdity of the thought—rather used up, as it were. On the other hand, a star that was scarcely noticeable might not have the strength needed for a wish of this magnitude.

She had resisted the urge to use her telescope, positioned as always in her room directly behind the open balcony doors, to select a star. It didn't seem quite in the proper spirit to use the telescope for this purpose, although the spyglass that she'd discovered as a child in her father's desk, the very instrument that had begun her study of the stars, might be acceptable. The spyglass had apparently once been used by a sea captain or sailor or perhaps even a pirate, something of that nature, and therefore carried a sense of romance that might suit this endeavor. Even now, the instrument was within reach on the table beside the doors to the balcony. Still, this wasn't science, and science should have nothing to do with it. This was magic or perhaps faith or even—she grimaced—desperation.

"I should perhaps explain the situation before we continue. I am, well, the last of my kind." Felicity sighed in an overly dramatic manner. But then this did seem to call for an excess of drama. "Who would have imagined that I would be the last among those girls I shared my first season with to remain unmarried? If I had been unkind enough to have wagered—although I would never have done such a thing, but if I had—I would have placed my money on Mary St. James."

Mary was a quiet, unassuming girl with an unexceptional appearance and a dowry to match. But Mary had snared the heir to a dukedom—a distant heir but an heir nonetheless—when their first season had barely begun. Now she had two children and a third on the way.

Felicity shook her head. "What on earth happened to the years between then and now? This will be my sixth season." She thought for a moment. "No, my fifth, I missed last year. Grand tour, you know. Quite lovely, really. And I am ever so much more cultured and polished now." She wrinkled her nose. "Not that I expect it to make much difference."

Still, she had noticed an increase in attention from the gentlemen present at the handful of social events she had attended thus far this season. Perhaps the polish acquired in travel did indeed matter. She certainly felt more assured and confident than she had in the past. And her Italian was much improved as well.

Felicity rested her back against the doorjamb. "Eugenia says"—she glanced at the star—"Eugenia Wentwhistle, or rather Lady Kilbourne now, my dearest friend in the world, says my expectations are entirely too high. And if I truly wish to marry—and have no doubt of that, I do wish to marry—I shall lower my standards. I will concede her point, but I really don't think I am particularly difficult to please."

The star twinkled down at her in silent disbelief.

"I admit that I have met any number of pleasant enough gentlemen who would serve adequately in the position of husband, but regardless of title or wealth or appearance, none has ever struck me as anything other than ordinary and really rather dull. Even when, on occasion, I have allowed one to steal a kiss"—she glanced at the star apologetically—"which one would have thought would have been exciting by the very nature of the illicitness of the act itself, it was never the least bit exciting, nor was it particularly interesting."

Worse yet, when she had looked into the eyes of these pleasant enough but unexceptional prospective husbands, she saw nothing but years ahead of a pleasant enough but unexceptional existence. Precisely like the unexciting, staid, and dull life that oddly enough seemed to well suit her parents.

"Sometimes I wonder if I am truly their child," she said ruefully. "If perhaps explorers or adventurers or at the very least dreamers deposited me as an infant on their doorstep. Not that I don't love them with my whole heart," she said quickly. "They're quite wonderful, all in all. Why, they've never pressured me to marry, whereas Eugenia's parents were quite beside themselves at the thought of having a spinster daughter on their hands for the rest of her days. So I am extremely fortunate. Still, they are content with their lot in life." She blew a long breath. "Their terribly ordinary, eminently forgettable, and not the tiniest bit exciting lot in life." It was a lot Felicity saw herself heading directly toward.

"So there you have it. And here we are." She fixed the star—her star—with a steady eye. "I need help, and you are my last resort because I have no idea what to do now."

In truth, this was the first real step she'd taken—if indeed wishing could be considered real—to find the type of husband she wanted. Oh, certainly, it had taken her several seasons to realize she had no interest in the gentlemen who routinely made her acquaintance. And a few more seasons to understand why. Then there was the year when she'd actively sought the acquaintance of men of a scholarly nature in hopes that a shared interest in the heavens would provide a certain element of excitement, but in that she had proven sadly mistaken. Beyond discussion of constellations, the astronomers she'd met were extraordinarily dull. And most of the past year had been spent on a grand tour of Europe, with two of her younger cousins and an assembly of older female relations, during which she'd met any number of interesting gentlemen with a significant potential for excitement, yet none of them seemed quite right.

"I'm not simply wishing for a husband. I should make that clear. I could have a husband; I have had offers. Perfectly acceptable offers. What I want... what I'm wishing for..." Felicity straightened and squared her shoulders. "Is a future that's not staid and boring and ordinary.

"I want a man who will make the rest of my days an adventure. The grandest of adventures. That's what I wish." Felicity paused. "If you please."

She held her breath. She wasn't entirely sure what would happen now although she wouldn't be at all surprised if the perfect man dropped from the sky onto her balcony. Perhaps a French musketeer? D'Artagnan preferably. Or an Edmond Dantès? Or an armor-clad knight, although that might make rather a lot of noise when he landed, and it was very late in the night or quite early in the morning, depending on one's point of view.

Felicity sighed. This was absurd. Even if her wish were to come true, it certainly wouldn't happen immediately. It simply made sense that something as imprecise as a wish wouldn't be granted at once, if at all. It would need time for whatever power granted such things to evaluate her need and worthiness and who knew what else. Still...

"As much as I hate to appear impatient," Felicity said in a pleasant tone, "I would appreciate some haste on your part. I do want to marry, and if I have to settle for an ordinary life, I should decide that fairly soon and make my peace with it."

A dog barked somewhere in the distance. She ignored it.

"Unfortunately, I am of an age where I cannot expect acceptable offers to continue indefinitely. And I admit, there are some suitable gentlemen as yet unwed."

The dog continued its tirade, accompanied now by shouts. Felicity rolled her gaze toward the heavens. Goodness, you would think people would be more considerate of their neighbors at this time of night.

"As I was saying, if my wish is not to be granted, then I really should accept that my life is going to be unexceptional. I should therefore get on with it and find a gentleman of good family, acceptable fortune, and, if at all possible, pleasant appearance. I really would prefer not—"

The unmistakable sound of a shot rang out in the night.

Felicity started and, without thinking, leaned over the balustrade and peered in the direction of the noise, ignoring the voice in the back of her head that warned it might well be better upon hearing shots to take precautions rather than give in to curiosity. A tall wall separated her family's garden from that of their neighbors, Lord and Lady Pomfrey, but from her balcony she had an excellent vantage point. The lights flickered on in an upstairs room, and she could make out the distinct figure of a man climbing down the ivy that covered the Pomfreys' house.

Felicity gasped. A burglar, no doubt. Caught in the act of robbing Lady Pomfrey's jewels or the Pomfreys' collection of art or something equally valuable. The figure ran across the Pomfreys' lawn, his white shirt illuminated by the starlight, and vanished behind the wall. *Her wall!* Felicity's heart caught in her throat. Good Lord, he wasn't coming here, was he? She grabbed her spyglass and hefted it in her hand. It was brass and quite heavy. She had never considered it a weapon before but it certainly could be.

Shouts caught her attention, and she could see two figures in the window. Even from this distance, it was apparent they were arguing. Why on earth would one argue about a burglar? And shouldn't there be servants all over the grounds by now giving chase?

Unless it wasn't a burglar at all. There certainly were enough rumors about Lady Pomfrey's, well, *interests.* Still, it could be a burglar, and one should know for certain if only to protect one's home and family. Even as Felicity raised the spyglass to her eye, she knew observing her neighbors thusly was completely improper, quite rude, and, in a moral sense, absolutely wrong. She fully intended to chastise herself about it later.

She stepped back into the deeper shadows of her room, grateful she had not lit a lamp that would expose her presence, extended the spyglass, and focused on the window. Lord and Lady Pomfrey were indeed arguing. Why, His Lordship was the color of overripe plums, although that might have been a trick of light and distance. One would think if one had a wife like Lady Pomfrey, and from all she had heard Lord Pomfrey was no better, one would be used to middle-of-the-night incidents like this and would take them in stride. Of course, regardless of their individual activities, it could well be that His Lordship was not at all pleased to come upon his wife in the act of whatever she was in the act of with a—

Good Lord, where was the burglar?

Felicity scanned the area and caught a blurred glimpse of someone dropping from the top of the wall into the garden. *Her garden!* She ignored a rising sense of panic. One should keep one's head at a time like this when it was critical to properly evaluate a situation. She found the figure through the spyglass and adjusted the focus. It was far too dark to make out his features, and he did blend in rather well with the shrubbery at the base of the wall in spite of his shirt. Still, she could tell he was tall, and even in the inadequate light cast by the stars, she noted impressively broad shoulders and—

And he was staring straight at her! The immediate temptation was to step back, deeper into the shadows, but Felicity held her ground. She was made of sterner stuff than to retreat, and hadn't she just been wishing for excitement? Regardless, he couldn't possibly see her. There was no light on in the room behind her and the starlight was entirely too dim to—

"I say," he called in a stage whisper, "is it safe?"

Dear Lord, he could see her! For a moment she considered ignoring him completely and slipping back into the safety of her rooms. But that would be the height of cowardice. Besides, what she did or did not do scarcely mattered. *She* was precisely where she was supposed to be. *He* was the interloper.

"Miss," he hissed from the darkness.

She lowered the spyglass reluctantly and matched her tone to his. "What do you mean, *safe*?"

"I should think *safe* would be fairly obvious." There was a distinct hint of annoyance in the man's voice, although it was a cultured, refined voice. Any lingering thoughts as to whether he was indeed a burglar vanished, although he could have been a well-bred burglar. A duke fallen on hard times or a prince trying to retrieve royal jewels from Lady Pomfrey's boudoir or—

"Safe specifically as in is anyone coming after me? Have they set the dogs on me?"

She raised a brow. "You're rather impatient, given your position at the moment."

"One tends to be impatient when one has been shot at, forced to climb down a building, scaled a wall, and lost one's favorite coat in the process, all with the proverbial hounds of hell nipping at one's heels."

"They don't have hounds," she murmured. "Or dogs of any kind."

"I was certain I heard dogs." He stepped away from the shrubbery and closer toward her house.

"Oh, there are any number of dogs in the neighborhood, all of whom were probably aroused by tonight's activities, but Lord and Lady Pomfrey don't have dogs, although I suppose you were speaking metaphorically. I daresay there are no hounds of hell in London at all. Even if they did have hounds or dogs, I should imagine Lady Pomfrey would have something quite small and furry and not at all capable of climbing walls. Although now that I think about it, dogs generally can't climb walls so you would indeed be safe."

"This might well be the strangest conversation I have ever had," he muttered, and she wasn't at all sure he was speaking to her. He came closer. "Coupled with one of the stranger evenings. Not the beginning, of course—"

"Yes, well . . ." She cleared her throat. "Perhaps it might be best if you didn't—"

"Quite."

He was right; the conversation was odd and abruptly uncomfortable. It struck her how terribly improper it was as well. Why, she was in her nightclothes chatting with a man who, while probably not a burglar, was certainly not to be trusted. She glanced at the neighboring property. Their Lordships could still be seen in the window but there was no rush of torch-bearing servants headed toward the wall. "It appears to me that you are indeed safe."

"Excellent." He chuckled. "That's that then."

"Is it?" She stared down at him. "Have you no shame? No morals whatsoever?"

"What do you mean?" he said cautiously.

"I mean—" She thought for a moment. "I suppose before I make any accusations regarding your morals, I should determine if you are or are not a burglar."

"Fair enough." She could hear the grin in his voice. "I can assure you I am most certainly not a burglar."

"Are you sure?"

"Absolutely."

"Why should I believe you?"

"Good point. I have no idea." He thought for a moment. "I would think, if I were a burglar, I probably wouldn't be taking the time to chat with you. Furthermore, if I were a burglar, I certainly wouldn't be plying my trade with the lady of the house present. It's obviously a sure way to get caught."

"That would depend on whether you were a good burglar."

"Oh, I would be a very good burglar. However, I am not."

She sighed. "No, I don't suppose you are."

"You sound disappointed," he said slowly.

"Not precisely. One should never be disappointed to learn one's home and family are safe."

He stepped nearer and stared up at her. He was almost directly beneath the balcony now. She couldn't make out his features but his voice was surprisingly nice. "And yet you definitely sound disappointed."

"Well, if you're not a burglar then you . . . It scarcely matters."

"I should be happy to rob your house if you wish."

She scoffed. "Don't be absurd. I have no desire for you or anyone to rob my house."

"That is a relief. I haven't the faintest idea how to properly rob a house, and I should hate to be found out." He chuckled. "A man could get shot that way."

"A distinct possibility." Indeed, there was an antique dueling pistol in the top drawer of her nightstand at this very moment. She had purchased it after a nasty incident in Venice and had kept it beside her bed ever since. It was of sentimental value more than true protection, really, although a pistol close at hand made her feel a little adventurous. Odd that she hadn't remembered it before now. Of course, the weight of the spyglass still in her hand was reassuring.

"Now then, as we have resolved that question I should like—"

"As we have established that you probably are not a burglar, I assume you were"—Felicity wrinkled her nose—"dallying with Lady Pomfrey?"

Silence greeted her question, then a resigned sigh drifted upward. "Dallying is as good a word as any."

"That's rather reprehensible of you, isn't it?"

He paused. "Is it?"

"Absolutely." She collapsed the spyglass in a measured, methodical manner and searched for the right words. It wasn't every day she chastised a man for scandalous behavior. "Lady Pomfrey is a married woman. Therefore your actions were indeed reprehensible. Morally, that is."

"Do you think so?"

She nodded. "I do."

"I see." He paused for a long moment. "I, however, do not."

She snorted in disbelief. "You can't possibly disagree. Your behavior is improper and immoral and—"

"Aha. That's where you're wrong."

"I most certainly am not."

"Oh but you are." An annoying note of triumph rang in his voice. "You see, I am not married."

She furrowed her brow in confusion. "What does that have to do with anything?"

"I am not married, which means I have not broken any sort of vow of fidelity or loyalty or whatever else one promises when shackling one's life forever to a spouse." He shrugged. "My morals therefore are not in question."

She gasped. "Surely you don't believe that?"

"Surely I do. I take my word, and any promises I might make, up to and including marriage vows—which I have never taken nor do I have any intention of taking in the foreseeable future—quite seriously. Honoring my word is my responsibility, my solemn duty, as it were. However, the actions others take in regard to whatever promises they might make are not my responsibility."

"Come now. You bear some culpability. Lady Pomfrey couldn't dally by herself."

"I wouldn't wager on—never mind." He choked back a laugh. "Now then, if there's nothing else—"

"You are a man of questionable morals, aren't you?"

"I suppose that depends on your point of view. I have no question at all about my morals. And while I would love to continue to debate my behavior and the ethical considerations regarding that behavior, I should take my leave."

"Indeed you should," she murmured, struck by a vague sense of disappointment. It was ridiculous, even if this—or rather, he—was the most interesting thing to happen in her life in some time. Or ever.

"Unless you plan to summon the authorities and have me arrested?"

"Don't be absurd. If I had wanted to summon the authorities I would have done so by now." While it was highly improper for a man who had just escaped the justifiable wrath of an irate husband to be under her balcony in the middle of the night, it was probably not worthy of arrest. Apparently, though, this adventure had come to an end. Pity. She gestured at the far side of the garden. "If you head toward the break in the top of the wall, you'll find a gate a few feet away. It leads to the mews and the passage to the street."

"What break?"

"There." She waved again. "You can see it from here, edged against the night sky. It's just above the border of tall hedges over there."

"I can't see it; it's dark. And I daresay I wouldn't be able to see it from down here anyway." He blew a frustrated breath and moved to the trellis. "Damnation, it's been a hell of a night."

"Indeed it has." She peered over the side of the balcony. "What are you doing?"

"I'm climbing up your trellis."

Felicity ignored the thrill that ran up her spine, whether of fear or excitement, she wasn't entirely certain. Probably a bit of both. "Is that wise?"

"It is if I'm to see where this blasted gate of yours is and get out of here."

"Perhaps if you looked a bit harder." She backed away from the balcony, struck by the realization that she could indeed be in danger. She gripped the spyglass tighter and clutched it to her chest, its weight a comfort and a reassurance. It could indeed serve as a more than adequate weapon and put a nasty dent in a man's skull. Beyond that, she had no doubt as to her ability to scream if necessary. "I really don't think you should come—"

"If you're fearing for your virtue, you needn't." An arm appeared over the balustrade, and her breath caught. Dear Lord, he was far faster than she'd expected. Although she shouldn't have been surprised. The man had already climbed down one building, sprinted across a lawn, and scaled a wall, not to mention whatever other activities he might have engaged in previously, and he hadn't seemed the least bit out of breath.

He hauled himself onto the balcony, planted his feet on the floor, and straightened. She was right; he was tall. Nearly a head taller than she, and she was of above average height. It was far too dark to see his features well, but what she could make out was quite nice. Of course in the light of day he could well be hideous, although she doubted Lady Pomfrey would ever be involved with an unattractive man. Regardless, his smile would be wicked and no doubt irresistible. If she knew nothing else about him, she knew that.

"I am far too tired to engage in anything other than sleep, which I intend to do the moment I am in my own bed."

"I wasn't the least bit worried," she said in a lofty manner.

"Then why are you armed?" He nodded at the spyglass in her hands.

"This?" She shifted the spyglass from one hand to the other. "This is simply an old spyglass that once belonged to a seafaring relative."

"A spyglass?" He glanced from the instrument in her hands to her telescope. "And I see you have a larger telescope as well."

"I study the stars. I find them fascinating."

He laughed. "As fascinating as your neighbors?"

Heat flashed up her face. "I am an astronomer. Amateur, admittedly, but an astronomer nonetheless. I do not study my neighbors!"

"No?"

"I will admit that once I heard shouting and shots I did wish to see what was happening, but I do not make a habit of peeking in other people's houses."

He snorted in obvious disbelief and turned away

to study the garden wall. At this particular moment she regretted that she hadn't bashed him with the spyglass, and noted that it was not too late to do so. Of course, if she rendered him unconscious he would probably be discovered and her reputation would be shattered, as he was obviously a man of disrepute and—

"You're foolish not to be worried, you know. Speaking to a stranger of questionable morals in the middle of the night and allowing him to enter your bedchamber—"

"I allowed nothing of the sort." Indignation sounded in her voice. "You took liberties that were not granted to you. You climbed into my garden un-invited and now, again uninvited, you appear in my room and—"

"Yes, well, that is just the kind of thing a man of questionable morals does." He nodded. "I see the break in the wall now and how to get to it, so I shall bid you good night."

She huffed. "Go on, then."

"Before I once again take to the trellis, I should like to thank you for your assistance."

She shrugged. "I really didn't do anything."

A grin sounded in his voice. "Precisely. And it is most appreciated." Without warning he stepped closer, took her free hand in his, and raised it to his lips. "My dear girl, if you were my younger sister I would make certain you were locked up for the better part of the next year to ensure there would be no repetition of tonight's incident."

"Would you?" She raised a brow. "If it were my younger sister I would make certain she was armed with something other than a spyglass should there be a repetition of tonight's incident."

"Well said." He laughed, released her hand, and stepped to the balcony. He swung a leg over the side and reached for the trellis. "Oh, and one more thing. Do try to keep men of questionable morals from climbing into your bedchamber in the future. At least until you are of an age to understand exactly what the consequences of questionable morals might be." With that, he disappeared into the night. Only the sound of rustling leaves indicated he had been there at all.

"Of an age . . ." She stared for a moment, then laughed. The silly man thought she was a child. Certainly in the dark with her eminently practical nightclothes and her hair down, plus her telescope and spyglass, she probably did indeed look like a mere girl.

A thump sounded somewhere below her, followed by a muffled profanity. She moved to the balcony and leaned over. "Are you all right?"

"My bloody shoe caught in your blasted trellis and now I can't find the damnable thing."

She stifled a giggle. "Sir, your language."

"My apologies," he said in a clipped tone. "Apparently my indignities were not complete until now, and I am to be forced to hobble through the streets with only one shoe."

"Divine retribution, do you think? For your sins?"

For a moment only silence greeted her comment. Then a reluctant chuckle drifted up to her. "Undoubtedly."

With that he sauntered across the lawn, and a moment later, blended into the shrubbery at the base of the wall. He would have no problem finding the gate now.

She pulled a chair onto the balcony, sank down into it, rested her elbows on the cold stone balustrade, and propped her chin in her hands. This—he—truly had had all the elements of an adventure. There'd been excitement and not knowing what might happen next and a definite hint of danger. And oddly enough, her hand was still warm where he had kissed it. She couldn't help but wonder how his lips might feel.

Life with him would certainly never be staid and boring and ordinary.

Felicity smiled slowly and rose to her feet. She searched the sky and found the star she had wished on.

"I should start by saying how grateful I am for your prompt attention to my wish. He shall do nicely. Certainly he needs some reformation, a great deal of work, really, but that shall add to the challenge and, frankly, the fun. And I have no doubt he will be fun. Oh, he's not exactly what I'd hoped for. All that questionable morals business. But he does seem to have a certain sense of honor, twisted yes, but it is there. He shall definitely never be dull.

"Now then, if you could see your way clear for one more tiny, insignificant request." She drew a deep breath and smiled hopefully. "I should very much like to know his name."

$\mathcal{T}wo$

*What a gentleman really wants is the freedom
to do as he chooses, when he chooses, for as long
as he chooses.*
The Honorable Mr. Nigel Cavendish

"So." Sinclair stood with a glass of champagne in
his hand and a look of amusement in his eye.
"You were rescued by a little girl."

"I wouldn't call her a little girl," Nigel said casually and studied the swirl of dancers moving to the familiar strains of a popular Strauss waltz. He hadn't particularly wanted to attend tonight's ball and was here only at his mother's insistence. She had pointed out that it was best to appear in public as soon as possible after incidents such as the one three nights ago with Lord and Lady Pomfrey to defuse the possibility of scandal. Or, rather, the probability of scandal.

Nigel had thought he had escaped that misadventure unscathed and unnoticed. After all, Lady Pomfrey certainly would not want her indiscretions exposed. And as Lord Pomfrey had returned home straight from the arms of an actress of considerable reputation that had nothing to do with her skills on the stage, he too would wish to avoid public exposure. Nigel had simply, once again, failed to take into account how quickly information passed from one household to another thanks to London's vast community of servants. Maids and footmen, valets and cooks all derived great amusement from the antics of the upper classes. Nigel bit back an unrepentant grin. He certainly did his part to entertain the masses. Indeed, he considered it a sort of responsibility. *Noblesse oblige*, as it were.

"She came up nearly to my nose, far too tall to be too young. And she was extraordinarily bright or perhaps simply precocious." Nigel chuckled at the memory. "She gave as good as she got. I warned her against allowing men of questionable morals into her bedchamber, and she accused me of being a man of questionable morals."

The American laughed. "She *was* bright."

"Indeed she was. And most amusing as well." In truth, if the circumstances had been different, Nigel would have quite enjoyed sparring with the girl. There was something about her he liked. Something beyond her ability to keep her head when confronted with a strange man in the middle of the night in her garden. She obviously had courage, even if misplaced. The girl should have been more cautious.

Norcroft drew his brows together. "A little girl, you say?"

"No, I did not say a little girl. Sinclair said a little girl. I said she was young." Nigel nodded at a cluster of chattering young women. "Younger than the current crop of newly introduced husband hunters, I should think. Probably my youngest sister's age, sixteen or so, although I admit it was difficult to tell. It was extremely dark. The only reason she caught my attention at all was because she wore a voluminous white gown or robe or something of that nature that fairly glowed in the starlight."

"And this was the house directly beside Lord Pomfrey's?" Norcroft asked.

Nigel nodded. "To the east."

Norcroft stared at him for a moment, then grinned. "That's Lord Dunbury's house."

Nigel narrowed his gaze. "Why are you smirking like that?"

"Lord Dunbury's daughter, his only daughter, his only child, is Lady Felicity Melville." Norcroft's grin broadened. "And she is no little girl."

Nigel sipped his champagne. "I said she was young."

"Young being relative, especially in this case." Norcroft chuckled.

Sinclair raised a brow. "How old is she?"

"I'm not sure exactly." Norcroft thought for a moment. "In her early twenties, I think."

"Utter nonsense." Nigel scoffed. "I don't believe you for a moment. I can certainly tell a girl from a woman."

"Even in the dark?" Sinclair said.

Nigel grinned. "Especially in the dark."

"Not this time." Norcroft scanned the crowd, then nudged his friend with his elbow and nodded toward the far side of the dance floor. "That's her. The woman dancing with Beckham. That's Lady Felicity."

Nigel's gaze followed his friend's. Norcroft was right. Lady Felicity was certainly not a girl. She was, as he already knew, tall, and he had surmised the dark color of her hair. He had not suspected the shapeliness of her figure, even if she was a bit slender for his tastes. He couldn't make out her features at this distance, but there was something in the graceful way she moved that struck him, as if dancing was as natural to her as her next breath. Not that it mattered. She was an unmarried woman—or rather as she was still Lady Felicity Melville, a never married woman—and as such not the type of female that interested him. Not this year. Still, he would like to see her face.

"How well do you know her?" He directed his words to Norcroft but his gaze remained fixed on Lady Felicity.

His friend hesitated.

Nigel slanted him a curious glance. "That well?"

"No, not at all," Norcroft said quickly. "Well, that

is. In point of fact, I scarcely know her at all although we have been acquainted for years. My mother and hers are friends, and periodically my mother will drop her name as a potential bride."

"And you are not interested?"

"I have never had the opportunity to be interested or not interested. She is pleasant enough, in both appearance and nature, and she's never said or acted in any overt manner, but I have always come away from our dance or conversation or what-have-you with the vague impression that she found me less than"—Norcroft's brows drew together in annoyance—"interesting."

Sinclair laughed. "Nothing like a woman finding a man boring to dissuade him from furthering his acquaintance."

"It does tend to dampen one's enthusiasm," Norcroft muttered.

"I daresay she wouldn't find me boring," Nigel murmured, still studying the lady in question. "Introduce me."

"Why?" Suspicion sounded in Norcroft's voice. "She's not your type."

Nigel glanced at the other man. "Why not?"

"Because she is not married nor has she ever been married," Norcroft said. "And I am fairly certain she wishes to rectify that."

"A virgin looking for a husband? No, not that." Sinclair shook his head mournfully. "Cavendish has made his views perfectly clear about involvement with virgins. Particularly virgins who wish to marry, as all well-bred, socially conscious virgins wish to do."

"Indeed I have," Nigel said firmly. "Marriage-minded virgins, as well as members of their families—especially their mothers—are to be avoided at all costs. However, I have no intention of involvement of any kind with this particular virgin beyond a simple conversation. I am curious; there's nothing more to it than that." Lady Felicity laughed at something Beckham said, and Nigel wondered what she found amusing. "When I thought she was a girl, her behavior could be excused. Her youth and inexperience precluded her from realizing the danger presented by a man of questionable morals."

"A scoundrel, you mean?" Sinclair said. "A rascal? Even a rogue?"

"All of those and unabashedly so." Nigel rather liked being known as a scoundrel, rascal, or rogue. In truth, it kept all but the most determined marriage-seeking virgins—and apparently Lady Felicity could be counted among their number—at bay, and kept their mothers at bay as well. At some point, when he was ready for marriage, he was confident his name, wealth, and position would overcome any reluctance caused by his reputation. But that time was far in the future. "What has piqued my curiosity was why a young woman who should certainly have known better given her age did not sound an alarm when she saw me drop into her garden. Or when I approached her balcony. Or when I climbed her trellis."

"Perhaps she didn't know you were a scoundrel?" Sinclair said helpfully.

Norcroft scoffed. "She saw the man come straight from Lady Pomfrey's window, with dogs in hot pursuit—"

"There were no dogs," Nigel murmured.

Norcroft ignored him. "Only a scoundrel—indeed a scoundrel of the worst sort—would be in such a position in the first place."

"Thank you for putting it so succinctly," Nigel said wryly.

Norcroft grinned. "You are most welcome."

"Therefore one wonders what our Lady Felicity was thinking, doesn't one?" Nigel said thoughtfully.

His friends exchanged glances. Sinclair shrugged. "I don't."

"Neither do I," Norcroft added firmly.

"I do. And I intend to find out. A few moments of casual conversation will no doubt satisfy my curiosity. Besides, I should thank her for her assistance." Nigel downed the rest of his wine and handed the empty glass to a passing waiter. "If you would be so kind as to introduce us."

Norcroft shook his head. "I don't think this is a good idea."

"It's an excellent idea." Nigel raised an amused brow. "Are you concerned about me? Or her?"

"I am most certainly concerned although I am not certain who I am concerned for. Both, I should think."

"Surely you can't imagine any harm could come to Lady Felicity from a mere introduction?"

"Don't be absurd. I suspect Lady Felicity is well able to take care of herself." Norcroft studied the other man, then blew a resigned breath. "I simply have the oddest vision in my head of two immovable objects crashing head on into one another."

"Couldn't happen." Sinclair idly sipped his champagne. "Immovable objects can't crash into one another. They're immovable."

"Exactly." Nigel adjusted the cuffs of his shirt. "Now, introduce me to the immovable Lady Felicity."

Good Lord, he was heading directly toward her!

Well, not directly toward her, Felicity amended. The scandalous Mr. Cavendish was skirting the perimeter of the ballroom floor accompanied by Lord Norcroft, but they were definitely headed in her direction. Not that she would ever allow Mr. Cavendish to know that she had noticed him in any way whatsoever but of course she had. She had been aware of the very moment he had entered the ballroom, as well as his extended conversation with Lord Norcroft and another man. Still, this wasn't at all what she had planned. She was not yet prepared for their first real encounter.

She laughed at something her partner said and was, as always, grateful for the ability to appear to be paying rapt attention even while her mind was somewhere else entirely. It was a skill her mother had encouraged. "My dear girl," her mother had said, "one should never allow a boring gentlemen to know just how boring he is. It's not at all nice. However, neither is it necessary to allow oneself to be trapped by ennui when one could be engaging in much more interesting thoughts."

Lord Beckham was nice enough and an excellent dancer as well but he wasn't, nor, she suspected, could he ever be—and no doubt he had no wish to be—the Honorable Mr. Nigel Cavendish. Even if honorable was an official designation due to his position as the son of a viscount rather than a descriptive term regarding his character.

It had been remarkably easy to discover his name after his appearance in her garden three nights ago. The next morning she had simply mentioned to her maid, Nancy, that she had heard a commotion at Lord and Lady Pomfrey's the night before. Nancy had heard from Bridget, the downstairs parlormaid, who had received her information from Cook, who had an ongoing flirtation with the greengrocer who also provided fresh produce to the Pomfrey house, exactly what had transpired and the name of the scoundrel involved. Nancy, though well trained and always cognizant of her place, was never reluctant to gossip with just the tiniest bit of encouragement. Apparently Mr. Cavendish's activities were an ongoing source of amusement below stairs throughout London, and Nancy was a fount of information.

Felicity learned he was currently residing with his parents, Lord and Lady Cavendish, in their grand home in Mayfair only because the residence he had previously inhabited, a house loaned to him by the Marquess of Helmsley, had been damaged by fire. Nancy spun an altogether unbelievable story about Mr. Cavendish and an actress and a parrot that made no sense whatsoever but was fascinating nonetheless. The maid furthermore said he had been residing in the marquess's house because his own was under repair due to an incident of flooding, *also* of a suspicious nature.

Nancy delivered these stories and several others in a manner that clearly indicated what she thought of men who dallied with actresses, with or without parrots. Felicity was certain each and every tale was exaggerated and Mr. Cavendish's exploits had gained a great deal in the telling and retelling, although there was undoubtedly a kernel of truth in the accounts. Still, Felicity noted that not one of Nancy's stories involved women who were not widowed, or married with questionable reputations, or on the stage. While he had been involved in any number of scandalous escapades, none had led to the ruination of women who were not previously inclined in that direction. Obviously, for a scoundrel, Mr. Cavendish did indeed have some scruples. A clear indication that he simply needed the right woman to start him on the path to reform.

Felicity Constance Evanston Melville was the right woman.

The music drew to a close, and Lord Beckham led her off the floor.

"Is it me?" Lord Beckham asked in a casual manner.

"Is what you, my lord?" Felicity said pleasantly, noting Mr. Cavendish's approach behind His Lordship.

"I have the impression your mind was not entirely on our dance." He cast her a curious smile. "Or on me."

"Nonsense, my lord." She ignored a stab of guilt. He was a nice man, after all. She favored him with her brightest smile. "I was simply captivated by your charm, and therefore it was all I could do to concentrate on the steps and not fumble about. Gossips would surely attribute that to an excess of spirits and assume you had plied me with alcohol to enable you to have your way with me. My reputation would be shattered, and the blame would be laid on you. No." She heaved a dramatic sigh. "If I have seemed inattentive it was only to save us both from complete and utter disgrace."

He stared at her for a moment, then laughed. "Very good."

She grinned. "Thank you."

He studied her curiously. "I know we have danced together and spoken in the past, but I must confess I don't recall you being quite so . . ."

"Polished?" She raised a brow.

He chuckled. "I was going to say enchanting, but polished suits as well."

She leaned toward him in a confidential manner. "It's the travel, you know. There's nothing quite like

new experiences and new places to take a . . . a . . ."
She thought for a moment. "A stone plucked from the
earth and turn it into something nicely decora—"

"A gem, Lady Felicity." Lord Beckham lifted her
hand to his lips. "A jewel, exquisite, lovely, and
nearly flawless."

She laughed. "As delightful as that is to hear, I
should tell you I have any number of dreadful flaws."

"Ahem." A throat being cleared sounded behind
Lord Beckham. He cast her a reluctant glance, released her hand, and turned.

"Good evening, Beckham," Lord Norcroft said.

Beckham smiled. "Norcroft. Good to see you."

"Good evening, Lady Felicity." Norcroft nodded a
bow.

"Good evening, my lord." Felicity extended her
hand and tried not to notice Mr. Cavendish beside
Norcroft. What was she going to say to him?

"You are looking exceptionally lovely tonight," Norcroft murmured over her hand.

She laughed lightly. "And you are as charming as
ever, my lord."

Norcroft smiled and released her hand. "Allow
me to introduce an old friend of mine, Mr. Nigel
Cavendish." Felicity held her breath and forced a
pleasant, impersonal smile. "Mr. Cavendish, this is
Lady Felicity Melville."

"An honor, my lady." Mr. Cavendish took her hand
and raised it to his lips. She wondered that she didn't
melt into a small puddle at his feet.

He was quite as handsome as she thought a

rogue—at least a successful rogue—should be. His jaw was nicely square, with a distinctly determined set to it. His hair was dark, a walnut color, and with a slight unruly hint of curl. The kind of hair a woman wanted to run her fingers through just to see if it was as thick and lush as it appeared. His nose was the tiniest bit crooked, which enhanced rather than detracted from his appearance and made him seem just a touch dangerous. But it was his eyes, clear and blue as a summer sky, with a spark of amusement in their depths, that made him appear truly wicked. As if he knew precisely what a woman wanted and was more than willing to provide it.

"Mr. Cavendish." She met his gaze directly, and a delightful shiver ran through her. He stared at her as if he was momentarily confused by what he saw. It was most disconcerting. She resisted the urge to pat her hair or check her clothing to see if her gown had vanished from her body or a tree had sprouted from her head.

"Mr. Cavendish?" she said again and pulled her hand from his.

"Would you honor me with this dance?" he blurted. She had expected him to be much more practiced than this but the man seemed positively befuddled. It was surprisingly gratifying, and her nerves vanished.

"This dance?" Her brow quirked upward.

"It is as good a dance as any. Unless, of course, you have already promised this dance." He leaned slightly closer and lowered his voice. "In which case I shall ask for the next, and if that one is taken, the one following, and the one after that, and so on until you agree to dance with me."

Now that was the charming devil she had anticipated. "Or until we run out of dances."

"I shall arrange for the musicians to continue forever if need be," he said staunchly.

"You are determined."

He smiled an easy, confident smile. Obviously whatever had perplexed him had disappeared. "Indeed I am."

Norcroft cleared his throat. Odd, Felicity had nearly forgotten anyone else was here.

"I believe I see someone I have been meaning to speak with," Beckham said smoothly. His gaze met Felicity's. "I do hope you will save another dance for me."

"Of course, my lord." She cast him a genuine smile.

Beckham nodded and took his leave. Mr. Cavendish glanced at Norcroft.

"I too believe I have spotted someone . . ." Norcroft sighed. "Never mind." He smiled at Felicity, threw a warning glance at his friend, turned, and disappeared into the crowd.

Felicity directed her gaze toward Mr. Cavendish. "Am I mistaken or doesn't Lord Norcroft trust you?"

"I assure you, in the midst of a crowded ballroom I am most trustworthy."

She doubted that. "And elsewhere?"

"Elsewhere is a different matter." Mr. Cavendish offered her his arm. "Shall we?" He escorted her onto the dance floor, and they took their place amid the kaleidoscope of dancers moving to the strains of yet another waltz.

He glanced down at her. "Lady Felicity."

"Mr. Cavendish," she said politely. One would have thought they were conversing on a public street rather than in each other's arms. There was absolutely no indication in his words or his eyes that he had ever seen her before. Of course, it was entirely possible he might not know that she was the woman on the balcony. Certainly she had made the effort to find out who he was, but perhaps he hadn't made a similar effort. He had, after all, thought she was a mere girl. His asking for an introduction could be no more than a coincidence.

He studied her carefully. "You have no idea who I am, do you?"

"I know who you are. I can't imagine anyone in London who hears even the least bit of gossip doesn't know who you are," she said coolly. "You are the Honorable Mr. Cavendish, son of Viscount Cavendish."

"Well yes, that, but that's not precisely what I meant." His gaze searched hers, and at once she realized he knew who she was just as she knew who he was.

She bit back a satisfied grin. "I am well aware of what you meant, and again, I know exactly who you are." She smiled in a cordial manner even if it was somewhat difficult to keep her wits about her while dancing in his arms. The man smelled as good as he looked. "However, I must confess, I find it most taxing to attempt a conversation and not stumble through the steps of the dance at the same time. So if you don't mind—"

"Oh, but I do mind." Determination sounded in his voice. "And as waltzes are exceptionally plentiful at a ball hosted by Lord Denton, as he quite enjoys both the tempo of the dance and the proximity to his partner, I would much prefer to talk. But if it is awkward for you . . ." Without warning, he smoothly steered her off the dance floor and ushered her out an open terrace door. "We can speak elsewhere."

She glanced over her shoulder. "I daresay this isn't especially proper."

"Not especially."

"One wonders if you are as trustworthy on a terrace as you are in a ballroom."

"Not if I have a choice. However." He gestured at the terrace. While not nearly as crowded as the ballroom behind them, it was by no means empty. Clusters of guests stood chattering away, illuminated by dozens of blazing candelabras. Waiters bearing trays of champagne wound their way around those enjoying the uncharacteristically warm spring night and disappeared in and out of the stuffy ballroom. "As we are in plain sight, I have little alternative but to be trustworthy and completely honorable."

"Yes, of course," she murmured, ignoring the vaguest sense of disappointment. Not that she was prepared to be alone with him. Still . . .

He raised a brow. "Unless you would prefer to find a more secluded spot? There are any number of nooks in the shadows of this terrace as well as in the garden below."

"This will serve, but I do so appreciate the offer," she said, ignoring the fact that that had indeed crossed her mind. "Do you know them all? The secluded nooks, that is."

"Not all." He led her to an open spot along the terrace balustrade. A good six feet would separate them from any of the other guests, far enough away to have a private conversation, yet easily observed to avoid any suggestion of improper behavior. "A fair number perhaps. I have been to my share of Lady Denton's balls."

"And do you know the secluded spots off the terrace of, oh, say, Effington House? Or Shelburne House? Or Hamilton House?"

"I pride myself on knowing the secluded spots on any terrace I might find myself on under the stars with a beautiful woman." He flashed her a wicked grin. "One never knows when such knowledge might come in handy."

She laughed.

"You find that amusing?" He accepted two glasses of champagne from a waiter and handed her one.

"I do indeed."

"Why?" He sipped his champagne and studied her.

"Why? I'm not sure exactly." She thought for a moment. "I suppose it's because I have had very little occasion to converse with a man of your nature. It's really somewhat thrilling and most amusing."

"A man of my nature?" he said slowly.

She nodded in a noncommittal manner.

"Dare I ask what, precisely, is a man of my nature?"

"Are you sure you wish to know?"

"I do know. What I am curious about is your perception of my nature."

"Do you wish for honesty then?" She sipped her champagne and gazed at him over the rim of her glass. "Or flattery?"

"One always prefers flattery to honesty, but for now"—he shrugged—"honesty will suffice."

"Very well." She considered him for a long moment and wondered exactly how candid she should be. She had always believed in honesty. Perhaps it was time to put that belief to the test. "You are the type of gentleman, and I use the term in its loosest definition, that mothers warn their daughters about. If it weren't for the stature of your family name and your wealth you would be ostracized from polite society."

He winced. "I should have chosen flattery."

"However," she continued, "as the world is a most peculiar place, you are actually viewed as reformable. Even desirable."

"Because of the aforementioned name and wealth and title?"

"I didn't mention title, although I suppose I should have. Therefore your misdeeds, for lack of a better term, have little effect on your future." She raised her glass to him. "You, Mr. Cavendish, are quite a catch."

He grinned. "I knew that."

"No doubt," she murmured.

He drew his brows together. "Are you always this honest?"

"Always?" She tilted her head and considered the question. "Perhaps not always, but most of the time, I should think. Generally there is no reason not to be honest. And in a situation like this, where I gave you the option of honesty or flattery and you chose honesty, well, I really had no choice but to be completely candid, did I?"

He chuckled. "Even if it hurt?"

"Especially if it hurt. It probably did you a world of good." She studied him with a skeptical eye. "I can't imagine you are the least bit pained by my assessment. It can't possibly have come as a surprise. You did say you were aware of your own nature."

"Nonetheless, I am deeply wounded," he said staunchly. "Why, I may never recover."

She laughed again. The man definitely needed work, but he had a great deal of potential.

He raised a brow. "Now you find my pain amusing as well?"

"I find your acting amusing."

"Really?" He frowned in a mock-serious manner. "I thought I was most convincing."

"No doubt you have had considerable practice in deception. At least if gossip is to be believed." She turned and gazed out at the starlit skies. "It's a lovely night, isn't it?"

"Lovely," he murmured, and she knew without looking he was staring at her. "You do not like me very much, do you?"

She glanced at him. "Do you wish for honesty again?"

"I would be wise to ask for flattery," he muttered, then sighed. "However, honesty it is."

"Excellent choice. Well then." She drew a deep breath. "I'm not entirely certain whether I like you or I dislike you at this point. I scarcely know you." She met his gaze firmly. "I do find you most intriguing."

"Intriguing and amusing? I could scarcely ask for more."

She turned her attention back to the heavens. "I imagine most women find you amusing and intriguing."

"I'm not sure . . ."

"Oh come now, Mr. Cavendish. A man with a reputation like yours does not acquire a reputation like yours by being dull and ordinary."

"I never said I was dull and ordinary."

"No, you're quite adventurous."

"Well, I—"

"You break society's rules whenever the fancy strikes you without so much as a by-your-leave and act only as your own misplaced sense of behavior dictates."

"I wouldn't say—"

"You, Mr. Cavendish, are really quite infamous."

Indignation pounded in his voice. "I scarcely think—"

"I have your shoe," she said abruptly.

"What?"

"Your shoe. The one you caught in the trellis."

He stared at her for a long moment, then slowly smiled. "You did recognize me, then."

She shook her head. "No, I didn't, although I might well have recognized you by voice alone if given the opportunity."

"Then how—"

"Goodness, Mr. Cavendish, one would think your intelligence was in question as well as your morals." She scoffed. "I daresay there are few who do not know about your late-night encounter with Lord Pomfrey's dueling pistol, not to mention the assignation that preceded it with Lady Pomfrey."

"It was a bad night in so many ways," he murmured.

"I should think so."

"Your behavior was not exactly above reproach," he said under his breath.

She gasped and turned toward him. "My behavior?"

"It was questionable when I thought you were a mere girl. Now that I realize your true age . . ." He shrugged.

"I did nothing improper whatsoever!"

He leaned toward her. "If you do not lower your

voice, my lady, you will have each and every person on this far too busy terrace moving ever closer to us in hopes of overhearing precisely what impropriety the infamous Mr. Cavendish is accusing the immovable Lady Felicity of."

"Immovable?" She widened her eyes. "Why would you call me immovable?"

"A comment Norcroft made. It scarcely matters at the moment, although I assure you it was meant as a compliment."

"Was it?" She wasn't at all sure if she liked being called immovable. "I'm not certain it sounds like a compliment."

"It was," he said firmly. "And you are changing the subject."

"Yes, I suppose I am." She drew a deep breath. "You're right about the other night as well. I was completely improper. I should have raised an alarm. Called for the authorities. Screamed for assistance. At the very least I should have shot you myself."

He chuckled. "Now that would have been proper."

She sniffed. "I shall remember that next time."

"Oh, there will be no next time."

"You have given up dallying with married women?"

"I have given up Lady Pomfrey."

She scoffed. "Don't tell me you've reformed."

"I have no intention of reforming at the moment, and I see no need to do so. Aside from an enjoyment of certain members of the opposite sex—enjoyment that I might add is mutual—as well as a penchant for gambling—in which I typically win nearly as often as I lose—and an overindulgence in spirits, I am not unlike many men of my age and position."

She stared in disbelief. "You say that as if the fact that you are not unique in your disrepute makes your behavior acceptable."

"Perhaps not acceptable, but as you yourself said, forgivable. I am yet a young man. I have my entire life to reform. Besides, as you said, I am a catch."

"The magnitude of your arrogance is astonishing," she said dryly.

"Thank you yet again." He signaled to a waiter and exchanged their empty glasses for fresh ones.

She sipped her champagne and studied him curiously. "Why did you seek me out tonight?"

"Tonight? Well . . ."

"I am not the type of woman you usually pursue."

"I'm not . . ." He shook his head. "Curiosity, I suppose. When I thought you were a girl, your behavior—"

"My not revealing your presence at the top of my lungs, you mean?"

"Among other things, which I attributed at the time to the fact that you did not know any better. However, when I learned of your true age—"

"When you realized your mistake."

"Yes, of course, my mistake. I was curious as to what kind of woman would not be terrified by an obvious scoundrel climbing onto her balcony."

She drew her brows together. "Why would I be terrified?"

He paused. "Concern for your virtue, that sort of thing."

She choked back a laugh. "Concern for my virtue?"

"Yes, of course," he said firmly. "There you were, an unmarried lady of good family, on your balcony in the middle of the night, in your nightclothes, I might add, and you see a man of questionable moral character climb out of the window of a neighbor's house and make his way to your balcony. A sensible young woman would be terrified."

"I was not unprepared to defend myself."

He scoffed. "With what? Your telescope?"

She shrugged. "It's brass and quite heavy."

"Even so—"

She leaned toward him and lowered her voice. "What if I'm not sensible?"

He started. "What do you mean?"

"I mean just what I said. What if I'm not sensible? Or rather, what if I've tired of being sensible?" She straightened and set her glass on the balustrade. "I have always believed in science, in rational, sensible, irrefutable facts. Take the stars, for example." She nodded toward the night sky. "Their study is one of observation of what is, and yet throughout history many people have believed they are mystical, even divine. Part and parcel of the rule of the universe, as it were.

"I have never believed in silly nonsense like magic or fate, omens or signs. You, Mr. Cavendish"—she met his gaze—"have persuaded me otherwise."

"I have?" he said slowly.

"Indeed you have." She wasn't at all sure this was the right moment to tell him he was the answer to her wish. That she had decided his appearance in the night was fate. No, the scandalous Mr. Cavendish would run screaming into the night if he realized she had set her cap for him. Besides, it only seemed prudent to get to know him a bit better before letting him in on her plans. His fate, as it were. But in some odd way, she already knew, without question, without doubt, he was the man for her. Her fate. And she did like him so far.

"Do you care to elaborate?"

She picked up her glass and took a long sip of champagne, then shook her head. "No."

He frowned. "No?"

"No."

He narrowed his eyes. "Will you ever?"

"My dear Mr. Cavendish." She looked into his eyes and smiled in a slow, provocative manner that came from somewhere deep inside her she had never known existed but was delighted with nonetheless. "You may count on it."

Three

What a man really wants is to know that his son is up to the task of carrying on his name in an honorable manner. And to know as well he has produced not merely an heir but a good man.

Edmund, Viscount Cavendish

"*P*leasant," Nigel muttered to himself and handed his hat and coat to a footman in the foyer of Cavendish House. "I'd scarcely call her pleasant."

"Beg pardon, sir," the footman said cautiously. "Were you addressing me?"

"George." Nigel frowned at the young man. "It is George, isn't it?"

"Yes, my lord."

"Very well then, George, let me give you a piece of

advice. The next time a friend, even a very good friend, introduces you to a woman he describes as no more than pleasant"—he narrowed his gaze— "do not hesitate. Run for your very life."

George stared at him as if he had serious questions about the state of Nigel's sanity. "Very well, sir, I shall."

"See that you do." Nigel nodded and headed toward the stairs.

Lady Felicity's cryptic comment and her refusal to explain lingered in his mind. No, it had taken up permanent residence. He wasn't sure why or how, but he was certain it boded no good. He'd had no opportunity to quiz her further; she'd been actively sought by various gentlemen following their conversation and he'd lost sight of her. She'd no doubt gone home, probably accompanied by her parents. Nothing at all sinister in that. Nonetheless, he'd had the distinct impression she was avoiding him. Damnation. What was the woman up to? It couldn't be some sort of extortion. Everyone in the world apparently already knew most of the details about that unpleasantness the other night. And disclosing her own role would only bring disgrace upon her head. Still, there was something . . . "Pleasant, my ass," he muttered.

It wasn't that Lady Felicity wasn't, although *pleasant* was not even remotely an accurate term. In appearance alone she was far more than merely pleasant. Oh, certainly, at first glance she might appear unexceptional, but upon closer observation one discovered her slender figure was nicely curved and rounded in all the appropriate places. Her hair was not at all the nondescript brown he had originally thought but a medley of shades ranging from mahogany to dark chocolate. The features of her face were indeed *pleasant* enough unless one happened to look into her eyes. Bloody hell, he'd feared he'd drown in those eyes, in an endless pool of deep, rich brown sparked by intelligence and barely concealed amusement. He had never thought of brown as being at all remarkable but then he'd never before gazed into the eyes of Lady Felicity Melville. For a moment, he'd quite lost his senses. He couldn't recall anything similar ever happening to him before, even with the most beautiful women. It was extremely unsettling.

Beyond that, the lady had a presence about her of confidence, even determination. If *pleasant* was too feeble a description, *immovable* seemed entirely accurate. And yet this air of complete assurance carried with it a hint of something distinctly sensual and utterly feminine. She was, well, *ripe*. He couldn't understand why Norcroft was oblivious to it, or rather, to her. It was obvious Beckham was aware of it, or rather, of her.

Lady Felicity Melville might well be the most dangerous female Nigel had ever met.

"Sir," George called from behind him.

Nigel paused on the stairs. "Yes?"

"Your father requested that you join him should you come in at a . . . a . . ." The servant searched for the right words.

"Decent hour?" Nigel suggested.

"Early hour, I believe His Lordship said, sir," George said with a note of relief. "He is in the library."

"Pity I didn't stay out later then." Nigel blew a long breath and started toward the library. "Thank you, George."

Nigel had expected a summons to the library for further discussion ever since his parents had learned of the incident with Lady Pomfrey. Blast it all. It was exceedingly difficult for a man of thirty years to live under his parents' watchful eyes, if only temporarily. Thank God, repairs on his own house would be completed within the week. He looked forward to being master of his life again. Why, his parents treated him like an unruly child. A voice in the back of his head noted he often acted like an unruly child. As he always did when his conscience made its unwelcome presence known, he ignored it. Besides, there would come a time when he would have to accept the responsibility of title and family. Until then, why shouldn't he enjoy himself?

His father, no doubt, had different ideas.

Nigel braced himself and pushed open the door to the library. The long, book-lined room with its floor-to-ceiling windows was bright and cheery in the light of day and, in spite of its size, surprisingly cozy at night. Even the portraits of ancestors hung in the spaces between the windows and behind the desk were somewhat comforting in spite of the forbidding expressions on the faces of many of the members of the preceding generations. His father sat directly in front of the largest gallery wall, behind the massive desk that had been his father's and his father's before him, writing in a large ledger.

"You're home early this evening," his father said without looking up.

"It does seem wrong somehow, doesn't it?" Nigel said lightly and strolled across the room to a table where a decanter of brandy and glasses awaited. "I shall take care in the future to see that it doesn't happen again."

"Imagine my surprise," his father murmured, his attention still on the book before him. Between his political activities, running the family estates, including a centuries-old castle in constant need of repair, and a fair number of business investments, Viscount Cavendish had a great many irons in the fire. A great many *successful* irons. His would be difficult shoes to fill. Not that Nigel expected, or wished, to fill them for many years to come. While his father was in his sixties, he remained strong and healthy and vibrant.

Nigel filled two glasses, crossed the room, placed one within his father's reach, then settled into the comfortable chair positioned in front of the desk. It was the same chair in the same position that he had always sat in when having serious, and just as often, not so serious, discussions with his father since he'd been old enough to do so. Nigel suspected the same chair, or one very much like it, had served a similar purpose when his grandfather had been the one seated behind the desk. Nigel took a slow sip of the brandy and savored the warmth and the mellow sting of the liquor.

He father closed the book, set it to one side, and reached for his drink. "There is nothing like a glass of fine brandy at the end of a day."

"Indeed." Nigel paused. "You wished to speak to me."

The viscount settled back in his chair and studied his son. "I did."

Nigel drew a deep breath. "If it's about that unfortunate incident with Lord and Lady Pomfrey, I can assure you I have no intention—"

"Alfred Pomfrey is a lecherous idiot and deserves what he gets for marrying a woman half his age. Letitia Pomfrey is a tart. She was a tart as a girl and a tart she remains."

Nigel stared at his father, then grinned with as much relief as humor. "I've always been rather fond of tarts."

"Most men are. However, in the future might I suggest that you confine your preferences to tarts of the baked cherry variety as opposed to those of the married variety."

"Cherry and marry?" If his father could joke, this discussion might not be as dire as Nigel had anticipated. "Well said, Father, well said indeed."

"Thank you." His father smiled slightly, his tone deceptively mild. "You do understand, the failings of Lord and Lady Pomfrey in no way excuse your own behavior."

Nigel winced to himself. "Of course not, sir."

"What are your plans, my boy?"

"My plans? Well . . ." Nigel thought for a moment. "I had planned on a ride in the park the first thing in the morning. Then I thought I would visit my tailor. And afterward—"

"Your plans for your life, Nigel."

"My life?" Nigel frowned. "I'm not sure what you're asking."

"What I'm asking is whether or not you intend to continue to squander your intelligence, your time, and your money—my money, really—in the pursuit of mindless pleasures as well as the Lady Pomfreys of the world."

Nigel took a long pull of his brandy, as much to avoid the question as to consider an answer, although evasion seemed the best, or at least the easiest, course. "If I recall the stories I've heard, sir, you were not substantially less enamored of the pursuit of pleasure when you were my age than I am."

"When I was your age I had already served in Her Majesty's army, lost a father and two older brothers, and come into a title I had not expected. I do not deny that I engaged in any number of less than reputable activities along the way. Nonetheless, when put in the proper perspective, one might say I had well earned whatever frivolous pastimes I might have enjoyed." The elder Cavendish fixed him with a firm stare. "You, my boy, are a different matter entirely."

"What, would you have me join the army then, Father?" Nigel said in a casual manner. "Go off to this new war we're engaged in? Fight the Russians?"

The expression in his father's eyes hardened but his tone remained mild. "Given a choice, I would not have either of my sons experience war."

Viscount Cavendish rarely spoke of his time spent fighting Napoleon's troops in Spain in his youth. But Nigel had heard stories of his father's courage and military prowess. Edmund Cavendish's leadership ability and skill on the battlefield had earned him any number of medals and commendations, as well as the love and respect of his men. Indeed, many had called him hero. His father had brushed off the designation, saying the difference between a hero and a coward often came down to nothing more than a single moment in time.

"The difference is in the choice one makes in a fraction of a second," the viscount had once told his sons. "Those we call heroes rarely pause to consider the consequences, while the coward thinks entirely too much. One might say the coward exhibits great intelligence while the hero none at all."

Regardless of his own experience, or perhaps because of it, Viscount Cavendish's voice was among the loudest of those few raised now in protest of war. Futile, of course, as anti-Russian sentiment in Britain was at a fever pitch.

The older man shook his head. "This, more than many others, is a foolish war."

"Because it's over the superficial issue of the question of who has the right to the keys of the Church of the Nativity in Bethlehem?"

"Superficial is entirely accurate. Religion is now,

as it has ever been, merely an excuse." His father swirled the brandy in his glass in a thoughtful manner. "The French wish to regain the influence lost after Napoleon's defeat. The Russians want to solidify their own position, and if expansion of their power can be accomplished at the same time, so much the better. Turkey can barely cope with its internal affairs let alone international issues, and the British are concerned with all of it and its effect on our own interests."

Nigel chuckled. "Odd to realize we are aligned with the French in this."

"Indeed it is." His father snorted. "We have long been natural enemies." He studied his son. "But you understand all of this, don't you?"

"It's rather like a tangle of string, isn't it? Once you sort out one end, it's not especially difficult to untangle the rest."

"You have an excellent mind, Nigel. I have long wondered why you prefer to have people think you don't."

Nigel started to deny his father's charge, then shrugged. "I cannot help what people think of me."

"Of course you can." His father leaned forward. "You give the world the impression that you have nothing in your head save the next wager or the next woman. Why?"

Nigel raised his glass. "Don't forget the next bottle of wine. Or in this case brandy."

"A serious answer, if you please."

"I don't really like serious answers. They're so . . . so . . ." Nigel grinned. "Serious."

His father arched a brow.

"Very well then." Nigel thought for a moment. "It's easier, I suppose, to live down to people's expectations rather than live up to them."

"And you feel people have great expectations of you, then?"

Nigel met his father's gaze. "You do." For a long moment neither said a word, then Nigel blew a resigned breath. "I regret that I have disappointed you."

Surprise washed across his father's face. "You think that, do you?"

Nigel shrugged. "You just said as much. You pointed out that at my age you had already—"

"It was a different time, a different world." The elder Cavendish shook his head. "If you took my words to mean I am disappointed in you, my apologies. That was neither my meaning nor my intention."

Nigel chose his words carefully. "Then you are not disappointed?"

"Not yet." His father smiled and relaxed back in his chair. "Have you never wondered why I have never seriously chastised you for your behavior, as scandalous as it has been at times?"

"I wouldn't use the word *never*," Nigel murmured, the memory of any number of *chastisements* flitting through his mind.

The viscount laughed. "Perhaps *never* is the wrong word, but you must admit, the repercussions of your actions on my part have been relatively mild."

"Yes, well . . ."

"I have never cut off your funding, banished you to the country, or any other number of actions I could have taken to curb your antics."

"No, I suppose—"

"Do you wish to know why?"

"I still wish to know why you consider the actions you have taken, in regard to my antics, as you put it, as mild," Nigel said under his breath.

"It is precisely because of my past that I am so tolerant of yours. Oh, not the amusements and carousing that you have pointed out but the seriousness of it. My past, that is." His father finished the rest of his brandy and looked pointedly at the glass. Nigel obediently got to his feet and fetched the decanter. He refilled his father's glass and his own, then took his seat. The older man nodded his thanks and continued. "I never expected to be the next viscount, you know. My oldest brother, Arthur, had been trained since birth for the position. Since I was the third son, my father was happy to purchase my commission. After all, I was expendable."

Nigel stared at his father. Talk of his family was rarer, if possible, than discussion of his life in the military. "Father, you needn't—"

"Ah, but I never have, Nigel, and perhaps it's time. Past time, really. There are things you should know."

An odd weight settled in the pit of Nigel's stomach, but he kept his tone light. "Secrets, Father? Family skeletons and all that?"

The older man chuckled. "Nothing so dramatic,

I'm afraid." He paused a moment as if reflecting on the past, then continued. "I thought the army a glorious career for a man in my position and went off gladly to fight the French. Let me tell you, my boy, the concept of war is far more glorious than the reality of it."

"Yes, sir."

"At any rate, my father still had his heir and a spare to boot, even if Lionel, my other brother, hadn't a serious bone in his body. His was an existence even more frivolous than yours."

Nigel smiled weakly.

"He was great fun, Lionel, that is. While Arthur was intent upon duty and responsibility, Lionel thought of little more than his next game of chance or his next amorous conquest. You could not have found two men whose natures were more in opposition than Lionel and Arthur, and yet they were fond of one another. We were all fond of one another. There is a bond between brothers . . ." His father smiled in a sad, wistful sort of way that Nigel could not recall ever having seen before. "I worshipped Lionel, but then everyone did, even Arthur in spite of his disapproval of Lionel's behavior and his own serious nature. You remind me of Lionel a great deal."

Nigel's gaze shifted to the small portrait of Lionel that hung to the right of his father. "Because I look like him?"

"The resemblance is remarkable, but no, that's not what I meant."

"Then I fear that is not a compliment."

"Oh, but it is. He was not wicked in nature, simply fun-loving. Lionel was amusing and clever and somehow made you think the world was not as dire a place with him in it. Unfortunately he was foolhardy and reckless as well. He met his fate in a duel at the hands of a jealous husband."

Nigel resisted the urge to squirm in his seat.

"I was in Spain when he died. By the time I received word of Lionel's death, a sudden illness had taken my father's life as well. Still, Arthur did not urge me to come home. What was the point? He was now the viscount, and with his usual air of efficiency appeared to handle the title and its accompanying responsibilities with the capability expected of him. He certainly had no need of my assistance. Unfortunately, there was more of appearance than substance to my brother's abilities. As I was later to learn, my father's affairs were in something of a mess when he died. Arthur did the best he could, I think, but he was not up to the task. And when he died, it fell to me." He glanced at his son. "He died after he was thrown by a horse. Were you aware of that?"

"Vaguely." Nigel's knowledge of his father's family was little more than dim recollections of chance comments.

"Arthur was an excellent horseman. No one sat a horse as he did." The viscount paused. "It was a curious way for him to meet his fate."

Nigel stared at his father. "Do you suspect it was other than an accident?"

The older man shook his head. "Not really, but as

I said, given Arthur's skill, it was odd." His father drew a deep breath. "Needless to say, I returned home at once. I was shocked to discover the sorry state of the family's finances. Arthur had made no progress in that respect. Indeed, there was a fair amount of evidence to indicate he had no idea what to do. So it fell to me. I worked, borrowed, sold some property and used the proceeds to invest in estate improvements, and I did what men in my position have always done. I found a wife with excellent connections and an impressive dowry."

"I was always under the impression yours and Mother's was a love match," Nigel said slowly.

"It was ultimately." His father chuckled. "But I did not begin my pursuit of her because she was pretty and clever, although that certainly made it much easier, but because she had what I needed: position and fortune. Even so, I knew she was the only woman in the world for me the moment I looked into her eyes."

"Her eyes?" Nigel drew his brows together. "What about her eyes?"

"They were, indeed they remain, a blue so deep a man could surely drown in them and go to his death a happy man. Haven't you ever noticed your mother's eyes?"

"Apparently not," Nigel murmured, and took a bracing swallow of his brandy. Oh, he knew his mother's eyes were blue but they'd never struck him as being especially remarkable. She was his mother, after all, and perhaps one wouldn't notice such a thing about one's mother.

He'd certainly noticed Lady Felicity's eyes. Not that she was the one woman in the world for him. Far from it. He had no intention of settling for one woman just yet. Someday perhaps, but not now. No, as enticing as her brown eyes were, as appealing as her appearance was, as intriguing as her manner might be, Lady Felicity Melville was absolutely not the right woman for him. Not in any kind of permanent sense. He had rules about women like her. Young, unmarried, well-bred virgins. The Lady Felicitys of the world had only one thing on their minds when it came to eligible men like him. That alone was enough to dissuade him from ever seeing her again. Cryptic comments or not, it would be best to avoid Lady Felicity from this point forward.

"Your mother's wisdom and courage were as much help to me as her money. Today the family fortune is once again on sound footing. When it is placed in your hands"—his gaze met his son's—"your job will be substantially easier than mine was."

"How do you know I won't muck it up?"

"I have every confidence in you."

Misplaced, no doubt. Nigel kept the thought to himself. He'd had no idea his father held him in such high regard. It was both surprising and gratifying. Still, it was probably no more than parental affection or fatherly optimism. Nigel had certainly done nothing to earn it.

"However, I do not wish you to come into your inheritance unprepared." The viscount tapped his finger on a leather-bound notebook. "This details the family's assets, including all property as well as various ventures in which I have invested." He slid the notebook across the desk toward Nigel.

"How interesting." Nigel slid the notebook back toward his father.

"Study it." The viscount again pushed the book toward his son. "I want you to become familiar with the family's interests over the next fortnight or so. Then you'll begin spending a least a portion of each day here. In six weeks you'll be thirty-one years of age. At that time, I will hand over management of the majority of all this to you."

"What?" Nigel jerked upright in his chair. "You can't possibly be serious?"

"Oh, but I am." The older man sipped his brandy and considered his son with obvious amusement. "Would you prefer to wait until I die?"

"Don't be absurd." Nigel jumped to his feet and paced the room. "But no one turns over management of family affairs to a son before . . . Well, it simply isn't done."

"You thought you'd have more time, didn't you?"

"Yes. A great deal more time." Nigel ran his hand through his hair and struggled against a rising sense of panic.

His father shrugged. "You have six weeks."

Nigel stared. "That's scarcely any time at all."

"It's more than you would receive if—"

Nigel braced his hands on the desk and leaned toward his father. "I'm not ready for this."

"No one ever is."

"But what if I fail miserably? Lose the entire fortune? Plunge the family into poverty." Nigel's voice rose. "Or worse? You have the futures of two other children to consider. Why, Robin is barely in his twenties and Phoebe is only sixteen. Whatever I do will surely affect their lives. No doubt adversely."

"Robin is a scholar and is destined to remain a scholar. His head as well as his heart is in the study of antiquities. Scholars are notorious for having little interest in anything save the subject they pursue. Maintaining such a life is not especially costly. As for Phoebe . . ." He blew a resigned breath. "Well, daughters, especially daughters as fond of lovely things as she is, are extremely expensive. At least until they wed; then they become another man's problem. I can tell you my expenses became considerably less once Madeline was married."

"Have you mentioned this plan of yours to Maddy?"

"It's none of her concern. She is married to a fine man and has a family of her own."

"Still, she is my twin sister and I should think—"

"I should think she of all people would applaud my decision. I suspect she too thinks it's time for you to begin bearing the responsibilities that are your birthright," the viscount said firmly. "Nigel, I have no intention of running off to the south of Italy with your mother and leaving you entirely to your own devices. I shall be here to advise you and guide you. But I will warn you, your mother has always wished to travel the world, and I want to indulge her before we are too old to do so."

Nigel stared at his father for a long moment. "Why are you doing this to me?"

The viscount laughed. "I'm not doing anything to you that will not happen eventually. As it is, you will have my guidance and not be left to flounder on your own." His expression sobered. "I should apologize to you as well, I think."

Nigel huffed. "At the very least."

"Not about thrusting this responsibility onto your shoulders. I believe it's time for that. But for allowing you to live your life thus far without a mind for anything beyond fun and frolic. I suppose I did so because I did not have the same opportunity at your age to be without a care in the world. I must admit, I have rather enjoyed watching your escapades."

"Then you shall no doubt enjoy the next six weeks." Nigel straightened and squared his shoulders. "I warn you, Father, I plan on having a rousing good time."

The viscount rose to his feet. "I expect no less."

"There might even be a minor scandal or two."

His father nodded. "I would not be at all surprised."

"I could even take up with Lady Pomfrey again," Nigel threatened.

The older man stifled a grin.

"Well, perhaps not Lady Pomfrey," Nigel muttered. "But someone equally as notorious."

"Or more so. One should always strive for the

best." The viscount picked up the notebook and handed it to his son. "One last thing."

Nigel cast a disgusted look at the notebook in his hand and grimaced. "There's more?"

"You should, in these next six weeks, casually begin looking for a wife as well."

"Oh no." Nigel shook his head vehemently. "I have no desire to be shackled to one woman for the rest of my days as of yet, and I suspect I will be no more ready in six weeks than I am today. I am less ready for a wife than I am for this."

"It was simply a suggestion," his father said mildly.

"And I shall take it as such." Nigel blew a resigned breath. "You're certain about all of this, then? If you wish to reconsider . . ."

"I never reconsider good decisions. I have absolutely no doubts as to this course. I have every confidence in you, my boy, as does your mother. The only one who doesn't"—affection shone in the older man's eyes—"is you."

Four

What a sister really wants is to be helpful.
Madeline, the Countess of Windham

"You what?" The Countess of Windham, Madeline Windham née Cavendish, stared at her guest as if she had suddenly sprouted wings and a tail.

Felicity resisted the urge to glance over her shoulder to see if indeed she had and instead cast Lady Windham her brightest smile. "I intend to marry your brother."

Lady Windham's eyes widened with delight. "You plan to marry Robin? How wonderful."

It was Felicity's turn to stare. "Who is Robin?"

"My brother, of course. Robin, or rather, Robert Cavendish."

"Dear Lord." Sheer embarrassment swept through Felicity. "My apologies, Lady Windham. Apparently I have made a dreadful mistake." How could her information be so wrong? Felicity rose to her feet. It was bad enough that she had the nerve to call on Nigel's sister in the first place, but to call on the wrong woman entirely put this encounter in the category of humiliations she would never forget. The sooner she could take her leave, the better. "I was given to believe that you were the sister, indeed I was told you were the twin sister of Mr. Nigel Cavendish."

Lady Windham choked. "You were speaking of Nigel? Nigel Cavendish?"

"Yes?" Felicity said slowly.

"Have you actually met Nigel Cavendish?"

Felicity nodded. "Yes."

"And you still want to marry him?"

"Yes," Felicity said firmly. Her resolve to marry Nigel was only strengthened by the time spent with him last night. There was simply something about the man. It made no sense but there it was. Still, she did wish to know a bit more about him than could be gathered simply from the gossip of servants. "Are you then a relation? Was I right about that at least?"

"Oh, you were right about everything. I am indeed Nigel's sister as well as Robin's. When you said you wished to marry my brother, I simply assumed you were speaking of Robin because he is the sort of man women do wish to marry, whereas Nigel, well, Nigel is the kind of man marriage-minded women tend to avoid. Nigel is not at all inclined toward marriage, and he makes no attempt to hide that fact." Lady Windham gestured at the spot Felicity had just vacated. "Now do sit down, my dear. We have a great deal to talk about."

"I would so appreciate it." Felicity sank back down on the brocade settee with a sigh of relief. "I can't tell you how embarrassed I was at the thought that I had come to the wrong person."

"You have definitely come to the right person." Lady Windham studied her curiously. "Might I ask how you know Nigel? You don't seem at all the type of woman he is usually interested in."

"Oh, he's not interested in me," Felicity said quickly. "At least not yet. Although with any luck at all, he might be a tiny bit intrigued."

"But you intend to marry him nonetheless?" Lady Windham said slowly.

"Indeed I do."

"Why?" Lady Windham's eyes narrowed. "If your interest is merely due to his position as my father's heir, then I—"

"But it isn't," Felicity said quickly. "Although admittedly it was something of a relief to learn he was of good family and prospects instead of a common burglar or thief or number of other things I initially thought he might be."

"I can see where it would be," Lady Windham murmured. "Where did you say you met my brother?"

"I didn't. But I suppose there would be no harm in telling you. You are his sister." Felicity wasn't quite sure how to explain the circumstances of her first meeting with Nigel. She drew a deep breath. "You see, I am something of an astronomer, nothing but an amateur really, although it is a passion of mine. Several evenings ago, the sky was exceptionally clear, and one should take advantage of clear nights, particularly in London. Not so much in the country where clear nights are not as rare. So naturally I was on my balcony with my telescope and I was studying the stars. Not really studying, if truth were told, but—"

"My dear." Lady Windham leaned closer and laid a hand on Felicity's arm. "You're babbling. Perhaps if you came to the point?"

"Yes, of course. You should know I am not usually a babbler. I tend to be quite well spoken but I do seem to be somewhat nervous. Very well then. The point, as it were." Felicity paused to gather her thoughts. "You see, my house is separated from Lord and Lady Pomfrey's by nothing more than an expanse of lawn and a garden wall. And on the evening in question—"

Lady Windham thrust out her hand. "Stop. I've heard quite enough. I can well imagine the rest, and do believe me, I have an excellent imagination. And this . . . this . . . this meeting?"

Felicity nodded.

Doubt crossed Lady Windham's face. "This convinced you that you wished to marry him?"

It did sound rather absurd. Felicity smiled weakly.

"More or less. I did speak with him again last night at Lady Denton's ball."

"I see." Lady Windham smiled pleasantly. "Might I ask you if there is any insanity in your family?

"Not that I am an aware of."

"And there isn't . . . That is, you and Nigel haven't . . . On the night you met . . . Given the odd circumstances . . . Oh dear." Lady Windham sighed. "I don't know how to put this delicately. You're not . . . compromised?"

"Com—" Felicity gasped. Heat washed up her face. "Good Lord, no! He and I have barely danced together."

"Good." Lady Windham breathed a sigh of relief. "I do apologize, but given Nigel's well-earned reputation . . ." Her brows drew together. "If you're not insane or ruined, why on earth would someone like you wish to marry someone like Nigel?"

"Someone like me?" Felicity brushed aside a twinge of annoyance and kept her tone cool. "Is there something wrong with me?"

"Not at all, and therein lies my confusion. You appear to be quite acceptable, practically perfect at least in regards to a potential wife. You may well be the answer to my prayers." She studied Felicity with a critical eye. "You're attractive but not overly so. You're of good family. Your demeanor is proper but not too proper. Obviously, otherwise you certainly wouldn't be here."

Felicity raised a brow. "And that's good? I've always considered that more of a flaw than anything else."

Lady Windham shook her head. "Not for someone interested in marrying Nigel. Too proper won't do for him at all." She glanced at Felicity's calling card still in her hand. "Your family name is vaguely familiar." She looked up. "You're the daughter of the Earl of Dunbury then?"

Felicity nodded.

"I don't know your parents but then I don't know *of* them either, which is probably to your, or rather their, credit." Lady Windham set down the card and again considered Felicity. "I'm not certain why I know nothing about you, however. I've been keeping my eyes open for a prospective bride for my brother for years. Nigel, that is. Robin will present an entirely different sort of problem as he is completely wrapped up in his books, but then he is not nearly as old as Nigel. I can't believe you escaped my notice."

"I spent most of last year abroad, and before that, well, I might not have been especially noticeable."

Lady Windham scoffed. "I can't imagine that."

"Thank you?" Felicity wasn't sure if she should be flattered or offended.

"My dear girl, that was indeed a compliment. You're eminently noticeable. Beyond that, you've decided you want Nigel and you're taking steps toward that goal. It's quite admirable and I applaud you. The last thing Nigel needs in a wife is some insipid little beauty with no mind of her own who will do precisely what he wants without question. He would be bored to tears within a month. But what I still don't understand is"—her brow furrowed—"why Nigel?"

"Why Nigel?" Felicity wasn't sure anything she might say would make sense, but then what about her conviction that Nigel was the right man for her did? She certainly couldn't tell his sister she had been wishing for an exciting man when he had magically appeared in her life. No, that might well make Lady Windham reconsider her query about insanity in Felicity's family. "You must admit he's quite handsome and extremely charming."

Lady Windham waved away the comment. "Nigel has perfected charming to the level of fine art. And in spite of your intention to marry my brother, you strike me as a fairly sensible young woman. Sensible young women are not swayed by handsome charmers with wicked reputations."

"He's clever and witty, and intelligent as well, I think."

Lady Windham stared at her. "You noticed that? It has always seemed to me that Nigel goes to extremes to avoid any display of intelligence."

"Does he?" Felicity widened her eyes. "How very strange. Why would one wish to be thought a fool when one so obviously isn't?"

"My brother is . . . I'm not sure how to put it." Lady Windham thought for a moment. "He has always been well aware that he is our father's heir and the next viscount. My father is extremely intelligent and capable, whether that involves leading men into battle or management of the family estates or politics. In truth, he is the kind of man legends are made of. It's rather daunting to be the heir to a legend. Nigel fears he cannot live up to Father's standards, and therefore he makes no attempt to do so."

"I see," Felicity murmured. She never would have imagined this man who exuded confidence had even the least bit of doubt as to anything about himself. Her heart twisted for him.

"But surely there's more?" Lady Windham said. "As to why you wish to marry him."

"I think, in spite of his reputation, that he is a good and honorable man. Furthermore, I suspect life with Mr. Cavendish will never be dull."

"You have a point there. But as perceptive as you are, and I must admit you have ascertained his character with surprising accuracy, you've only met him twice. How can you be certain he is the right man for you?"

Because I wished for him and there he was. "I don't know why I'm so certain, I just am." Felicity shrugged. "It sounds absurd, I know. I might add I have never been so confident of anything in my life. I know I should have been terrified when he climbed onto my balcony—"

"Dear Lord." Lady Windham rolled her gaze toward the ceiling.

"But I wasn't. And last night, when I met him again, well, my heart thudded and my mouth was dry and I wanted nothing more than to fling myself into his arms. For the rest of my days. I can tell you nothing like that has ever happened to me before. Beyond that he seems . . . right. I can't explain it any better than that. I've never felt that sense of rightness about any man. It seems a feeling one should not ignore. Ultimately, I believe"—she met Lady Windham's gaze firmly—"he is my fate."

"Fate? I see." Lady Felicity thought for a long moment, then drew a deep breath. "Well, I, for one, do believe in fate. I always have. It explains so much in life. And there are stranger things than meeting the right man when he"—she winced—"climbs over your balcony in the dead of night. I believe as well that my brother needs a good, sensible, proper—"

"But not too proper?"

"No." Lady Windham smiled. "A not too proper woman to set him on the right path. It will be a great deal of work, you know. Reforming my brother. He shall not go down the road of acceptable behavior willingly. Are you up for the task?"

Felicity raised her chin. "I am."

"Excellent."

"Then." Felicity held her breath. "You're not concerned that I do not know him well? Well enough for marriage, that is?"

Lady Windham scoffed. "The idea that one should know one's husband well before marriage is utter nonsense. I scarcely knew my husband at all when we wed, and we have been blissfully happy for nearly ten years now." She leaned toward Felicity as if imparting a great secret. "One never truly knows a man until one marries him anyway. I have often thought the less one knows of one's spouse, at least in the beginning, the better off one is. It makes life together a constant discovery. Oh, certainly one should be confident that one's choice is a good and honorable man. You have already realized that about Nigel and if you had any doubt at all, I am more than willing to reassure you." She smiled. "There now. Is that what you came to find out? Does that relieve your mind?"

"You have indeed confirmed what I already felt." Felicity blew a long breath. "That in itself is exceptionally odd. I have always thought of myself as sensible and practical until recently when I realized that I wanted something more than a sensible, practical life. Precisely the moment when I met your brother." She shook her head. "It makes no sense at all. But somehow . . ."

"Somehow with Nigel everything is different." Lady Windham beamed. "That's how it is, my dear, when one finds the right man."

A discreet knock at the parlor door heralded the entry of a maid bearing a tray with tea and biscuits. She placed the tray on a table beside Lady Windham's chair and silently took her leave. Lady Windham poured the tea, handed a cup to Felicity, and settled back in her chair.

"Now, might I ask what is your plan?"

"Why, my plan is to marry Mr. Cavendish," Felicity said firmly.

"First of all, if you are to marry Nigel, I think it's perfectly acceptable for you to refer to him as Nigel, at least between us. And, as we are to be sisters, you should call me Madeline and I shall call you Felicity."

Felicity smiled. "I should like that, Madeline."

"Secondly, your intention to marry Nigel is a goal

not a plan." Madeline stirred sugar into her tea in a measured manner. "You don't have a plan, do you?"

"Of course I have a plan. It's a very good plan." Felicity struggled to come up with something, anything that sounded even remotely like a plan. Even a bad plan would be better than no plan at all. At once, she realized she did have at least the beginnings of a plan. "My plan was to seek the advice of someone who knows Nigel very well." She grinned. "You."

"Very good. That is indeed an excellent plan." Madeline returned her grin. "A woman who is sensible and practical joining forces with one has known him since before birth—why, poor Nigel doesn't stand a chance. We shall have you married before the season ends."

"I don't want to force him into marriage," Felicity said quickly. "I want him to want to marry me."

"Oh, a forced marriage won't do at all. Nigel would dig his heels in like a willful pony. We shall make certain you are not put in a position where your reputation might be at stake, which shouldn't be the least bit difficult. As I said, you are not the sort of woman Nigel usually pursues."

Felicity sighed. "I know."

"But you are the type of woman he will want to marry. We just have to make him see that."

"Is that all?" Felicity said weakly. "It seems an impossible goal."

"I didn't say it will be easy. Nigel is very resistant

to marriage." Madeline sipped her tea thoughtfully. "You say he was intrigued by you?"

"Oh, I think so." Indeed, after their parting last night she was well aware that he had attempted to seek her out again, and she had made certain she was not available before she had left the ball for home. "In fact, I am fairly certain of it."

"Good." Madeline's eyes narrowed in a thoughtful manner. "I think the first thing I need to do is find out just how intrigued he is. I'm not sure Nigel has been intrigued by a respectable young woman before. This is extremely interesting and a very good sign."

"Do you think so?"

"I do." Madeline nodded firmly. "Now, before we go any further, I need to know everything that's transpired between the two of you."

Felicity widened her eyes. "Everything?"

"Every detail." A wicked look shone in Madeline's eye, and Felicity realized it was the same wicked look she'd noted in Nigel's eye. While there was a vague similarity in coloring, Nigel's twin didn't look the least bit like him. Except for the twinkle in her eye. The Countess of Windham would be the perfect ally.

For the next few minutes Madeline listened thoughtfully while Felicity detailed every moment of her conversations with Nigel, concluding with her comment to him that perhaps she didn't wish to be sensible and her avoidance of him for the rest of the evening.

"Oh, that's very good," Madeline said approvingly. "There's nothing that drives Nigel mad faster than a puzzle he cannot figure out. You've made an excellent start." She thought for a moment. "It seems to me the thing to do now is to continue on the path you have started. We shall make certain you are in attendance at every social event he attends. As the season is well under way, that shouldn't be at all difficult."

"I can't imagine Nigel is the type who attends the same sort of occasions I am invited to. Mine seem so"—Felicity wrinkled her nose—"proper."

"Fortunately for us, the attendance of social events during the season is one of the few areas Nigel has accepted as his duty as the future viscount. It's not at all difficult for him, really, as Nigel has always loved a good party. We shall coordinate your social calendar with his. I am assuming, as an eligible young woman of good family, you have been invited to everything worth being invited to."

"I think so."

"Good." Madeline nodded. "And I shall make certain you receive an invitation to anything you have not yet been invited to."

"So the idea is to put myself in his path at every turn," Felicity said slowly.

"I admit it sounds somewhat feeble, but the best plans are those that tend not to be overly complicated."

"And then what?"

"Well, the rest is up to you." Madeline lifted her

shoulder in a casual shrug. "You've already caught his attention. You need to continue to do so while ignoring him at the same time."

Felicity's brow furrowed. "What?"

"It's a question of balance. Simply put, you must tempt him while not appearing to be especially interested in him." She chuckled. "Nigel's never had a woman he's been interested in not be interested in him in return. That too will drive him mad."

"I don't know that I wish to drive him mad," Felicity said quickly.

"Of course you do. Only when he is totally and completely insane will he realize that in spite of his aversion to marriage, if he wants you in his life—and he will—marriage is his only option."

"It doesn't seem especially honest though, does it?" Felicity murmured. "It's rather calculating and devious."

"That's the beauty of it. One must be calculating and devious when the right man enters your life and has no idea that he is the right man. Especially men who are not interested in marriage. As for honesty." Madeline cast her a look that could only be called pitying. "Honesty between men and women is highly overrated. There is certainly a time and a place for honesty, but one must choose those times and places carefully."

Felicity stared. She wasn't at all sure what to say. Honesty had always struck her as rather important. Still, Madeline knew Nigel better than anyone, and if a certain amount of deceit was needed to win his hand, then deceit it would be. She drew a deep breath. "Very well.

"Excellent." Madeline beamed. "Fate is all well and good, my dear, and as much as I fervently believe in destiny and what have you, one cannot count on providence alone. Besides, whereas the ancients believed the fates to be lovely women, scantily clad, I have always thought of fate as something or rather someone entirely different. When you consider the nature of fate, there is an excellent argument to be made that fate is, in truth, male."

Felicity raised a brow. "Male?"

"When you think about it, men are prone to grand pronouncements without any real attempt to see them through to their conclusion. Just decreeing this and decreeing that without any thought as to how to get to whatever has been decreed. No, I think fate is definitely a man. And just like any man, needs the helping hand of a good woman." The Countess of Windham sipped her tea and considered her future sister-in-law with a satisfied smile. "And I do so love to be helpful."

"What am I to do?" Nigel paced the width of Maddy's parlor. He had spent a long, sleepless night wrestling with the weight of the responsibilities he had known would come someday. He just wasn't prepared for someday to come quite so soon. He had intended to unburden himself to his sister first thing in the morning, but he hadn't fallen asleep until past dawn and had slept far later than he had wished. He paused and met his twin's gaze. "What am I to do?

"Oh, I don't know. Stop repeating yourself? Accept your responsibilities? Behave like an adult? Grow up?" Maddy smiled in a pleasant manner. He knew that smile. Pleasant wasn't at all the sentiment behind it. Was he destined to be plagued by women who were considered pleasant but in truth were something entirely different? He ignored the thought. He didn't need to be distracted by the ever-present image of Lady Felicity in his head.

"That's easy for you to say." Nigel continued his pacing. "You're a success at your chosen profession."

"My chosen profession?" Maddy quirked a brow. "What, pray tell, is my chosen profession?"

"You know." Nigel gestured impatiently. "Countess, hostess, wife, mother. You have what? Seventeen children now?"

"Five." She huffed. "As you well know. It only seems like seventeen on occasion."

"No, my dear sister. On occasion it seems like forty." Even now, he could not resist the opportunity to tease Maddy about her brood: five boys, including a set of twins. If truth were told, he was fond of his nephews, although he usually preferred them in small doses and at a reasonable distance. Still, there were moments when he quite enjoyed their presence. His sister would say—had said repeatedly—that was because he was little more than a small child himself.

"Regardless, wife and mother is no more my chosen profession than becoming the next viscount and head of the family is yours."

"It suits you though," he muttered. "You're very good at it."

"Thank God. But perhaps it only suits me, indeed perhaps it only suits most women, because we have no real choice. It's not as if there were legitimate professions open to us. Oh, certainly we are permitted to dabble in the arts. And if one is poor but well bred, one can become a teacher in a boarding school or a governess for disgracefully low wages and less respect."

"And do you pay your governesses disgracefully low wages?"

"I pay my governesses the equivalent of their weight in gold." She sighed. "Each and every one of them."

It was an ongoing source of amusement to Nigel that his sister was unable to keep a governess for any length of time regardless of how well she paid. Her children were, to say the least, high-spirited.

"I love my children. I adore my husband. I relish my position in society, and all in all I am quite satisfied with my life. Still, it would have been nice to have had a true choice. To have been able to become something other than what I was expected to be." There was a wistful note in his sister's voice he'd never noticed before.

He raised a brow. "And what would you have become?"

"Oh, I don't know." She thought for a moment. "I should have liked to have attended Oxford as you did. It would be great fun, I think, to be in politics or study the law. Or the sciences. I would have enjoyed becoming, oh, say, an astronomer."

"An astronomer." He stared at his sister. "Why would you say that?"

"No reason in particular." She smiled in a too innocent manner. "It just came to mind."

He narrowed his gaze. Nothing *just came to mind* when it came to his sister. "I don't believe you."

"Nonetheless, it's true. It simply strikes me that it must be quite fascinating to study the stars. Even romantic. Spending your nights gazing up at the heavens through the eyepiece of a telescope. On a balcony perhaps."

Lady Felicity had both a telescope and a balcony and was, in fact, the only person he knew who did, although admittedly, aside from Robin, his circle of acquaintances did not include those of a scholarly or scientific nature. To hear now that his sister was apparently so inclined was completely out of character. What—or perhaps who—had put such a notion in her head?

He narrowed his gaze. "Madeline, what do you know?"

"I know any number of things, brother dear. First and foremost, you"—she met his gaze firmly—"you are as frightened as a rabbit by this decision of Father's and—"

"Of course I'm frightened. And with good reason.

I shall surely plunge the whole family into abject poverty and—"

"*And*, as I was saying before you so rudely interrupted me, you are the only one who thinks so. The only one who thinks you are not well up to the task. Father would never make such a decision if he had any doubts about your abilities whatsoever." Her tone softened. "Nigel, you've been trained for this from the time you were old enough to walk. Your entire life has been spent in preparation to become the next viscount."

"I don't seem to have learned much," he said under his breath.

"I suspect you've learned more than you think. Honestly, Nigel, sometimes your behavior is no better than Edward's and he's only nine. No. I take that back." She glared at her brother. "Sometimes your behavior is substantially less mature than my oldest son's or his younger brothers."

"Thank you. That is precisely what I need to hear." Sarcasm sounded in his voice.

"It is indeed what you needed to hear," she snapped. "I daresay you haven't heard it enough.

"That I behave like a child?"

"Yes!"

"Well, damn it all, Maddy, I feel like a child." He sank into the chair closest to his sister. "I feel completely unprepared and totally incompetent."

"That may well be one of the stupidest things you've ever said, and you have long made a habit of saying stupid things."

"Again, my thanks." He glared at his sister. "Motherhood has changed you, Maddy, and not for the better, I might add. You used to be far more sympathetic to my problems than you are now."

"I've become quite skilled at dealing with small children and their problems. *Your problems*, as you put it, are not nearly as great as your apprehension. Father is certainly not going to toss you in the water and allow you to sink or swim on your own. He'll be right by your side. Nigel." She blew an exasperated breath. "From the time you finished school until now, Father has allowed you free rein to do exactly as you please, has he not? He has not requested anything of you—"

"I am expected to make an appearance at each and every social event deemed of importance by Mother," he muttered.

"Poor, poor Nigel." Maddy rested the back of her hand against her forehead in a gesture of feigned sympathy. He wanted nothing more than to revert to childhood and yank her hair. "Forced to go to one party after another for the sake of appearances and respectability and spending the rest of his time in scandalous activities and one liaison after another with equally scandalous women."

"It's a difficult job, keeping up appearances, that is." Nigel slumped back in his chair and grinned. "I'm exhausted."

"Have you considered that in addition to your new responsibilities it's past time you acquired a wife as well?"

"No," he said quickly, ignoring the vision of Lady Felicity that arose unbidden in his mind. Since he'd met her again last night and discovered she was not the girl he had thought, she had come to mind with annoying frequency. Even during his sleepless night, when he hadn't been considering the ramifications of his father's decision, she'd been in his head. And oddly enough, he saw her not as she'd been on that infamous first night but as she might have been. On her balcony, with her white nightclothes shifting in the slight breeze, clinging to every delightful curve just long enough to tease and tantalize and—he shook his head. "I most certainly have not nor do I intend to do so."

"You can't put it off forever, you know. You will need a wife eventually. Children, an heir."

"Couldn't I just take one of yours?" He forced a light tone to his voice. "You have more than enough."

She raised a brow.

He sighed. "I have no interest in those sweet young things that are routinely paraded before me every season. And only, I might add, because of my future position. And perhaps my face." He flashed his sister a wicked grin. "I do have a damn fine face."

"Although it's nothing compared to your arrogance," she said sweetly.

"If one is going to do something, one should do it well." He rested his head on the back of the chair and stared up at the coffered ceiling. "They are all so well bred, so well behaved, so eager to please. So bloody perfect. There isn't the least bit of fun in any one of them, you know."

She snorted. "I certainly do. I was once one of them."

"Not at all, Maddy. You always gave gentlemen the vague, but nonetheless distinct, idea that there was something just a bit improper about you, a scandalous nature lurking just beneath the surface."

"Nonsense. It was only my relationship with you that made it appear so. Guilt by association and all that. My behavior was always above reproach." He could hear the smile in her voice. "Well, perhaps not always."

He laughed, then sobered. "I don't want a wife at all at the moment, but when I do, I want one who isn't perfect. Who has a few flaws. And a mind as well. I can't imagine anything more deadly than spending the rest of my days with a woman who does nothing but agree with me." He paused for a moment, then raised his head and grinned. "No. Let me amend that. I can't imagine anything more deadly than spending the rest of my days with one woman and one woman alone."

"And yet many men do," Maddy said in a dry tone.

"Saints, Maddy." He sat upright in his chair. "Each and every one. Most especially your husband." He shook his head. "I've lived with you. I know how difficult you can be."

"However, I am not the problem, am I?" She smiled in an overly pleasant manner.

"No." He sighed. "I am. It's bloody awkward to be the problem and know it."

He fell silent for a long moment. Maddy was right, of course; his father was not a fool. He wouldn't do anything to jeopardize the family's future. If his father thought Nigel could take on this challenge, no doubt Nigel could. Regardless, for the first time in his life he found himself questioning his father's judgment. Admittedly that was perhaps more an indication of his own lack of confidence than a lack of faith in his father's competency. Still, acknowledging the problem did nothing to solve it.

It was time, he supposed. Maddy was right about that too. Better now when he had his father's guidance than upon his death. Besides, just as Maddy had had no real choice as to her ultimate lot in life, neither did he.

He blew a resigned breath. "I'd best get on with it then, hadn't I?"

Maddy studied him with obvious suspicion. "Get on with what?"

"All of it." He shrugged. "Taking over for Father. Fulfilling my destiny, my fate as it were."

"Ah yes, your fate," Maddy said brightly. "One cannot fight fate. And I should think fate would include a wife."

"No. Eventually but not yet." He shook his head. "I am not about to take on yet another responsibility. I shall spend the time before our birthday familiarizing myself with the family interests as Father requested. But I fully intend as well to live these next six weeks as if they were my last. Which in many respects"—he grimaced—"they are."

"And no doubt you shall have a grand time." She leaned forward and patted his arm. "And speaking of grand times, you haven't forgotten that my party is the week after next, have you?"

"The party you used to give in celebration of our birthday until you decided you no longer wished to mark another year publicly?"

She ignored the sarcasm in his tone. "The very one."

He bit back a grin. "I would never forget about one of your parties. Especially the one which does not recognize that another year has passed."

"I can count on your presence then? You will be here?"

"I wouldn't miss it. Will it be as small and intimate as usual?" It was difficult to ask the question with a straight face. Maddy didn't know the meaning of small and intimate when it came to parties. In that she took after their mother.

"Smaller. Only fifty or sixty of our closest friends." She wrinkled her nose. "When one is firmly ensconced in one's fortieth decade one tends to trim one's entertaining."

"Fortieth?" He laughed. "That would make us four hundred years old. You meant fourth."

"Fourth, fortieth, it scarcely matters." She waved

away the comment. "When one approaches a birthday, any birthday, one becomes conscious of how very quickly time passes. How fleeting life truly is."

He stared at his sister. "That's remarkably philosophical of you. What has brought this on?"

"I suppose Father's decision, his figurative passing of the torch, has made me realize he will not be with us forever. Nor will Mother."

"I hadn't thought of that," Nigel said quietly and grimaced to himself. He'd been so occupied with his own concerns, he hadn't for a moment stopped to realize that even as healthy as his parents appeared, there would come a day when they were no longer here. A day that grew inevitably nearer with every passing year.

"I should think Father's dearest wish would be to see you settled."

He nodded. "As head of the family."

"With a wife and children of your own," she said firmly.

"And it's a wish I shall fulfill." He grinned. "Someday."

Maddy huffed with exasperation. "You are so annoying."

"One does what one can." He smiled in a pleasant manner and changed the topic. "Now then, are your plans for the party in order? Do you need my assistance in any way?"

"Your assistance." She scoffed. "What assistance could you lend?"

"None whatsoever." He shrugged. "I just thought I'd offer. I do like to be of help, you know."

"In that, brother dear"—she smiled slowly—"we remain very much alike."

Five

What a woman really wants is a husband.
Preferably one who is easily trained.
Eugenia, Lady Kilbourne

*L*ady Felicity strolled along the garden path looking not unlike a blossom herself, a virtual
flower of femininity in a color Nigel suspected was
peach although he wasn't entirely sure and didn't
particularly care. *A ripe peach.* The thought popped
into his head and he immediately banished it. If he
started thinking of her as a ripe peach, who knew
what would happen next. He'd always been fond of
peaches.

Nigel smoothly stepped to her side. "I have begun
to suspect in recent days"—he peered under her

fringed parasol—"that you are following me," he said with all the charm he could muster although he was, in truth, somewhat annoyed.

He'd noticed Lady Felicity at every social event he'd been to in the past two weeks. Indeed, it seemed he couldn't turn around lately without seeing the blasted woman. It could be simple coincidence but he doubted it. He'd been so very *aware* of her. She'd been at Lady Fenwick's ball and Lord Pemberton's musicale. He'd spotted her at the theater and at a charity event for homeless orphans—where he had wondered, as he did every year, if there were indeed orphans who weren't homeless—and at a masked ball at Vauxhall although he couldn't be entirely sure it was she. But while he saw her everywhere, *she* hadn't seemed to have noticed him at all. That too was most annoying. He wasn't sure why he had sought her out now although he suspected he was simply tired of being ignored.

"What a remarkable coincidence, Mr. Cavendish." She smiled pleasantly. "As I have begun to suspect you of following me. And here you are again."

"Everyone worth his salt attends Mr. Burnfield-White's garden party," he said in a manner far more defensive than he wished. As if he had something to defend. "Yet I have never seen you here."

"Perhaps you have never noticed as I have attended this particular event every year since I have been old enough to do so." She paused. "With the exception, of course, of last year."

"What happened last year?"

"I was out of the country, a grand tour, as it were, of the continent."

"Did you enjoy it?"

"I did indeed. The Alps, the Greek isles, and most especially Italy. There is something about travel that puts one's own life in a different perspective. It seems to me, we are very narrow-minded in England about what is the proper and improper way to live. What is civilized and what is not. If one is open to new ways of thinking, travel expands one's mind." She glanced at him. "Don't you agree, Mr. Cavendish?"

"Most definitely," he murmured although he'd really never given it much thought.

She raised a brow. "You seem uncertain. Have you traveled to any extent, Mr. Cavendish?"

"Of course." He scoffed. "I went on a grand tour after university. It was most . . . *extensive.*" The details of which were somewhat hazy as much of the tour had been spent in a constant state of drunken revelry. He did remember having a bang-up good time though.

"Where did you enjoy most?"

"Italy," he said without thinking. "Venice in particular."

"Why?"

Now that was an awkward question. His stay in Venice had been especially scandalous and a great deal of fun. From what he could remember. "The history of the place, obviously. The art and architecture. It's a unique city and culturally most enlightening."

"Indeed." An amused twinkle gleamed in her dark

eyes. "And I thought you'd say the people of Venice. The vaguely sensual air of the city itself. The hint of high-spirited decadence, as if life itself was all in fun."

He stared. Lady Felicity was certainly full of surprises. "Yes, well, that too."

She laughed, a forthright, honest laugh. As if she had nothing to hide and truly enjoyed a good laugh.

He glanced around and realized the walkway they were on had curved to parallel the river. They were out of earshot of the throng of other guests but well within sight. Nothing at all improper about this, and his opportunity to determine if she was deliberately crossing his path, and if so, why. "Might I accompany you?"

"I believe you already are," she said coolly.

"So it appears." He paused. "Do you mind?"

She stopped and studied him, her gaze entirely too assessing, as if she were determining if he was worthy of accompanying her. *At least she doesn't find me dull.* Not that it mattered. "I should quite enjoy your company, Mr. Cavendish."

He chuckled. "I feared for a moment you were going to say no."

"For a moment, I was," she said lightly and resumed walking. He stared after her and she glanced back at him over her shoulder. "Are you coming then?"

"Yes, of course," he murmured and quickly returned to her side. "Why?"

"Why did I consider not allowing you to walk with me?"

He nodded.

"You have a scandalous reputation, and I don't know that it's beneficial to be seen in your company. Furthermore, I'm not sure it's a good idea to encourage your attentions," she said in a lofty manner.

"My attentions?" His brow rose. "I'm not giving you my attentions."

She scoffed. "Of course you are. You sought me out today—"

"Just to talk."

"And you have been following me—"

Indignation swept through him. "I most certainly have not!"

"Then how do you explain the fact that everywhere I seem to go, you are there as well?"

"Coincidence," he said firmly, ignoring that he had dismissed coincidence when it came to the question of her following him. "Nothing more than that. It is the beginning of the season after all, and it's not uncommon to run into the same people over and over again."

"Possibly," she said in a manner that indicated she didn't believe him at all.

"Lady Felicity, I assure you I am not following you!"

She ignored him. "You could simply ask to call on me, you know, and eliminate this nonsense altogether."

"I have no intention—"

"Of course that wouldn't be as much fun, would it?" she said more to herself than to him. "This way, all this 'you're here, I'm here but we're pretending not to see one another' does give it a slightly forbidden aspect, does it not?"

"No," he snapped. "I mean yes. I mean—" He blew a frustrated breath. "I have no desire to call on you."

She pulled up short and stared at him. "You don't? Not at all?"

Her brown eyes were wide and completely enchanting, and once again that drowning sensation struck him. He swallowed hard. "I have no wish to offend you."

"And yet." She raised her chin. Dear Lord, was the woman going to cry? He wasn't at all sure he could bear up under an onslaught of tears from those eyes.

"See here, Lady Felicity, you are quite lovely and very bright and altogether charming."

"And yet," she said again.

"To call on you would indicate an interest on my part beyond a mere conversation or dance at a ball or stroll in a garden."

"An interest?" She raised a brow.

"Yes. In something, well, of a permanent nature." He shook his head. "I am not at all ready for something of a permanent nature."

"Are you speaking of marriage?"

He nodded. "Exactly."

She stared. "You cannot even say the word?"

"Of course I can say the word." He scoffed. "Marriage. See, there I've said it. I can say it again if you like."

"No, once was quite enough." She thought for a moment. "Why would calling on me necessarily mean your intention was marriage?"

"It's obvious, isn't it?" He shook his head. "You are a young woman of marriageable age, of good family and equally good reputation. You are everything a man would want in a wife if a man was looking for a wife, which, at the moment, I am not."

"I see." She narrowed her eyes. "I am not the type of woman you would typically call on."

"I wouldn't—"

"Come now, Mr. Cavendish, we are both aware of your reputation. I daresay you wouldn't hesitate to call on me if I were a widow with a proclivity toward adventures of an amorous nature."

"Well, I—"

"Or a bored matron with a penchant toward illicit affairs."

"See here, I—"

"Or not a virgin."

"Lady Felicity!" Shock stole his breath and he gasped. "That's entirely improper!"

"What? The comment or the word?"

"Both!"

"It's simply a word, Mr. Cavendish. Much as marriage is simply a word."

"They are not simply words, they are states

of . . . of existence." Good God, he sounded like a pompous idiot.

She shrugged. "And easily changed."

"Lady Felicity!"

"Have I shocked you? I would not think a man like you would be easily shocked."

"I am not easily shocked, and yes, you have," he said in a manner far loftier than he had ever used before. But then he had never had a conversation quite like this before.

"I was not offering myself to you if that's what you were thinking." Her expression was composed, but there was a definite hint of amusement in her eyes.

"Good Lord." He closed his eyes to pray for strength, but an image of an indecently clad Lady Felicity offering herself to him in the midst of a bed covered with peaches popped into his head. He snapped his eyes open. "By no means was I thinking that."

"Oh." Was it his imagination, or was there the slightest touch of disappointment in her voice. "Good, because that would indeed be improper. And unlike you, I am most interested in marriage." She smiled and resumed walking.

He trailed after her. "I knew you were."

"Why?"

"It's not as if you have a real choice." His sister's words rang in his head. "The only position open to a young woman of your station in life is marriage."

She cast him a curious glance. "You sound almost sympathetic."

"I am, I think. I am in precisely the same position. I am the heir of a viscount and my future is laid out for me." He shrugged. "My younger brother, however, has choices in life. He is of a scholarly nature and is pursuing his passion for ancient civilizations. On the other hand, one of my sisters is already well married and my younger sister will be expected to do the same when she is old enough." He adopted a casual tone. "I have recently learned my sister, my twin sister, that is, has an interest in astronomy. You have an interest in astronomy, do you not?"

"Indeed I do. Yet another coincidence, do you think?"

He studied her for a moment. It had been exceptionally odd that his sister had mentioned astronomy, but then it could be that he was seeing things that did not exist because he was so very aware of one particular astronomer. "Probably."

"I should pay a call on her," Lady Felicity said brightly. "It appears we have much in common, although there are any number of women who have a serious interest in the heavens. Today and in the past. Did you know that more than two thousand years ago a lady, Hypatia of Alexandria, studied the stars?"

"I had no idea," he murmured.

"And Caroline Herschel, who lived in Bath, was the first woman to discover a comet, oh, seventy-some years ago. She discovered eight, all in all, and three nebulae. Why, her star catalogues were published by the Royal Society."

"You don't say." Not that he particularly cared, but Lady Felicity's passion for her subject was mesmerizing. He wondered what else she might have a passion for.

"Miss Herschel was even made an honorary member of the Royal Astronomical Society." She wrinkled her nose. "Honorary because they don't accept female members."

"How antiquarian of them." It did seem somewhat unfair that someone with the accomplishments of a Miss Herschel would be denied membership simply because of her gender.

"And an American, Maria Mitchell, discovered a new comet just seven years ago."

"And?"

"And"—she drew her brows together—"and what?"

"Are there more? Women astronomers, that is?"

"Most certainly. There is—" She winced. "Oh dear. I've been going on and on, haven't I?"

"A bit, but it was most enlightening. Your passion is admirable."

"My passion tends to carry me away," she said in an apologetic manner.

"Does it?" Once again the image of a peach-covered Lady Felicity popped into his head. He cleared his throat. "You are exceptionally well versed on the subject."

"Not at all." She shook her head. "I am simply a dabbler. I can identify a fair number of the various stars and planets but I am not a serious scientist."

"Still, your knowledge—"

"Is minimal," she said firmly. "I do, however, enjoy knowing that I am not the only female intrigued by gazing up at the heavens. It is a pursuit that is at once precise and somewhat magical, if one believed in things like magic."

"Do you?"

She hesitated. "No, of course not. How absurd."

"If I recall correctly, you told me that I had changed your mind about things like magic."

She shrugged dismissively. "Flirtatious banter, Mr. Cavendish, nothing more than that, and, as such, quite meaningless. Surely you have engaged in flirtatious banter on occasion?"

"On occasion."

"But allow me to ask you the same question. Do you believe in magic?"

"I don't know. I've never given it much thought." Yet another thing he had never reflected upon. It struck him that there might well be any number of issues Lady Felicity had given thought to that had never so much as crossed his mind. She was much more intelligent than most women of his acquaintance, although admittedly he had never been overly interested in a woman's mind. He felt like something of an uninformed dolt.

"What have you given much thought to, Mr. Cavendish?"

"I was just wondering the same thing myself," he said with a dry chuckle. "I thought about a great many things during my school years. Art, literature, philosophy. I can recall having passionate philosophical debates about whether ideals or realities shape the course of history. Now . . ."

"Now you are far too busy living your life rather than studying about life. In many ways it would be quite admirable." A slight smile curved the corners of her lips. "If that life wasn't so scandalous."

"Fun though." He grinned.

"No doubt." She thought for a moment. "I suppose that's why I enjoyed travel so much. I was living my life rather than waiting for something to happen." She sighed. "But then the lot of women like myself is to wait for life to happen to them rather than going out and living it as you have done."

"I don't understand."

She smiled. "Neither do I." She chose her words with care. "It seems to me that women—how did you put it? Ah yes. Women of good family and good reputation, trained to be everything a man would want in a wife, spend the first part of our lives waiting to be selected, as it were, by an appropriate man, whereupon we will spend the remainder of our lives being precisely that good wife that we are expected to be. It's all very proper and respectable and, from what I have seen, quite, quite dull."

He chuckled. "Surely it's not that bad."

She cast him a skeptical glance.

"But you said you wish to marry."

"Of course I wish to marry. As you said: I have no real choice."

"If you had a choice? If you could do whatever you wished?" He wasn't sure why he wanted to know but he did. "Would you pursue astronomy as something more than a dabbler?"

"Probably. Although if the entire world were open to me . . ."

A thoughtful light sparked in her eye. "I should wish to do something rather more adventurous than simply study the stars. Sail to them, perhaps."

He laughed. "I daresay that would be adventurous. Impossible but adventurous."

"Then I shall have to sail somewhere else," she said with a laugh. "The South Seas, possibly, in search of primitive tribes. Headhunters and the like. Oh, that would be exciting. Or I should like to explore the jungles of darkest Africa. Or search for the hidden riches of the pharaohs in Egypt."

"Have you always had this desire for adventure?"

"I'm not sure." She considered the question for a moment. "I think it was always there but it seems to have grown in me in recent years. I suspect it was travel that brought it to a head. Seeing new places, meeting new people, that sort of thing. Now I find I don't wish to settle for an ordinary life although I daresay I shall."

"I doubt your life would ever be ordinary," he said gallantly and realized as he said the words he did indeed mean them.

"It's kind of you to say but"—she shook her head—

"this is my fifth season, not including last year, and if I am going to marry at all I should do so soon." She slanted him a pointed look. "And I *do* intend to marry."

"Yes, I believe you mentioned that."

She stopped and turned toward him, her gaze meeting his. "And what, Mr. Cavendish, would you do if you could do anything in the world? What would you be?"

"Better," he said without thinking and then cringed to himself. Why on earth had he said that?

"Better?" She studied him, and for a moment he had the oddest sensation she could see right through him. "Better in a moral sense?"

"My morals are just fine, thank you," he said firmly, then paused. "At least they have suited me thus far."

"Then what did you mean by better?"

"I don't know. It was a silly thing to say. I have no idea why I did so."

"Surely you have some idea why—"

"No." He shook his head and offered her his arm. "Would you care for some refreshment? I find I am somewhat parched from our walk."

"Are you?" She took his arm. "And I thought you were simply changing the subject away from something you would prefer not to talk about."

"That too." He chuckled. "But I am thirsty."

They turned off the path and started across the vast expanse of lawn that led to the tents that stood along the back of the appropriately grand Burnfield-White house. There were tables as well on the terrace that overlooked the tents, and nearby a wooden floor had been laid across one section of the grass for the dancing that would begin when the late afternoon drifted into evening and the lanterns were lit. Guests milled about between the tables and beneath the tents. Others strolled through the well-tended plantings. A spirited game of croquet occupied a laughing crowd off to one side of the wide lawn.

Edgar Burnfield-White's annual garden party was a marathon that began in midday and typically ended near dawn. The length of the event, coupled with the vast amounts of spirits imbibed and the sheer number of guests attending, virtually guaranteed there would be at least one noteworthy incident, and usually more, for gossips to dwell on in the coming weeks. Affairs both public and private had started and ended here. Scandalous behavior, again both public and private, regularly occurred. Those who were married and unmarried and various combinations thereof were routinely discovered in compromising situations. And yet the Burnfield—White garden party was not considered especially scandalous. Indeed, even the loftiest members of society considered it an event not to be missed. Why, one never knew what might happen, and one would hate to miss being on hand when it did.

"Lady Felicity," Nigel began.

"Mr. Cavendish," she said at the same time.

They laughed and he tried again. "It seems to me

in these past few minutes we have forged a sort of friendship."

"Why, yes, I believe we have."

"In the spirit of which I should very much like you to call me Nigel."

"I'd like that especially as I have been thinking of you as Nigel all along." She smiled in an innocent manner. "Why, every time I have seen you following me I have thought, 'There's Nigel again.'"

"I have not . . ." He sighed. "Coincidence, Felicity, nothing more than that."

"There are some who say there is no such thing as coincidence. That everything we do, everything that happens to us, is preordained by some greater power."

"Are you speaking of fate?"

"Yes, I suppose I am." She paused. "Do you believe in fate, Nigel?"

He chuckled. "I must confess I have given fate no more thought than I have given magic or the benefits of travel or any number of other things."

She met his gaze firmly. "You should, Nigel. You should give it serious thought. It is well worth thinking about." Her gaze slid past him and she nodded. "I see a friend I have not seen in some time and I believe she wishes to speak to me."

He turned in the direction of her gaze. A short, roundish young woman dressed in a multitude of flounces and lace headed toward them. If Felicity resembled a blossom, this creature looked very much like a full-blown bouquet. "You mean the determined-looking female bearing down on us?"

Felicity nodded. "She is my dearest friend, and determined is an apt description. If you will excuse me I shall head her off and save you the inquisition she surely has in mind."

He raised a brow. "Inquisition?"

"Most definitely." Felicity's gaze stayed on her approaching friend. "Eugenia wed last year and is bound and determined to see me married as well. The mere fact that you and I are walking together has no doubt set off her matchmatching instincts like a vulture scenting fresh prey."

"Ouch." He winced. "That's far too vivid a picture."

"But accurate nonetheless," Felicity said under her breath. "You see, Eugenia, who is really a dear, feels I should lower my standards when it comes to a match. She feels any husband is better than no husband."

"And obviously you disagree."

"Indeed I do." Her jaw set in a stubborn line. "I have no intention of spending the rest of my days trapped in a dull, boring, predictable life with a dull, boring, predictable husband. No marriage is better than that kind of marriage. Make no mistake, Nigel"— a firm note sounded in her voice—"I do wish to marry and I do intend to marry, but marriage simply for the sake of marriage will not do. I would rather spend the remainder of my life alone staring at the stars than wondering what I have missed."

"I see," he murmured. He wasn't sure he'd ever met a woman quite as forthright as Felicity Melville. And he certainly had never spoken as freely with any other woman as he had with her. Perhaps it was her outspoken nature that had led him to be as candid with her as he had. Regardless of the reason, it was at once refreshing and more than a bit confusing.

"Now then." She drew a deep breath and squared her shoulders. "We shall part here and I shall spare you her inevitable quizzing as to your intentions."

"Which I don't have," he said quickly.

"I believe we have established that," she said in a wry tone, nodded, and started to leave.

"Felicity." Impulsively he took her hand and raised it to his lips. "I cannot think of anything worse than you lowering your standards."

"You may rest assured, Nigel." She cast him a brilliant smile that did the oddest thing to the pit of his stomach. "I do not intend to."

"What on earth were you doing with that man?" Eugenia said the moment she reached Felicity. "Do you know who that is?"

"And good afternoon to you too, Eugenia." Felicity smiled at her friend and continued to stroll in the direction of the refreshment tables. She was every bit as thirsty as Nigel had claimed to be, and there was the strangest feeling in the pit of her stomach. More to do, she suspected, with Nigel's presence than with the fact that she had not yet partaken of any of the delicacies offered by Mr. Burnfield-White's excellent kitchen staff. "I'm famished. I feel as if I haven't eaten for a week. Are you hungry?"

"I'm always hungry," Eugenia muttered and fell in step beside her. "But you are avoiding the subject. Whatever are you thinking? Being seen in the company of Nigel Cavendish?"

Felicity grinned. "Are you afraid he'll ravish me on the spot?"

"Yes!" Eugenia huffed, then sighed. "Well, perhaps not. You are not the type of woman a man like Nigel Cavendish typically pursues."

"So I've been told."

They reached a table laid out with fruits and pastries and all manner of tempting delights. There would be a more extensive supper later in the evening and yet another at midnight. Mr. Burnfield-White did not stint on quality or quantity when it came to food or entertainment or anything else at this annual soiree. The man himself was something of an enigma. He was the youngest son of a marquess with a fortune that came from his mother's side of his family as well as from his first two wives. Mr. Burnfield-White himself was a charming man of about forty years. Aside from his penchant for large, elaborate parties, he was said to be somewhat reserved. Felicity had met him, of course, but she could not claim to know him and had on occasion wondered if anyone truly did.

"Well?" An insistent note sounded in Eugenia's voice, and Felicity wouldn't have been the least bit surprised if the other woman had stomped her foot. "Aren't you going to say anything?"

Felicity handed her parasol to a nearby servant, picked up a plate, and surveyed the offerings. "The strawberries look good." She selected two, placed them on her plate, then took a third for good measure. "What do you want me to say?"

"I want you to tell me what you were doing with Nigel Cavendish." Eugenia fairly hissed the words, which would have been more effective had she not been piling her own plate with fruit tarts and cakes.

"I wasn't *doing* anything." Felicity selected a peach tart. "I was just speaking with him." She paused and watched Eugenia take a bite from an iced raspberry cake. "I find him fascinating."

"Fascin—" Eugenia choked and coughed and turned a rather remarkable shade of red, somewhat darker than the color of the cake but complementary nonetheless. Felicity patted her on the back and signaled a servant for a glass of lemonade. She handed her friend the drink, and Eugenia gulped it down, then glared. "You did that on purpose."

"Not entirely." Felicity smiled apologetically. "I am sorry but I couldn't help myself. You were being so . . . so . . ."

"Concerned?" Eugenia snapped.

"Scandalized," Felicity said firmly.

"I am scandalized. Felicity." Eugenia pressed her lips together in the manner of a chastising governess. "You cannot afford to be wasting your time with a man like Nigel Cavendish. He has an appalling reputation and has been the center of one scandal after another. Are you aware of that?"

"I believe I've heard it mentioned." Felicity took a bite of a strawberry. It tasted as good as it looked. She wondered if she could get Nigel to join her for a meal later. Just as a friend, of course. For now.

"There isn't anyone who hasn't heard. The man is infamous for his affairs and his . . . his . . . well, any number of things too improper to mention." Eugenia popped the rest of the tart in her mouth.

"Still, you must admit he's quite a catch." Felicity's gaze wandered past her friend to the far side of the lawn, where she caught a glimpse of Nigel speaking with a group of gentlemen including Lord Norcroft. "I think he has a great deal of potential."

"Utter rubbish." Eugenia snorted. "It would take a lifetime to reform a man like that."

"I believe that a lifetime is precisely the length of a marriage," Felicity murmured.

"Good God!" Eugenia's eyes widened, and Felicity feared they might pop right out of her head. It was an interesting, if somewhat gruesome, image. "You've set your cap for him!"

Felicity forced a laugh and prayed for strength. "Don't be absurd." She set her plate down, grabbed Eugenia's elbow, and directed her away from the table and any number of guests who might be more than a little interested in their conversation. Burnfield-White's garden party was well known as an event where one could effortlessly pick up all sorts of scandalous information simply by lingering near the refreshment tables. "If you do not lower your voice, you'll attract no end of attention. I would prefer that the center of gossip at this year's garden party be someone other than myself."

"But"—Eugenia glanced at her plate—"I wasn't finished."

"No, I didn't think you were." Felicity smiled and nodded a greeting to those they passed but continued to steer Eugenia to a point where they would not be overheard. Nigel was right. No one would dare to miss Mr. Burnfield-White's garden party. Nearly every face she and Eugenia passed was familiar. And no doubt each and every one was curious as to where Lady Felicity and Lady Kilbourne were going with such a determined step.

They reached the rose garden, where the low bushes made it easy to spot any curious eavesdropper. Felicity released Eugenia in front of a stone bench. "There. Now you may finish."

"I am no longer hungry," Eugenia said in a lofty manner and set her plate on the bench. "However." She clasped her hands together in front of her. "I am by no means finished discussing Nigel Cavendish."

"Imagine my surprise."

"Are you or are you not"—Eugenia fixed her with a firm gaze—"pursuing Nigel Cavendish?"

"I am not," Felicity said without hesitation and noted to herself that it wasn't actually a lie. While she was determined to marry him, she wasn't pursuing him in the strictest definition of the word. What she was doing was encouraging him to pursue her. As such it was a different thing entirely.

Eugenia narrowed her gaze. "I don't believe you."

Felicity laughed. "Why on earth not?"

"Because I know you. I've known you since our first season and I have never once seen you spend as much time with any gentleman as I saw you spend with Mr. Cavendish today."

"Nonsense." Felicity scoffed. "I was barely with him for more than a few minutes. And we were never out of sight."

"It scarcely matters. The man is a scoundrel."

"But a scoundrel with outstanding prospects," Felicity said with a grin.

"Even so, it takes a great deal of time and effort to reform a rogue of his nature. Time, my dear friend, that you simply don't have. This is your sixth season."

"Fifth," Felicity murmured. "I missed last year."

"Precisely my point."

"What if I don't wish to reform him? What if I like him exactly as he is?"

Eugenia gasped. "You can't mean that."

"I'm not saying that I have any plans whatsoever in regards to Mr. Cavendish—"

"I should hope not!"

"But if I did," Felicity continued, "it seems to me that the very appeal of a man like him lies in what you see as his flaws."

"What everyone sees as his flaws."

"So why on earth would I, or any woman, for that matter, wish to change the very thing that attracted them in the first place?"

Eugenia stared in disbelief. "Because . . . because . . ."

"Yes?"

"Because . . . he's not suitable for marriage, that's why." Eugenia shook her head in an ominous manner. "If he does not change his ways, he shall surely break the heart of any woman foolish enough to marry him. Tigers never change their spots you know."

"Leopards."

Eugenia drew her brows together. "What?"

"Leopards," Felicity said. "Leopards have spots. You said tigers. Tigers have stripes."

"Tigers, leopards, it's of no consequence." Eugenia waved off the comment. "The point is the important thing, and you know what I meant. A beast is a beast and cannot change who he is."

"I'm not sure Mr. Cavendish is a beast," Felicity said mildly. "He does seem to have some moral standards. As you've pointed out, I am not the type of woman he typically expresses an interest in. And in not one of the stories or gossip I've heard about him have I ever heard that he has ruined anyone."

"There's always a first time," Eugenia said darkly.

Felicity studied her friend. "Is your opinion of me that low then? Do you think that I am stupid? That I would allow myself to be ruined?"

"No, of course not." Eugenia sighed. "You are probably the most intelligent woman I know. But intelligence flies out the window in the face of love."

Felicity laughed. "Love has not been mentioned."

"See that it isn't! When he marries, as he is certain to do eventually, it will surely be to some meek, pretty little thing without a brain in her head who will be so pleased to be the next Viscountess Cavendish, she will overlook his indiscretions and other scandalous activities. It's what men of his type do. I know you. You would not stand for that kind of behavior. Which means you would be terribly unhappy and your very life would be a misery."

Felicity stared. "What a lovely picture you paint."

"It's a picture painted over and over and one I should not like to see you in the middle of. Felicity . . ." Eugenia's voice softened "I have met several very nice gentlemen, friends of my husband, that I should like you to meet. They're pleasant, not at all disreputable, and quite suitable for marriage."

"Quite suitable for marriage? That sounds very much like describing a horse as quite suitable for the park, but one wouldn't want to wager on him in a race."

"That's completely inappropriate." Eugenia sniffed. "But accurate. One doesn't want a racehorse for a husband."

"One doesn't want a draft horse either," Felicity said dryly.

"No, what one wants is a nice, sensible, horse for everyday outings. Broken well to the saddle and not prone to high-strung behavior. Exactly like my Albert."

"I daresay Albert would not take kindly to being compared to a sensible horse." Although, if Felicity thought about it, dear, pleasant Albert might not mind being compared to a well-trained horse at all. "Besides, Eugenia, I have met any number of horses broken to the bit in these last seasons, and not one has been especially interested in me as . . ." Felicity bit back a grin. "As a rider."

"That's because you haven't been interested in the ride," Eugenia snapped, then gasped. "Did I say that?"

Felicity laughed. "You did indeed."

"You are a bad influence on me, you know." Eugenia struggled against a smile, but then Felicity had always been able to make Eugenia smile.

The two women could not have been more dissimilar. Not merely in appearance but in character as well. Eugenia was short and blond and prone to plumpness, with a creamy complexion and voluptuous figure. She could certainly advise Felicity to lower her standards, but if truth were told, Eugenia had never considered lowering hers. While she had pursued marriage with a single-minded determination, had indeed received several offers through the years, she had stood her ground until she had found the one man she wanted. That it had turned out to be Lord Kilbourne, Albert, a sensible, respectable sort of man with a quiet manner and equally quiet—though surprisingly quick—wit, surprised everyone, including Eugenia herself.

"Whatever makes you think these pleasant, reputable friends of Albert's would be the least bit interested in me?" Felicity crossed her arms over her chest. "Through five seasons I've received very little interest whatsoever."

"Probably because you expressed no interest in

them. Have you ever considered that while you were finding them tedious, they were finding you equally dull?"

"No. I can't imagine such a thing." Indignation sounded in Felicity's voice. "I am exceptionally interesting. I am an excellent conversationalist. I have a well-developed sense of humor. I can be quite charming."

Eugenia raised a brow.

"I *can.*"

"When you wish to be."

"Well, of course, when I wish to be. And if a gentlemen isn't at all interesting, then I see no reason to waste my time . . . what I mean to say . . ." Felicity wrinkled her nose. "Oh dear."

Eugenia smirked.

"I am dull?" Felicity winced.

"You *were* dull."

A horrible thought struck her. "Did you think I was dull?"

"I'm your dearest friend, I would never think such a thing. However, *was* is the significant word here." Eugenia studied Felicity. "But you've changed. I noticed it as soon as I saw you again. It's all that travel and the continent and whatever, I suppose. And from what I've seen this season so far, gentlemen have noticed it as well."

"What do you mean by changed?" Felicity said slowly.

"There's an air about you of confidence, perhaps, or polish, refinement maybe. I don't know. It's as if you know a secret the rest of us do not and you do not intend to tell."

"Do you think so?" Felicity tried and failed to hold back a grin. This was much better than being dull. "A secret no one else knows? I rather like that."

"I thought you would." Eugenia cast her a reluctant smile. "In addition, you've done something this season I've never seen you do before."

"I have?"

Eugenia nodded. "You've been flirting. I don't believe I've ever seen you flirt before."

Felicity laughed. "What nonsense. Of course I have flirted before. I have always flirted. Why, I'm an incorrigible flirt."

Eugenia snorted. "You've never considered any man worth the trouble."

"Surely not. That can't possibly be true. Why, I can name any number of flirtations, serious flirtations at that, from long before this year." Still, now that the question was raised, Felicity couldn't quite recall any specific instances of having flirted before this season. Certainly she had flirted with any number of men on her travels. There was the son of a French count, and a quite handsome Italian nobleman, and that charming composer in Vienna. And since her return, she had most definitely flirted with Lord Beckham and the very pleasant Mr. Copcorne at the theater and Sir Kenneth at a masquerade, although, upon reflection, it might not have been Sir Kenneth at all. And every conversation she'd had with Nigel thus far had had a definite element of flirtation. Why, none of it had taken any effort at all. And she had definitely noted gentlemen being far more attentive this year.

"For a woman who claims to want to marry, you've never put any effort into it whatsoever."

Felicity shook her head. "I never realized it, but apparently not. Why haven't you told me this before?"

"Oh, I don't know," Eugenia said in an offhand manner and picked up a tart from her plate on the bench. "It didn't seem important."

Felicity studied the other woman for a long moment. Eugenia always tended to eat when she was disconcerted about something. "Eugenia?"

Eugenia took a large bite of the tart. "Hmm?"

Felicity took the now half-eaten pastry from her friend's hand and tossed it into the bushes. "What are you trying not to say?"

Eugenia swallowed and cast a longing glance at the tart. "Do keep in mind that I am your friend."

"I will."

The oddest look of what appeared to be guilt crossed her face. "Your dearest friend in the entire world."

Felicity narrowed her eyes. "Eugenia?"

"I didn't say anything for a number of reasons." Eugenia paused to choose her words. "First of all, you weren't nearly as eager to marry as I was, so it really didn't seem necessary to say anything. And secondly . . ."

"Go on."

"Frankly." Eugenia drew a deep breath. "I was afraid if you made any effort at all, no one would pay the least bit of attention to me."

"What are you talking about?" Felicity stared in disbelief.

"You're tall and slender and far prettier than you've ever thought in a Greek statue sort of way."

"Me? A Greek statue?" Felicity scoffed. "That's the silliest thing I've ever heard."

"It's not at all silly. And the image is only enhanced by the somewhat aloof, disinterested manner you've always had."

Felicity winced. "Immovable?"

"Precisely." Eugenia shrugged. "As we were always together, I did fear if you were more approachable I would pale in comparison and no one would notice me."

"Not notice you? Men have always fallen over themselves to get to you. You're petite and blond and you have"—Felicity gestured at Eugenia's chest—"those."

Eugenia glanced down at her chest. "They have served me well. Regardless"—Eugenia met her friend's gaze—"you were everything I wanted to be. I admit it, I was jealous."

"You were jealous of me? Me?"

"Yes." Eugenia's face twisted in an expression of abject remorse and sheer misery. "Can you ever forgive me?"

"Forgive you?" Felicity stared at her friend for a long moment. Who would have imagined that in those years, while Felicity would have given a great deal to have Eugenia's curves and bubbly charm, Eugenia was envying Felicity's form and manner.

"Well?" Eugenia's voice rose.

"It seems to me," Felicity said slowly, "all you've really done is to spare my feelings by not telling me how truly dull I was—"

"Not to me," Eugenia said quickly. "I've always thought you were extremely interesting."

"—and not mention that, in your opinion, I made no effort to attract or charm gentlemen, and was, in fact"—Felicity wrinkled her nose—"immovable."

Eugenia moaned. "And I am truly sorry."

"You needn't be." Felicity sighed. "I probably wouldn't have believed you anyway."

"Then you do forgive me?"

"Aside from your jealousy, which I find more flattering than anything else, there is really nothing to forgive."

"Thank goodness." Eugenia breathed a sigh of relief. "I have been concerned about this for some time. I felt quite awful about it, and I should like to make it up to you."

"Would you?"

"I would indeed." Eugenia nodded vigorously. "In any manner that I can. You are my dearest friend in the world, after all."

"Yes, yes, I know." Felicity considered the possibilities. She wasn't at all sure how she might be able to use Eugenia's help, but Albert was another matter entirely. And while she didn't have a plan for either of them at the moment, a pledge of assistance would be a nice weapon to have. "Anything at all?"

Eugenia raised her chin. "Absolutely."

"Without question?"

Eugenia clapped her hand over her heart. "Without so much as a moment of hesitation."

"Excellent." Felicity grinned, took hold of Eugenie's shoulders, and turned her around to face the crowd across the lawn. "Do you see Mr. Cavendish over there."

"Yes," Eugenia said slowly.

Felicity leaned close and said softly into her friend's ear. "I intend to marry him."

Eugenia groaned. "No."

"Yes. I am as resolved to marry Mr. Cavendish as you were to marry Albert."

"But Albert is so . . . so . . . wonderful."

"As is Mr. Cavendish." Felicity's gaze lingered on Nigel, and her heart actually fluttered. "And you are going to help me."

Eugenia's shoulders stiffened. "I will not."

"Oh but you will. Because you are my dearest friend in the world. And because some of those secrets I appear to be keeping"—she lowered her voice and resisted the urge to laugh—"are yours."

Eugenia gasped. "You wouldn't."

"I might."

"Very well then," Eugenia snapped and jerked out of Felicity's grasp. "What do you want me to do?"

"I don't know yet. I simply want you to be ready to lend assistance should I need it."

"I think this is a horrendous mistake." Eugenia blew a resigned breath. "But apparently I have no choice." She drew her brows together. "Would you really tell my secrets?"

Felicity grinned. "Only to Albert."

Eugenia narrowed her eyes. "You are a wicked, wicked woman, Felicity Melville. You and Mr. Cavendish probably deserve one another."

"Oh my dear Eugenia." Felicity laughed. "I am counting on it."

Six

What a mother really wants are children who are healthy and intelligent. Regardless of the price.
Madeline, the Countess of Windham

"You!"

Nigel froze on the steps leading down to his sister's ballroom. "What have I done now?"

"Nothing at all, *today*," Maddy snapped, looking more than a little frazzled. Odd, Maddy always had everything well under control before the beginning of a party but right now she had a cape on over her gown, her gloves in her hand, and looked like she was about to leave. Or flee. She drew a deep breath, obviously for calm. "I am simply grateful to see you."

"You don't sound especially grateful. I'm not merely

here but I am a good half an hour early. You couldn't possibly ask for more." He glanced around the all but deserted ballroom. No servants bustled about, no musicians tuned their instruments, no extravagant urns of flowers were in evidence. "Too early, perhaps?"

"It's a disaster, Nigel, an utter disaster." Maddy squared her shoulders and determination sparked in her eyes. "Regardless, I have everything well in hand."

"Do you?" He raised a skeptical brow.

"I do." She started past him, pulling on one glove. "Now then, I need you to stay here and—"

"Where are you going? And what is going on here?" He waved at the ballroom. "I must say this doesn't look at all like a party is about to begin."

"That's because it isn't. At least not here." Maddy blew a frustrated breath. "The party has been moved to Cavendish House. Mother offered to have it there the moment she heard what happened."

"What on earth did happen?"

She grit her teeth. "We had a flood."

"Ouch." He winced. "I know how nasty floods can be. It took months to get my house back in order. I just moved back in this week and—" He stopped and studied his sister. "Why are you glaring at me like that?"

"Did you or did you not give my boys toy boats?"

Nigel wasn't entirely sure if he should confess although it did seem innocent enough. Still . . . "Yes?"

"And what did you tell them when you gave them

those . . . those"—she waved her glove at him—
"*boats*?"

"I told them I had great fun sailing boats on the ponds in the parks when I was a boy."

"And?"

"And I told them on occasion I would . . ." At once he remembered exactly what he had said and the rapt expressions on the faces of his nephews as they had hung on every word.

"On occasion you would float them in bathtubs?" She fairly spit out the words.

"On occasion," he said weakly.

She narrowed her eyes. "They decided that occasion was today. Suffice it to say there was something of an overflow."

"I say, Maddy, you can't blame this on me," he said with an appropriate level of indignation. "Where was their governess?"

"Packing!" She closed her eyes, obviously to pray for strength. She drew a breath. "Apparently, the boys decided they needed sailors for their boats and frogs would do nicely."

"Frogs?" He shook his head. "On my word, I never mentioned frogs." Oh he might have mentioned frogs at some point, although he was fairly sure it was not in connection with boats. Rather clever thinking on the part of his nephews though. One had to give the little devils their due. "Where did they get them?"

"The garden probably. I don't know and I don't care." She huffed. "They decided they needed a place to keep the frogs until the boats sailed and chose

Miss Everett's room. Needless, to say, the poor woman was distinctly unnerved when she opened her door to be confronted by frogs. Frogs!"

"How many?" he said without thinking. Judging by his sister's expression, it was not the right question to ask.

"She said hundreds although I doubt there were that many. The boys claim there were no more than a half a dozen, but while they are prone to exaggeration, in situations like this they do tend to underestimate." She bit her lip, and Nigel wasn't sure if it was to keep from screaming or laughing. "We haven't found them all."

"That is a problem," Nigel murmured.

"I would prefer not to have my guests find frogs in the punch bowl." She was definitely trying not to laugh.

He grinned. "It would be quite a sight though."

"This isn't the least bit amusing. I am furious." She paused, then sighed. "Perhaps it is a little amusing, although it would be far funnier if it had happened to someone else. Between the frogs and the flood . . ." She shook her head in disbelief. "The water, by the way, flowed into the upstairs hall and down the back stairs as well as leaking through to the lower floor. I have several floors and ceilings that now need to be repaired. Once we discovered the boys' seafaring exploits and the extent of the problem, I realized I couldn't possibly have the party here. Why, a good portion of my staff spent much of the day trying to mitigate the damage."

"You could have canceled," he said mildly.

She stared at him as if he had just suggested slaughtering innocents. "It's *my* party. *Our* party really. I have given it every year since my marriage. I would have to be run over by a carriage and breathing my last before I would think of canceling it, and even then I would expect someone"—she shot him a pointed glance—"to bravely carry on in my place."

He nodded in a somber manner. "In the midst of mourning your loss, of course."

"Well, I wouldn't expect you to enjoy yourself." She again started off. "Most of the servants have already gone to Mother's. Those that remain are finishing packing up the food in the kitchen. Mother sent notes to all the guests informing them of the change in location." She shook her head in amazement. "Only Mother could manage that. I have no idea how she does it but I am eternally grateful that she does."

He trailed after her. "But why am I to stay here?"

"There's every possibility some of those invited did not receive Mother's note and they may well come here. I need you to send them on to Cavendish House."

"Can't a servant do that? Your butler perhaps?"

"He's accompanying me. There will still be a footman here, but it would be terribly impolite to greet a guest with only a footman."

"No it wouldn't," he muttered. "What about your husband?"

"He's already gone," she said over her shoulder.

A horrid thought struck him. "You're not leaving me alone with the children, are you?"

"I would never do that to the boys although it would certainly serve you right. They are firmly established in the old nursery at Cavendish House."

"Maddy!"

She turned on her heel and glared at him. "In ways too numerous to count, the blame for this can be placed firmly on your head. I need someone from the family to be here in my stead. Surely you can do this one little thing for your sister? Your twin sister. Who once shared a womb with you!"

He stared at her and realized further argument was futile. "It will be my pleasure," he said with a weak smile. "Just how long am I to be exiled here?"

She thought for a moment. "No more than an hour I think." She nodded. "Yes, that will be more than sufficient. After all, this isn't a ball where people can drift in and out all evening. It's a small, intimate—"

Nigel snorted. "Only fifty or so of our closest friends."

"—gathering. To be more than an hour late for such an event would deserve to be greeted by no more than a footman." Maddy glanced behind him at the empty ballroom and heaved a wistful sigh. "It would have been quite grand, you know. There was to be dancing after dinner and the library was to be set for cards for those who prefer games to dancing. I had even arranged for two separate sets of musicians so there would be music throughout the evening."

"It was grand last year and it will be again next

year and it will be every bit as smashing tonight. Tonight"—he took his sister's hands, raised them to his lips, and met her gaze firmly—"will be different but no less wonderful because regardless of where it is, it is still a Countess of Windham affair."

"You are a charming rogue. It explains so much." She kissed his cheek, pulled her hands from his, and started toward the entry. "One hour, Nigel. I expect to see you at Cavendish House no more than a quarter of an hour after that. This is to mark your birthday as well as mine, remember."

"Unofficially, of course."

"Absolutely. I do not celebrate birthdays publicly."

He chuckled. "Precisely why the party is weeks removed from the actual date of our birth. And what will my loving sister do if I'm late?"

"I don't know but I can assure you it will be vindictive and quite painful," she tossed over her shoulder. "And will make you rue the day you ever so much as heard the word *frog*."

He laughed and called after her. "Don't you want to know why I was early?"

"No!"

"I just wanted to tell you, you were right."

"I'm always right," she called back. The next moment, she swept through the front door, manned by the lone remaining footman, accompanied by her butler and a few other servants. The door shut firmly behind her.

Nigel glanced at the ballroom and grinned. The more he thought about it, the more he'd wager the idea of frogs on boats came from Maddy's husband, although he'd never tell his sister his suspicions. Still, no one could handle Maddy the way Gerard did. Probably one of the reasons she'd married him even if she'd never admit such a thing.

He started to step down into the ballroom, then thought better of it, turned, and headed toward the library. Gerard had an excellent library if not quite the size of that at Cavendish House. No doubt there was something of interest there to pass the next hour with. Preferably a treatise on estate management or investments or finance or any number of other topics that might help him in his study of the family inter-ests. He stepped into the library and scanned the volumes neatly arranged by category. Nigel wasn't especially organized himself—his own library was a haphazard arrangement where philosophy might well be shelved beside poetry, next to ancient history, flanked by current novels—but he did appreciate or-ganization in others, particularly when it made his own life easier.

He'd started studying the notebooks his father had given him, with great reluctance at first, and, much to his surprise, had found it all, well, interest-ing. The family's interests were admittedly compli-cated and would take some effort to master, but Nigel was having little difficulty understanding his father's style of management. He was starting to be-lieve, if only a little, that he might well be able to take his father's place without disaster befalling the family.

Maddy was right about that. Pity she hadn't stayed long enough to hear him admit it. It certainly would have made up for the flood and the frogs. Not entirely, perhaps, but it would have given her enormous satisfaction. Maddy loved being right.

He stepped to a shelf of books on finance and banking and perused the titles. An annoying thought struck him, and he firmly thrust it to the back of his mind. Still, he couldn't completely ignore one insistent question.

What else might his sister be right about?

Felicity stared in horror at the empty ballroom. Dear Lord, did she have the wrong night? It would serve her right after convincing her parents there was no real harm in allowing her to attend Madeline's party alone. After all, she was of age and had traveled extensively without them. She ignored the fact that she'd been well chaperoned. Besides, she'd pointed out, they didn't know Lady Windham and had been surprised by the invitation in the first place.

This was obviously divine retribution for her sins although she couldn't remember anything she'd done that would merit embarrassment of this magnitude. She'd never made a mistake like this before. Indeed, she was certain Madeline's party was two days after Mr. Burnfield-White's garden party. Perhaps she had read the invitation wrong? She should have realized her error when there was no long line of carriages depositing guests. She simply assumed it was, as Madeline had said, a small affair.

Regardless of the reason, there was obviously no party in progress, and from the looks of it, nothing planned. At least not for tonight. If she hurried, she could be back in her carriage before the somewhat confused footman who had answered the door and taken her wrap recovered his wits and returned from wherever he had scurried off to. As supportive of Felicity's plans as Madeline was, even she might think it overeager for Felicity to arrive on the wrong night. She ignored the nasty thought that perhaps she had missed it—and the opportunity to be with Nigel again—altogether.

She hadn't seen him since their encounter at Mr. Burnfield-White's unless one counted the fact that he was constantly present in her thoughts and in her dreams, in which case she was scarcely ever without him. Eugenia had brought up the idea of love, and until then Felicity hadn't considered love at all. Still, what else but love would account for it? She wished to be with him every minute. To spend her days in his company and her nights in his arms. To have his children and share his life and grow old by his side. She'd never felt anything like this before. This ache, this longing, this need. She'd no more believed in love at first sight than she'd believed in magic or fate until he climbed over her wall and into her life. It was as if she could not be fully whole without him, as if he were a missing part of her. It was exceedingly strange. Felicity had always thought of herself as complete and independent. Now there was a hole in her world only he could fill. It was not at all rational and made no sense whatsoever. But then perhaps love wasn't supposed to make sense. And surely this must be love.

Still, until he felt the same, it was best not to appear too enthusiastic, although it was much harder than she had expected to act as if she wasn't the least bit interested in him, when all she wanted was to fling herself into his arms. Aloof but amused was Madeline's advice, so aloof but amused Felicity would be. And aloof had no business being here in the wrong place at the wrong time.

She turned and headed back toward the front door, grateful that in this particular house the ballroom was directly across from the entry at the opposite side of a grand, galleried salon. With luck, she could be out the door before anyone knew she was here. Felicity sent a prayer heavenward that her driver had not yet left.

"I would wager you did not receive word," the familiar voice sounded somewhere in the shadows off to her right.

She drew a deep breath and adopted a pleasant smile. "I suspect I would be wise not to accept that wager. Word about what?"

Nigel stepped from the shadows, a book in his hand. "My mother sent a note to all of my sister's guests saying tonight's party had been moved to Cavendish House."

"Oh dear." She shook her head. "No, I didn't receive anything of the sort."

"It was inevitable, I suppose, that in a gathering

of this size—only my sister would call it small and intimate, by the way—someone would be missed." He stepped closer. "I didn't realize you knew my sister."

"We've only recently met," she said quickly. "You did say we had a lot in common."

"Yes, I suppose I did," he murmured and studied her thoughtfully.

At once she realized they were all but alone here. Highly improper, even scandalous. Still, it was an innocent mistake. At least on her part. "If I might be so bold as to ask why, if the party has been moved, you are here?"

"I've been exiled for the moment." He grinned. "Penance for my sins."

She raised a brow. "All of them? It's to be a lengthy exile then?"

"Good God, it would, wouldn't it?" He chuckled. "No, my exile only continues another half an hour or so. I am to stay here and direct any guests who arrive on to Cavendish House."

"Dare I ask what particular sin prompted your exile?"

"It was harmless enough, at least it seemed so at first. Some time ago, I gave her boys toy boats, as I had quite enjoyed sailing boats on ponds myself as a boy. Apparently I also mentioned that I had enjoyed sailing them in bathtubs as well. Boys, being what boys are, decided to follow in my footsteps with rather unfortunate results."

She winced. "I see."

"A rather nasty flood, from what I understand." He paused. "And then there were the frogs."

"Frogs?"

"To sail the boats."

"Of course," she said faintly.

"The frogs were not my idea." His voice was firm but there was a definite twinkle in his eye. "It seems many of them escaped and are even now running free through the house."

"And your sister blames you?"

He nodded in a solemn manner. "I am the reason for the flood and the frogs. It sounds rather biblical, doesn't it?"

"All you need now is famine." She tilted her head and considered him. "You don't seem overly contrite for a man responsible for a disaster of biblical proportions."

"Oh, but I am." He heaved a dramatic sigh. "I am wracked with guilt."

She bit back a smile. "Wracked?"

"Perhaps not wracked but I am sorry. Extremely sorry." His gaze met hers, and they burst into laughter.

"Will your sister forgive you?" Felicity said, sniffing back a laugh.

"Probably." He grinned. "She always does."

"I should leave you to your exile then." Felicity stepped toward the door.

"No, stay," he said, looking somewhat surprised at

his own words, then he smiled. "I would appreciate the company. And I can then accompany you to Cavendish House."

"It wouldn't be at all proper, you know." She shook her head. "We are very nearly alone here."

"Nonsense. There's a footman at the door behind you."

She glanced over her shoulder. The bewildered footman had once again taken up his position by the door.

"And any number of servants still in the kitchen. I would be happy to call them in to chaperone if you are afraid to be alone with me."

"I have been alone with you before," she said pointedly. "In circumstances far more scandalous than this."

"And I was a perfect gentleman."

"Perfect?"

"Well, with you."

She laughed. "You thought I was a child." She studied him curiously. "For a man who does not wish to marry, are you not at all concerned about being caught in a compromising situation with a woman who does wish to marry?"

"I assure you, Felicity, I have no intention of behaving in a manner that would be considered the least bit compromising."

She waved at the book in his hand. "Don't you have reading to help pass the time?"

He grimaced. "This particular book will not help the time pass but rather stretch it out endlessly." He tossed the book onto a nearby bench, took her hand, and raised it to his lips. "Do save me, Felicity, from the tedium of *Modern Methods of Soil Conservation.* You have my word I shall be the epitome of propriety at all times."

She gazed into his blue eyes and said the first thing that came into her head. "Pity." She resisted the urge to laugh at the startled expression on his face, pulled her hand from his, and moved away. She glanced around the grand salon. "What a lovely home this is."

"Yes, it is," he said, the faintest hint of confusion in his voice. Good. She quite liked confusing him. "Maddy married well."

"As was expected," Felicity murmured and wandered to the arched entry of the ballroom. She gazed out over the grand room with its classically styled paintings on the ceiling and deep, gilded moldings. "Is she happy, do you think?"

"Happy?" he said from behind her.

"With her life, I mean."

"Well, she has a husband she loves and five little boys she adores." He stepped to her side and looked out over the ballroom. "Although perhaps not at the moment."

Felicity laughed.

"As for the rest of her life . . ." Nigel paused for a long moment. "A few weeks ago I would have answered without question, but then I had never given it much thought. Now . . ."

"Now?" She turned toward him. He stood entirely

too close to her than was proper, or perhaps she stood entirely too close to him. Regardless, she had no desire to move.

"Now I realize how very lucky my sister is. She has indeed found happiness within the very narrow confines we allow women in this world."

If she leaned toward him the tiniest bit, it wouldn't take any effort at all for him to lean forward as well and kiss her. "Do you think those restrictions too narrow, then? Should your sister have been allowed to become whatever in life she wished?"

"Yes." He paused. "And no."

"No?" She wondered how it would feel to have his lips on hers.

"I do feel a woman's primary responsibility in life is to be a good wife and mother. However"—he drew a deep breath—"you, as well as my sister, have recently made me realize that perhaps it isn't entirely fair to restrict the use of intelligent minds to the male of the species alone."

"That's very . . ." She searched for the right word. It was difficult to think with him so very close. "Progressive of you."

"It seems my thinking has changed on a number of issues of late." His gaze searched hers.

"Oh?" Her voice had the oddest breathless quality.

"I have begun to wonder if I am not quite as incompetent as I have always thought I was." His gaze drifted to her lips and back to her eyes.

She swallowed hard. "I suspect no one thought that but you."

"I doubt it. I have made no effort to encourage anyone to think otherwise."

"I have never thought that." Her heart thudded in her chest.

He bent his head closer to hers. "But you scarcely know me."

"And yet . . ." She raised her face to his. There was no more than a breath, a word, a sigh between his lips and hers.

"And yet . . ." His lips brushed hers.

"Beg pardon, sir." A voice sounded from across the ballroom.

Nigel straightened and at once stepped back. A man carrying a violin case hurried across the floor toward them.

Nigel drew a deep breath. "May I help you?"

"I do hope so. None of them in the kitchen seemed to know much of anything but they're all running around like chickens without their heads so I figured someone in here might help. We are, or were, supposed to play at a party here tonight. I know we're a bit late, for the start of things, that is, but we were told we would be playing later as there was to be other music as well, so . . ." The musician shook his head. "We could have the wrong date or house or—"

"We?" Nigel asked.

"Four of us of altogether, sir." The man, obviously the leader of the quartet, nodded toward the back of the ballroom where three other musicians waited anxiously.

Nigel glanced at Felicity. "Apparently you are not

the only one who is unaware of the change of location." He turned toward the musician. "My good
man, you are indeed in the right place at the right
time but due to circumstances"—he flashed Felicity
a quick grin—"of a divine nature, the right place has
become the wrong place."

The man's brows drew together in confusion.
"What?"

Felicity stepped forward. "Lady Windham's party
has been moved to a different location."

"I see." The musician's expression lightened. "Well
then, if you would be so kind as to direct us, we'll be
off."

"Certainly, I . . ." Nigel paused. "I say, would you
do something for me before you go?"

"Of course, sir," the other man said slowly, obviously concerned about Nigel's *something*. "But we
should be on our way."

Nigel waved off the objection. "I shall take full responsibility. Besides, you said you were not expected
to play until later in the evening." He turned to Felicity and swept a polished bow. "My dear Lady Felicity,
would you do me the very great honor of allowing me
the first dance?"

She raised a brow. "Here?"

"We have the ballroom. We certainly have the
time." He waved at the musicians. "And now we have
the music."

"Beg pardon, sir." Unease sounded in the musician's voice. "But we did contract to play—"

"For my sister, yes, and you shall. But first"—his gaze met Felicity's and her heart leaped—"you shall play for us."

"Sir, I—"

"I shall pay you whatever my sister is paying you, and as you will still be able to play for her, you shall make twice as much for scarcely any additional work."

"One moment, sir." The musician hurried off to join his friends.

Nigel watched the discussion among the small group. "What do you think, Felicity?"

"About whether they'll play for us or about whether our dancing here alone is completely inappropriate and the stuff scandal and gossip is made of?"

He slanted an amused glance at her. "Are you afraid of scandal then?"

"I am afraid of what scandal leads to. I rather enjoy my small place in society, and I should hate to be ostracized. There is that matter of my desire to marry, you know." She shook her head. "What will people think if we are caught?"

"They will think I am the cleverest fellow to have arranged a private dance with you."

"Given your reputation, they will think seduction is in the air."

He choked. "Seduction?"

"It's just a word, Nigel. Good Lord," she said under her breath, "one would think you were the virgin and I was the miscreant."

"Felicity!" Shock sounded in his voice, but there was a distinct smile in his eyes.

"You and I both know seduction, real or imagined, of someone like me—marriageable, of good family, untouched as it were—would lead to a forced marriage. And you have no desire for marriage."

"But you desire marriage."

"Indeed I do but I never said I desired it with you."

He stared in indignation. "What's wrong with me? If I recall, you said I was a catch."

"I didn't say I wished to catch you."

"You said I was reformable and desirable." He nodded. "I remember that distinctly.

"Yes, well, it would take a great deal of effort. I'm not at all sure you're worth the trouble."

He leaned toward her and lowered his voice. "I assure you, I am well worth the trouble."

"My lord." The musician approached, accompanied by two of his friends. "We've agreed, but if it meets with your approval, only the two violins and viola will play. It takes too long to get the cello out of its case. And just one piece, then we must be on our way."

"Excellent." Nigel grinned. "How fast can you be ready?"

The man nodded to his friends and all three set their cases on the floor, pulled out their instruments, and prepared to play. The leader propped his violin under his chin. "Is that fast enough for you, sir?"

"Aren't you going to tune the instruments?" Felicity asked.

"It'll take time and"—the musician grinned—"it will cost you extra."

"In that case, we shall take what we can," Nigel said firmly. "A waltz, if you please." He held his hand out to Felicity. "Now then, let me ask once more, will you do me the honor of this dance?"

It was undoubtedly a mistake, and even though Nigel didn't mean it as such, perhaps the most romantic thing she could have imagined. Of course, a man like Nigel was probably as skilled at romance as he was at everything else that had to do with relations between men and women. She ignored the question of exactly what *everything* truly meant.

She cast him a brilliant smile and put her hand in his. "I can't think of anything I should like more."

At once the strains of a popular waltz filled the air. She moved into his arms, and if he held her longer than was strictly necessary before he started to whirl her about the floor, it was no more than a moment and she might have been mistaken. Or it might have been that, given the type of man he was, that fraction of a second was part and parcel of his flirtatious manner. Regardless, it made her stomach flutter and warmed her to her very soul.

"I've never danced in an empty ballroom before." Nigel grinned. "I rather like not having to worry about accidentally careening into another couple."

She laughed. "I can't imagine you careening into anyone, accidentally or otherwise."

"Oh, the occasional collision has its uses."

"No doubt." He led her through a complicated step, and she moved with him as if they had danced together always. Forever. "You're an excellent dancer."

"Only when I have an excellent partner." His gaze met hers, and amusement showed in his blue eyes. "Practically perfect, I would say."

"Practically perfect." She chose her words with care. "It seems to me when one finds a partner who is practically perfect, one should take advantage of it."

His grip tightened the tiniest bit. "Absolutely."

"Such a match does not come along often."

"No, it does not."

"One would be a fool to let a practically perfect partner slip away."

"The worst sort of fool." He raised a brow. "I thought you did not like to talk when you danced?"

"Without the possibility of collision it's not at all difficult to do both." She met his gaze firmly. "Nigel, I have a confession to make."

"Excellent." He grinned in a wicked manner. "I do so enjoy confessions from lovely women."

"I wasn't entirely honest a moment ago."

"Oh?"

"I think you would be worth the trouble."

He laughed. "I knew it."

"As well as the effort." She braced herself. "My effort."

"Your effort?" His brows drew together in confusion, then realization dawned in his eyes. He stopped abruptly and she stumbled forward. He steadied her, then took a step back. "What do you mean?"

"Exactly what I said. You might well be worth the trouble and the effort." She drew a deep breath. "You did agree with me that when one finds a match who is practically perfect, one should do something about it."

He stared. "I was speaking of dancing."

"And I was speaking of . . . of "—she shrugged—"everything else. Life, as it were."

"Life?" The rising pitch of his voice coupled with the horror in his eyes might have been amusing under other circumstances. "Life?"

"Life," she said firmly.

"Life?" he croaked.

"Nigel." She leaned toward him. "The music has ended and those gentlemen are no doubt waiting for payment and directions to Cavendish House. You should see to them." She smiled pleasantly. "I shall wait here."

"Of course," he said, a stunned look still on his face, and strode off toward the musicians. A low, muttered "life" lingered in his wake.

She resisted the impulse to laugh. It was the oddest thing. She certainly hadn't planned to tell him anything at all about her feelings and indeed had been distinctly nervous as she'd done so in anticipation of his response. Which was very much as she had expected. Yet the moment the words were out of her mouth, absolute calm and complete confidence had replaced any trepidation she'd felt. In spite of what she and Madeline had discussed, she knew without doubt complete honesty was the right way to win Nigel. At least at the moment.

He completed his transaction with the musicians and stalked back toward her, determination in his step. His expression was stern, and it made him, if possible, even more attractive. A weaker woman would have backed down at the look in his eye. It was the tiniest bit dangerous and completely thrilling. Certainly this would not be easy, but she had never anticipated anything about Nigel would be easy.

He stopped in front of her, a far more respectable distance than at any other time thus far this evening. "When you say life, surely you're not speaking of marriage?"

She favored him with her brightest smile. "Surely I am."

"With me?"

"Practically perfect, that's what you said." She nodded. "And I quite agree."

"I believe I have made my position on marriage clear," he said in a forbidding manner she disregarded completely.

"As have I."

He stared in disbelief. "But I don't wish to be married. Not now, not yet. I am not ready for marriage."

"I daresay few people are."

"Let me be perfectly honest with you, Felicity." He paused. "I find you quite attractive and most desirable."

"As I find you." She leaned toward him in a confidential manner. "You are most suitable, and even your reputation doesn't scare me at all."

"That's somewhat gratifying, I suppose," he muttered. "I will even admit that, in recent days, you seem to have lingered in my mind rather more than I would like."

She beamed. "How delightful."

"It's not delightful at all," he snapped. "It's bloody well annoying."

"Well, I find it delightful," she said firmly. "Have you dreamed about me as well?"

"No!" He closed his eyes for a moment, as if to pray for strength. "Perhaps. Once or twice."

"Or every night?"

He glared.

"If we are being honest with one another, and you did say you were being perfectly honest," she said quickly, "then you must admit you have never had a woman linger in your mind like this before."

"Aha. I have you there." He crossed his arms over his chest. "I have had any number of women fill my thoughts. All sorts of thoughts. Wicked, lascivious thoughts of lust and desire and the like."

"Lust and desire?" She waved off his comment. "Two more words that don't shock me in the least." She thought for a moment. "And have you had such thoughts about me?"

He paused for no more than a fraction of a second, but it was enough. "Certainly not."

She laughed. "I don't believe you."

His eyes narrowed. "Believe this, then. I do not dally with . . . with . . ."

"Marriageable virgins?"

His jaw clenched. "Yes."

"Why not?"

"Because they want *marriage*!" He fairly spit the word. "And I do not!"

She scoffed. "Utter nonsense."

He stared. "You're mad, aren't you? Completely insane."

"I don't think so, although it is a possibility, I suppose." She sighed. "My dearest friend probably thinks I am. She has warned me about you."

"You should listen to her."

"Where would be the fun in that?" She shook her head. "No, Nigel, my mind is made up. It was fate that led you over my garden wall that night, and as much as I have never especially believed in fate, it does seem to me when it smacks you in the face, you would be a fool to ignore it."

"Fate has nothing to do with this!"

"There is the chance you could be right, but I don't think so. You have already admitted you have been thinking about me—"

He snorted.

"Dreaming about me."

He scoffed.

"Following me."

"I most certainly have not!"

"Lusting over me."

"Now see here, Felicity—"

"No, you see here, Nigel." She stepped closer and shook her finger at him. "You admit you want me. You further admit, or at least imply, that the only way to have me is marriage. Therefore, the only logical—"

"No." He grabbed her hand. "I do not want marriage." He yanked her into his arms. "But I do want you." He crushed his lips to hers in a kiss obviously meant to punish or perhaps frighten her. It was at once shocking and exhilarating. She realized he expected her to fight him, to pull away and run shrieking from the room in virginal terror. She had no intention of doing anything of the sort. She threw her arms around his neck and melted into his embrace. His kiss softened, deepened. Her mouth opened to his, and his tongue met hers. Sheer excitement swept through her. Aching need swelled inside her and she wanted more, much, much more. This, no doubt, was lust and desire. And it was exquisite.

He pulled his head away from hers and stared into her eyes. "I want you out of my life."

"Never," she said with a breathless smile.

He stared at her intently, then released her and stepped back. "There can be no more of this."

"No?" She touched her finger to her lips and realized her hand was trembling. And realized as well his gaze was fixed on her lips. "I rather liked it. Didn't you?"

"Yes, I liked it." He huffed. "It was exceptional. One would think you've had a great deal of practice."

"Not at all. Oh, I've been kissed on occasion, but

not enough to develop any skill at it. I think I'm simply an adept student and most willing to learn." She gave him a pleasant smile, as if they were discussing something of no more importance than the prospects of rain. "What do you think?"

"I think you are the most dangerous woman I have ever met," he said sharply, then blew a long breath. "I will admit, Felicity, that I do indeed want you. More and more each time we meet. Which is precisely why I shall avoid you from this moment on. I am a weak man when it comes to matters of the flesh, and I cannot continue to resist my desire and your . . . your . . ."

"My what?" she said helpfully.

"Your willingness to learn!" He grimaced. "I will not be the cause of your ruin and I will not be forced into marriage."

"I have no intention of forcing you into anything, nor will I permit my own ruin, and I have as much to say about it as you do. Besides"—she raised a shoulder in a casual shrug—"it was only a kiss. A very nice kiss, I grant you, and as much as I enjoyed it, I suspect you can do better."

"Better?" His brows rose. "Better?"

"Much better." She stifled a laugh. He was so very indignant. "Of course, the gossip could be wrong. Gossip is usually exaggerated. I have often wondered if the truth of any matter is more—"

"I told you this was the wrong night." An elderly male voice sounded from the entry of the ballroom.

"Good God, what now," Nigel muttered and turned toward the entry.

"Nigel Cavendish, is that you?" A lady of advanced age stood at the top of the steps leading down to the ballroom and waved. Beside her stood an equally elderly gentlemen.

"Indeed it is, Lady Fernwood." Nigel offered Felicity his arm and lowered his voice. "This discussion is at an end."

"Or not," she murmured.

He shot her a sharp glance, then escorted her across the floor and up the steps. Upon closer inspection the elderly couple looked even older than they had appeared from across the room. Somewhere in that vague area between seventy years and forever. Still, they were distinguished and quite charming.

"Lady Fernwood." Nigel took her hand and raised it to his lips. "You are more beautiful than ever."

The aged woman laughed. "Indeed I am."

Nigel turned to her husband. "You are looking exceptionally well this evening, sir."

The old man snorted. "Have you gone blind? I'm dying, boy, any fool can see that."

"We're all dying, dear," Lady Fernwood said and patted her husband's arm. "Although I daresay you will outlive us all." She turned an assessing eye toward Felicity. "And this is?"

"Lady Fernwood, Lord Fernwood," Nigel said in an impeccably proper tone, "may I present Lady Felicity Melville. Lady Felicity, Lady Fernwood is my late grandmother's cousin."

Felicity bobbed a polite curtsy. "My lord, my lady, it is an honor to meet you."

"Melville?" Lord Fernwood squinted at her. "Daughter of the Earl of Dunbury, are you? A rascal if ever I met one."

"My father? A rascal?" Felicity laughed. "I assure you, you have him confused with someone else."

"Don't get confused," the elderly man muttered.

"Of course you do," Lady Fernwood said. "Regardless, water under the bridge and all that." Her surprisingly sharp gaze slid from Felicity to Nigel and then to the empty ballroom. "All alone, are you, Nigel? Someone of a suspicious mind might assume something of an improper nature is occurring. I do hope such a person would be wrong."

"Such a person would definitely be wrong." Nigel's voice was firm.

"Let us hope so." Lady Fernwood glanced again at the ballroom and shook her head. "While I myself am not usually prone to confusion, I must admit I am perplexed at the moment. Have we indeed come on the wrong night?"

"Not at all," Nigel said and quickly explained the situation. "We were just about to leave for Cavendish House."

Felicity raised a brow. "Is your exile over then? I thought it was longer."

"I have declared it over," Nigel said firmly.

"Then we must all go together." Lady Fernwood smiled at Felicity. "We have the town carriage tonight, and there's more than enough room. It's really far too big for the two of us, but Lord Fernwood insists."

"Like my comfort," the old man said under his breath. "Don't want to be stuffed in some little pony cart."

"No one will stuff you anywhere, dear." Her gaze caught Felicity's, and a twinkle sparked in her eyes. "Although the idea does have merits."

Lord Fernwood cackled. "She's still got spirit." He winked at Nigel. "It's why I keep her." He nodded toward Felicity. "This one got spirit, boy?"

"Without a doubt," Nigel said wryly.

"Not surprised." Lord Fernwood shook his head. "Expect as much from Dunbury's girl."

"Perhaps on the way to Cavendish House you can tell me your remembrances of my father." She couldn't recall her father, or her mother for that matter, ever discussing their youth. She had assumed it was un-eventful. Now it seemed their past might be far more interesting than their present. "I suspect you have some entertaining stories."

Lord Fernwood chuckled. "Indeed I do. Why, I could tell you—"

Lady Fernwood cleared her throat.

"Wouldn't do, of course." The elderly man sighed with regret. "Proper thing like yourself, wouldn't do at all."

They moved toward the front door. Felicity collected her wrap and Nigel offered his arm to Lady Fernwood. "Shall we?"

The older lady beamed up at him. Apparently no

woman, regardless of age, was immune to Nigel's charm. "We shall indeed."

Lord Fernwood placed Felicity's hand in the crook of his elbow and grinned at her. The old man didn't seem quite as feeble now as he had a few moments ago. "Always did like a woman with spirit."

"I do hope I won't disappoint you," Felicity said with all the spirit she could muster and wondered if she should sit as far away from the old man in the carriage as possible.

"He thinks he's still the rake he used to be but he's harmless," Lady Fernwood said over her shoulder as she passed through the open door.

"Harmless?" Lord Fernwood scoffed and leaned toward Felicity. "She doesn't think so."

Lady Fernwood laughed.

"Think there'll be cards tonight, Cavendish?" Lord Fernwood asked. He and Felicity followed Nigel and Lady Fernwood down the front steps to the waiting carriage.

"My sister has arranged for a card room, no doubt, specifically with you in mind, sir," Nigel said.

"Damn fine girl, your sister. Lady Fernwood and I love a rousing game." Lord Fernwood cast Felicity a speculative look. "I'd wager a small fortune you play cards."

Felicity stared in surprise. "Why yes, I do."

The old man's bushy brow rose. "Dunbury teach you?"

Felicity nodded. In fact, she and her father had

played at least three times a week since she'd been old enough to hold the cards. Her father had played monthly with a group of friends who had played together for as long as she could remember, but that was the limit of his card playing. He'd not only taught her how to play, and play well, but he'd taught her that one should never wager more than one was willing to lose. As she grew older, she realized it was a lesson for life even more than for cards.

"Thought as much." Lord Fernwood nodded. "We'll play then, the four of us. You'll play too, Cavendish."

Nigel paused, then sighed slightly in resignation. "Of course, sir."

She choked back a laugh. So much for Nigel's vow to avoid her from now on. Bless Lord Fernwood's demanding little soul.

"Won Lady Fernwood in a card game, you know," Lord Fernwood said to Felicity.

Lady Fernwood paused on the top step of the carriage and looked back at her husband. "You most certainly did not." She cast Felicity a wicked smile. "I won him."

Felicity laughed and stepped back to allow Nigel to assist the older man into the carriage. She glanced up at the sky. It was only dusk but the sky was clear. It would be a perfect night to star gaze.

"Are you looking for something in particular?" Nigel said.

"Indeed, I am." She looked in the direction of the star she had wished on the night they had met and smiled her thanks, then met Nigel's gaze directly. "And I do believe I have found it."

Seven

What a woman really wants is a man with a wicked look in his eye for her and her alone, from the first moment he sees her to the last. No matter low long that may be.

Lady Fernwood

*B*loody hell, what had he gotten himself into?

Nigel smiled and nodded and even managed to make passable conversation, although his mind was anywhere but on those who were confident they had his complete attention.

She wanted to marry *him*? *Him?* How had this happened? He'd always been so very careful, but then he'd never encountered anyone like Lady Felicity Melville before. She was outspoken and candid and far more clever than any woman had a right to be.

Nigel had encouraged her, he knew that. Even as he was warning himself to stay away from her, he couldn't help migrating toward her. Like a goose heading toward warmer climes in autumn. He had sought her out at Lady Denton's ball, simple curiosity really, and at Burnfield-White's, curiosity again, nothing more than that, and tonight . . . *Tonight*! What had he been thinking? All that nonsense, romantic nonsense at that, about her keeping him company and then paying the musicians so that they could dance. He groaned to himself. No wonder the woman wanted him.

Nigel moved through the crowded salon, responding absently to a greeting here, a comment there, and steadfastly refused to glance in Felicity's direction. Although he did, of course, constantly. And every time he looked at her, she would glance at him and meet his gaze. If was as if she could feel his gaze upon her. And she would smile a rather secret sort of smile that might well warm his heart under other circumstances but right now struck terror into his very soul. Damnation. Thank God dinner would be served soon and he would have companions to distract him, although he doubted the ability of even the most fascinating of Maddy's guests to do so.

Nigel had to admit he wanted Felicity as well, a great deal, actually. That was the crux of the problem. How could a man who did not wish to marry have anything at all to do with an unmarried young woman? He couldn't. It was as simple as that. He knew the rules, his own as well as society's. Society said honorable men did not take advantage of innocents. And if they did—through passion or love and whatever other irresistible forces ruled the male of the species on such occasions—the right thing to do, the proper thing to do, the *honorable* thing to do was to marry the innocent in question. Or the no longer innocent, as it were. That was precisely why he had always avoided innocents. Marriageable women of good families. *Virgins.*

In spite of his many relationships with members of the fairer sex, he did consider himself an honorable man. Why, he had never once had an affair with a woman who wasn't already a woman of the world. Women who had their own resources and wanted nothing more from him than he did from them. Oh, certainly, there had been the occasional young widows who had become overenthusiastic and brought up the subject of marriage. Nigel had always managed to convince them that they were happier without a husband than they had been with one. In truth, married women were easier in every respect. They typically had an arrangement with their husbands and had no desire beyond a pleasant interlude. The only problem there was that, now and again, he would become involved with a woman who was not entirely honest about her husband's view of her infidelities. Those nearly always resulted in incidents like that at Lady Pomfrey's. Indeed, he counted himself lucky that he had never actually been injured in such an occurrence, although admittedly he had lost numerous pieces of clothing through the years. He still had not yet retrieved his shoe.

Blast it all, regardless of how much he wanted her, he wasn't ready for marriage. Besides, he still had a good three weeks before his birthday marked his complete immersion into the family's business affairs, and he intended to enjoy each and every minute of it. He was not about to be smitten by a virgin with seductive brown eyes who kissed like it was a natural gift and molded her body to his in a way that was at once innocent and enticing and—

"Might I borrow my brother for a moment?" Maddy's overly bright tone broke into his thoughts and yanked him back to the here and now.

"Yes, of course," the lady he'd been talking with said. "We were just having the most wonderful conversation." She placed a hand on his arm and fluttered her lashes at him. "We must continue it later."

"It would be my pleasure," he said smoothly although he hadn't the least idea either what he'd said or who she was.

Maddy laughed lightly, hooked her arm through his, and steered him toward the nearest exit. "She's married, Nigel," she said under her breath. "Not that that has ever deterred you in the past."

"I don't even recall speaking to her," Nigel murmured. "Good God, I might have said anything."

"And you probably did." The pleasant smile on her face belied the sharp tone of her voice. She briskly led him behind a row of potted palms to a concealed servants' door, opened it, and practically shoved him into a back corridor, then closed the door firmly behind her. "What in the name of all that's holy is the matter with you?"

"The matter with me?" he said cautiously. "I don't know what you mean."

She glared at him. "Something has happened. You haven't been your usual self from the moment you arrived here tonight. I've been watching you. Oh, you've acted politely enough but there's a vague air of preoccupation about you." She shook her finger at him. "I count on you to be charming and gracious and amusing. Your usual roguish self, as it were."

"And I'm not?"

"You most certainly are not," she said sharply. "It's as if you're here but your mind is somewhere else entirely. I want to know where and I want to know now."

"Why?" He shrugged. "If indeed I am preoccupied but if I have been polite as well, why does it matter what is on my mind?"

"For one thing, we are about to go into dinner and if you are going to be less than engaging, I shall have to rearrange the seating and place you between people who won't notice or care. For another"—her tone softened—"I am worried about you. You are not behaving like yourself at all. I've never seen you this way and it's most distressing."

"Yes, well, I've never been this way." He ran his hand through his hair. "It is indeed most distressing."

She stared at him with concern. "What on earth has happened?"

"There is a lady—"

She snorted. "There always is."

"—who wishes to marry me."

"That's what has you all tied in knots?" She stared in obvious disbelief. "I daresay there are any number of women who have wanted to marry you."

"Not at all," he said loftily. "I have gone to great efforts to make certain of that. I have made my attitude toward marriage clear from the start of any involvement and I have never been involved with a woman who had a serious wish to marry."

"And this one does?"

He heaved a frustrated sigh. "This one definitely does."

"I hate to sound unsympathetic but I'm afraid I don't see why this is such a problem. It's not as if she can marry you without your consent."

"No, of course not," he muttered. Maddy was right. Marriage was a consensual sort of thing. Felicity couldn't bash him over the head and drag him unconscious in front of a minister. "She did say she would never force me into marriage."

"Force you into marriage?" Maddy's eyes narrowed. "Have you done something scandalous, more scandalous than usual, I mean, that might force you to marry this woman?"

"No." *Not yet.*

"I still don't understand . . ." She paused. "Exactly who are we speaking about?"

"Lady Felicity Melville."

"Fel— Lady Felicity?" Maddy brightened. "Why, she's a lovely young woman." She shook her head. "You could certainly do worse."

"I could not do at all!" He stared at his sister. "I don't wish to marry. Not now and not in the foreseeable future."

"Why not?"

"I believe we've had this discussion before."

"And I daresay we'll have it again," she snapped. "Why don't you wish to marry?

"I'm . . . I'm not ready." Even as he said the words he knew he sounded like a petulant child.

"Don't be absurd." She waved off the comment. "You're as ready as anyone ever is. Besides, marriage is never something one is truly ready for. You simply hold your breath and jump in. Like jumping into a vat of cold water. After the initial shock, it's really quite pleasant. Certainly there are sacrifices." She pinned him with a firm look. "You will have to give up other women. I realize some men don't but—"

"When the day comes, I fully intend to be faithful," he said firmly. "Marriage vows are every bit as much a pledge of honor as any other promise. I am a man of my word."

"And yet you've never hesitated to assist a married woman in breaking that same pledge," Maddy said mildly.

"It was not my pledge." Damnation, he did sound like a child.

"So speaks the man of honor." She considered him

for a long moment. "Well, I for one think Lady Felicity is perfect for you."

"I didn't realize you knew her until tonight."

She shrugged. "One meets any number of people. I find her quite interesting. She's something of an amateur astronomer, you know."

"I am aware of that." At once the image of Felicity, clad in an ethereal Grecian gown like the ancient astronomer she had mentioned, bathed in the glow of the stars and gazing up at the heavens, popped into his head. His stomach tightened.

"I'm thinking of purchasing a telescope for myself," Maddy said thoughtfully. "Perhaps Lady Felicity could advise me."

"No," he snapped.

"Why not?"

"That would only serve to encourage her." He shook his head. "You seeking her advice on telescopes or anything else could be inferred as approval of her attempt to trap me into marriage."

"Is she attempting to trap you into marriage then? I though you said she would never force you to marry?"

"She wouldn't. And admittedly, it might be inaccurate to say she is attempting to trap me. In truth, she's done nothing beyond tell me she wishes to marry me. She's been annoyingly honest." He blew a long breath. "She thinks I am her fate."

"Oh, well, that's something else entirely." Maddy shrugged. "One can't fight fate."

"I can!" He glared. "This has nothing to do with fate. This has to do with . . . with . . ."

"With what?"

"I don't know but I refuse to accept that my future, particularly in regards to marriage, is contingent upon the whims of something I cannot control."

"Fate is rather unyielding that way. You must admit the idea of marrying Lady Felicity is interesting, though," she said thoughtfully. "She's everything you said you wanted, and she would make you an excellent wife."

"Or rather she would if I were in the market for a wife." He clenched his teeth. "Which I'm not."

She ignored him. "You told me you didn't want a perfect wife, you wanted a woman with flaws. Lady Felicity strikes me as having any number of flaws."

"I wouldn't say any number," he said grudgingly, "but certainly one or two. She is exceptionally stubborn and rather more outspoken than is proper."

"She is intelligent. Extremely, I think. I believe you said you did want a woman with a mind."

"Yes, yes." He gestured dismissively. "She is clever enough. She thinks about a great number of things. She has opinions on nearly everything. Indeed, she has made me realize I scarcely think about anything whatsoever."

"I see."

He narrowed his eyes. "What do you see?"

"You're obviously taken with her."

"I am not!"

"My mistake. Now that I think about it, she's not suited for you at all." Maddy shook her head. "For one thing she is entirely too tall."

"She is not. She's quite a good height."

"And somewhat too slender."

"She has an extremely nice figure."

"Her hair is a rather nondescript brown and her eyes . . ." Maddy scoffed. "Well, they're brown as well."

"They're not merely brown," he said indignantly. "They're a sable, deep and rich and endless. Why, a man could lose his soul in those eyes and not regret the loss for a moment."

Maddy raised a brow.

"Not that I have," Nigel said quickly. "I'm simply relating my unbiased observations as a man who appreciates the finer qualities of a woman."

Maddy smirked. "I never for a moment thought otherwise."

"Hah." He aimed an accusing finger at her. "I know that look. You think I'm smitten with her. Head over heels. Perhaps even in love."

"I never said that."

"You didn't have to. I can see it on your face. I'm not, so you can put that thought out of your head right now. Felicity means nothing to me whatsoever. I can well live my life without her, and I have every intention of doing so. I do not want a wife, and therefore any further involvement with her is at an end. I intend to avoid her entirely from now on." He paused. "Well?"

"Well what?"

"Aren't you going to say anything?"

"I'm not sure I need to. You seem to have covered everything extremely well." She smiled pleasantly.

Suspicion narrowed his eyes. It wasn't like his sister to concede a point this easily. "I don't believe you."

"It scarcely matters whether you believe me or not. Or whether I believe you. It seems to me the most important question is one neither of us has touched on."

He was almost afraid to ask. "And what, dear sister, would that be?"

"It's obvious, at least to someone who knows you as well as I do, and possibly even to the most casual of observers, that your reaction to this young woman's desire to marry you is out of all proportion to her crime."

He snorted. "I don't think—"

Maddy held out her hand to stop him. "In a situation like this, I would have expected you to make light of the lady's wishes and turn her away firmly but gently with your usual good humor. I would further expect that, in the process, you would somehow convince her that not only were you unsuitable for marriage, but that she was the one to come to that realization, and furthermore that it was her idea to turn you away."

"Certainly, I could—"

"However, as you have not done so, and have instead acted in a manner completely foreign to your nature, it would seem to me, darling brother Nigel, the real question you should concern yourself with"— she smiled a slow, wickedly knowing smile that was all the more terrifying because he had seen a smile very much like it in his own mirror—"is why."

"Why?" Nigel said to himself. "Why, why, why?"

"Did you say something, Mr. Cavendish?" the lady to his right asked. She was a widow around his age, with a lush beauty and a speculative gleam in her eye. Exactly his type of woman. Why, he should be charming her right now with an eye toward something of greater interest later. Yet it was all he could do to maintain a semblance of coherent conversation.

"Nothing," he said with a polite smile. "Nothing at all."

"Oh." She leaned forward in a provocative manner. "Are you certain? I could have sworn you said something."

He stared at her for a moment, waiting for the surge of desire he usually felt when a woman this lovely and this eager flirted with him. Nothing. What had Felicity done to him? Damn the woman anyway. He resisted the urge to glance to where she was seated, directly across the table from him. And damn his sister too. She'd told him she hadn't seated Felicity next to him, but she failed to mention she had placed Felicity where he couldn't fail to notice her every move. Not that he cared.

"No." He shook his head with more regret than she would ever know. "I am sorry."

"As am I," the lady said curtly, and pointedly turned her back to him to speak to the man on her right.

The lady on his left was similarly engaged with the gentleman beside her. Maddy was right. He might well be polite but he wasn't the least bit charming or engaging tonight. Under other circumstances, by this point in the dinner—he glanced at the barely touched quail on his plate—the third or possibly the fourth course, he would have thoroughly conquered the ladies on either side of him and had one wondering if his reputation was well earned and the other planning to find out for herself. His heart simply wasn't in it tonight. Blast it all. Look at what the mere discussion of marriage did to a man. His resolve to avoid it hardened.

He shot an annoyed glance at Felicity, the source of all his trouble, who was too busy conversing with Norcroft beside her to pay Nigel any notice at all. Judging by the expression on her face and the way her eyes would widen and she would lean toward Norcroft ever so slightly, not to mention her occasional light laughter, she apparently no longer found him dull. Norcroft didn't seem the least bit bored either. At least she wasn't paying any attention to Beckham, seated to her left, at the moment. Not that she hadn't spent part of the soup course, and nearly all of the fish, hanging on the man's every word. Nigel wouldn't have thought it of her, indeed until tonight the idea hadn't entered his head, but Felicity Melville was an accomplished flirt. When one thought about it, it was surprising that she hadn't found a husband before now. Why, just look at Norcroft and Beckham. They had both fallen under her spell. Well, Nigel Cavendish was made of sterner stuff.

"What say you, Cavendish, do you agree with Beckham?" Norcroft said.

Nigel stared at his friend. He had no idea what they'd been talking about. "I'm not entirely certain. It's a . . . a difficult question to answer." Made all the more difficult by not knowing what the subject under discussion was. "Want do you think, Lady Felicity, do you agree?"

Beckham snorted.

"Do I agree?" Her brow rose. "As it was my contention that started the debate in the first place, obviously I do not agree with Lord Beckham."

"However, she does agree with me, or rather"—Norcroft grinned—"I agree with her."

"I think Cavendish is trying to curry favor with Lady Felicity by evading the question," Beckham said. "By not saying anything, he doesn't have to disagree with her."

"Nonsense. I daresay Mr. Cavendish doesn't worry about disagreeing with me at all." An amused smile quirked the corners of Felicity's mouth as if she knew full well he had not been following the conversation. "And surely you do have an opinion as to whether Mr. Robert Browning or Mrs. Elizabeth Barrett Browning is the better poet."

Poetry? They were discussing poetry? Relief washed through him. He could certainly discuss poetry.

"Unless of course it's a topic you have never given any particular thought to." A definite challenge sounded in Felicity's voice.

"I admit I have not given it a great deal of thought." He shrugged. "However, I am familiar with the works of both husband and wife." He paused to consider the issue and come up with some sort of lucid answer, straining to recall anything he had ever heard about the works of the Brownings. After all, he wasn't an idiot, he did have discussions of an intellectual nature on occasion. He couldn't recall a recent one at the moment but surely he had had them. "I believe," he said slowly, "Mrs. Browning has been hailed as one of England's most gifted poets. While Mr. Browning's works have yet to receive the public acclaim of his wife's, he is gaining respect from critics."

"Very good, Mr. Cavendish," Felicity murmured.

"Yes, yes, that's fine, but what do *you* think, Cavendish?" Beckham pressed the question. "What's *your* assessment? Whose work do *you* think is best?"

"The lady's or her husband's?" Norcroft grinned. "The man's or the woman's?" Obviously Felicity had expressed her opinion, and Nigel would wager it was in favor of Mrs. Browning.

"As much as I am scarcely ever reticent to articulate my views, in this case I believe it's not possible to express a definitive opinion," Nigel said in an offhand way. "I must admit, I quite enjoy Mrs. Browning's work and I think, today, she might well be the better of the two." He resisted the urge to smirk. That was good.

Norcroft raised his glass. "Well said, Cavendish."

"However," Nigel continued in an authoritative manner that he quite enjoyed. "I think as well there is an excellent argument to be made that Mr. Browning's work continues to develop. A decade from now, we might well laud him as one of this country's finest poets. Only time will tell which of the two is better." That was very good indeed.

"So today you think Mrs. Browning is the better of them but next year you might well change your mind." Felicity laughed. "What a clever answer, Mr. Cavendish."

Norcroft cast him an admiring look. "Exceptionally clever. I had no idea you could be that clever."

Beckham scoffed. "Too clever, I'd say. Cavendish has managed to agree with everyone by leaving the answer to the future. To fate, as it were."

"Fate?" Felicity's eye's sparkled. "I don't think Mr. Cavendish believes in fate."

"I most certainly do not," Nigel said firmly. "I refuse to believe what happens to us is predestined and out of the control of individuals. That choice has been taken out of our hands."

"What of you, Lady Felicity?" Norcroft said. "Do you believe in fate?"

Her gaze met Nigel's. "I didn't, but recent events have convinced me otherwise."

Nigel stared at her for a moment. If he did not get her out of his life, he was as good as married. Even if he found her damn near irresistible, even if she might well be the perfect woman for him, the perfect wife, he would be the one to pick when he wed and to whom. Not Felicity. Not his sister. And certainly not fate.

An idea popped into his head. Odd or brilliant, he wasn't sure, but it was certainly worth trying. "If indeed," he said slowly, "everything lies in the hand of fate, would you risk all on choosing one path over another? One door over another? One turn of the card?"

"Feast or famine," Beckham murmured.

"One could argue that the path or the door or the card you chose is the one you are destined to choose," Norcroft said mildly. "So, in truth, there is no risk."

Nigel ignored him. "But if indeed fate is already determined, then you shouldn't hesitate to wager on the proper path or door or card because the outcome—whether you will win or lose—has already been determined."

"I suppose"—Felicity chose her words with care—"it very much depends on whether you are clever enough to recognize what fate has in store for you. If you are confident that you do indeed understand your own destiny, then I would say yes. One would not hesitate."

"Let us not speak in generalities." He studied her intently. "As someone who believes in fate, who believes in destiny, would you hesitate?"

"My father taught me never to wager more than I could afford to lose," she said coolly.

Beckham chuckled. "Excellent answer."

Norcroft's gaze flicked between Nigel and Felicity. "But nearly as evasive as Cavendish's."

"You're right, my lord, it is evasive. Very well." Felicity's gaze locked with Nigel's. "No, I would not hesitate. Not for an instant."

They stared at each other for a long moment. Norcroft cleared his throat, and the connection between them was broken.

"If you are finished, sir," a footman behind him said coolly.

"Yes, thank you," Nigel murmured, glancing at the barely touched quail as the servant removed the plate. A pity, really; he usually loved quail.

Across the table, servants were removing plates in preparation for the next course. Felicity was already involved in a new conversation with Norcroft and didn't so much as glance his way. But then he hadn't expected her to. He had thrown down a gauntlet and she had picked it up. There was nothing more to do until the battle itself.

Her trust in fate would be her downfall. He now knew how to get her out of his life, and he didn't have the slightest doubt as to his success. Still, he had to wonder why, at this very moment, he didn't feel at all triumphant but rather had a queasy sensation in the pit of his stomach, as if he'd eaten something not quite right. It was absurd, of course; he had nothing to feel sick about. Nothing to regret. Nigel would avoid marriage and put the too tempting Lady Felicity out of his reach and out of his head. He would get exactly what he wanted.

And he did want Felicity Melville out of his life. Didn't he?

* * *

What was Nigel up to? Felicity glanced at him over her cards. Whatever it was, she suspected he would reveal it soon.

"Your turn, dear," Lady Fernwood said.

"Of course," Felicity murmured and played a card.

Nigel had been quite charming after dinner. Not at all the befuddled, sputtering creature he had become when she'd told him of her desire to marry him. No, he was the smooth, polished Nigel described in lurid detail by gossip and reputation. He had a plan, she was sure of it. It was apparent by the confident, self-satisfied look in his eye. She suspected it had come to him sometime during the discussion of the Brownings and fate. Before that, he was distinctly preoccupied and overly quiet. Afterward, well, if he had given the lady sitting on his right any more flirtatious encouragement, she would have leaned so close to him that her bosoms would have fallen right out of her gown and plopped onto his plate. The blasted man probably would have enjoyed that too.

"Damnation, girl," Lord Fernwood snapped. "Pay attention to the game."

"Sorry," she said under her breath, not that she needed to pay any particular attention even to play well. She knew the game by heart. She'd started playing whist with her father before she could read.

Felicity hadn't had a moment alone with Nigel since they had arrived at Cavendish House. He had actively avoided her before dinner, and immediately afterward, Lord and Lady Fernwood had reminded them of their promise to play cards. Nigel had escorted Lady Fernwood into the library, where tables had been arranged, and Felicity had again found herself on Lord Fernwood's arm.

Nigel had done nothing untoward through the three hands they'd already played. Indeed, a casual observer might think the foursome was quite a congenial group, with the older couple far more competitive than she had expected. She glanced at Nigel. The man was taking great pains not to look at her, but a smug smile teased the corners of his mouth. It boded no good, that smile; she was certain of it. But until he actually revealed his plan, the reason for that smile, there was nothing she could do to counter it. Not knowing what he had in mind might well drive her mad. Therefore . . .

She drew a deep breath. "What is your plan, Mr. Cavendish?"

"My plan, Lady Felicity"—he played a card—"is to win."

Lord Fernwood snorted. "That's why we play, boy. To win."

"Now, now, my lord," Lady Fernwood said absently. "Winning is not paramount. It is equally important to play the game with skill and honor."

"Rubbish." The older man scoffed. "The sole purpose is to win." He slapped down a card, and a moment later claimed the trick as well as the victory. Lord Fernwood cackled with delight. "And so we have."

"Well played, sir." Nigel grinned at his partner.

"You do realize you have merely won this hand." Lady Fernwood slanted a pointed gaze at her husband. "The game itself is still at stake. The points are very nearly evenly divided. And, as Lady Felicity is an excellent player, I have no doubt we shall be triumphant in the end."

Felicity smiled at the older lady. "I am confident of it."

"I suspect it will come down to this hand," Nigel said mildly. It was his turn to deal, and he did so with an elegant efficiency. She watched his hands, strong and deft and skillful, deliver the cards to each player and wondered how those hands would feel touching her. Strong and deft and skillful. "Perhaps"—he paused in the deal, and her gaze jerked to his—"we should make a wager on it."

"A wager," she said slowly. So this was what he was up to. Perhaps the man didn't realize she was as skilled as she was. Admittedly her mind hadn't been fully on the game, although it would be now. "What kind of wager?"

"I don't know." He shrugged and continued dealing. "Something interesting, I should think."

"Don't like wagering for big sums." Lord Fernwood shook his head. "Had my share of that in my youth."

"Besides," Lady Fernwood added. "It's not as exciting when one doesn't need the money if one wins and can afford the loss if one loses. No, money won't do at all. But I agree we should wager something interesting. I know." She smiled at her husband. "If

Lady Felicity and I win, you and I shall spend the winter in Spain."

"I hate Spain. Always have, always will." Lord Fernwood narrowed his eyes and studied his wife. "But I'll agree. And if Cavendish and I win—"

"When we win, sir," Nigel said firmly.

"When we win." The old man nodded in agreement. "You will agree to sponsor my niece's daughter for her first season next spring and allow the rest of her family to reside with us for the duration of the season."

"Oh dear." Lady Fernwood winced. "That's asking rather a lot."

Lord Fernwood grinned. "Spain is asking rather a lot."

Lady Fernwood leaned over the table toward Felicity. "It's not that I wouldn't enjoy shepherding a young woman through the season. Indeed, I did that for several of my nieces many years ago. But these are Lord Fernwood's relations." She shuddered. "They're truly annoying creatures, the entire family. The father is pompous, the girl is horribly spoiled, and her mother is a particularly unpleasant sort."

"One can't choose one's family," Lord Fernwood said with a shake of his head. "I don't like them much either but it doesn't matter. Family is family."

"Excellent." Nigel nodded. "Now you both have something interesting at stake."

"And what shall we wager, Mr. Cavendish?" Felicity said lightly and held her breath. "You and I? What do you want from me?"

"Why don't you just wager a night in her bed and be done with it," Lord Fernwood muttered.

Felicity stared.

Nigel choked.

"My lord!" Lady Fernwood glared at her husband. "That's entirely improper and you well know it."

"Of course it's improper, but have you seen the way he looks at her? The man is all but drooling over the girl." The elderly man shook his head. "Might as well bed her and get it over with I say. What we would have done in my day."

"We most certainly would not." Indignation rang in Lady Fernwood's voice, then she paused to consider the question. "No." She shook her head firmly. "I was right in the first place. We would not."

"Bedding Lady Felicity would lead to commitments I am not prepared to make," Nigel said coolly. "You see, Lady Felicity has gotten it into her head that I am the man she is to marry."

"Oh how wonderful, Nigel." Lady Fernwood beamed. "She is a lovely young woman and no doubt will make you an excellent wife."

Felicity smiled but held her tongue. Anything she said now might well make matters worse. But it was worth noting that Nigel didn't deny Lord Fernwood's comment regarding drooling.

"Perhaps." Nigel shook his head. "But I am not interested in marriage at the present time."

"You should be." Lady Fernwood's brow furrowed. "Goodness, Nigel, if someone as well bred and pleasant as Lady Felicity wishes to marry you, in spite of your very naughty reputation, you should thank your lucky stars and snatch her up before someone else does."

"Unfortunately, Mr. Cavendish does not share your views." Felicity studied him for a moment. Whatever he had in mind was certain to be significant. Why, it was only a few hours ago that the man had said he wanted her out of his life. This was his opportunity to accomplish just that. Not that she was worried. He was skilled with cards but she was better. Not merely at whist but, she suspected, at this other game they played as well. In spite of his vast experience with women, he had never played for stakes like these before, never played with a virgin determined to marry him before. Felicity stifled a grin at the thought. A determined virgin was indeed a powerful force. "Very well then, what do you want to wager?"

Nigel lowered his voice and leaned toward her. "I fully admit to you, Felicity, that I cannot get you out of my head. I desire you in a way I'm not sure I have ever wanted a woman before. I have no idea if that's due to the fact that I cannot have you, or the fact that you seem to be everywhere I look, or something altogether different, although I refuse to believe fate is involved. Such desire on my part will surely lead to your ruin—"

"So you simply have my best interests at heart?" she said softly. "How very noble of you."

"Sounded noble to me," Lord Fernwood said in an aside to his wife.

"Hush," Lady Fernwood said.

Nigel ignored Felicity's comment. "And your ruin will inevitably result in marriage. I do not wish for marriage." He straightened. "If we win, Lady Felicity must leave London."

Felicity gasped. "You're exiling me?"

Nigel shrugged. "Only for the remainder of the season."

"But it's the height of the season. She'll have no chance of finding anyone to marry if you force her to leave town." Lady Fernwood shook her head reprovingly. "That's rather vile of you, Nigel. I should tell your mother."

"You won't tell anyone." Lord Fernwood's voice was firm. "Indeed, I think all the revelations at this table should be kept between us." He turned toward Felicity and met her gaze directly. "I agree with Lady Fernwood. You would make Nigel an admirable wife—"

"See here, sir," Nigel cut in.

Lord Fernwood ignored him. "This wager will take a great deal of courage, my dear. I would expect courage to run in your blood. Does it?"

"I don't know if it does or not, my lord." Felicity smiled slowly. "But I do have every confidence in my skill."

"Well, I shall do my best to make certain we win." Lady Fernwood nodded. "I strongly suggest, since Felicity's stake is her own exile, which might well affect the rest of her life, Nigel's wager be equally as great. His freedom perhaps."

"If we lose, he should have to marry her." Lord Fernwood chuckled. "Seems only fair to me."

Nigel paused, met Felicity's gaze, then nodded slowly. "I agree."

"But I do not." Felicity waved off his offer as if it were of no significance whatsoever and prayed she was not making a mistake. "I have no desire to make you marry me against your will."

"I know you've said that but this wouldn't be against my will exactly. I have agreed to the stakes." Nigel's brows drew together. "I thought marriage was what you wanted."

"Oh, I do. And I still believe you and I are fated to be together. Nothing has changed that. Indeed, your comments tonight have only strengthened that belief."

Nigel shook his head. "Then I don't understand."

"Men rarely do," Lady Fernwood murmured.

"I understand," Lord Fernwood said under his breath.

"You are a rare gem, my lord." Lady Fernwood cast her husband an affectionate smile.

Nigel stared. "Then what do you want if you win?"

"A keepsake," Felicity said without thinking. "Something to remind me of you when you are not following me around."

"You've been following her?" Lady Fernwood huffed.

"Bad form, Cavendish." Lord Fernwood shook his head in disgust.

"I have not been following her," Night said sharply. "We have tended to be in the same places at the same times, but I assure you it is nothing more than mere coincidence."

"Or fate," Lady Fernwood said softly.

"The small portrait of you that hangs behind the desk over there." Felicity pointed to the portrait she had noted upon their entry into the library. "It's a remarkable likeness. Quite well done, I think. That's what you will wager."

"Oh, that's not—" Lady Fernwood started.

"Accepted," Nigel said firmly. "Now, shall we begin?"

Felicity picked up her cards and studied them carefully. It was not a bad hand. An overwhelming desire to grin swept through her, but she maintained a passive expression. Indeed, she'd been exceptionally lucky in the deal. Fate, no doubt. Still, it would be an interesting game. Lord and Lady Fernwood were both very good players and Nigel was excellent as well. But, especially with these cards, Felicity would be better.

They played with a calm concentration and very few words save when Nigel or Felicity claimed the trick. The men won the first two tricks, the ladies the next three, and the wins went back and forth from then on. The players were well matched, and Felicity thought Lady Fernwood played even better than she had thus far tonight, while Lord Fernwood seemed a touch off. Of course, Felicity could be mistaken. She was surprisingly nervous herself. Midway through the game, the score was even. Nigel was intent upon the play of the cards, his expression bordering on grim. Did he fear he would lose or was he concerned that he might win?

With four cards left to play, and the gentlemen one point ahead, Nigel paused. His gaze met Felicity's. "Lady Fernwood is right. This wager I have proposed is vile of me. I am willing to call an end to this right now and abandon the wager. I'm confident Lord and Lady Fernwood will approve."

"I will not." Lord Fernwood huffed.

"Quiet," his wife snapped.

"Why, Mr. Cavendish?" Felicity smiled pleasantly. "Do you fear you'll lose?"

"I am very much afraid"—he shook his head—"I may win."

Their gazes locked for a long moment. Regret shone in his eyes. It might well have been the loveliest thing she had ever seen. Her heart warmed.

"That's not the way the game is played, Nigel," Felicity said firmly. "One doesn't try to end the play if one doesn't like the cards. Even for the best of intentions."

"Very well then." He studied her for a moment longer, then shrugged. "Let us continue."

The men won the next trick and Lady Fernwood cast Felicity a look of sympathy, or perhaps it was dread at the thought of next year's season. Felicity simply nodded her acknowledgment, considered the cards in her hands, and resisted the urge to smirk. The game was hers.

The ladies took the next trick, and the next, and with Felicity's last card played, the final trick and the game.

"Brilliant, my dear." Lady Fernwood beamed.

"Never suspected she held those back. Damn fine job, girl." Lord Fernwood nodded. "Your father would be proud."

Nigel stared at the cards on the table in disbelief, then shifted his gaze to Felicity. "You won."

"Yes, I know." She patted his hand. "That was *my* plan."

"You beat me." Disbelief sounded in his voice.

"Yes, I did." She cast him her brightest smile. "It was most exhilarating."

"Fate," he said under his breath. The poor man looked positively stunned. "Bloody hell."

"Nigel," Lady Fernwood said sharply.

"I should like my painting now, if you please," Felicity said politely.

"The painting?" A queasy look passed over Nigel's face. "About the painting . . ."

"I don't want to hear anything about the painting. It is mine now and"—she smiled—"I want it."

"Now? Tonight." Nigel shook his head in a regretful manner. "Oh, I don't think tonight is a good idea."

She drew her brows together. "When would you have made me leave London had you won?"

"Certainly not tonight," he said, as if offended she would suggest such a thing.

"I'm not entirely sure I believe you, Mr. Cavendish." She leaned toward him over the table. "Regardless, I want the portrait and I want it now."

"I really don't think—"

"Now, Nigel."

"As you wish, Lady Felicity." Nigel nodded curtly, got to his feet, and strode across the room to the portrait on the wall.

Lady Fernwood leaned close to Felicity and lowered her voice. "Nicely played, my dear."

Felicity directed her voice to the older woman but her gaze remained on Nigel. "You're referring to the cards, I assume."

"What else?" Lady Fernwood paused. "You do realize he does not own that painting."

Felicity nodded. "Then he should not have wagered it."

"He will have to get it back."

"I'm counting on it."

"He cannot avoid you if he is trying to convince you to give him back the painting. I daresay it will take an extraordinary amount of time and effort on his part. Why, the two of you will be together constantly." Lady Fernwood chuckled. "Nicely played indeed."

"Thank you but I have simply won the opening hand. The game, Lady Fernwood"—Felicity grinned—"has only just begun."

Eight

*What a man really wants is not to be treated as
if he were an idiot. Even when, on occasion, he
might well be.*

The Honorable Mr. Nigel Cavendish

"We need to talk," Nigel said out of the corner
of his mouth and escorted Felicity from the
library. Her hand was tucked into the crook of his
arm, and they trailed after Lord and Lady Fernwood.

"What have you done with my painting?" She
knew full well he had handed it to a servant and
wouldn't have been at all surprised if the man had
been instructed to spirit it away for safekeeping from
its new owner.

"I am having it wrapped for you." He clenched his jaw. "You simply can't waltz out of someone's home with a portrait under your arm."

"It is a very small portrait."

"Nonetheless, your possession of it would be noticed."

"You're right of course," she said in a somber manner. "That would attract no end of unwanted attention and any number of unwanted questions as well, I would imagine. It might be rather awkward to explain why I am the new owner of a family portrait. Although there is another explanation which would be just as awkward."

"I doubt it," he muttered.

She bit back a smile. "I did have a great-aunt who tended to—what was the word she used? Ah yes, liberate items from homes she visited."

He frowned. "She did what?"

"She took things. Interesting items that struck her fancy. She once smuggled a marble bust out of a duke's country house. No one ever could figure out how she did it." She lowered her voice in a confidential manner. "She did carry a rather large bag with her though. It was always assumed it was for needlework. I daresay she took a painting or two in her time."

"That's precisely what we need to talk about," he said in a clipped tone.

"My great-aunt's larcenous escapades?"

He eyes narrowed but he didn't say a word. Felicity resisted the impulse to laugh.

Ahead of them, Lord and Lady Fernwood turned to the left toward the salon where guests had gathered for dancing but Nigel steered her firmly forward. She glanced in the direction the elderly couple had headed. "We're not going to dance then?"

"No," he said shortly.

"I would have much preferred to dance in the first place rather than play cards. You do recall cards were not my idea?"

"I do." He released her, pushed open a door, and gestured for her to enter.

She stepped into a small salon, a room obviously designed for family rather than visitors. He snapped the door closed behind her. She raised a brow. "Are you about to have your way with me?"

He ignored her. "Felicity, I wish to discuss the painting."

"Does this mean you're not about to have your way with me?"

"Yes," he snapped. "I mean no." He glared. "I mean I wish to discuss the painting, my painting—"

"My painting now."

"Or rather my family's painting, nothing more than that."

"What a shame." She trailed her fingers along the back of a sofa. "I had rather hoped, given all that you've admitted to your feelings for me—"

He gasped. "I don't have feelings for you."

"Desire is a feeling, Nigel, you can't deny that. As for the painting, I see nothing to discuss. You wagered it. I won it." She shrugged. "I want it."

Nigel grimaced. "If truth were told, it wasn't exactly mine to wager."

"Then you shouldn't have done so."

"Because it isn't mine"—he chose his words with care—"I can't really give it to you."

"You're not giving it to me, I won it. I gather that your father is the true owner of the painting?"

Nigel nodded.

"I suspect he would require you to live up to your obligation." She stepped toward the door. "Shall we ask him?"

"No." Nigel moved to block her way. "I would prefer my father, as well as everyone else in my family, know nothing of this incident."

"You don't think Lord and Lady Fernwood will say anything?"

"I'll speak to them."

"Surely someone will notice a gap on the wall?"

"I hadn't thought of that." He considered her for a long moment and it was apparent he was trying to think of something to convince her to give up her claim on the painting. "You do realize the portrait is not of me?"

"I had suspected as much although the resemblance is remarkable. The difference is in the hair, you know. The style in the painting is terribly old-fashioned." She studied his hair in an assessing manner. "Yours is quite stylish. Nonetheless, the portrait will remind me of you and so I shall treasure it always. Now." She stepped toward the door. "The hour is growing late, and as much as I would like to stay and dance for a bit, I think it's best if I take my leave. If you would call for my carriage and fetch my painting, I shall be on my way."

"Not yet." Again he blocked the way and narrowed his eyes. "How did you manage to beat me?"

She smirked. "I'm very good."

"*I'm* very good."

She shrugged. "I'm better."

He paused. "Did you notice Lord Fernwood's play in that last hand was not up to his usual standards?"

"It's to be expected. The man is getting on in years."

"Regardless." A casual note sounded in his voice. "Even though I was his partner, I wonder if he wasn't on your side."

Felicity widened her eyes. "Are you accusing His Lordship of cheating? For me?"

"No." Nigel drew the word out slowly until it very much sounded like yes. "But he did agree with Lady Fernwood that you would make me an excellent wife."

"I daresay any number of people would agree with Lady Fernwood about that. I will make you an excellent wife."

He ignored the comment. "And it was his suggestion I should have to marry you if I lost."

"I can't believe you would accuse that dear old man of such a thing." She cast Nigel an indignant glare.

"I'm not really accusing, merely speculating."

"I wouldn't let Lord Fernwood know of your *speculation* if I were you." She shook her head. "Impugning his honor like that. Why, the old gentleman is likely to challenge you to a duel. And dueling with a man of his age would only make your already bad reputation worse. What if he were to win?"

He scoffed. "He wouldn't win."

"I did."

"And I still don't understand how," he said sharply.

"In an entirely fair manner and with a skill superior to yours." She rolled her gaze toward the ceiling. "Do tell me, what bothers you more? The fact that you were beaten at cards, clearly a man's game, by a woman? Or the fact that you were beaten by me?"

"Neither bothers me more. I find them both equally annoying."

"Accept it, Nigel. You lost, I won. Accept it and give me my painting."

"Felicity."

She shook her head. "One should never wager more than one can afford to lose."

"I never thought I'd lose!"

"Furthermore, one should never wager an item that isn't his in the first place."

"Did your father tell you that too?" Sarcasm edged his words.

"No, he didn't need to." She shrugged. "It just makes sense."

"Felicity," a pleading note sounded in his voice. "I

cannot honor that wager. I beg of you, do not take the painting."

"Let me ask you this." She studied him curiously. "If you had won, and I had begged you not to make me leave London for the rest of the season, would you have forgiven the wager? Allowed me to stay?"

He paused and she could almost see the gears of his mind debating the correct response. At last he sighed. "Probably not."

"How very honest of you to admit it."

"I have my moments," he muttered.

"I am confident of it." She considered him for a moment. The poor man did seem rather wretched about the whole thing. Her intent wasn't to make him miserable. Still, he was the one who had started it all with his terribly clever wager to get her out of London. He should be made to pay for it. "I will not relinquish my claim on the painting." She paused. "Tonight. However you may call on me tomorrow."

His expression brightened. "And you'll give me the painting then?"

"I didn't say that. I shall consider the question tonight and discuss it with you tomorrow."

"But you won't give me the painting?" he said slowly.

"Not tomorrow," she said brightly. "And probably not the day after. But perhaps next week. Or even next month."

"I see." He stared at her then chuckled. "Apparently I will be calling on you after all. Very well, but understand it will only be for the purpose of convincing you to relinquish the painting."

"In the meantime, I shall keep it safe. I shall sleep with it under my pillow perhaps."

He shook his head. "I daresay that wouldn't be the least bit comfortable."

"No, you're right." She thought for a moment. "Beside my bed then. Where it will be the last thing I see at night and the first thing I see in the morning."

He raised a brow. "I'm flattered."

"I simply think I should get used to seeing your face night and day." She cast him a wicked grin. "In my bedchamber."

"You really believe this, don't you?" His gaze searched hers. "This idea of fate. Of you and I destined to be together."

I wished for you and there you were. What else could it be but fate? Or magic. "I know it sounds absurd." She raised her chin. "But yes, I do."

"It doesn't sound quite as absurd as it once did." He shook his head in obvious disbelief. "I should have won that game."

"But you didn't and I did. Now I have a painting that you want. To get it back you are going to have to spend a great deal of time with me. And eventually you will come to the realization that—"

"Yes, yes, I know." He sighed. "We are meant for one another."

"Exactly. Now then, if you will step aside, I shall

take my leave." He stepped away from the door and grabbed the handle to open it.

"One moment, if you please." Impulsively she grabbed the lapels of his jacket, pulled him close, and pressed her lips to his, hard. The warmth of his lips on hers washed through her, and she wondered that her knees didn't buckle beneath her. She pulled away. "Not quite as nice as the last time." She patted his lapels and stepped back. "But worth the effort." She turned toward the door.

"Not really. However." He grabbed her arm and pulled her back into his arms. "This is worth the effort." He pressed his lips to hers, and she surrendered herself to the sheer enjoyment of his kiss.

Surely this was desire. This odd yearning that filled her when he so much as touched her hand. That held her in its grip when their lips touched, when his body pressed against hers. That banished all rational thought from her mind and left her wanting him and everything wanting him meant.

He drew his head back and sighed. "Didn't I say there would be no more of this?"

"If you did, I can't recall. Admittedly." She smiled weakly. "I can't seem to recall much of anything when you kiss me."

"That's most gratifying," he murmured.

She leaned toward him. "Perhaps another kiss might restore my memory."

His gaze shifted to her lips. For a moment she thought he would indeed kiss her again. Then he shook his head as if to clear it, stepped back, and looked at her in a firm manner. "You have won this hand, Felicity, but I assure you, the game is nowhere near over."

"My dear Mr. Cavendish." Felicity favored him with her most innocent smile. "I certainly hope not."

This might well be the stupidest thing he had ever done.

No. Nigel stared up at Felicity's balcony. He had done far stupider things, although at the moment he couldn't think of any. The smart thing, the clever thing, the thing any intelligent man would do would be to play Felicity's game and best her at it, eventually convincing her to return the portrait. Of course a truly intelligent man would not be in this mess in the first place. Even so, he was smart enough to realize that the last thing he needed was to be in her company. The more he was around the blasted woman, the more he wanted her. He already liked her, a great deal really. In truth, aside from that annoying business of her wanting to marry him, there was nothing about the woman to dislike. She was intelligent and amusing and perceptive. But like and lust were a dangerous combination. He knew his own weaknesses, and Felicity Melville had moved to the top of the list. Eventually, if he didn't get her out of his life, he would succumb to his desires, and any scandal he had been involved in in the past would pale in comparison.

He moved quietly to the trellis that led to her balcony. She'd been home for hours and was surely fast asleep by now. Regardless, he could wait no longer. It would be dawn soon. Still, aside from the faint light from the stars, it was damnably dark. It couldn't be helped, he supposed. If he didn't recover the portrait of his uncle tonight, tomorrow he would start down the inevitable path to marriage.

Beyond that, he wanted the painting back in its place before his father noted its absence. In the weeks since he had started studying the family accounts, he and his father had grown closer. Nigel had begun to realize that in spite of his many transgressions, his father did indeed have confidence in his abilities, intelligence, and judgment. Discovering Nigel had wagered and, worse, lost the portrait of his father's beloved brother would only disappoint his father. Nigel would do whatever he had to do to assure that did not happen.

He took a firm grip on the trellis and started to climb. Would it be so very bad to marry Felicity? The question arose unbidden in his mind. To possess that willing body, taste those luscious lips, drown in those amazing eyes? For the rest of his days? No, of course it wouldn't if one were ready to marry, if one wanted to marry. Perhaps someday. *Someday, she might well have found someone else.* A sharp pang of regret stabbed him. He brushed it aside.

Nigel reached the balcony and pulled himself over the balustrade, landing lightly on his feet. Thank God one of the French doors to her room was open slightly to catch the night breeze. He carefully pushed the door wider and slipped through the opening, then paused to allow his eyes to adjust to the even deeper darkness of her bedroom.

She'd said she would keep the painting beside her bed. He hadn't seen any of her room the last time he was here but he assumed the bed was probably on the far side of the chamber. That was often the case when a lady's bedroom had a balcony. He'd found such an arrangement most convenient in the past.

Nigel inched his way across the room in a slightly crouched position, hands stretched out in front of him. The moment he found the bed, he would feel his way around it and from there explore the room one grope at a time. It wasn't a good plan, but it was all he had. He refused to consider the tempting body that occupied the bed. In truth, he was better at escaping from bedrooms than he was at breaking into them. He'd certainly never, well, *robbed* a lady's room before and he had only the vaguest idea of what he was doing. Still, as long as he didn't get caught, he was probably doing it correctly. What he really needed was light but he didn't dare light a lamp. Who knew what Felicity might do if she found him here?

His foot snagged on something unsteady and he realized it was her telescope. He reached out and caught it before it could clatter to the floor. He breathed a silent sigh of relief. One obstacle avoided, but who knew how many others there might be in this room.

"I suggest you not take another step." Felicity's clear, firm voice rang out in the night. "I have a pistol and as you're nicely silhouetted by the light from the balcony, I should be able to do a great deal of harm when I shoot you. And I am an excellent shot."

Obviously he was not doing this correctly. Nigel groaned. "Why does that not surprise me?"

"Nigel?"

A match flared and she lit a lamp on the table by her bed. Felicity scrambled out of bed and stared at him. She was tousled and rumpled as one would expect a woman just roused from her bed, and looked at once innocent and sensual and utterly irresistible.

Except for the look in her eye of course.

She glared. "What are you doing here?"

He glared right back. "You don't really have a pistol, do you?"

"Of course I do. I keep it in the drawer in the table beside my bed. I had it in my hand a minute ago. It's here somewhere." She leaned over the bed and dug among the bedclothes, her long white gown clinging to her in completely inappropriate places. He swallowed hard and tried to ignore the way the fabric caressed and revealed and— "There it is." She held up a large pistol. "I told you I had it."

He scoffed. "That's a dueling pistol. Antique at that. And it only has one shot."

She smiled. "I only need one shot."

"It's rather ornate, isn't it? For a serious weapon, that is."

"It will do the job." She studied the weapon in her hand. "And I think it's quite lovely. All that carving and filigree."

"I daresay I shall regret the question," Nigel said wryly, "but why do you keep a pistol in a drawer beside your bed?"

"An unpleasant incident in Italy." She shrugged. "Scarcely worth mentioning. Besides, one never knows who might climb over one's balcony in the middle of the night."

"It's nearly dawn," he said without thinking.

"I scarcely think the fact that it will soon be daylight puts your presence here in the category of a proper social call." She narrowed her eyes. "Why are you here?"

He didn't like the casual way she waved the pistol around. The bloody thing could go off. For all he knew, it wasn't even loaded, although he would wager if Felicity had a pistol, it was probably loaded. She wouldn't see the point otherwise.

"You can put that down now."

"Can I?" She studied him thoughtfully. "What if you have come to ravish me? I should need the pistol then."

He adopted a lofty manner. "I assure you, that is not my purpose."

She smiled in a wicked manner. "Are you certain?"

"I have never been more certain in my life. Ravishment is not my intention. However." He stared at her, and his restraint snapped. He stepped toward her. "My *desire*, my sincere and heartfelt *desire*"—he moved closer—"right here and right now"—he was a scant step in front of her now, her gaze locked with his—"is to rip that surprisingly sheer garment from your body, toss you onto that bed, and indeed ravish you from head to toe. I wish to make love to you until you are too exhausted to do so much as stand without support. Until you call out my name in your dreams and reach for me in your sleep. Until you can think of no one and nothing beyond the touch of my hand, the caress of my lips. And that, Felicity, is what I want."

"Oh." Her eyes were wide and she stared at him. "I thought you wanted the painting."

He blew a frustrated breath. "I do want the painting."

"I believe we've been all through this." Her voice was cool but there was a slight shake to it that was most gratifying. She stepped around him and moved toward the balcony and away from the bed. Excellent idea. "I won it, I have possession of it, it's mine. And should you attempt to take it from me"—she hefted the pistol in her hand, and he winced—"I shall be forced to stop you."

"I would never take it from you." Although admittedly the thought had occurred to him that he could simply grab the painting, toss it over the balcony, and then scramble down the trellis. That was contingent, of course, on locating it in the first place. He glanced around the room. "Where is the painting?"

"You needn't worry. It's safe."

"I thought you wished it to be the last thing you saw at night and the first thing you saw in the morning?"

"It sounded so good when I said it," she murmured.

"But obviously you were not entirely sincere."

"I have been sincere about everything regarding you and me," she said staunchly. "Whereas you—"

"That's not fair, Felicity. I have been honest with you from the start."

"You never said the painting was not yours to wager."

"Nor did I say it was."

She studied him for a moment. "You must want it very badly to risk sneaking into my room at this hour. Why?"

"Aside from the fact that it was not mine to wager?"

She nodded.

He blew a resigned breath. "The portrait is of my uncle. My father was very close to him. He died at a young age, and the painting means a great deal to my father." He might as well be honest. He doubted anything else would be as effective with Felicity. "In recent weeks my father and I have grown closer. I would hate for him to know what a stupid thing I did in wagering the painting." Nigel shook his head. "I have long believed that the way I have lived my life thus far was a disappointment to my father. It's only recently that I have learned that was not the case."

"It's a minor mistake though, Nigel, isn't it? In the scheme of things, that is?"

"Yes and no. The painting has great sentimental value but it's not the loss of the painting itself that's significant. I'm not sure I can explain." He thought for a moment. "The wager we made was more than foolish. It was wrong of me to ask you to leave London. I panicked at the thought of your desire to marry me and the only thing I could think of to save myself was to get rid of you. It was the act of a coward. What I asked you to wager coupled with wagering the portrait, well"—he cast her a reluctant smile—"if I were the father of a son who did that I would be disappointed in his actions and his judgment."

"I see," she said softly. "There's nothing to be done then, is there?"

"What do you mean?"

"Certainly you may have the painting back."

"Felicity." Relief rushed through him, and he stepped toward her. "I shall substitute something else for the painting. Whatever you wish."

"I wish . . ." She stared at him for a long moment. "Is the thought of marrying me so repugnant to you then?"

"It's not you," he said quickly. "I believe I've made my feelings about you perfectly clear."

"Yes, yes." She huffed and waved the pistol in the air. "You want me in your bed but not as your wife."

"And you will have it no other way." He shook his head. "And I would have it no other way. I will not have your ruin on my head."

She paused. "What if I would?"

"Would what?" he said slowly.

"Would have it another way? What if I am willing to share your bed without benefit of marriage?" Her gaze met his. "What then?"

He shook his head. "I could not allow that."

"Why?"

"Because your life would be ruined. You want marriage and all that goes with it. Someday I shall be ready for marriage but not now."

"What if I were married? What if I were to marry"—she thought for a moment—"oh, say, Lord Norcroft. Tomorrow. Would you then be willing to share my bed?"

"No!" Shock sounded in his voice. "I can't believe you would suggest such a thing."

"And I can't believe you would dismiss it. It's not as if you have moral standards that preclude bedding married women. You told me yourself that they were not your marriage vows being broken." She narrowed her eyes. "It is because I would be married to Norcroft—"

"He is one of my oldest friends," Nigel said staunchly. "I would never—"

"Or is it because it's me? Lord knows you've never hesitated before when it has come to a married woman."

He stared at her and had no idea what to say.

"I thought as much." She blew a long breath. "You may have the painting back. In that and in everything else between us, you may declare victory."

"What?"

"I surrender. I give up." She raised her shoulder in a resigned shrug. "I have found the one man I could spend the rest of my days with. Indeed, the man fate has intended me for, and if I can't have him, if he doesn't want me"—utter defeat sounded in her voice—"then I shall have no one at all. You want me out of your life and I shall accommodate you."

"Felicity." Good God, what had he done? Fear gripped him. He stepped toward her and held out his hand, forcing a calm note to his voice. "Give me the pistol."

Her brows drew together and she stared at him. "I'm not going to shoot myself if that's what you were thinking."

"No, not at all." He breathed a sigh of relief.

"I would never shoot myself over you." She scoffed. "I might shoot you but I would never shoot myself."

"I didn't think that for a moment." Although of course he had. He wasn't at all sure if it was good to know she wouldn't shoot herself but would apparently not hesitate to shoot him.

"It is nice to know that you don't wish me dead. However." She squared her shoulders. "I shall do all in my power from this point forward to avoid your presence. I might well leave London after all. Go to the country, rusticate among the fields and forests and gaze at the stars. I'll throw myself into my work. Possibly discover a comet or two myself."

"Felicity, you don't have to—"

"Oh, but I do. You see, Nigel, just as you have admitted to wanting me, I want you every bit as much. I have grown to care for you, deeply. I think I did from the moment you appeared over the garden wall. Seeing you as often as we have seen one another of late would only serve to remind me of what I can't have." She drew a deep breath. "A few minutes ago you asked what I wanted in place of the painting. Anything I wished, you said."

"Yes?" He held his breath.

"I wish." Her gaze met his directly. "I wish I'd never met you."

"Felicity."

"You should go now." A defeated note sounded in her voice. What had he done to her? This wasn't the Felicity he knew. "The way you came, I think. Quickly, before the sun is up. I shall send the painting back to Cavendish House this morning."

"I can't," he said without thinking and realized it was true. "I can't leave you this way."

"And what way would you leave me?" Her eyes glistened but her voice was harsh. "In a crowded ballroom? On a garden path? After a private dance together?"

"I don't know."

"Go, Nigel, please. Just go."

He started toward the balcony, then stopped. "This is farewell then?"

"So it appears."

"May I . . ." He knew it was a mistake but he couldn't seem to stop himself. "May I kiss you?"

"Why?" The word sounded as though it had been ripped from her soul.

"Because I shall miss you." His voice held a quiet calm he didn't quite feel. He stared into her eyes, and a heavy weight settled in the pit of his stomach, as if he were doing something terribly, irrevocably wrong. "Because in spite of my aversion to marriage, in spite of my refusal to take advantage of you, I shall miss those few moments when I held you in my arms."

She stared at him for a long moment, and he realized he would never lose himself in those eyes again. "Very well then." She stepped to him and raised her face to his. "Kiss me, Nigel. And remember it well."

"Felicity," he said softly and bent his lips to hers in a kiss gentle and sweet. A kiss of farewell. Desire surged through him, made all the more powerful by denial. In spite of his best intentions, he wrapped his arms around her and pulled her tighter against him. The heat of her body through the thin fabric of her gown spread through him and flamed his passion, warmed his soul. How could he be such a fool? A small moan sounded deep in her throat, and she responded hungrily to his kiss. If he didn't let her go now, it would be too late. He'd never let her go. He'd take her to her bed and that would be that. And wouldn't it be glorious. Her free hand wrapped around his neck and her mouth opened to his. Dimly he realized her other hand still held the pistol.

The moment the thought occurred to him, the gun slipped from her grasp.

Nine

What a father really wants is a man who will make his daughter happy. Or, barring that, a daughter who is a good shot.

William, the Earl of Dunbury

*T*he instant the shot rang out Felicity realized how very bad the situation would look to a casual observer. The next thing she thought was that one really couldn't fight fate.

Still, there was a chance the shot would go unnoticed. It hadn't sounded all that loud, scarcely more than a pop. Unfortunately, the bullet hit a large jardinière she'd always been exceptionally fond of, which shattered with an impressive explosion she would never have imagined. Even so, it was still possible no one heard, but Nigel jumped away from her as if he had been shot or she were the one who had just exploded, tripped over the telescope, lost his balance, and staggered backward uncontrollably. She reached out to grab for him but was too late. He smashed through the French doors, his momentum carrying him across the small balcony and over the edge. Felicity stared in horror and did the only thing a young woman could do if she saw the love of her life more than likely fall to his death. She opened her mouth and screamed.

The next moment her bedroom door slammed open and her father rushed into the room, her mother a scant step behind.

"What in the name of all that's holy is going on here?" With one glance her father took in the pistol on the floor, the shattered jardinière, and the broken balcony door. His eyes widened. "Felicity?"

"It's Nigel, Father." Felicity flew to the balcony and peered over the edge. "Nigel? Can you hear me? Are you all right?"

"Nigel?" Her father's voice rose and he moved to her side. "Who in the name of all that's holy is Nigel?"

"I have no idea," her mother said, hurrying to Felicity's other side. "Is he alive?"

"Nigel Cavendish, Father. And I do hope he's alive." Felicity leaned over the balustrade but it was entirely too dark to see a thing. "Nigel?"

"Nigel Cavendish?" Father's voice rose. "*The* Nigel Cavendish?"

"I suspect so." A speculative note sounded in her mother's voice. "That answers one question."

"It answers nothing," Father snapped. "Nigel Cavendish!" He said Nigel's name as if it left a nasty taste in his mouth.

"Yes, Father, Nigel Cavendish," Felicity said sharply. *"The Nigel Cavendish,* and he might well be breathing his last at this very moment!" A moan sounded from below, and Felicity breathed a sigh of relief. "Thank the heavens, he is alive."

"Nigel Cavendish," her father muttered.

"I'll send someone to help him at once." Her mother turned and started across the room. "I daresay no one is asleep at this point anyway."

"Nigel?" Fear squeezed her heart. Even if he was alive, he might be seriously hurt. "Do say something. Anything."

Nigel's faint voice sounded from below. "There are thorns in this bush."

"The bushes! Yes of course, I had forgotten about the bushes. Thank God. Nigel," she called. "Did the bushes break your fall?"

"I would be surprised if they didn't break something." Nigel groaned. "But no, I don't think I'm seriously injured, however I could use some assistance. I seem to be trapped. The thorns, you know."

"The thorns are the least of your worries, Mr. Cavendish." Father's angry voice echoed in the night.

Nigel paused, then his voice drifted up to them. "Lord Dunbury, I presume?"

"Apparently that's not all you presume," Father

said in a hard voice. Felicity winced. She had rarely heard that tone from her father. On those few occasion when she had, her mild, unassuming father was a force to be reckoned with.

"Poor Nigel," she murmured. Not only did he probably have any number of bruises and scrapes to deal with; he had her father to face as well. She noted movement on the ground and realized help had arrived. She had to go to him, to see for herself how badly he was hurt. Felicity straightened, turned away from the balustrade, and stepped into her room.

Her father blocked her way. "I assume there is a rational explanation for all of this."

She nodded firmly. "Absolutely."

He chose his words with care. "You can explain his presence in your room in the middle of the night—"

"It's dawn now," she said helpfully.

"Which begs the question of how long he has been in your room," Father said sharply. "Only a fool would sneak into a lady's bedchamber this close to dawn."

"He wasn't thinking clearly," she murmured.

Father stared at her for a long moment. "I never expected behavior like this from you, Felicity. I never imagined you would become involved with a man of Cavendish's reputation. I thought you had a good head on your shoulders."

"I do." She huffed. "Keep in mind, Father, I didn't climb into his room. And you should know he was not invited."

"Oh, that's a different story altogether then. This becomes nothing more than a social faux pas. No more significant than if he had arrived at a ball he did not receive an invitation for." Sarcasm rang in his voice. "Why, we can simply forget the entire incident ever happened."

"Could we?" she asked hopefully.

"No, we most definitely cannot!" He glared at her. "A man, especially a man of Cavendish's reputation, found in a young woman's room in the dead of night—"

"He wasn't actually found in my room—"

Father clenched his jaw. "Let me rephrase that then. A man found in the bushes beneath a young woman's balcony because he has fallen off the balcony—"

"That is more accurate," she said under her breath.

"—must be held accountable. There is a penalty to be paid for such misadventure."

She sniffed. "I would prefer not to think of myself as a penalty." She wrinkled her nose. "So you are saying we can't forget all about this then?"

"Absolutely not!" He stared at her as if she had lost her mind. "Are you mad? Every servant in the house is no doubt awake by now. By morning, every servant in every house in the neighborhood will know about this. By afternoon, it will be all over town. A man falling from a woman's balcony after a shot is heard is the sort of thing gossips dream about. Add a midget and a monkey and it would be the stuff legends are made of!"

She drew her brows together in confusion. "A midget and a monkey?"

"It's not significant." He waved off the question, and once again she realized there was far more to her quiet, sedate parents than she had ever dreamed. "Felicity." He forced a note of calm to his voice. "Your reputation will be in shreds. Any remaining hope of a decent match for you will vanish. Your future will be destroyed."

"Am I, well, ruined then?" She held her breath.

"I don't know," he snapped. "Are you?"

"Of course not," she said indignantly. "Not in the true definition of the word anyway. Nothing of real significance happened."

"That's something to be grateful for, I suppose, although in this world it scarcely matters. Appearance is every bit as devastating as the act itself." He considered her for a moment. "Before we go any further I should ask you if you have feelings for this man."

She met her father's gaze firmly. "Yes, Father, I do."

"I see. That's that then." Father started toward the door. "I shall speak with Mr. Cavendish at once and hope he is not too injured for an immediate wedding."

"I'm coming with you." She snatched her robe from the foot of her bed, shrugged into it, and started after him.

"That's not entirely proper in situations like this." Father cast her a stern glance. "Matters of this nature are best handled by men."

"That's utter nonsense, and furthermore, I don't care." She raised her chin. "It is my life, after all, and I should have a say in it."

"As you wish." The slightest hint of a smile touched her father's lips. "Does Mr. Cavendish have any idea what he's in for?"

Felicity glanced at the pistol on the floor, the broken pottery, and the shattered door, and thought of the thorns in the bushes below the balcony. "By now, I fear he might have some idea."

"*Fear* is the pertinent word." Father sighed. "Come along then. Let's see to your young man."

"Oh, he's not really my young man." She trailed behind him.

Father snorted. "He is now."

It was, all things considered, a surprisingly cordial affair. If one could call the sunrise meeting of an earl whose daughter's reputation was about to be destroyed with the son of a viscount who had brought about said destruction cordial. Still, no fisticuffs were thrown, no voices were raised, and not another shot was fired. Father was firm, Mother was calm, Nigel was respectful and polite and never once mentioned how he was not ready for marriage. Felicity, however, kept her hands firmly clenched in her lap in an effort to ease the butterflies that had taken up residency in her stomach.

It was decided that it would be best to move as quickly as possible in hopes of stifling the spread of gossip. Not that there was any real chance of that. As

Father had said, this story was entirely too juicy to ignore. They agreed that Nigel would speak to his family at once, and as soon as a special license could be arranged, Felicity and Nigel would be wed here at home. Father had muttered they should have the ceremony in the garden beneath the balcony but Mother had pointed out that would call attention to the circumstances. Nigel and Felicity would be man and wife within days.

All in all, it was polite and mercifully brief. When everything that needed to be said had been said, Felicity's parents left the soon-to-be-wed couple alone, pointedly leaving the door to the parlor open a crack.

"Well, that wasn't nearly as awkward as I feared it might be," Felicity murmured. "I had always imagined, in a situation like this, Father would shoot the man involved or at the very least, thrash—"

"You said you would never force me to marry you." Nigel turned an icy glare on her. "Never, you said. I remember that distinctly."

"I don't believe I ever said never," she murmured.

"It was implied!" Anger rang in his voice.

"Well, I'm not forcing you to marry me."

"Your father is." He fairly spat the words.

"He is not. Circumstances are," she said firmly

"You dropped that pistol on purpose knowing full well it would go off!"

"I did not." Indignation swept through her. "It slipped from my hand through no fault of my own. Indeed, what made it slip from my hand was your doing."

"You let me kiss you," he snapped.

"You asked to kiss me!" She shook her head. "You can't blame me for this. It was your fault entirely."

He gasped. "My fault? Who dropped the pistol?"

"Who climbed into whose window? Who wagered a painting he didn't own? Who tried to get whom to leave London?" Her own anger rose. "Who climbed over whose garden wall in the first place?"

"Who dropped the bloody gun?"

"I wished I'd shot you with it instead!"

"That might well have been better!" He drew a deep breath. "Perhaps you never said never but you did say you had no intention of forcing me into marriage. Can you deny that?"

"No, I don't deny that. I'm quite certain I said something very much like it."

"But you didn't mean it."

"Of course I meant it. If you recall, not more than an hour ago I was giving you up entirely. Vowing never to see you again. *Kissing you farewell!*"

"Hah!"

She ignored him. "But I never said—and here *never* is completely accurate—that I wouldn't expect you to marry me if I were ruined!"

He scoffed. "You're scarcely ruined."

"How ruined do I have to be?" She planted her hands on her hips and glared at him. "Would you be less angry, less indignant about all this if you had actually climbed into my bed? If you had made love to me until—how did you phrase it? Ah yes." She grit her teeth. "Until I am too exhausted to stand. Would you feel better if you had had your way with me?"

He narrowed his eyes. "Yes!"

"Well then you should have taken the opportunity when it presented itself!"

"I was being honorable," he said in a lofty manner. "I was thinking of you."

"You were thinking of avoiding precisely the situation we now find ourselves caught in." She folded her arms over her chest and paced the room. "I have no desire to marry a man who doesn't want me, but now there is no choice. My reputation will be destroyed. You well know how servants talk and how quickly a story like this will spread." She shook her head. "Within a few hours all of London will know that the infamous Mr. Cavendish was discovered leaving Lady Felicity Melville's bedroom." She narrowed her gaze. "And shots were fired."

"*One* shot."

"By the time the gossips finish, it will be cannon fire!"

"I don't know why you're so upset. You get exactly what you wanted. You get to marry me."

She stopped and stared at him. "Oh, lucky, lucky me!" She heaved a frustrated sigh. "I didn't want you to *have* to marry me. I wanted you to *choose* to marry me. It's a different thing entirely."

He blew a resigned breath. "You do understand that it's not you specifically that I'm opposed to. It's marriage in general."

"Oh, well, that makes all the difference in the world, doesn't it?"

"I actually like you," he muttered.

"Again, lucky me!" Her gaze met his, and she stared at him for a long moment. At last she sighed. "This is not what I wanted."

"Regardless, this is what you, what we, will have." He shrugged. "There is nothing to be done about it."

"Nigel." She raised her chin and squared her shoulders. "You don't have to marry me."

"Of course I do." He scoffed. "Regardless of what did or did not happen between us, your reputation is destroyed and I am to blame. In spite of my past, I do consider myself an honorable man. Therefore there is no choice but to marry. I am not happy with the cir-cumstances but"—he spread his hands in a helpless gesture—"there you have it."

"What if I refuse?" she said quietly. "What if I de-cide I would rather live the rest of my days alone than with a man who does not wish to marry me?"

"Don't." His voice was grim.

His gaze met hers, and she saw nothing in his eyes save anger and resignation. Her heart sank.

"We probably will not speak again until the cere-mony," he said, his tone polite and cool. "Until then." He nodded curtly and headed for the door.

"Nigel." She started toward him.

"Yes?" He glanced back at her.

"I . . ." She wanted him to take her in his arms. To tell her, somehow, all would be well between them.

That they would be happy. But the words would not come. "Take care."

He nodded again and left the room.

Felicity sank onto the nearest sofa and buried her face in her hands. Dear Lord, how had things gone so horribly wrong? She was about to marry the man she loved, the man she was fated to spend the rest of her days with, and she'd never felt so wretched in her life. He claimed to like her but the look in his eye belied that. How could she enter marriage with a man who did not wish to be wed?

She'd believe they were fated to be together. And surely it was fate that had set recent events in motion. But what if her destiny was not to spend the rest of her days happily with the man she loved, but rather to live a miserable existence with a man who resented her very presence? How long would it be before Nigel's resentment turned to dislike and finally hate? How long until she grew to despise him as well?

"Dear heart." Her mother sat down beside her and wrapped her arm around her daughter. Felicity hadn't even noticed her return. "It's really not as bad as all that."

"Not as bad as all that?" Felicity raised her head and stared at her mother. "How could it possibly be any worse?"

"You love him, don't you?"

Felicity sighed. "Yes."

"And he cares for you, doesn't he?"

"No. Not at all." Felicity shook her head. "He

wants me in . . . in a carnal sense but nothing more than that."

"That is a great deal," Mother said firmly. "And an excellent place to start."

Felicity's eyes widened. "Surely you're not serious?"

"Oh, but I am. The physical relationship between a man and a woman is most extraordinary." She paused. "We should talk about that in detail before the wedding."

"Should we?" Felicity said faintly. She had learned a great deal about the relations between men and women during her travels, as one of her somewhat unconventional chaperones felt the best way to arm her charges against the wickedness of men was with knowledge. The very idea of speaking with her mother about such things now was unnerving.

"Oh my, yes. The more you know, the less likely you are to be apprehensive. Besides, it can be most enjoyable, and I daresay, given Mr. Cavendish's extensive reputation, he should be quite skilled—"

"Mother!"

"Have I shocked you?"

"A little."

Her mother studied her for a moment. "I know you think your father and I are quite a stodgy, boring old couple."

"No." Felicity said staunchly. "Not at all."

"It's kind of you to say but in many ways we are. Now at any rate. It was quite a different story in our youth." A wicked twinkle shone in her mother's eyes. "I daresay, those details would indeed shock you."

Felicity smiled weakly.

"But that's beside the point. Suffice it to say, I know of a long list of happy marriages that began with little more than lust and desire. Love, my dearest, can grow from even the naughtiest beginnings."

Felicity shook her head. "But Nigel doesn't want to get married."

"Few men do."

"He is being forced to marry and he hates me for it."

"Don't be absurd. He doesn't hate you at all. Felicity." Her mother took her hands and looked firmly into her eyes. "No one is truly forcing him to do anything. Your father has not put a gun to his head, although I suspect he would have liked to."

"Nigel's sense of honor will not permit him to abandon me."

"It sounds so good, doesn't it? An honorable man does the honorable thing." Mother scoffed. "I can tell you any number of stories about so called honorable men who did *not* do the honorable thing in circumstances like this. If Mr. Cavendish did not have some feelings for you, he would be on his way out of the country at this very moment."

"Do you think so?"

Mother nodded. "I do. And I am confident that all will turn out well."

"Are you?"

"Felicity, if I had any doubts whatsoever, regardless

of the consequences, I would not allow this marriage." She gazed into her daughter's eyes. "I would lock you in your room if necessary to keep it from happening. And for good measure"—she smiled in a pleasant manner—"I would have the balcony ripped from the side of the house as well."

"And you do intend to marry this young woman?" Nigel's father said in a thoughtful tone, but then he had been quiet and reflective throughout Nigel's recitation of the details leading up to this point. He sat behind his desk considering his son in a calm manner that made Nigel want to squirm. A feeling not eased in the least by his mother's steady perusal from a chair off to one side of the desk.

"I do, sir." Nigel sat in the chair facing his father's desk and shrugged. "I see no other option."

His father raised a brow. "Are you being forced to marry then? By her family, that is?"

"It certainly feels that way." In spite of what he'd said to Felicity, upon further reflection, Nigel acknowledged there had been no real force involved. His anger had dimmed since this morning and he had realized that, for the most part, he had brought this on himself. Every bit of it. He sighed. "But no, I'm not. Her father simply made it clear that I was expected to marry her."

"Understandable." The viscount nodded. "Go on."

"I don't have a choice though, Father, do I?" Nigel leaned forward in his chair. "In spite of the apparently irrelevant truth that nothing of significance happened last night, the mere fact that I was discovered in circumstances of a scandalous—"

"Highly scandalous," his mother murmured.

"Highly scandalous nature," Nigel continued, "will, if it hasn't already, destroy Lady Felicity's reputation. Her chances for any kind of acceptable marriage are over. I cannot abandon her to a"—the word caught in his throat—"*fate* that is entirely the result of my stupid actions."

"I see," his father said.

"Do you love her?" his mother asked.

"Love is of little relevance at this point, my dear." His father shrugged. "Whether he does or doesn't scarcely matters."

"I suppose you're right. Nonetheless, I for one am quite pleased at this unexpected turn of events," his mother said firmly. "I met the young woman last night and I must say I liked her at once." She glanced at her husband. "You met her as well, dear, remember? The tall one with the small bosoms and the charming laugh. And she has the most unique eyes."

"I didn't think her bosoms . . ." His father cleared his throat. "I did meet her and yes, she impressed me as well. Lovely girl. Exceptionally clever too, I thought."

"You undoubtedly could do worse, Nigel, and Lord knows I thought you would." His mother shook her head. "To be perfectly honest, I think she is the one who could have done better."

"Better than me?" Nigel said indignantly. "I'm your son."

"She is the daughter of an earl, with a tidy dowry I would assume, and I've never heard so much as a whisper about her. And while you have good prospects, you are a scoundrel with an absolutely dismal reputation." His mother pinned him with a firm gaze. "You are exceptionally lucky to have found her."

"I don't feel lucky," Nigel muttered and ignored the fact that just possibly his mother was right. He stared at her in disbelief. "Aren't you upset about all this? The circumstances? The scandal?"

"It's not as if scandal was new to you. But of course it's distressing. Most distressing." She waved away the comment. "One never wants to have a wedding under these conditions but it can't be helped. And, frankly, Nigel, I am relieved. I couldn't have chosen a better match for you. She'll make you a perfect wife."

"So I've been told," he said under his breath.

The viscountess rose, her husband and son promptly getting to their feet. "I realize it's still early, but I am going to fetch your sister and we shall both pay a call on Lady Felicity and Lady Dunbury at once. There is much we need to discuss if we are to have a wedding in the next few days." She favored her son with a brilliant smile. "There is nothing quite as exhilarating as putting together a proper wedding at a moment's notice. I should thank you for this but"—her eyes narrowed—"I shall restrain." With that she swept from the room.

Nigel sank down in his seat and stared at his father. "Well?"

His father settled in his own chair, leaned back, and folded his hands together. "Well what?"

"Isn't there more you wish to say to me? Chastise me? Reprimand me? Cut off my funds? Exile me to the country? Something?" Nigel braced himself. "Go on. I deserve it."

"Very well." His father thought for a moment. "You are marrying the girl."

"Yes?"

"You have accepted your responsibilities in this matter."

Nigel nodded. "Yes?"

"Your behavior, after the fact as it were, can only be described as honorable."

"I would hope so," Nigel muttered.

"Then I see nothing to reprimand you about."

"Nothing?" Nigel stared. "Nothing at all?"

"While your behavior in the past has been anything but exemplary, you've never before been in a situation where the consequences have been as severe as in this particular instance. Where a lady's future was at risk."

"And?" Nigel held his breath.

"And I must say"—his father's gaze met his—"I have never been more proud of you than I am right now."

"Proud of me?" Nigel shook his head. "I have made a mess of it all. Of my life. Of Felicity's life. Of everything."

The viscount chuckled. "And yet you are ending up with an exceptional young woman who will make you a fine wife. You have landed on your feet, my boy, and you have done so by doing the right thing. You've accepted your responsibilities like the man I've always known you could be. I am indeed proud."

"Proud," Nigel said under his breath. Who would have thought?

"Now that that's settled"—his father opened a notebook and paged through it—"I should like to discuss a question that's arisen regarding the estate tenants, one in particular."

Nigel pulled his chair closer to the desk, and a moment later father and son were both immersed in the details of running a country estate. Still, Nigel couldn't quite put all that had happened out of his head.

He had always known scandalous involvement with a lady of Felicity's position and background would ultimately result in marriage. Precisely why he had avoided such women—virgins—in the first place. He had never questioned that he would indeed do the proper thing should circumstances require it. And if he were honest with himself, the fact that the lady involved was Felicity Melville made it somewhat more palatable.

Still, he could not ignore this terrible feeling of being trapped. Like a beast captured in a cage. He would no doubt be put on display at any minute. As much as he realized he was at fault for all this, he couldn't help but blame Felicity as well. It was irrational, he knew, but there it was. At least he would at last have Felicity in his bed. There was something to be said for that.

This was perhaps the most significant scandal of his life, in terms of the repercussions, but no one seemed particularly upset. His mother was pleased at the thought of her new daughter-in-law. His father was proud of his actions. Maddy would certainly be delighted at the end result. Felicity wasn't especially happy at the moment, but ultimately she was getting what she wanted. Was he the only one dismayed at this turn of events?

It was as if the entire world was in a conspiracy to take control of his life. To make him into something he wasn't ready to be. It had started with his father easing him into the family's business affairs and now . . . now he was to be married whether he wished it or not. And while he could have fought it, any protest on his part would have only made matters worse. No, an honorable man did the honorable thing. Even if it killed him.

Still, he didn't like the feeling that his life was out of his hands. He didn't like it one bit. And it was past time he did something about it.

Ten

What a mother really wants is a daughter who will not make the same mistakes she did. Or barring that, a life for her daughter that will turn out as nicely as hers has.

Evangeline, the Countess of Dunbury

Felicity glanced around the large entry hall at Cavendish House and handed her wrap to a footman. She couldn't recall ever having been quite this nervous. Certainly brides were supposed to be nervous but the wedding wasn't until tomorrow. By tomorrow she'd be a small, quivering pool of sheer anxiety. If she survived tonight.

Tonight she and her parents were to dine with Nigel's family. There was nothing really to be nervous about. Her mother and Lady Cavendish had discovered they had a great deal in common and had already become fast friends. Apparently there was something about planning their children's wedding that brought women together. One would have thought this was a long-awaited affair instead of a hurried marriage of necessity.

No one expressed a single doubt that all would ultimately turn out well. Madeline had assured her that Nigel would come around eventually, and she knew him better than anyone. But in that she had more confidence than Felicity.

To all appearances, the only member of Nigel's family not pleased about his impending nuptials was Nigel himself. She hadn't seen him since they had agreed to marry two days ago. It struck her that her nervous state had little to do with meeting the rest of his family and everything to do with seeing Nigel again. The man who would soon be her husband, for better or for worse. Felicity drew a deep breath, and they were shown into a salon.

"There you are!" Lady Cavendish hurried across the room to greet them, Viscount Cavendish at her side. She kissed Felicity's cheeks. "My dear girl, you look lovely tonight."

Lady Cavendish turned to Felicity's mother. "Evangeline, I am not sure you have met my husband."

"I have but it was a very long time ago." Her mother's eyes sparkled with amusement. "How are you, Edmund?"

"Excellent, Evie." *Evie?* Felicity had never heard

anyone except her father call her mother *Evie*. The viscount took her mother's hands and raised them to his lips, his gaze never leaving hers. "You have not changed a bit."

Her mother laughed. "Nonsense. I am considerably older, and if I am inclined to forget, the mirror reminds me every day."

"You are as exquisite as ever." *Exquisite*? Her mother? She'd never thought of her mother as exquisite although now that she considered it, her mother was indeed a lovely woman who wore her age well.

"Apparently you do know one another," Lady Cavendish murmured, her eyes wide with curiosity.

Lord Cavendish dropped *Evie*'s hands and turned to her father. "Dunbury."

Father nodded. "Cavendish."

"It seems history repeats itself," Lord Cavendish said somberly.

"Indeed it does." Father studied the other man. "You have done well, Cavendish."

The viscount shrugged. "I have spent these last thirty some years making a name for myself whereas you have spent them"—he broke into a wide grin—"living yours down."

Father laughed and gripped Lord Cavendish's hand. Nigel's father clapped the earl on the back and the men broke into the kind of lighthearted conversation that can only be had between friends too long apart.

Lady Cavendish raised a brow. "Apparently you all know one another."

"It was a long time ago, Charlotte. Scarcely worth

mentioning." Her mother tucked Lady Cavendish's hand in the crook of her arm and turned her away from the men and toward the other guests. "Water under the bridge and all that."

"What did Lord Cavendish mean about history repeating itself?" Felicity followed her mother.

"It's not the least bit important dear," her mother said lightly.

"More water under the bridge?" Felicity asked.

"Exactly." Her mother nodded and directed her attention to Lady Cavendish.

Felicity had heard that phrase several times in recent days and always in reference to her parents. One had to wonder just how deep that stream might be. Once again, she realized there was much about her parents' lives she didn't know.

Madeline and Lord Windham were present, as were Nigel's brother, Robin, a tall young man who was very much the image of his brother; and Phoebe, Nigel's younger sister. She was a pretty girl, and from the practiced tilt of her smile and the look in her eyes, Felicity suspected Lady Cavendish would have her hands full when Phoebe entered society. There were a dozen or so other assorted relatives, a gathering small by Cavendish standards, Madeline had said. The only member of the family who was conspicuously absent was Nigel.

Madeline greeted her with a kiss on the cheek. "Nigel isn't here."

"So I see." An uneasy feeling settled in the pit of Felicity's stomach. "Where is he?"

Madeline pressed her lips together in a firm line. "I have no idea."

"You don't think he's left the country or something of that nature?"

"No, I'm sure it's nothing of the sort," Madeline said firmly. "His wedding is tomorrow. He's agreed to marry you, and I'm confident he will do so. He has always been a man of his word."

"And so I remain." Nigel's voice sounded behind them.

Felicity turned toward him, and her heart skipped a beat. She hadn't realized she had missed him so much. She hated the way they'd left each other; far too much remained unsettled between them. They had so much to talk about and had had no opportunity to do so.

"My apologies. I had a previous engagement and was delayed. Madeline." He gave his sister a quick kiss on the cheek.

She raised a brow. "Madeline?"

He ignored her, turned to Felicity, took her hand, and raised it to his lips. "You are looking well this evening."

There was the faintest air of cigar smoke and brandy about him. "Thank you, Nigel."

"I should greet your parents." He smiled pleasantly and turned away.

Madeline watched him move across the room. "He is up to something."

"Surely not," Felicity said, although she agreed with Madeline. There was something not quite right about Nigel tonight. "Perhaps he's just nervous. I know I am." Across the room, Nigel kissed her mother's hand. "But he seems polite enough, quite pleasant really." Nigel said something that brought a smile to her mother's face and a laugh from Lady Cavendish. "He's being most charming."

"Nigel is nothing if not charming." Madeline studied her brother. "There's something brewing in that wicked little head of his. I don't trust him."

"I do," Felicity said staunchly.

"I'm not sure you should." Madeline sighed. "Still, you really have no other choice, I suppose."

"No." Felicity watched the tall, handsome man who would soon be her husband. He was indeed utterly charming and most engaging. Why, any woman not long dead in her grave would be hard-pressed not to succumb to that knowing smile and the wicked twinkle in his eye. Still, she had a dreadful feeling of impending doom. "No." She sighed. "I don't suppose I do."

"It's a sad state of affairs when the most notable thing about your own wedding is the unexpected discovery that your parents are old friends," Felicity said under her breath.

Nigel glanced at her from his seat on the other side of the carriage. "My apologies, did you say something?"

She bit back a sarcastic retort and instead smiled pleasantly. "No, nothing. Nothing at all."

Her new husband smiled in an absent manner and turned his attention back to the passing scenery.

Felicity clenched her jaw and stared unseeing at the streets outside the carriage. It was a short ride from her house to Nigel's town house, her new home, and while she wasn't at all sure what awaited her there, she was impatient to be alone with her husband and at last find out what he'd been planning. She had no doubt he was planning something. Wicked little head was right. She'd had quite enough, thank you, of the overly polite, well-mannered Nigel he had abruptly become.

He had been practically perfect last night, charming and quite delightful. But she hadn't had so much as a moment alone with him. His behavior toward her had been pleasant enough in an impersonal sort of way. The flirtatious Nigel who had stolen her heart was nowhere to be seen. Immediately after dinner, he had claimed there was much he needed to settle before the wedding, made his excuses to all, kissed her blasted hand again, and taken his leave. Felicity hadn't next seen him until the ceremony today.

The wedding itself was something of a miracle. She wasn't sure how it all had been arranged but Mother had long said if one had enough power and money, one could do practically anything. Between her mother the countess and her mother-in-law the viscountess, there was enough money and power to move continents. Remarkably, it had been a lovely occasion with far more guests than Felicity had expected, including Eugenia and her husband. Eugenia had wisely restrained from saying anything even remotely suggesting she had predicted Felicity would come to this end, and Felicity was most grateful for that. The ceremony was brief, concluding with a terribly proper and quite disappointing kiss between the newly wedded couple, then a too long luncheon with endless toasts and well wishes. Nigel had been, through it all, the perfect groom, the perfect match, the perfect everything. She should have shot him when she'd had the chance.

Last night she'd been nervous and apprehensive about being with Nigel again. Today she been confused and more than a little concerned about his state of mind. Now she was annoyed, frustrated, and angry.

The carriage pulled up to a pleasant, well-tended house in a terrace near Russell Square. Felicity knew it had recently undergone repairs, and although most of her things had been brought here yesterday, she had yet to see it for herself. Nigel helped her from the carriage, and she resisted the urge to slap his hand away.

Blast it all, his wasn't the only life that had been abruptly rearranged. Certainly she had always wished to marry. And yes, he was the one she had wanted to marry. And indeed she truly believed they were fated to be together. One could say as well that she and his sister had plotted to bring him to this point, although it was a meager plot. Felicity hadn't followed Madeline's advice well at all, and giving him no choice but to marry was never part of their plan. Regardless, she hadn't wanted Nigel this way. She'd been as reluctant to marry him under these circumstances as he'd been to marry her. Well, perhaps not quite as reluctant, but reluctant. And she'd had no more choice in the matter than he had. Why, she should be the one to be aloof and remote and perfectly polite. And treat him as if he were a stranger.

Nigel escorted her into the house. In the front entry his staff lined up to be introduced, although *staff* was not entirely accurate. Aside from Nigel's long-time valet, there were a half-dozen servants on loan from Lady Cavendish. Nigel's mother had explained that most of Nigel's servants had found new positions after the flood. One of Felicity's first duties as the lady of the house would be to hire a new staff.

After the introductions, Felicity turned to her husband. "Would you show me around?"

"I'm certain Mrs. Fleming"—Nigel gestured at the assistant housekeeper from Cavendish House—"would be happy to accommodate you."

The servants exchanged glances. Felicity gritted her teeth but kept a smile on her face. "I would much prefer that you do so."

"As you wish." He dismissed the servants, then led her to a door off the entry and pushed it open. "This is the dining room."

It was a lovely, warm, wood-paneled room with a sideboard, a large table, and seating for perhaps a dozen people. Felicity had the distinct impression that it was seldom used.

"Very nice," she said, noting what changes needed to be made to properly entertain.

The only other room on the ground floor was a library. Not as large or elaborate as her father's or the one at Cavendish House, it was still well furnished and lined with book-filled shelves reaching nearly to the ceiling. Felicity wondered how many Nigel had actually read. There was a faint odor of tobacco and musty pages in the air. It was a pleasant smell, reminiscent of companionable evenings in front of the fire with a good book or a game of chess. Or cards.

"I like this room a great deal and I like it as it is. This room," Nigel said firmly, "is not to be touched."

She raised a brow. "Touched?"

"Changed. I expect you will wish to make any number of changes in the house. It's your right, after all, and I have no objection. When I originally purchased the house it was fully furnished, and I never got around to making any significant changes. Then there was the flood. While the repairs have been completed, there's a great deal that still needs to be done." He waved absently. "Furnishings and the like."

"I think this room is perfect just as it is." She shook her head. "I see no reason to change it."

"Good." He turned and led her up the stairs to the spacious first floor landing and pushed open large double doors. "This is the front parlor." He nodded at a set of matching doors on the connecting wall. "It opens to the back parlor."

"How convenient," she murmured and stepped into the room. It was a good-sized room, and she noted that with the doors to the back parlor opened, the space would nearly double. The walls were freshly plastered and painted, the woodwork pristine, and the fireplace mantel newly installed. She glanced at her husband. "It's empty."

"These rooms and those on the second floor were the ones most seriously damaged. I am scarcely ever here and I tend to take most of my meals out so the lack of furnishings is of no concern to me." He smiled politely. "I'm certain my sister or my mother would be happy to assist you in purchasing whatever you wish."

"Whatever I wish?" She stared at him. "You want no say in how I furnish these rooms?"

He shrugged. "I have every confidence you will do an excellent job."

"I'm so pleased I have your confidence," she snapped, turned on her heel, and stepped back into the hall. "I assume the bedrooms are upstairs?"

He nodded.

She narrowed her eyes. "Are they unfurnished as well?"

"Not exactly."

She started up the stairs, Nigel trailing behind her. It wasn't the lack of furnishings that infuriated her, she was well up to the task of refurbishing the house, but his overly polite demeanor. His aloof manner. As if he didn't care. About the house. About her.

She refused to consider the idea that perhaps he didn't.

She pushed open the first door she came to.

"This is my room," he said behind her.

This room too had been freshly painted and did hold a large clothespress, a wing chair, and an enormous, heavily carved bed, which simply reeked of scandalous adventure. Still, there was a temporary air about the place. "How long have you lived here?"

"Excluding the months the house was under repair?" He thought for a moment. "Six or seven years, I think."

"You've certainly left your mark on it."

"I said I am rarely here." He nodded at a door beside the clothespress. "That door is to the dressing room, which connects to the second bedroom. Your room."

"My room?" She started toward the dressing room. "And is my room furnished as well?"

"I don't know that *furnished* is the appropriate word," he murmured after her.

She pushed open the door to her room and pulled up short. There was indeed a wardrobe here but that was all, unless one counted the stacks of boxes filled with her things, the telescope planted in the center of the room, and her prized celestial globe as furnishings. "There's no bed, Nigel." She whirled around and faced him. "Where I am to sleep?"

"I thought you would sleep in my bed," he said coolly.

"With you?" She scoffed. "Not bloody likely."

He raised a brow. "Felicity, your language. I'm shocked." He paused for a moment. "You're perfectly safe. I have no intention of sleeping there."

"Where do you intend to sleep?"

"Elsewhere. I haven't decided yet. I thought I might take a room at my club."

"You don't plan to stay in this house?" Her eyes widened. "This is your home. Our home now. And you are my husband."

"And you are my wife. Yet a moment ago you said you would not share my bed."

"It was the only weapon at my disposal. Not that it seems to have mattered." She waved off the comment. "I was angry. I'm still angry."

His eyes narrowed. "Why should *you* be angry?"

"Why? Oh, let me think." She pushed past him and stalked back into his room. "First of all, you've scarcely said more than a handful of words to me, with the exception of our marriage vows, since the night you fell off the balcony. You've treated me as if I were a stranger. A stranger you have no desire to know. And in spite of the fact that you have said, with alarming frequency I might add, how much you want me, you don't even plan to"—she gestured at the bed—"make a proper wife of me."

"I didn't say that exactly." He folded his arms across his chest and leaned against the doorjamb.

"You said you were going to sleep elsewhere."

"The pertinent word there is *sleep*."

"Oh, I see. You intend to . . . to . . . enjoy yourself—"

"I rather hope you'll enjoy it as well," he said with his familiar wicked smile.

"—and then be off to wherever it is you intend to go? Absolutely not." She shook her head. "I will not be treated the way you have treated women in the past. Having your way with them, then it's off to your club or your friends or the next woman. Usually with a husband in close pursuit and, no doubt, a parrot thrown in for good measure."

"You know a great deal about me." His tone was somber, but there was a definite gleam of amusement in his eye.

"Don't think this is funny because it's not. You've been most unpleasant, really quite horrible and—"

"I know and I am sorry," he said quietly.

"And thinking of no one but yourself—"

"My behavior has been unforgivable."

"And never for a moment realizing or admitting or understanding that I am in this as deeply as you are!"

He nodded. "I've been a cad."

"Admitting it doesn't negate the fact of it." She stared at him. "Just tell me why. At least give me that."

"I don't know." He blew a long breath. "As much as I would prefer not to be, I am still, well, angry."

"At me?"

"At everything. At the circumstances we find ourselves in. At"—he rolled his gaze toward the ceiling—"*fate*, if you will."

"I'm not especially delighted with fate at the

moment myself," she said under her breath. "This is not what I'd had in mind."

"I feel as though my life is out of my hands, Felicity. As if I no longer have any say whatsoever over my future. Over anything. It's annoying, it's frustrating, and I don't like it."

"Well, that's that then, isn't it?"

"What?"

"We can't have you unhappy, can we? To hell with how I feel."

A hint of a smile curved the corners of his mouth. She wanted to smack him. "Did you know you have the most appalling language when you're angry?"

"Apparently you bring out qualities in me I never suspected. Of course, I can't remember anyone ever treating me as badly or making me as angry before."

"I shall certainly remember this and try not to anger you in the future." He shook his head in a solemn manner. "It would be a bad influence on the children, you know."

"There shall be no children. There shall be no future. I have changed my mind," she said in a lofty manner. "I don't want to marry you after all."

He chuckled. "I'm afraid it's too late."

"Don't be absurd. We've not even been married a full day yet. Nothing has been done that cannot be undone."

He stared at her in amused disbelief. "This cannot be undone. Surely you understand that?"

"Nonsense, Nigel. There are ways. There must be.

What about annulment? If we don't"—she waved at the bed—"share."

"Not—" he gestured with a dramatic flourish toward the bed—"*sharing* is not grounds for annulment. Admittedly, Ruskin's wife is arguing the absence of sharing but then they've been married for six years, so the circumstances are entirely different. We've scarcely been married for six hours. However, not being able to share by one party or another is grounds."

"What?" She drew her brows together in confusion. Abruptly it dawned on Felicity exactly what he meant. What she hadn't learned on the continent, her mother had filled in. "Oh, I see." In spite of herself, she glanced at his trousers. "I don't suppose you—"

"Are you insane? I am not going to publicly admit to anyone that I cannot *share*."

She shrugged. "No one would believe it anyway. There is that reputation of yours."

"Who would have imagined it would one day come in handy."

"For you," she snapped, then drew a deep breath. "I don't want you to feel frustration or anger or that your life is out of your control. I don't want to feel any of that either. I had thought, or rather I had hoped that . . ."

"Go on."

"As we are in this together, I hoped we could weather it together. You might well feel you have no say in the decisions that now affect your life, but I feel"—she met his gaze directly—"that I have been abandoned."

"I did marry you."

"Certainly you haven't fled the country; that's not what I meant. Oh, I don't know." She wrapped her arms around herself and stared at him. "You've been remote and cold and impersonal. It's most unpleasant and frightening as well to think I am now married to a man who not only doesn't wish to be married but wants nothing to do with me."

"I see." He studied her for a long moment. "That's rather unfair, isn't it?"

"Regardless, I won't apologize for it. It's how I feel. How you have made me feel."

"No, I mean it's unfair of me."

"Yes, it is," she said staunchly. "Unfair and undeserved."

"For that you have my apologies." He blew a long breath. "But I am not ready to change my life. Nor do I wish to do so."

She glanced around the room. "Yes, well I can see where change of any sort might be difficult for you."

He bit back a smile.

She raised a brow. "Am I amusing you?"

"No. Or rather yes. I find your passion amusing." An intriguing look showed in his eye. "And quite provocative."

At once the mood in the room changed, charged with something very much like anticipation. Or desire. Dear Lord, as angry as he had made her, she still wanted him. Perhaps deep down inside she was a tart. Perhaps that's why fate had intended her for Nigel, a man who definitely appreciated a good tart.

"There is a benefit to all this, you know." His voice was warm and smooth, and he stepped toward her.

"A benefit?" She resisted the urge to step back. "What might that be?"

His gaze skimmed over her in an assessing manner, and she had the distinct impression she had just been seen without benefit of clothing. "I have always been fond of married women."

"So I've heard." She studied him with a slow and measured look. "What a remarkable coincidence, Mr. Cavendish. Today I find myself a married woman."

"Do you?" He moved closer, his gaze dropped to her lips and back to her eyes. "And do you have, oh, an arrangement with your husband?"

"An arrangement?" She swallowed hard. "What sort of arrangement?"

"You know the kind of thing." He rested his hands on her shoulders, then skimmed them up and down her arms in a slow and deliberate manner. "Where you and he go your separate ways as regards to"—he leaned closer and kissed the side of her neck—"amusements."

She choked. "Amusements?"

"Um-hm." He wrapped one arm around her and pulled her closer, his lips murmured against her neck. "Of an intimate nature."

She closed her eyes and lost herself in the feel of

his lips on her skin. He had the most remarkable lips. "I don't know."

He pushed the jacket of her dress off her shoulders and it fell to the floor, and still he continued to nibble on her neck. "You don't know what?"

"If I have an arrangement." His hands played over her back. Abruptly she felt cool air and realized he had undone the hooks on the back of her bodice with a skill any lady's maid would envy. "Is it necessary?"

"No." He smoothly drew her bodice off and tossed it aside, then bent to kiss the hollow of her throat. "But preferable."

Her head dropped back and his mouth dropped lower to kiss between her breasts and run his tongue along the sensitive flesh not covered by her corset. Instinctively she reached out and gripped his arms. She held her breath. "Why?"

"I should hate to be shot at." His voice was low and heavy with desire. He reached behind her and undid the hooks that held her skirt and petticoats in place. Then they too dropped to the floor. She stood before him now in little more than her corset and chemise and drawers, and she didn't care. He stepped back and shrugged out of his coat, his gaze as caressing as his hands.

"I don't think my husband would shoot anyone."

His coat joined her bodice on the floor and he yanked off his cravat. "Not even someone dallying with his wife?"

She kicked off her shoes, stepped over the clothes

mounded at her feet, and moved toward him. "I don't think he cares enough."

He pulled his shirt off over his head and let it fall. She stared at him for a moment, at his broad shoulders and finely muscled chest. At the way his body tapered from his shoulders to the waist of his trousers. She reached out and rested her hands on his bare skin and reveled in the heat of his flesh under her fingers.

His voice was rough. "I doubt that."

"Still . . ." She gazed into his eyes.

"Then he is a fool." He pulled her into his arms and his lips pressed to hers, hard and firm and demanding. Her mouth opened to his and his tongue met hers. He tasted vaguely of champagne and strawberries and of promises not yet made. And fate. She wrapped her arms around his neck and pushed her body tighter against his to savor his warmth and the hard planes of his body. His hands roamed over her back and lower to cup her buttocks, and she ground her hips against his. And felt the evidence of his arousal hard against her. She moaned with his need and her own.

Without warning he released her, swiftly undid the hooks of her corset, and threw the thing aside. Then picked her up, carried her to the bed, and laid her down.

"You should know," she said in a breathless voice, "I am not experienced at sharing."

He peeled off her stockings and caressed her

ankles and her calves. "Your husband has not done his duty then."

His hands drifted upward over her legs and her thighs. She resisted the urge to press her legs together and instead clenched her hands at her sides and waited. "He has been . . . preoccupied. With other matters."

He pulled the ribbon that held her drawers together, then pushed the opening wider, lowered his head, and kissed the bare flesh of her stomach. She sucked in a hard breath.

"Then he is indeed a fool," he said under his breath.

He straightened and slowly pulled her drawers apart and down to reveal her most private parts, and still she waited. He traced slow, infinitely slow circles on her stomach until she wanted to scream. Instead she held her breath and closed her eyes. His touch was light, barely perceptible, and yet the most intense thing she'd ever known. His hand drifted lower to the joining of her thighs, and they fell open of their own accord. His hand slipped between her legs and slid over that portion of her body only she had ever known. She moaned and arched upward, her hands clutching at the bedclothes. His fingers were slick with her own desire and slid over her slowly until the most exquisite tension pooled deep in her body.

He stopped then, and she gasped with loss and opened her eyes. Nigel was discarding the rest of his clothing, and curiosity dampened desire. She propped herself up on her elbows and stared. Rather rudely, she suspected, but she'd never seen a naked man before aside from those depicted in marble. There was no comparison really. There was the obvious absence of a fig leaf, of course. On the continent she had seen the occasional sculpture of a male god without a fig leaf, but one really did try not to stare at that particular area of a statue even if one couldn't help taking a peek or two. Carved in marble, that *appendage* had always appeared rather innocent and benign, not the least bit threatening. But then she had never seen a man's, well, *manhood* aimed directly at her before. In the flesh, so to speak.

"Are you quite through staring?" Amusement sounded in his voice.

Heat flushed her face and she looked up at him. "It's rather startling, isn't it?"

He raised a brow. "Startling? I don't think I've ever heard it described as startling before."

"Never?" Her gaze shifted back to his privates. "I should think startling would be the usual description."

"Felicity!"

"Are you overly large?" she said without thinking. "In comparison to other men, that is?"

"I don't think so although I have never compared myself to other men," he said wryly. "However, I have it on good authority that I am more than satisfactory in this particular area."

"References." She nodded thoughtfully.

He groaned. "Felicity."

"References are always helpful, Nigel." She scrambled to her knees. "Might I touch it?"

He made an odd sort of choking sound. "Please do."

She reached out and ran her fingers along the shaft. His member jerked and Nigel gasped. "How remarkable," she murmured and curled her hand around him. She hadn't expected it to be quite this hard and rigid and covered in flesh as smooth as silk. She glanced at his face. His eyes were closed and his lips were slightly parted. She squeezed gently, and his brow furrowed as if his entire being was focused on her touch. She slid her hand up and down the shaft and watched the expressions play across his face. This was exactly what he had done to her. Had she looked as engrossed as he did now? The oddest sense of power swept through her, and, with it, desire.

He grabbed her hand. "I think that's quite enough."

"Is it?" She shook off his grasp, then slid her hands up his chest, leaned forward, and brushed her lips across his. "I'm not sure it's nearly enough."

"Perhaps you're right." With a quick, deft movement, he pulled her hands from his chest, and trapped her wrists behind her back with one hand. With the other he unbuttoned her chemise.

"You're very good at that."

"I know." He released her hands, pushed her chemise off her shoulders, and let it fall. Then he cupped her breasts in his hands. He bent and took her nipple in his mouth, and she uttered a short gasp and arched toward him. He lavished attention on each breast in turn, and a delightful weakness spread through her. When at last he straightened, she collapsed slowly backward on the bed, and he climbed in beside her.

His mouth again claimed hers and his hand caressed her breasts and traveled lower in an easy exploration that was at once exciting and infuriating. And she ached for more. His hand drifted ever lower to slip between her legs, and he again found that remarkable spot that was the source of her pleasure. His fingers teased and toyed, and her breath came in short gasps. The world around her faded to a haze of sensation and need.

He slipped a finger into her and she held her breath. He eased it out and then slipped two into her, and she realized he was preparing her for what would come next. She could have told him he needn't do so. She was prepared, she was ready, and, dear Lord, she *wanted*. Still, it was the most extraordinary feeling, this invasion of his, and not at all unpleasant. His fingers continued to slide in and out and his thumb caressed that point of sheer pleasure, and again she found herself sliding into a world of utter sensation.

At last he spread her legs apart and settled between them, his member nudging hard against her.

He stared down at her. "I understand it may be painful for a woman, this first time, that is."

"But not the second?" She gazed up at him.

"I don't think so."

"Then dear, dear Nigel, let us hurry and get past the first." She arched her hips up to meet him. "Remember, I am willing to learn."

"And I am most willing to teach," he murmured. He eased himself into her with a steady motion until he paused, and she held her breath. Then he thrust hard, and a sharp pain stabbed her and she gasped. "Oh my."

He lay still deep within her, and her body throbbed around him. For a long moment he didn't move, then with a slow, deliberate movement he drew back and thrust forward again. The pain eased. He did it again, and whatever remnant of pain remained dissolved into pleasure.

This was quite extraordinary. In spite of what she'd been told she'd had no idea it would be this intense, this overwhelming, this consuming. With an instinct she'd never suspected, her body responded to his and she moved in a rhythm that matched his. Thrust for thrust, stroke for stroke. A tight hunger, an ache, a longing built within her as if she were climbing up a very tall hill toward something most amazing. And abruptly, the need within her exploded in a shattering spasm of exquisite delight that gripped her body in waves of pleasure and touched her soul. Dimly she heard him moan, and he thrust hard into her and she felt his body shudder against hers. Then he collapsed against her, his body hot and all-encompassing, and she could feel the beat of his heart against hers. And she had the most profound sense of peace and contentment, as if all were right with the world. And for now, at least, it was.

They lay still joined together for a long moment, her fingers trailing lightly over his back, his head buried in the crook of her neck, and she wished they could stay like this forever. It was quite remarkable. Perfect. Right.

"Well, I never quite expected . . ." She sighed.

He murmured against her neck. "I'm delighted that you are not disappointed."

"Not at all. It was . . ."

He raised his head and stared into her eyes. "Extraordinary."

"Extraordinary," she echoed.

He slid off her, shifting onto his side, and propped himself up on his elbow. A lazy smile curved his lips. "I'm glad you enjoyed it."

"Enjoyed it?" She laughed. "I daresay *enjoyed* is an understatement. You're really quite good at this, aren't you?"

His smile widened to a grin. "Anything worth doing is worth doing well. I try to give it my best." He studied her for a moment. "You do realize this changes nothing."

"Perhaps not for you, but I feel distinctly changed." She rolled over on her side, propped her head in her hand, and grinned at him. "Perhaps we could change again?"

He raised a brow. "Again?"

"As lovely as that was, I daresay you can do better."

"Better?"

"I am new to this but I suspect you were being remarkably restrained."

"Well, not remarkably." He chuckled. "I have never been with a woman who has had no experience before."

"A virgin, you mean." She reached out and trailed her fingers idly over his chest.

"Yes." He laughed and caught her hand. "A virgin."

"Were you disappointed?"

"No, not at all. It was"—he brought her hand to his lips—"wonderful. But then I had a virgin who was willing to learn."

"One should never underestimate the importance of being open to new experiences," she said primly. "And I have always relished new experiences."

She pushed him onto his back, then threw her leg over him and shifted until she straddled him. She sat up and grinned down at him in a wicked manner. "If the first time was wonderful, what do you think the second time will be?"

"The second time?"

"I think we should do it again." She ground her bottom against him. He grimaced with obvious pleasure. "What do you think?"

"I think that's an excellent idea." He wrapped his hands around her waist, lifted her slightly, and repositioned her until she felt his hard member between her legs, then slid her down to impale her. "Oh my." She caught her breath. "This is interesting."

"Is it?" He thrust upward.

She gasped. "Yes, it is. Yes, indeed."

He slid his hands slowly up her body to cup her breasts. His thumbs toyed with her nipples and his hips moved beneath hers.

She sucked in her breath. "Very interesting indeed."

"I thought you might like it," he murmured.

He slid one hand to her waist to steady her and slipped the other between her legs and caressed her even as his hips rocked beneath her, one steady stroke following another. Sensation assaulted her, assailed her, overwhelmed her until it became her entire world and she no longer knew who she was and didn't care. She existed only in the spiral of ever-increasing pleasure.

The strength to sit upright abandoned her, washed away by sheer delight, and she collapsed on top of him. And still his fingers moved in tandem with the strokes of his manhood and the beat of her heart and the pulse of her blood. Faster and harder and relentless, until he thrust into her with a moan and she felt him shake beneath her. And a moment later, her body too jerked and shuddered in exquisite release and glorious pleasure.

For long moments she lay on top of him, unwilling, unable to do more than try to breathe and revel in the feel of his naked body joined with hers.

He chuckled beneath her. "What are you thinking, Felicity Cavendish?"

"I'm thinking how very fortunate I am to have such a skilled teacher. And I'm thinking as well . . ." She sighed with utter contentment. "Mother was right."

Were all virgins insatiable or was it just those who were willing to learn? Nigel propped himself up on his elbow and watched his sleeping wife. The afternoon had turned to evening and the last lingering rays of the sun caressed her sleeping form. Lucky sun. How could anyone ever have thought she was merely pleasant? She was lovely beyond words. His stomach tightened. Apparently he was rather insatiable himself.

If Nigel had ever envisioned the consummation of a marriage, and indeed he never had, this certainly was not what he had imagined. Virgin or not, Felicity had an innate sensuality coupled with a unique enthusiasm. The last few hours had been extraordinary, and he suspected he would not be able to get enough of his new wife, at least not in bed. As for the rest of marriage . . .

He had to consider that this was indeed the hand of fate. What but fate could account for his losing the painting to her? Or the pistol discharge? Or the fact that she seemed to be everywhere he looked? Or any number of other odd, annoying coincidences. Even his own actions were suspect. Over and over he'd done things he shouldn't have because he simply wanted to be with the blasted woman. To talk to her or dance with her or kiss her in the shadows.

He sighed. They were bound together now, for good or ill and certainly forever. There was nothing to be done about it. But he'd meant it when he said he did not intend to change his life. This marriage had not been his choice. He acknowledged, if only to himself, that an intelligent man would make the best of it. But blast it all, it simply wasn't fair. Certainly it wasn't fair to Felicity either, but when all was said and done, regardless of the circumstances, she had been given exactly what she'd wanted. And he'd simply been caught. He ignored the thought that he'd been given her as well.

Damnation, it was his life. Surely he had the right to have some say in it. Desperation gripped him, squeezed his soul until he had to struggle to breathe. Desperate men took desperate measures. Accepting his marriage was accepting defeat. Accepting that he had absolutely no control over his life. Accepting that he was no more than a pawn in the hands of fate. Well, he wouldn't do it. Not now, not ever.

The thought struck him that only a fool would fight fate. Who knew what the cost for that might be? Didn't the gods strike down mortals foolish enough to defy them? And weren't the fates minor deities? And women as well?

Still, there was something to be said for resolve, for determination, for fortitude. He gazed at his wife lying beside him and tried to ignore the voice nagging at the back of his mind.

He was indeed a fool.

Eleven

What a man really wants is a woman with spirit. Keeps him young.
Lord Fernwood

*I*f she hadn't been ruined before she certainly was now. And a lovely ruination it had been. Felicity lay in the center of Nigel's bed and gazed unseeing at the ceiling, her lips curved in a satisfied smile. Even with her mother's reassurances, she'd had no idea lovemaking would be quite this delicious. Nigel was indeed an expert but there was something more to it than simply skill. When he'd touched her or had joined with her or had cried out her name in the throes of passion, Felicity had never felt so, well, loved before. Even if the word *love* had not been mentioned.

She sat up and stretched and glanced around the room. It was obviously late morning. She hadn't planned to sleep so late, but then she really hadn't had much sleep during the night. She grinned. Or yesterday afternoon, or last evening. She wondered idly where Nigel had gone to but wasn't at all worried by his absence. He would be back. She was certain of it. In the meantime, she was now the mistress of a house and had a great deal to do.

She threw back the covers and realized she didn't have a stitch on. That too made her grin. Imagine, here she was naked on the morning after her wedding and she didn't feel the least bit embarrassed or uncomfortable. In truth, she had the most wonderful sense of well-being and contentment. She was, she realized, happy. Truly, blissfully, extraordinarily happy.

She slid out of bed and winced. Dear Lord, she was as sore as if she had ridden a horse across the country. She laughed aloud at the comparison and wondered what Eugenia would think if she knew Felicity was now most interested in the ride. Still, it was a lovely soreness. Felicity discovered her robe on the lone chair in the room. She hoped it had been placed there by her husband and not a maid. She blushed at the very thought of someone other than Nigel seeing the state of the room at the moment. The clothes she'd worn yesterday were still scattered about the floor. The bedclothes were bunched and disheveled, indeed the bed looked like it had been the scene of a battle of epic proportions, which in many ways she supposed it had.

Felicity pulled on her robe and stepped through the dressing room into what would be her room. She chuckled. Even when a bed was installed, she had no intention of spending her nights there. No, she would be by Nigel's side in Nigel's bed. And given what they'd shared last night, he would have no objections. She was indeed willing to learn, and he had been a most attentive teacher. She could scarcely wait for her next lesson. She moved to the wardrobe and found her clothes had been unpacked and neatly arranged. She selected a day dress she could put on without the help of a maid. Once dressed, she would go downstairs and see what state the kitchen was in. With any luck at all the cook Lady Cavendish had loaned her had something prepared. Felicity was famished. Remarkable how passion did that to you. She had an idea as well about how to furnish this house quickly, if temporarily.

No, she wasn't concerned about where Nigel was at the moment. She was confident he cared for her far more than he was willing to admit. Yet. She glanced through the open dressing room doors to the bed and grinned. He would most certainly be back. And when he returned, perhaps he could ruin her again.

Nigel handed his hat and gloves to the footman George, on loan from his mother. It was evening when he had at last headed for home. Nigel had managed to stay away the entire day but it hadn't been easy.

"Lady Felicity is in the parlor, sir," George said. "She requests that you join her there when you arrive."

"In the parlor?" Nigel shook his head. "There's nothing in the parlor."

"Lady Felicity is in the parlor sir," George repeated, and Nigel could have sworn there was a hint of chastisement in his tone. Surely not. George was entirely too well trained for that. It was probably no more than Nigel's guilty conscience at work, although he had nothing to feel guilty about. Admittedly he'd felt a twinge of remorse when he'd realized that he should have proposed a wedding trip. Still, this had been no usual wedding, and one could not expect the usual to accompany it.

He had spent much of the day at Cavendish House doing precisely what he was expected to do: learning his trade as it were. His father had raised a brow at his son's appearance but hadn't said a word. Nigel had spent the remainder of the day at a club he maintained membership in, although rarely frequented, where he had, fortunately, not run into anyone inclined to join him. Precisely as he'd wanted it. He'd had a great deal to consider.

Now he had to face his—he gritted his teeth at the word—*wife.*

Nigel pushed open the doors to the parlor and pulled up short. He glanced around the room in confusion. "Have I gone mad and somehow stumbled into the wrong house?"

Felicity rose to her feet from a chair—*a chair?*— beside the fireplace. "Of course not, Nigel, this is your house."

"Is it?" His mouth dropped open and he stared.

Where it had been bare, the front parlor was now filled with chairs and sofas and tables. Paintings hung on the walls. Carpets were laid on the floor. Drapes adorned the windows. He stepped cautiously into the room. The doors were flung open to the back parlor, and that room was similarly furnished.

"I must say I'm pleased. It came together far better than I expected." Satisfaction sounded in Felicity's voice. "Do you like it?"

"Like it?" Nigel shook his head. "I'm not sure I believe it. How did you . . . Where did this . . ."

"It's all temporary, until I have the opportunity to purchase what is needed, but it will serve for now. Quite nicely too, I think. As for the how and where of it . . ." She surveyed the room like a general assessing her troops. "I started with my mother. She was more than willing to loan some pieces she had no need of at the moment. From there, I proceeded to your sister's house, and she too contributed to the cause. She accompanied me to Cavendish House, and the result"—she waved with a flourish at the parlors— "is what you see here."

"And you managed to get it all moved in and arranged?" he said slowly. "In just one day?"

"It wasn't easy, I can tell you that." She shook her head. "But between my mother and your mother and sister, resources were marshaled and this is the end result. It's quite amazing what determined women can accomplish."

"Frightening really," he murmured. "Is the rest of the house—"

"Dear Lord, no." She scoffed. "This was all we could manage for the moment and all we need for now anyway." She moved to him, rested her hands on his chest, and gazed up at him, a distinctly wicked light in her eye. "Besides, we only need one bed, don't we?"

He stared down at her and tried to ignore the way her warm body pressed against his and the memory of just how responsive that body could be. He drew a deep breath, removed her hands, and stepped back. "One bed should suffice."

"It should, should it?" She studied him cautiously. "Has something happened?"

"Not at all. We simply have matters we need to discuss, Felicity." He groaned to himself. How could he sound so pompous? So asinine?

She crossed her arms over her chest. "Do we?"

"We do." He waved at the nearest sofa. "Perhaps you would care to sit down."

"Oh, I think I should remain on my feet for this."

"Very well." He clasped his hands behind his back and paced the room. "I have given a great deal of thought to our situation."

"Our situation?" Her eyes narrowed. "Our marriage, you mean?"

"Yes, of course, our"—he paused—"*marriage.*"

"You are going to have to learn to say the word without choking, you know."

"I can say the word. I say it all the time. And in recent days I seem to have said it a great deal." He stopped in midstride and met her gaze firmly. "Admittedly there are moments when it catches in my throat."

Her brow rose. "And this is one of them?"

"Apparently," he muttered and resumed pacing. "Felicity—"

"You said that."

"And I am saying it again." He cleared his throat. "Felicity—"

"I think I shall sit down after all," she said lightly, moved to a red brocade sofa that looked vaguely familiar, and sat down, spreading her skirts around her.

He clenched his jaw. "Are you finished?"

She smoothed the fabric of her skirts. "Yes, I think so." Felicity looked up at him and smiled pleasantly. "Do go on."

"I intend to." He huffed. "As I was saying, Felicity—"

"Ahem." She cleared her throat and cast him a pointed glance.

"Very well, I shall skip that part," he said sharply, then drew a deep breath. "Fel—" He winced.

She stifled a laugh.

He stared at her. "This is not the least bit amusing."

"No." She stared at him for a long moment, then sighed. "I don't suppose it is. Go on."

"Thank you." He resumed pacing. This was extraordinarily difficult, and she hadn't made it any better by her constant interruptions. Still, now that he had her complete attention he wasn't sure how to begin. It might be best to just plunge ahead. "As you know, I had no interest in marriage."

"I daresay everyone in the world knows that," she said under her breath. "It was not a well-kept secret."

He ignored her. "In truth, I had actively avoided it as well as any situation that might lead to marriage."

"You mean situations like falling off a balcony in the middle of the night?" Her eyes widened in an innocent manner. "The balcony of a virgin?"

"Exactly." He cast her a stern look. "However, in spite of my best efforts, I now find myself married regardless of my wishes."

She smiled. "Fate."

He nodded. "I agree."

She stared. "What do you mean, you agree?"

"Denying the facts of the matter do not make them any less accurate. I have accepted that there might well have been a greater force than I at work here." He drew his brows together in an effort to look serious. "From the first moment we met, I was a boulder rolling downhill, unstoppable, with ever greater momentum until inevitably I smacked into—"

"Me?"

"Marriage," he said firmly, then nodded. "And you."

"I'm so glad you accept it, Nigel. Fate, that is." Felicity beamed and rose to her feet. "I know marriage isn't exactly what—"

"Please allow me to finish." He gestured for her to retake her seat. She sank back down onto the sofa like a deflated balloon. He pushed the image out of his mind. Her spirits might be deflated soon enough anyway. Still, for his own sake, it had to be done. "While I realize you do care for me . . ."

"Yes," she said slowly.

"And I do like you as well . . ."

"Go on."

"I have made a decision regarding our—"

"Marriage?"

"I was going to say it." He huffed. "Although it's more regarding our lives than marriage as such." He drew a deep breath. "My life, really."

"Your life?"

He nodded. "I told you last night, I did not intend to change my life."

She studied him closely. "I'm not sure I understand what you're saying."

"Even though we are now married, I do not intend to change my behavior. My life. My activities." He smiled pleasantly. "Does that explain it?"

"Not exactly."

"You once said that I was reformable but that I wasn't worth the effort. As I have no intention of reforming, I have saved you a great deal of trouble."

"You have no intention of—what?" She rose to her feet.

"You can certainly change whatever you wish in the house with the exception of the library, of course, and"—he pinned her with a no-nonsense look—"me."

She stared in shocked disbelief, but then he expected that she would. Still, now that he had managed to say the words, he felt, well, good. Exhilarated. In command. Exactly how a man in his position should feel. Now that he had said his piece, made his announcement, there was a certain sense of power, of control. Yes, his life was back in his hands where it bloody well belonged.

"Now then." He smiled in a pleasant manner. "I shall be taking dinner out this evening at my club."

"Before you go." Her manner was as pleasant as his. "Might I ask a few questions?"

"Certainly." He could afford to be generous. While she, and fate, had won the battles up to now, he was going to win the war. "Anything you wish."

"Thank you." She thought for a moment. "First of all, how long do you intend to live your life in the manner in which you always have?"

"I hadn't really thought of a time period." He shrugged. "Indefinitely, I suppose." A brilliant idea struck him. "Or until I reach the point when I *wish* to be married. Yes, that's good. It's bound to happen sometime, you know. Then, conveniently enough, I will already be married and I already have you."

"That is convenient," she murmured. "Tell me, what exactly does this life of yours involve? Drinking? Gambling? Carousing with your friends? Coming in at all hours of the night? Activities of that nature, I assume."

He waved offhandedly. "Yes, yes, all of that."

"What about women?"

He frowned. "What about women?"

"You have always had a particular fondness for women."

"I haven't considered the question of women in regards to this. But I have always believed marriage vows are as sacred as a man's word. I see nothing to change that now. Therefore." He nodded firmly. "There shall be no other women. That much I am willing to change about my life."

"How very gracious of you."

He stared at her for a long moment. "There's no need for sarcasm, Felicity."

"Really? And I thought there was every need for sarcasm."

"I am just trying to make the best of a bad situation."

"A bad situation?" Her voice was cool. "Last night was a bad situation? And yesterday afternoon? And again just before dawn?"

"Absolutely." He caught her expression and shook his head. "*Not*. Absolutely not. Yesterday and last night and this morning were delightful. Why, I probably couldn't have enjoyed it more if I hadn't been with my own wife."

"But as I am your wife it's a bad situation?"

He drew his brows together. "You're putting words in my mouth, Felicity. I don't mean to say that you are a bad situation. I've said before that I quite like you. And I certainly have no complaints about sharing your bed. I mean the circumstances we find ourselves in—"

"You mean marriage?"

"Yes. Even you have to admit the situation is not ideal."

"Let me make certain I understand." She thought for a moment. "You intend to continue your activities exactly as before but you will curtail those involving other women—"

"Eliminate," he corrected.

"My apologies, eliminate those involving other women and share my bed exclusively. You will do as you wish and then come home to me."

"That's it exactly." He grinned. "It solves all our problems."

"Not entirely." She considered him for a moment. "While you are living your life as you please, what am I to do?"

"Why, whatever you wish I suppose. You are now the mistress of a house, a house that needs a great deal of work and substantial management. That should occupy a considerable amount of your time."

"And in the evening?"

"I've thought of that," he said in a smug manner. "You can devote yourself to your work. To astronomy.

You may study the stars all you wish. Perhaps discover a new comet yourself."

"I see." She paused, obviously to ponder his announcement and realize it was the perfect solution. "You have given this a great deal of thought, haven't you?"

"Indeed, I have thought of little else."

"I admit it is an interesting proposal," she said thoughtfully.

"It's not a proposal. It is how I have decided things shall be." There was an authoritarian note in his voice that under other circumstances would have appalled him but at the moment sounded appropriate. After all, she was his wife.

"Then I have no choice?"

Still, it was perhaps wise not to answer that question directly. "I have made my decision."

"I see. Very well then." She stepped into the hall and called down the stairs. "George, would you call for my carriage."

He frowned. "Where are you going at this hour?"

"Out."

"I suspected that but out where?"

She shrugged. "I'm not sure yet. I shall decide when I get there. But I'm certain it shall be a great deal of fun."

He stared. "I don't understand."

"It's very simple, Nigel. I have long wanted a life of adventure and excitement. You have now provided me the means for such a life." She cast him a brilliant smile. "And I do thank you for it."

"What do you mean?"

"I mean if your life of fun and frolic is too very dear to abandon, I should experience the appeal of it myself."

"What?"

She studied him carefully. "I expect you drink a great deal."

"Perhaps," he said slowly.

"Then I shall do likewise. And you gamble considerably?"

"Not considerably but—"

"Then I shall do the same." She leaned toward him in a confidential manner. "Although I daresay I'll win."

He sputtered.

"You spend a great deal of time at your club?"

"Aha, I have you there. You don't have a club."

"I don't have a club. Yet. Although I'm certain I can find one. Surely there are ladies' clubs?"

He scoffed. "I've never heard of such a thing. Certainly there are ladies' clubs devoted to gardening or charities or something of that nature but not to . . . to . . ."

"Drinking and gambling and carousing?"

"Yes!"

"Then I shall have to start one." She beamed. "What an excellent idea. A place where ladies can escape from their husbands and drink to excess and gamble away all their pin money. Oh, it shall be great fun."

"Felicity!"

"Eugenia will join, I'm certain of that. She loves a wickedly expensive game of chance. And your sister will definitely be interested."

"I will not permit—"

"Anything I wished," she cut in. "That's what you said. I may spend my time doing anything I wished."

"Within reason!"

"Whose reason? Yours? You never said that." She shook her head. "I only intend to follow your example. You can scarcely complain about that."

"But—"

"Now one last thing." Her brow furrowed. "About other women."

"I said I have given up other women," he said staunchly.

"Perhaps we should reconsider that."

His eyes widened with disbelief. "You're saying you would accept my sharing the bed of other women?"

"Only if I can share the bed of other men." She gasped and her eyes widened. "We could have an arrangement! What a lovely idea!"

He could barely choke out the words. "An arrangement?"

"Yes indeed. You know, one of those things where you will not shoot my"—she smiled sweetly—lovers.

"Lovers!"

"Well, I shall surely have more than one. And I would prefer to keep them from being shot.

Especially if they are skilled in matters of . . . of the mattress."

He stared in horror.

"You have quite whetted my appetite for amorous pursuits, you know. Indeed, you've opened my eyes to an entirely new world. And as proficient as you are, I cannot help but wonder what the skills of other men are like."

"Felicity!" Shock sounded in his voice.

"I am most willing to learn if you recall. Although I would like to avoid undue scandal. Oh wait." She met his gaze directly. "Scandal has always been part and parcel of your life, therefore I shouldn't avoid it at all."

"There shall be no arrangement!" He clenched his fists by his sides. "I shall give up other women and you shall give up other men."

"I can't give up what I've never had." She shrugged. "Perhaps that part of making the best of a bad situation should wait until I have."

"Absolutely not. I will not have my wife—"

She raised a brow.

He narrowed his gaze. "I see exactly what you're doing Felicity, and it won't work."

"Nigel, you have gone on and on about how unfair the circumstances we find ourselves in have been to you. In the interest of fairness, if you are allowed to live your life in whatever way you see fit, I should be allowed to do so as well. It's only"—she paused to emphasize the word—"*fair*. If you wish to lead separate lives, so be it." She turned and headed down the stairs. "I shall see you, well, whenever I see you then. Do have a pleasant evening."

A moment later he heard the door downstairs open and close and she was gone.

What in the name of all that was holy had just happened here? Nigel moved to the nearest chair and collapsed into it. He had intended to seize back control of his life. And indeed he had done so. He was now free to resume his life precisely as it had been before their marriage, with the exception of amorous pursuits. And those he was more than willing—indeed eager—to restrict to Felicity alone.

As for the rest of it, he had gotten exactly what he'd wanted, but he'd never imagined she'd want it as well. He'd thought she'd be annoyed or upset, even angry. He was prepared for that. But he'd never dreamed she would decide to follow in his footsteps. Well, he wouldn't allow it.

Nigel got to his feet and started after her. The very thought of her drinking and gambling and doing everything else he wouldn't hesitate to do was outrageous. He'd stop her right now.

Still . . . he paused in the doorway. Felicity was a clever woman. Very clever. She obviously thought if she turned the tables on him, he'd back down. More than likely she had no intention of actually engaging in the behavior she had threatened. It was obviously a bluff on her part. He'd wager serious sums that she was even now on her way to Lady Kilbourne's house to pour out her complaints about her new husband.

Of course, that was exactly what she was doing. He chuckled to himself. She was playing this the same way she played cards, keeping her trump cards close to her in anticipation of the last trick. What she didn't know was that the last trick had indeed been played and he had won. He just had to wait for her to realize it.

Nigel may have been manipulated by fate, but he wasn't going to be manipulated by his wife as well. Not bloody likely. He knew her well enough to know, regardless of how outspoken she was or how flirtatious, she was not the type of woman to do the type of things she'd threatened. As for other men, the very idea was absurd. No, she was definitely bluffing, and he could wait until she stopped pretending to follow his example. No matter how long it took.

Nigel absolutely refused to consider the possibility that there was so much as the slightest chance he might just be wrong.

"Obviously my brother has gone mad." Madeline watched her new sister-in-law pace her parlor. "Or you have. How could you have agreed to such a thing?"

"I didn't agree. And what was I supposed to do?" Felicity shook her head. "I suspect he expected an argument or tears or something quite emotional." She paused and met Madeline's gaze. "I refused to give him that. It seemed at the time that turning the tables was the best strategy."

"Probably," Madeline said thoughtfully. "Although many women would have accepted their husband's pronouncement."

Felicity stared. "Accepted that he will go on with this life exactly as he always has with the exception of coming home to my bed?" Felicity snorted. "Not bloody likely."

"Good for you." Madeline beamed. "I knew you were the right woman for Nigel."

"Unfortunately your brother doesn't feel the same." She sat down on the sofa beside her sister-in-law. "He says he likes me and it was quite obvious that he *enjoyed* me."

"Did you enjoy him as well?"

"Dear Lord yes," Felicity said without thinking. Heat rushed up her face.

Madeline laughed. "It's nothing to be embarrassed about. I think a husband and wife should enjoy one another. Besides, it keeps the husband in the bed he should be in."

"That's something at any rate."

"I should have expected this." Madeline sighed. "Nigel's reaction, that is."

"The fact that he feels his life has been taken out of his hands?"

Madeline nodded. "Nigel has always been used to doing precisely as he wished without particular regard to responsibility or duty. It's only recently that that has changed."

"You mean marriage."

"No, actually I don't. You see a few weeks ago,

Father began turning over management of the family's affairs to him. Responsibilities Nigel knew he'd have to take on when Father died, but he assumed he'd have years until he reached that point. Given Father's accomplishments, my brother was terrified of stepping into his shoes. But he's doing very well from what Mother has told me. He seems to have a natural aptitude for it. One might say it's in his blood. Father's quite proud of him. Of course, the only one who thought he wasn't up to it was Nigel himself."

"Nigel mentioned that he and his father have recently grown closer."

Madeline nodded. "I think they have. They've been spending a great deal of time together, more than ever before, I think. Although they have never had a bad relationship. They've never been at odds the way so many fathers and sons tend to be. Father has always been tolerant of Nigel's misadventures, and I think the tiniest bit amused as well, although I'm certain Nigel has no idea of that. Nigel and I turn"—she winced—"thirty-one in a few weeks. At that time, Father is putting management of the family interests entirely in Nigel's hands, whether he wants it or not."

"I see," Felicity said slowly. "He has no choice then."

"None whatsoever." Madeline shook her head. "It is his lot in life." She paused. "He didn't have a say in Father's decision nor did he really have a say in marrying you."

"And following on the heels of one part of his life

being taken from his hands, it makes a certain amount of sense that he would fight to remain in charge of another part."

"Yes, well, understanding the situation doesn't make it any better, does it?"

"Not really." Poor Nigel, no wonder the man felt trapped. Between his father's edict and his being forced into marriage, Felicity could well understand his analogy about being a boulder rolling downhill. Good Lord, in recent weeks Nigel had been more of an avalanche than a mere boulder. "So what am I to do? The last thing I want, the last thing I've ever wanted, is for him to be unhappy."

"And he won't be," Madeline said firmly, then grimaced. "Eventually."

Felicity raised a skeptical brow.

"Come now, Felicity. It's not as bad as all that. He does like you and he likes being in your bed—"

"But he doesn't like being married to me."

"Nonsense. He's barely been married to you for more than a day. He can't know at this point whether he likes being married to you or not."

"But—"

"He doesn't like the *idea* of marriage. He doesn't like *being made* to marry. And he doesn't like *being forced* to give up a way of life that was very nearly at an end anyway." Madeline sighed. "What my brother really doesn't like is growing up, but it's time. Past time."

Felicity spread her hands in a helpless gesture. "Then am I to wait for him to realize that?"

Madeline snorted. "Lord help us, no. Who knows how long it might take Nigel to come to his senses. And I can't see you being the kind of dutiful wife patiently waiting with open arms for your husband to come home from his carousing."

Felicity wrinkled her nose. "Yet another flaw in my character."

"Don't be absurd. That kind of wife wouldn't suit Nigel at all. In fact, I wouldn't be at all surprised if his little announcement about living his own life wasn't as much a challenge to you as anything else. I think my brother would have been disappointed if you had meekly acquiesced to his decree. Now then." She studied Felicity for a moment. "I suspect you don't have a plan."

"Other than coming directly to you." Felicity smiled weakly. "No."

"I did like that idea about a ladies' club. Somewhere for ladies to spend their evenings when their husbands are out doing whatever it is they do."

Felicity shook her head. "It was the first thing that popped into my head. I wasn't serious about it."

"Perhaps you should be."

"It is an interesting proposition, I suppose, but it would take a great deal of time and effort to arrange something like that." She got to her feet and resumed pacing. "No, I suspect I need to move quickly."

"You're probably right. The longer you allow Nigel to have his own way, the more he will come to expect it." Madeline shrugged. "Perhaps at some later point we can do something about a ladies' club."

"Which still leaves us at today." Felicity couldn't recall ever feeling this helpless before. As if her very life was out of her control, out of her hands. She could understand how Nigel had felt the very same thing and could understand as well his response to it.

"It does, doesn't it?" Madeline rose, clasped her hands behind her back, and paced, in precisely the same manner her brother did, in a pattern perpendicular to Felicity's.

For long moments neither said a word. It struck Felicity that someone walking in on them right now might think it rather comical to see Lady Windham and Lady Felicity pacing in counterpoint to one another. Indeed, it had all the appearance of a lighthearted theatrical farce. Pity, there was nothing lighthearted about it. No, her heart was heavy and leaden and wretched. Still, this was not the time to give up. After all, she was married to him, probably for the rest of her days. And he did like her. The situation could definitely be worse.

Madeline stopped and looked at her. "The way I see it, you have two choices."

"I do?"

"Of course. You can accept Nigel's edict and concern yourself with nothing more than furnishing his home and managing his household so that he doesn't have a care in world and welcome him with a joyful smile to your bed every night."

Felicity scoffed. "And my second choice?"

"You can do exactly what you threatened to do."

Felicity stared at her sister-in-law. "I couldn't

possibly. I don't know the first thing about the kind of activities Nigel no doubt participates in."

"You play cards exceptionally well."

"I daresay I am up to Nigel's standards in that." Felicity waved off the comment. "But I certainly can't drink excessively." The few times she had overindulged in spirits came back to her, and she blanched at the memory. She had the most appalling tendency to speak her mind even more so than usual when she was inebriated. Precisely why she avoided excessive drink. "Beyond that, I honestly have no idea how a man like Nigel spends his time."

"Nor do I really. I should ask my husband." Madeline drew her brows together and considered the question. "I have always thought Nigel and his friends did little more than sit in their clubs, smoke cigars, gamble on cards or dice or simply ridiculous things like who will next have an affair with Lady Whomever or which actress will next catch Lord So-and-so's eye, gossipy things like that. They'll wager on nearly anything, I suspect. And then there is their inevitable pursuit of women."

"Which Nigel says he will abstain from in the future," Felicity said firmly.

"Yes, of course." Madeline studied her sister-in-law. "But you didn't agree to give up men."

"I can scarcely give up something I've never had. Aside from Nigel, that is. Besides, I have no interest in other men."

"Nigel doesn't know that."

"Yes, but—"

"You're missing the point, Felicity. You did not agree to abstain from amorous involvement with other men. Therefore—"

"You cannot be serious." Felicity widened her eyes in disbelief. "I couldn't possibly. Why, it would be wrong. Morally wrong. Besides, I love Nigel."

Madeline raised a brow. "You do, do you?"

"I do." Felicity had never said the words aloud before. "I think I have from the moment he climbed over my balcony."

"And I suspected as much from the moment you first asked for my help." Madeline grinned. "I couldn't imagine a woman not in love willing to pursue Nigel."

"And yet, loving him does me no good whatsoever." Felicity shook her head. "It scarcely matters whether I love him or not."

"Don't be absurd. It matters a great deal," Madeline said firmly. "It means you're not willing to give up on him."

"No I'm not. Never." Felicity gritted her teeth. "Whether he likes it or not."

"Excellent." Madeline nodded. "Now, regardless of how it might have sounded, I am not proposing you take up with other men, nor am I suggesting you do indeed emulate my brother's behavior. My suggestion is that you let him think you are."

"And how am I to do that?" Felicity crossed her

arms over her chest. "I can't simply vanish every evening and pretend that I am out and about. Where shall I go?"

Madeline grinned. "Here."

"That's very generous of you but—"

"And in coming here you will be doing exactly what your husband suggested."

Felicity drew her brows together in confusion. "I don't understand."

"Nigel suggested you throw yourself into your work, did he not?"

Felicity nodded.

"This is the perfect place to do exactly that." Excitement sparked in Madeline's eyes. "One of my husband's ancestors, several generations ago, fancied himself an artist. The room at the back of the house on the third floor has the most wonderful windows and skylights. In that room, you very much feel as if you are out of doors. It has some old furniture in it, but it's a very big room and it's not being used at the moment. I tend to keep it locked because little boys and large, tempting windows are not a good combination. I've never been up there at night but I think it might well be perfect—"

"For studying the stars!" Felicity cast her sister-in-law a delighted smile. "My word, I've never had my own observatory before. What a wonderful idea."

"I thought so," Madeline said modestly. "But the very best part about it is that you scarcely have to lie to Nigel regarding your activities at all. Why, you simply tell him you are off to pursue your own interests and leave it at that."

"And leave him to draw his own conclusions," Felicity said thoughtfully. "Yes, that might work."

"Of course it will work. In no time at all, Nigel will realize sharing a life with you is far preferable to living his own alone." Madeline turned and started toward the door. "Come along then. You should see your new observatory."

Felicity hurried after her. "We shall have to move my telescope here. And my globe and star charts."

"I have been thinking of purchasing a telescope myself," Madeline said over her shoulder. "Perhaps you can show me how to use it."

"Yes, of course." Felicity followed Madeline up the stairs. "It will be great fun to be able to share my interest with a friend."

"My dear girl, I'm not your friend." Madeline stopped a few steps in front of Felicity and leveled her a firm look. "*I* am your sister."

Felicity caught her breath. "I've never had a sister before."

"And I've never had a sister close to my own age before. I'm quite looking forward to it." Madeline nodded and started back up the stairs. "We have a great deal in common, I think. Not the least of which is my brother."

"Madeline," Felicity said slowly. "Nigel won't think you, I don't know, a traitor for your kindnesses toward me? After all, you are his twin."

"As such, I want only his happiness. And I shall do whatever I must to help ensure his happiness." Ahead of her, Madeline's voice rang with purpose. "And, especially when it comes to my brother, I do so love to be helpful."

Twelve

What a man really wants is the fortitude of character to admit when he's wrong.
The Honorable Mr. Nigel Cavendish

"You're joining me for breakfast?" Felicity said mildly, a piece of toast in one hand, a pen poised over a notebook in the other, correspondence in neat stacks beside the notebook.

"I'm hungry." Nigel seated himself in the chair at the head of the table for the first time.

"You've never joined me for breakfast before." She smiled pleasantly and turned her attention back to whatever she was writing. "You're usually off to Cavendish House by this hour of the morning."

"Yes, well, today, I'm hungry." He signaled to George to bring him a plate and wondered irritably when Felicity was going to hire servants to replace those from Cavendish House. After all, they'd been married a full week now. And a most annoying week it had been too.

"You came in rather late last night." He adopted an offhand manner, took a slice of toast from the rack on the table, and slathered it with jam.

"Did I? I hadn't noticed," she said, without looking up from the notebook. "You should try the jam. It's excellent."

He glared at the toast and viciously took a bite as if it were responsible for his troubles. It wasn't, of course, and the jam was indeed excellent. Not that even ambrosia from the gods would ease his foul mood. A mood that had grown worse with every passing day.

For the first few days after Nigel had declared he would not be changing his life, he was confident and not the least bit concerned about where Felicity was spending her evenings. He'd simply assumed she was at her parents' house or with her friend Lady Kilbourne. Or perhaps attending one party or another. He'd spent his nights at his favorite club with Norcroft and the American and whoever else happened along, in a pleasant haze of self-satisfaction. He was doing precisely as he pleased after all. He and Felicity had returned home each evening within a few minutes of each other and had promptly fallen into bed together, which had continued to be most extraordinary. Her willingness to learn was impressive and she was a very good student.

Beyond that, they'd have long discussions in those quiet hours of the night about all sorts of things he'd rarely considered. He'd come to enjoy that nearly as much as their lovemaking. He couldn't recall ever talking to a woman before, at least not about anything of significance. Felicity had a fine mind and a curious nature, and he found she stimulated his own intellect as nothing had since his school days.

By the third day, he had grown curious about how she was filling her evenings and had casually inquired as to her activities. She'd said she was pursuing her own interests, had promptly employed her mouth in a most inventive manner, and he had completely lost his train of thought. Every subsequent time he'd asked she'd either distracted him, although admittedly the distractions were usually most enjoyable, or had told him, politely but firmly, that he had exactly what he'd wanted and as she didn't ask about his activities, he had no right to ask about hers. He was fairly certain her nighttime endeavors did not involve men, although he could not quite get the fact that she had not agreed to give them up out of his head. It was enough to make a man jealous if a man was a jealous sort. All in all, it was most annoying. Another month of this and he'd go stark, raving mad.

George set a plate of coddled eggs, sausages, and bacon before him. It looked every bit as good as the jam had tasted. Perhaps he should begin taking breakfast here. That was one aspect of domesticity he wouldn't mind.

Even worse, with every passing day Nigel found he was enjoying himself less and less. His sense of triumph had faded. He had no heart for gambling and no interest in any of the other ways he had once spent his time. In truth, he couldn't seem to recall exactly what he used to do that was so worth fighting for. And even if he hadn't given up his more amorous adventures, no woman was nearly as interesting as the one waiting for him at home. Why, he'd actually taken to reading a book to while away the hours at his club on, of all things, the geography of the heavens.

That he wasn't enjoying the life he used to lead was a revelation. That he preferred Felicity above other women was not. He'd thought from the first that there was a distinct sensuality about her, a ripeness, as it were. There was as well a sweet aspect to her enthusiasm, an innocence, if one could use the word in this context, in her willingness to learn. What was a surprise was the realization that he could indeed spend the rest of his days with one woman, with this woman, and not regret it for a moment. And that was the greatest revelation of all.

"I am glad you joined me." Felicity set her pen and her toast down. "There are some things we must settle."

"Indeed there are," he said firmly. This was more like it. At last he was going to get answers to his questions. "It's past time too."

She cast him a curious look. "I didn't think you were that concerned about such matters."

"Well, I am." He had, no doubt, given her the impression he was not concerned, and perhaps he hadn't been a week ago. Now, however, was a different story. "Most concerned."

"Very well then." She shrugged. "I suppose I should I start with a confession."

"Aha!"

She raised a brow. "Aha?"

"Go on then." He crossed his arms over his chest. "Confess. I'm ready."

"As long as you're ready," she murmured and laid a hand on one of the stacks of correspondence. "In this pile are invitations addressed to me alone. My mother sent them on to me here." She moved her hand to the second stack. "This pile was addressed to you alone, and as it was apparent they were invitations, I took the liberty of opening them. I thought it was a wife's duty to do so. I hope you don't mind."

"That's it." He stared at her. "That's the confession? The entire confession? All of it? There's nothing more?"

She thought for a moment, then nodded. "Yes, that's it. This last stack are invitations addressed to both of us. They've all arrived within the past few days. Apparently we've become quite a popular couple." She smiled in a wry manner. "I daresay no one can believe the infamous Mr. Cavendish has finally wed."

"I can understand their doubt," he said under his breath. "And this is what you wished to discuss?"

"Well, we do need to decide which we plan to accept." She picked up the pen and tapped the notebook. "I have made some notations here regarding which events we were both invited to separately, before our marriage, that is, and then those that requested the presence of the Honorable Nigel Cavendish and the Lady Felicity Cavendish." She grinned. "I do like the way that sounds."

"It has a nice ring to it," he said grudgingly and realized he meant it. Blast it all, he did like the way it sounded. It sounded, well, right.

"Do you have any preferences? As to which invitations we accept, that is?"

"No." He sighed in surrender. "None whatsoever."

"I should hate to interfere with your"—she gestured aimlessly—"whatever it is you do in the evenings."

"Would you like to know?" He leaned toward her. "What I do in the evenings, that is?"

"Absolutely not." She shook her head in a firm manner. "It's none of my concern. Your life is your life." She paused. "As is mine."

He forced a casual note to his voice. "I should be happy to exchange information. As a gesture of . . . of goodwill between us."

Her brow furrowed. "Is there ill will between us then? I thought we were getting on extremely well together."

"We are but—"

"Although I will admit"—she lowered her voice in a confidential manner—"and you should like this as it is another confession, that I didn't think all this you-live-your-life-and-I-live-mine nonsense was going to work well at all. And in fact, I think it's worked famously."

"Still, I—"

"And the credit is due entirely to you, Nigel. You didn't want to be married, and this *arrangement*, as it were—" Her eyes widened. "Oh dear, you don't mind my calling it an arrangement, do you? I know you seemed somewhat sensitive about the word when we first discussed this."

"In truth I would prefer—"

"It is only a word after all, Nigel."

"Yes, but—"

"As I was saying, then, I think our arrangement has proven most beneficial to you given you did not wish to marry in the first place. It was really brilliant of you to think of it. Why, in many ways, you have every freedom you had before we wed. Which means you have no reason to feel, well, trapped is the only way to describe it, I suppose." She cast him a pleasant smile. "You don't feel trapped, do you?"

"No." He gritted his teeth. "I don't."

"Good. Now then." She glanced at the notebook. "It seems to me we have been remiss in this past week in regards to our social obligations. There were a few parties that I had been looking forward to, most especially the Charitable Society's ball, and I did hate to miss them but it couldn't be helped, I suppose."

"Then you haven't attended any social events?"

"Dear Lord, no." She shook her head. "I wouldn't dream of going without you. My appearance in public without my husband would only exacerbate the gossip about our unexpected marriage."

"Is gossip the only reason then?" he said casually. "For not attending, that is." *Or did you find something better to do?*

"Yes." She thought for a moment, then sighed. "And no."

"Yet another confession?"

She laughed. "You do like confessions, don't you?"

"I do. Almost as much as I like"—he paused to emphasize the word—"*honesty.*"

"I thought you preferred flattery to honesty?"

He narrowed his gaze. "Apparently marriage has changed me."

"Well then, in the interest of honesty, I will confess, yet again, that I haven't attended any social events without you because I didn't think"—she met his gaze directly—"that they'd be the least bit enjoyable without you."

He stared. "You didn't?"

"Of course I didn't, Nigel. I quite like your company. One of the reasons I regret missing the society's ball is that we have missed the chance to dance together again. We haven't danced very much at all and"—she cast him an affectionate smile that warmed his very heart—"I do love dancing with you."

"My apologies. I have been remiss in my duties." He pushed his chair back, rose to his feet, and held out his hand. "Dance with me now."

She laughed. "Don't be absurd, Nigel. One doesn't dance at breakfast. It simply isn't done."

"Then we shall be the first." He grabbed her hand, pulled her to her feet and into his arms. He stared into her brown eyes and wondered that he'd ever wanted to spend any time apart from her at all. And realized that he no longer did. "Dance with me, Felicity."

"What will the servants say?" Amusement rang in her voice.

"They will say, 'Why, isn't that Mr. Cavendish dancing with his wife at breakfast?'" He pulled her closer and spoke low into her ear. "Which is nothing compared to what they would say if I were to make love to you right here on the dining room table amid the breakfast dishes."

"Nigel! I'm shocked." The light in her eye belied her words.

"Not as shocked as they would be." He chuckled. "However, I shall settle for a dance at the moment."

"But there's no music."

"We don't need music. But I shall hum if you like." He hummed the strands of a waltz and twirled her around the dining room table. Her laughter echoed in the room, and it was all he could do to provide some semblance of a tune in spite of his own laughter and not trip over a chair at the same time. At last he spun her to a stop. He stepped back and swept a dramatic bow. "My dear Lady Felicity, my thanks for a breakfast dance I shall never forget."

She dropped a deep curtsy. "It was entirely my pleasure, Mr. Cavendish."

"Might I reserve the next dance?"

"The next dance? Let me think." Her brow furrowed with exaggerated thought, then she nodded. "Why yes, I believe I am free for the next dance."

"Excellent. Then I claim it as my own." His gaze met hers. "And every dance thereafter." The tone of his words was abruptly far more serious than he had intended, and yet somehow, perfect.

She caught her breath and stared at him. "Every dance?"

"Every one." He held out his hand. "Now, might I escort you back to your chair?"

"I should be delighted." There was a slight unsteadiness in her voice, as if she were as aware as he that something of great significance had just happened between them. She placed her hand in his and he led her back to her chair, seated her, then took his own seat.

"I've always liked dancing, you know," he said and attacked his breakfast. He was indeed hungry, far hungrier than he had thought. Obviously a breakfast dance and settling things with one's wife gave one an appetite. "This is very good. Do we have a cook now?"

"A cook's assistant really, Mrs. Fitzwilliam. She too is on loan from your mother. Although"—Felicity smiled in a sly manner—"I am going to make every effort to hire her away and keep her here."

"See that you do." He laughed, turned his attention back to his meal, and ignored the fact that things were scarcely settled.

"As for these invitations," Felicity began. "I think this one from . . ."

The food was indeed excellent. Mrs. Fitzwilliam was a rare jewel if this was an example of her skills. But the food paled in comparison to the company.

"And then I should hate to miss . . ."

The very idea that he would enjoy having breakfast with his *wife*, why, he grinned at the absurdity of it.

"Indeed that gathering is always most amusing and . . ."

And yet here he was, listening to her go on about what social engagements they would accept. It was surprisingly enjoyable. Perhaps he should indeed join her more often. Perhaps he should start taking all his meals here. Perhaps he should . . .

Perhaps he should stop being an idiot and accept that he was now a married man. Perhaps it was time to admit that he was wrong. He cringed to himself. No, he couldn't do that. He might well have been wrong, but admitting it would make him look like even more of a fool than he was. After all, he'd been so firm, so resolute, so . . . so . . . stupid.

No, he couldn't simply throw up his hands at the breakfast table and announce that he'd made a mistake. That he was now willing to fully share his life. That he no longer wished to live his own life apart from hers because he'd realized it wasn't anywhere near as enjoyable as he had once thought it. When all was said and done, it came down to a matter of his making the decisions that controlled his life. To admit he had made that decision and it was wrong, terribly, horribly wrong—

"So if we are to attend Lady Thomas's soiree then we shall have to miss . . ."

Still, why was it necessary to admit anything at all? Why couldn't he simply remain home in the evening? It would be his choice, after all. Not every night at first, a night here and a night there, not enough to attract her suspicion. More and more often. Until it became expected and not the least bit unusual. Until she forgot all about that business of separate lives.

"Nigel?"

Still, his staying in didn't mean she would as well. Although there was nothing in their arrangement that precluded their going out together.

"Nigel?"

"Yes, absolutely, without question." He nodded in a vigorous manner. "I think we should."

She stared at him. "Should what?"

"Should attend that"—he had no idea—"what was it you called it?"

"A soiree?"

"Yes, of course, the soiree. Given by Lady . . ."

She bit back a smile. "Sir Digby?"

"Yes, that's the one. Let me see your notes." She handed him the notebook. She'd made charts of all they'd been invited to. The woman was remarkably organized. "I think we should go to them all."

She laughed. "All of them? Why on earth would we want to go to all of them?"

"Why?" Why indeed? "Why . . . why to show the world that we have nothing to hide. Nothing dissipates scandal faster than the parties involved acting as if nothing out of the ordinary has happened. The more we appear in public, the less extraordinary our story will be." He scanned her list. "There's nothing for tomorrow night though."

"Imagine that."

"We shall have to make do, I suppose," he said under his breath. He could certainly propose something, but that might be suspicious. One more night of separate lives certainly wouldn't hurt. And it would make his plan seem all the more natural. "And where are we to go tonight?"

She stared at him. "I didn't think you'd wish to accompany me anywhere tonight."

"Nonsense. If we are to lay gossip to rest, there's no time like the present to begin." He studied her notes. "Here. Lord and Lady Treadwell's masquerade is tonight." He looked up at her. "It's quite the event of the season. I can't imagine you haven't been planning to attend for weeks now. Surely you already have a costume?"

"Well, yes, I do, but I thought—"

"What is it? Your costume that is."

"Titania, Queen of the Fairies." She paused. "From Shakespeare's *Midsummer Night's Dream*."

"I know that." He scoffed. "And obviously this is yet another instance of fate guiding our actions." He grinned. "I was planning on going as Oberon, King of the Fairies."

She snorted in disbelief. "No, you weren't. You're just saying that."

"I was and I am." He stood and grinned down at her. "You shall see tonight."

She cast him a curious look. "I can scarcely wait."

"I must be off. Father is expecting me." He took her hand and raised it to his lips. "Until tonight then."

The loveliest smile curved her lips. "Until tonight."

He nodded and stepped into the hall, where George handed him his hat and gloves. Of course he hadn't been planning to be the king of anything as ridiculous as fairies. He'd been planning on doing exactly as he usually did for this sort of thing; simply throw on a mask and be done with it. But if he was going to sweep his wife off her feet, and he wasn't sure when he had decided that but it did seem the best way to keep her by his side, then dressing like a fairy would be a step in the right direction. How hard could it be to come up with something that looked suitably fairylike? He had once, years ago, attended a party as Robin Hood. Surely that costume could be made to work for Oberon. Perhaps Norcroft could give him a hand. He'd always had an artistic streak.

George opened the front door a step ahead of him. Nigel nodded his thanks and stepped out onto the walk. Poor George seemed to be doing every job in the house. Felicity really did need to hire more servants. He must speak to her about it. But in the meantime, he had more pressing matters to concern himself with.

First and foremost, where in the hell was he going to find wings?

"You look like a pirate," Norcroft said idly.

"With wings," Sinclair added.

"Nonsense." Nigel surveyed Lord Treadwell's ballroom and signaled to a waiter, who at once hurried to the three men and exchanged their empty glasses of champagne with freshly filled ones. The ballroom doors were opened to the terrace and the horde of guests moved freely in and out. The ballroom itself was decorated to look like the out-of-doors with palms and ferns and all manner of potted plants. He had lost Felicity somewhere in the crowd but was certain he would find her shortly. While there were any number of Titanias here—apparently it was a popular costume—none was as tall and lovely as his. The very thought was enough to make his wings quiver in anticipation. He grinned. "I look like Oberon, King of the Fairies."

Norcroft snorted. "Or Nigel, Prince of the Fools."

Nigel shrugged, the weight of his wings bothersome against his back. They were made of gauze attached to a thin wooden frame and appeared light and airy but were, in truth, anything but. "Where did you get these things anyway?"

"I'm not sure." Norcroft studied Nigel's wings. "I asked my mother if she had any ideas regarding wings and she produced these." He reached up and flicked something off Nigel's right wing. "I think they were in the attic."

"They look"—Sinclair could barely choke out the words—"good on you. You should wear them more often."

Sinclair and Norcroft exchanged glances although it was difficult to tell for sure as both men had chosen to forgo costumes as such and simply wear masks. Their laughter, however, was unmistakable.

"Why aren't the two of you in costume?" Nigel asked irritably. "It is a masquerade after all."

"Once I loaned you the family wings, there was little point to it," Norcroft said. "Besides, we are eminently eligible unmarried men. Masquerade or not, we could wear almost anything we wish and still be welcomed with open arms."

"Whereas you are trying to impress a"—Sinclair paused for emphasis—"*wife.*"

Nigel raised a brow, although under his own mask it was probably a pointless gesture. "You told him?"

"I tried not to but"—Norcroft shook his head—"this was just too delicious to keep to myself."

"I'm not trying to impress . . ." Nigel chuckled. "Perhaps I am. I didn't really court her, you know. I just stumbled into this marriage."

"I think *fell* is a more appropriate word," Sinclair murmured.

"Or *toppled.*" Norcroft grinned. "Over the edge of a balcony."

"And now he's fallen again, hopelessly in love, that is." Sinclair heaved an overly dramatic sigh.

"Do you think so?" Nigel continued to scan the crowd, but Sinclair's words echoed in his mind. Was this indeed love? Certainly he wanted Felicity. In his bed obviously, but he'd wanted that from the start. Only recently had he realized he wanted her in his life as well.

"Let us consider the matter for a moment then, shall we?" Norcroft studied his friend. "To begin with, it was not quite a week ago that you were congratulating yourself for coming up with a brilliant plan—"

"Brilliant only in your own mind," Sinclair cut in.

Norcroft ignored him. "—to permit you to continue your wicked ways—"

"Not all of them," Nigel said under his breath.

"—and live your life precisely as you wished." Norcroft shook his head. "It didn't seem especially wise to us—"

Sinclair snorted. "It seemed pretty damn st—"

"Yet we held our tongues," Norcroft continued, "in the spirit of friendship."

"The spirit of male unity. It seemed the least we could do." Sinclair bit back a grin. "For the King of the Fairies."

Nigel sighed. "I admit that might have been a mistake."

"I should think so." Sinclair scoffed. "Winged pirates went out of fashion years ago."

"Not the costume." Nigel rolled his gaze toward

the ceiling. "My plan. Once I realized that there was a greater power at work here, fate, that is, I should have accepted that Felicity and I were destined to be together. Needless to say, being together in regards to a woman like Felicity means marriage and all that marriage entails. I shouldn't have fought it." He shook his head. "I should have embraced it."

"Embraced it?" Norcroft could barely choke out the words. "You? Embrace marriage?"

"Not marriage precisely, but marriage to Felicity. It's an entirely different thing altogether. Although we all are well aware marriage awaits each one of us eventually."

"Good God, he is the King of the Fairies." A stern note sounded in Sinclair's voice. "Out with it now. What have you done with Nigel Cavendish?"

"I suspect he has turned him into a husband." Norcroft sipped his champagne thoughtfully. "And a content one at that?"

"Not quite yet." It was startling to realize that he could indeed be content and happy with Felicity by his side for the rest of his days. "But I fully intend to be."

"I never thought I'd hear you say anything even remotely like that." Norcroft considered his friend for a long moment. "You've changed, Nigel. For the better, I think. Since you began work with your father, you've become a different man."

"Not nearly as amusing though," Sinclair said under his breath.

"I am sorry to disappoint you," Nigel said in a dry manner.

"I'm not." Sinclair's tone was abruptly sincere. "I haven't known you for long, but I must admit, when we first met, I thought surely you would come to a bad end."

"Shot by an angry husband," Norcroft said.

"Stabbed by an irate father," Sinclair chimed in.

"Set upon by thugs hired by an angry husband or an irate father," Norcroft continued.

"Poisoned by a spurned—"

"That's quite enough." Nigel grinned. "I will confess, though, none of those dire prospects were entirely out of the realm of possibility. Now, however . . ." He caught sight of Felicity across the room, speaking to an older gentleman he didn't know. How could anyone have ever thought her merely pleasant? "Now, gentlemen, I am ready."

"Ready?" Norcroft chuckled. "For what?"

"For all of it, Norcroft. For responsibility, for marriage, to take my place in the world." Nigel shook his head. "It's odd, though, isn't it? Less than a month ago I was terrified at the idea of filling my father's shoes and I had no interest in marriage whatsoever. Now . . ." His gaze drifted back to his wife.

"Now, old friend," Norcroft said softly, "everything has changed and you are the better for it."

"I am indeed." Nigel downed the rest of his champagne and set the glass on the tray of a conveniently passing waiter. "Gentlemen, if you will excuse me, I have a wife to enchant." He straightened his mask and shrugged his shoulders. "Blast it all. Sinclair, be a good fellow and adjust my wings."

Sinclair took a step back. "I'd rather not."

"I'll do it," Norcroft said, handed his glass to Sinclair, and moved to Nigel's back. "I daresay they need some adjustment. They look a bit crooked." Norcroft tugged at his wings. "There, that should do." Norcroft turned him around, clapped his hands on Nigel's shoulder, and stared him straight in the mask. "Go forth and claim your queen, oh King of the Fairies."

Sinclair bowed in an exaggerated manner. "And may all the power of the fairy kingdom be with you."

"Come now, gentlemen." Nigel flashed them a wicked grin. "I scarcely think I'll need it." He nodded and started off.

"You do realize you have forfeited your portion of the tontine," Sinclair called after him.

Behind him, Norcroft chuckled. "I don't think he cares."

"I can't possibly dance another step." Felicity laughed and took Nigel's arm.

"Fresh air then." He nodded and led her out of the ballroom and into the night.

The terrace was lit with flickering candles and bedecked with lanterns and urns of flowers and potted plants. Indeed, it appeared that Lady Treadwell had raided her conservatory and half a dozen others to create a fairyland of light and scent and magic. Overhead the stars twinkled, and they too became part of the magic of the night. And it was indeed a magical night.

Felicity slanted a quick glance at her husband. She wasn't at all sure what had come over Nigel tonight. Not that he hadn't always been charming and flirtatious. But tonight there was a subtle difference in his behavior. Tonight his charm, his flirtation was directed at her alone in a most personal manner. She wasn't sure why and was almost afraid to question it. This last week had certainly brought them closer. Not simply in an intimate sense, although that was quite extraordinary, but their physical relationship had led to long discussions while lying in bed of everything ranging from politics to philosophy. The man was far more intelligent than anyone gave him credit for. But then she'd known that from the beginning. She knew he'd accepted their marriage as a fact of life, in a rational, intellectual sense. What choice did either of them have anyway? Now she couldn't help but wonder if he were starting to accept it in his heart as well.

They paused in front of the balustrade that overlooked Lady Treadwell's garden. Below them the grounds were lit nearly as well as the terrace, and the sound of a fountain could be heard somewhere nearby.

Felicity gazed out over the garden and sighed with contentment. "It's a wonderful night, isn't it?"

"Indeed it is." His voice was low beside her.

She glanced at him. "You are exceptionally charming this evening."

"My dear Felicity, I am always exceptionally charming," he said in a lofty manner.

"And exceptionally flirtatious as well."

"That is entirely your doing." He leaned close and spoke softly into her ear. "I have always enjoyed flirting with fairy queens."

She laughed. "Do you realize your wings are crooked?"

"I'm not surprised." He pulled off his mask. "The blasted things are far heavier than they look."

She wiggled her shoulders. "Mine are extremely light."

"Yes, well, I am the king." He shook his head in a mournful manner. "It's a heavy burden to bear."

"The wings, you mean?"

"The wings are simply a symbol." A royal note sounded in his voice. "It's a difficult job, governing fairies, that is. They are quite an unruly lot. Always flitting about here and there. Getting caught in butterfly nets. Trapped under flowers. Being forced to grant wishes."

"Do fairies grant wishes, then?"

"Yes, of course. It stands to reason, doesn't it?" His brow furrowed. "Perhaps not all of them. Perhaps only"—he ginned—"the King of the Fairies can grant wishes. Do you have a wish you want granted?"

My wish has already been granted. She shook her head and laughed. "Not at the moment, but I shall keep it in mind should something occur to me."

"See that you do." A pompous note sounded in his voice as if he were indeed king.

She studied him curiously. "You've been very attentive tonight. You do realize everyone here has been watching us. Is that why?"

"Not at all. I expected as much but in truth I haven't noticed." He raised a brow. "Can't a man flirt with his own wife?"

"I daresay it isn't done that often."

"No, it isn't." His voice was abruptly serious. "I suppose that's why there are so many wives who look outside their marriage vows for flirtation. It strikes me that if men, as a whole, were more attentive to their wives, and perhaps remembered why they married them in the first place, there would be fewer"—he cleared his throat—"*arrangements*."

"Wisdom from experience," she murmured.

"One can only hope I have learned something." He paused. "You should know, Felicity, that I am not ashamed of my past behavior. Embarrassed perhaps by the stupidity of parts of it, but not ashamed. I was never involved with a woman who did not wish to be involved with me."

"Will you remember?" she said abruptly.

"Remember the women in my past?"

"No, of course not." She gestured in a dismissive manner. "I should prefer you forget them completely. I meant will you remember why we married?" She wasn't entirely sure how she wanted him to answer.

"Yes." He chuckled. "And no. Although it's quite an amusing story really, one we should tell our children someday."

"Our children," she said faintly.

"Of course, there will certainly be children." A wicked smile curved his lips, and the unmistakable feeling of desire pooled within her. Good Lord, would he always be able to do this to her with nothing more than a smile? She did hope so. "Between your willingness to learn and my ability to teach, I daresay we shall have a dozen or more."

"Or less."

"We shall leave it up to fate," he said firmly. "It has served us well thus far."

She cast him a curious glance. "Do you think so? Served us well, that is?"

"I didn't." He shrugged his wings. "But it appears I have changed my mind. You have changed my mind."

"Have I?" Her words had a slight breathless quality.

"Indeed you have." His gaze slid to her lips and back to her eyes. "Do you think people are watching us now?"

"Without a doubt."

"Do you care?"

She raised her chin. "Not at all."

"Would they notice, then, if I took you in my arms right here and kissed you?"

She leaned toward him. "I think that might well attract attention, yes."

"And scandal?"

"At the very least gossip." But well worth it. She wanted nothing more at the moment than for him to kiss her, here on the terrace, under the stars. Her stars. "What would people say?"

"Well they'd say, 'Look, that fairy king with the crooked wings is kissing his fairy queen.'"

"I suspect that's not all they'd say," she murmured.

"They might also say, 'Why, isn't that the infamous Mr. Cavendish kissing the immovable Lady Felicity Cavendish?'"

She swallowed hard. "They might say such a display explains their hasty wedding."

"Or they could say"—he gazed into her eyes—"'Why, they look as if they belong together.'"

Her breath caught. "Could they say that?"

"They could indeed." He untied her mask and gently pulled it off. "If they were perceptive and intelligent they would add, 'What a lucky man that Nigel Cavendish is. Why, he should thank'"—a slow smile spread across his face—"'*fate* for bringing her into his life.'"

"You would thank fate then?" she said slowly. "You no longer feel like a boulder rolling downhill?"

"Oh, I still feel like a boulder." He chuckled. "But I must confess I am beginning to enjoy the tumble."

Perhaps it was time to tell him fate had had a tiny bit of help. She straightened. "Nigel—"

"I never imagined I would and I didn't at first, of course. But I'm starting to see everything that's happened in a different light. One can't fight fate after all."

"No, but Nigel—"

"There's a purpose, a plan if you will. I see that now." He nodded firmly.

"Nigel—"

"In fact, at this very moment, even though the terrace is nearly as full as the ballroom itself, fate is compelling me to kiss you."

She surrendered. Obviously this was not the time to confess anything, let alone the role she had played in helping fate along. That could certainly wait until later. Until they had their first child perhaps. Or their third. Or until they were as old as Lord and Lady Fernwood. "One should never fight fate."

"As I have learned." He shrugged. "Resisting fate is futile."

"It will be most scandalous. A kiss here, that is."

"That's entirely part of the fun." He put his finger beneath her chin and tilted it upward. "Besides, the best way to dispel gossip about our marriage is to give the gossips something else to talk about." His lips brushed hers.

"Will we give them a great deal to talk about in the future?"

"With any luck at all."

"Individually, as Lord and Lady Pomfrey do?" She held her breath. "Or together?"

"You once told me you didn't want a dull, boring predictable life." His gaze locked with hers, his tone was somber. "I promise you now to do everything in my power—"

"As King of the Fairies?"

"As Nigel Cavendish, to keep our lives from ever being dull, boring, and predictable. To make each and every day an adventure. And I promise as well that we shall never be the least bit like Lord and Lady Pomfrey. Aside from everything else, Lord and Lady Pomfrey would never be caught kissing one another in public." He smiled. "Someone else perhaps, but never each other."

She drew a deep breath. "Then kiss me, Nigel, and let the scandal begin."

And he did, quite nicely and with a restrained but obvious passion that caused even the most forgiving of observers to raise a brow. And if, as the evening wore on, Felicity noticed any number of condemning looks at their improper display of affection, she noted as well an equal, if not greater, number that could only be described as envious of what she and Nigel appeared to have found that so many others had not.

Much later, when they had at last returned home and he had taken her to his bed, his kiss was every bit as exciting, his touch as skillful, his caress as arousing as before tonight, but there was a subtle change in their coupling. Their passion was somehow deeper, richer, forever. And when his body joined with hers, it was as if they were made one for the other, two halves of a whole at long last one. As if their bodies knew, long before their hearts, that they were indeed destined to be together. For now, for always.

And in those moments afterward, when she lay in

his arms, a deep joy filled her soul, and she wondered if anyone had ever been as happy as she was right now.

And wondered as well what the gossips would say about that.

Thirteen

What a lady really wants is love.
Lady Felicity Cavendish

*N*igel Cavendish was a new man.

At least he felt like a new man, and in many ways he suspected he was. Even his father had noted the change in his mood and had commented on it. They'd had a long talk then about the twists and turns life takes, about the responsibility inherent in position and even about fate. In many ways it was an odd talk, but then, since he'd begun his involvement in the family affairs, they'd talked more and more about things that had nothing to with the family's interests. Frequently the topic had been his father's life, and Nigel had heard all sorts of fascinating stories. Often they discussed the future. They would talk of politics or literature or art. Sometimes they'd talk about nothing of importance at all, and that too was satisfying.

The day had lasted much longer than either of them had expected. Between their wide-ranging talks and the work that needed to be dealt with, it was early evening when his father had declared they'd done enough for today. When Nigel had at last taken his leave, his father had clasped his hand and said he was proud of the person his son had become. And added that he had never doubted it.

That too made Nigel feel like a new man.

Now he was impatient to get home to his wife. If this blasted cab could manage to maneuver through the congested London streets a little faster, he'd be home by now. Last night had been, well, *magical* was the only word for it. At the ball and afterward in their bed, and still later holding her in his arms while she'd slept, he'd had the most profound sense of satisfaction and peace and perfection. As if it were all meant to be. Perhaps it was the lingering effects of last night or the talks today with his father, but Nigel had decided it was time for his own confession. Time to tell Felicity the last thing he wanted was to live his own life. Time to tell her he loved her.

He chuckled to himself. No doubt that would come as just as big a surprise to her as it had to him. Although it probably shouldn't have. Still, he'd never been in love before. Lust was another matter. He was well acquainted with lust. Love hadn't even occurred to him until Norcroft had mentioned it last night. But there wasn't so much as a doubt in his mind now. This was indeed love.

His cab stopped in front of his house just in time for him to note his own carriage pulling away. Blast it all, Felicity was obviously off to her evening of whatever it was she'd been doing. He hesitated, then told the driver to follow her carriage, at a discreet distance, of course. Now that their separate lives were at an end, what was the harm in finding out what she'd been up to? After all, he was more than willing to tell her what he did. He had nothing to hide. He ignored the unwelcome thought that perhaps she did.

Felicity's carriage pulled into a drive a half block in front of his cab and he watched her get out and hurry into a house. Abruptly he recognized the house as his sister's. He'd been too busy thinking about what Felicity was doing to notice their route. Unexpected relief flooded him. He hadn't realized he had been quite that concerned about Felicity's activities, but given the way it seemed a weight had lifted from his shoulders, obviously not knowing had indeed preyed on his mind.

Well, there was certainly nothing that said he couldn't call on his sister as well. He stepped out of the cab, paid the driver, and started toward the door. His presence was no more than a happy coincidence. One could even call it—he grinned at the thought— fate. Now that he was here, why, he could escort his wife home. And once home, as awkward as it might be, he would admit his mistake. Admit he'd been an idiot and recant his desire to lead separate lives. He would confess his love for her and ask her to forgive his stupidity.

He reached for the door knocker. And they would live happily for the rest of their days. There was no question of that.

After all, it was their fate.

"... and he further insisted that we attend every social event we've been invited to." Felicity paused for emphasis. "Together."

"Together?" Madeline raised a brow. "Oh, that is progress."

"And last night was..." Felicity wasn't entirely sure she wanted to share last night even with Madeline, who had indeed become the sister Felicity had never had.

She and Nigel had danced nearly forever and had laughed almost as much. There had even been a moment when she'd thought he would declare his feelings. Feelings that went beyond merely liking her. It was impossible to believe that he didn't feel something more. Something... wonderful. Especially after last night. And later, when he'd taken her in his arms... She sighed. "Perfect. Absolutely perfect."

"You're not going to give me any details, are you?"

Felicity grinned. "Absolutely not."

"That's as it should be. It's all working out beautifully, but then I always knew it would." Madeline beamed with satisfaction. "Is Nigel still curious about how you're spending your nights?"

"He asked again yesterday."

Her sister-in-law chuckled. "I would wager it's driving him mad. It's all very well and good to talk about a husband and wife living their own lives, but when it comes right down to the reality of it, no man wants his wife to live a life that excludes him. Beyond that, men, as a group, are insanely curious. More so than women, although they would, each and every one, deny it."

"Madeline," Felicity said slowly. "Do you think, if Nigel wants us to go everywhere together, as husband and wife that is, that he has had a change of heart?"

"Possibly."

"I think I should tell him." Felicity swept a wide gesture at the room that had become her observatory. One wall was hung with star charts. Stacks of notebooks sat on a table set up beside her telescope. Her celestial globe dominated one corner. "About all this, that is."

"Why?"

"I have always been honest with him."

Madeline raised a brow.

"More or less," Felicity said quickly. "I've never actually lied to him.

"And you're not lying to him now," Madeline said firmly.

"It certainly feels as though I am."

"Rubbish." Madeline cast her a pitying look. "You have no real experience with the way men think, do you?"

"I'm afraid not."

Madeline sighed. "You have so much to learn. Well, there's no time like the present to begin." She pinned Felicity with a pointed stare. "First of all, did he or did he not tell you that you should concentrate on your work?"

Felicity nodded. "He did."

"Are you or are you not doing exactly that?"

"I am. Why, I have nearly filled an entire notebook with observations."

"An unexpected benefit." Madeline nodded. "Now, have you even once lied to him about your activities?"

"Certainly not."

"So all you've ever really done is not tell him you're doing precisely what he told you to do in the first place." Madeline nodded with the satisfaction of a point well made.

"You're right." Felicity stared at her sister-in-law. "Why, I have done nothing wrong whatsoever. Whereas I have allowed him to . . . to . . ."

"Dictate to you?"

"That's it." Felicity punctuated her words with her finger. "Without so much as a—"

"Protest on your part?"

"Exactly." She shook her head in disbelief. "I've been an idiot."

"You are well matched," Madeline murmured.

Felicity's brows rose in indignation. "Pardon me?"

"I didn't mean that the way it sounded," Madeline said quickly. "I simply mean that in terms of love, you are both . . ." She thought for a moment. "Inexperienced. Yes, that's good. That's what I meant."

"Inexperienced?" Felicity snorted. "I daresay Nigel is the most experienced man I have ever met."

"In one respect, admittedly, but what I mean is that Nigel has never been in love before. He's never especially seen women as anything other than a romp, and a temporary one at that. And you've told me you've never felt about anyone the way you do about Nigel. You're both extremely inexperienced at this. At love, that is."

"You think he's in love with me?" Felicity held her breath.

Madeline stared in surprise. "My dear Felicity, don't you?"

"I don't know. Not really." She heaved a heartfelt sigh. "I simply hope."

"Well, there isn't a doubt in my mind." Madeline studied her sister-in-law. "You're very good for him, you know. You and the responsibilities Father has given him. I've noticed a distinct change in him of late. He's more . . ." She thought for a moment. "He's finally grown up, I think. Lord knows, it's past time. It would have happened eventually, I suppose. Still, I had begun to fear—"

"Good evening ladies." Nigel's voice sounded from the doorway.

"Nigel!" Felicity stared. So much for whether to tell her husband what she'd been doing.

"What are you doing here?" Madeline said sharply.

"Delighted to see you too." He strode into the room, a smug smile on his face. "I simply thought I would visit my sister, as my wife was not at home."

"I did not expect you to be home," Felicity said cautiously. "I thought you would be out tonight."

"And indeed I am out." He glanced around the room. "What on earth is going on here?"

"It's not precisely on earth," Madeline said under her breath.

"It's an observatory of sorts." Felicity paused. "My observatory."

"Your observatory?" He raised a curious brow. "I see." He glanced around the room, then wandered in an aimless manner toward the telescope. "It's a perfect room for it, isn't it?"

"Indeed it is." Felicity studied her husband. There was a thoughtful light in his eyes she didn't like one bit. What was the man thinking? "Your sister was kind enough to offer it to me for my work."

"My sister is nothing if not kind." He bent and gazed through the telescope. "Ursa Major, I see." He glanced at Felicity. "Specifically Benetnasch?"

Felicity stared at him. Benetnasch was a second magnitude star, the first in the handle of the Dipper. "How did you know?"

He straightened and shrugged. "You talk about the stars a great deal. And I have recently had the occasion to glance through a book or two on the subject."

Madeline snorted. "You?"

"Yes." A firm note sounded in his voice. His gaze moved slowly around the room. "This is quite remarkable. It must have taken a lot of time and effort."

"Not at all," Felicity said carefully. "It was simply a matter of moving my telescope and globe and charts and things here. It took no particular time at all."

He met her gaze. "Still, I didn't notice they were missing."

Felicity chose her words with care. "You have scarcely been at home to notice."

"Indeed." He chuckled in a sardonic manner. "How very clever of you both."

Madeline and Felicity exchanged glances.

He looked at Felicity. "You could have told me, you know."

"Yes." She sighed. "I probably could have."

"But," he said slowly, "that would have spoiled the fun, wouldn't it?"

Felicity caught her breath. "The fun?"

"It must have been quite enjoyable for the two of you to lead me to believe Felicity might be doing something untoward."

"We did nothing of the sort," Madeline said staunchly.

"You"—he nodded at his sister—"provided her with someplace to go and something to do—"

"You were the one who told her to pursue her stargazing while you were out living your life," Madeline said sharply.

He ignored her and directed his gaze toward Felicity. "And you."

Felicity narrowed her eyes. "I what?"

"You refused to tell me where you were at night."

She stared at him, an awful sensation growing in the pit of her stomach. "And?"

"And you knew it would drive me mad."

"Frankly, Nigel, I knew nothing of the sort." She raised her chin. "All I truly knew was that I was married to a man who did not wish to be married, who had furthermore said—no, announced—in no uncertain terms that he fully intended to act as if he were not married."

"And yet you didn't object." His tone was deceptively mild.

She stared in disbelief. "You gave me no choice."

"So you turned to my sister for help in deceiving me."

Felicity gasped. "Deceiving you? I have scarcely deceived you."

"That's rather harsh of you, Nigel, and not the least bit fair." Madeline glared at her brother.

"Isn't it?" He stared at his sister for a long moment. "Why did you invite Felicity to your party?"

"Why? Well, why does anyone invite anyone to a party?" A defensive note sounded in Madeline's voice. "I had met her and I thought—"

"When," he snapped.

"When what?" his sister asked.

"When did you meet her?"

"I don't know exactly." Madeline shrugged. "One meets so many people, particularly during the season, it's impossible to say with any precision exactly when one meets—"

"She met me when I came to her to tell her I intended to marry you." Felicity met Nigel's gaze directly. "The day after we met at Lady Denton's ball."

"Met again," Madeline muttered.

"I see." His eyes narrowed. "So from the very beginning the two of you have conspired to trap me into marriage."

Felicity stared. "Trap you?"

"We did nothing of the sort." Madeline scoffed. "I simply advised her—"

"Successfully!" He fairly spit out the word.

"If we were successful, it's because you couldn't resist her!" Madeline glared. "You were the one who sought her out over and over again."

"She was everywhere I looked!" Fury snapped in his eyes. "Everywhere I went. I could scarcely breathe without tripping over her."

Madeline snorted. "And trip you did. At every opportunity, I might add."

"Every opportunity you arranged." He gestured angrily. "You invited her to your party. You arranged for her to fail to receive a note about it being moved—"

Felicity looked at Madeline. "Did you?"

Madeline winced. "I might have."

"You made certain we would be alone together." His jaw clenched. "Was there really even a flood, Maddy?"

"Yes, of course there was a flood." Madeline huffed. "I would not go to the trouble of moving an entire party even for you. That was simply—"

"Fate?" He snorted in disdain. "I actually believed all that nonsense about fate but I daresay we can now call fate by its real names: Madeline and Felicity!"

Felicity stared with horror and a growing realiza-tion. This was never going to work. Nigel hadn't wanted marriage, and the fact that he wanted her scarcely mattered. He might well want her in his bed but he'd never wanted any woman permanently. And hadn't she told Eugenia that the appeal of a man like Nigel was the very things that made him unsuitable in the first place? What on earth made her think that he'd change simply because he'd taken vows?

"I wouldn't put the blame on fate or on us." Mad-eline aimed an accusing finger at her brother. "The blame here rests squarely with you. If you hadn't—"

"That's quite enough." A hard note sounded in Felicity's voice. "It scarcely matters who is at fault for what. There is only one thing that matters." She squared her shoulders. "This has been a mistake."

Nigel crossed his arms over his chest and glared. "I should say so!"

"Felicity?" Apprehension shone in Madeline's eyes, and she stepped toward her.

Felicity held out her hand to stop her. "I realize this is your house, but might we have a minute alone?"

Madeline's gaze met hers, and Felicity realized the other woman knew exactly what Felicity was thinking. "I don't think—"

"You've been most kind to me and I am extremely grateful." Felicity smiled at her sister-in-law. "Indeed, you've been all that a sister should be and I shall remember that always, but now I need to have a word with my"—she almost choked on the word—"husband."

Madeline moved to her and took her hands. Her gaze searched Felicity's. "Are you sure?"

"I'm not really sure of anything." Felicity forced a short laugh, an odd, mirthless sort of sound. "But I think this is what needs to be done."

Madeline stared at her for a moment longer, then pulled her into her arms and whispered into her ear. "Well, I for one shall never give up."

"I'm not giving up," Felicity said softly. "I am accepting the inevitable. Fate, if you will."

"Are you two plotting again?" Nigel said irritably.

"You should have shot him when you had the chance." Madeline gave her a quick hug, released her, and headed for the door. She cast her brother a scathing glance. "You are an idiot."

"Hah!" he snapped.

"Excellent answer," she muttered and took her leave.

"Well?" Nigel glared at Felicity. "Have you nothing to say?"

She stared at him for a long time. How could she possibly love him as much as she did and still do what she had to do? As much for herself as for him. She searched for the right words. "You should know the extent of our conspiracy, as you called it. There was very little to it. All your sister did was to make certain you and I were invited to the same social events. To put me in your path, as it were. The rest was up to—"

"Don't tell me fate."

"I wasn't going to." In the back of her mind she noted how remarkably calm and cool and unemotional she sounded. Odd, she'd had no idea she had that kind of strength. "I was going to say you. You approached me at the garden party. And the night of your sister's dinner—"

"When she arranged for us to be alone."

"You could have sent me on my way. But instead you . . ." She struggled for control. "Instead you danced with me."

"And what about the cards? And the wager?"

"The game was not prompted by anyone other than Lord and Lady Fernwood, and it's silly of you to imply that it was. Neither I nor your sister had anything to do with that. And the wager was entirely your doing."

"Because I wished to get you out of my life before"—his jaw clenched—"before something irrevocable happened. The life, I might add, Maddy assisted you in becoming part of. I would never have made such a wager if I had not been desperate."

"Desperate?" Her heart twisted.

"I knew my own nature." He shook his head. "And you were always there, and always so very tempting."

"I should be flattered, I suppose. No one has ever called me tempting before. Nonetheless." She drew a steadying breath. "You could have waited, at the very least for daylight, to get the painting. There was no need for you to climb my balcony."

"Admittedly that was a mistake—"

"One of many," she said in a cool tone.

"I never wanted this." He shook his head. "I never wanted marriage. I never wanted—"

"Me?" she snapped.

"Not as my wife!"

"No, of course not! That would have forced you to become an adult. To accept the responsibilities of your position and your life!"

"Which I was well prepared to do when the proper time came! Instead, thanks to you and my sister, the choices I should have made, the choices that were indeed mine to make, decisions about my life, were ripped out of my hands! I was forced into a—"

"I am so bloody tired of hearing about how poor Nigel was forced into a marriage he didn't want. Forced by his own actions and his own mistakes which he—you—so conveniently tend to forget." She whirled away from him, moved toward the windows, and gazed out at the night. "I've had more than enough."

"So they are *my* own actions and mistakes, are they?" Sarcasm dripped from his words. "And I thought I was being manipulated by fate."

"Let me tell you about fate, Nigel." She crossed her arms over her chest and stared up at the stars. She wished—no. Wishing had started all this in the first place. Now it was up to her to finish it. She drew a deep breath. "I believed everything I ever said about fate. I never once lied to you. Not about anything and certainly never about that. I did believe, I still do, that fate brought us together." She searched the heavens and found the star she had trusted with her hopes and dreams. "The night you first appeared in my garden, I had just done something incredibly foolish. I had wished on a star for a future that was not boring and ordinary. I wished for a man who would make the rest of my days an adventure. And then, as if by magic, there you were. And you were indeed exactly what I had wished for."

She turned to face him. "That, dear husband, was a dreadful, dreadful mistake. The biggest of my life, I think. It's true that one should be careful what one wishes for. I should never have wished for excitement and adventure. I should have wished for happiness." She met his gaze directly. "I should have wished for love."

He stared at her, a stunned expression on his face.

"The last thing I ever wanted was to make you unhappy, and certainly I never wanted unhappiness for myself. But apparently my happiness is contingent on yours."

His brows pulled together. "What?"

"I can't be happy if you aren't. It's as simple as that. And I refuse to live my life with a man who resents my presence in his. Therefore." She forced a smile. "I shall give you what you want. I shall remove myself from your life."

"Felicity." He moved toward her.

She stepped away. If he so much as touched her hand, she'd dissolve into a quivering mass of sorrow. "There's nothing more to say, Nigel. We don't want the same things. You want the freedom to do precisely what you wish. I want . . ." *You.* She shook her head. "I want someone who wants to make me as happy as I want to make him." She nodded and moved toward the door.

"Where are you going?"

She paused and looked back at him. "It's no longer any of your concern. And frankly, Nigel, you've forfeited the right to ask."

A moment later she was out the door and on her way down the stairs. She caught sight of Madeline out of the corner of her eye but refused to so much as hesitate. One sympathetic word from Madeline and she'd lose what little hold she still had on her emotions.

She reached the entry, accepted her wrap, hat, and gloves from a footman, and stepped out into the night. Her carriage, Nigel's carriage really, waited in front of the house. Madeline must have anticipated her leaving and had it brought around. Felicity would miss having a sister, but it couldn't be helped. She paused on the top of the steps leading to the drive and looked up at the sky.

This was it then. The end of an adventure that had begun on a starry night very much like this one. She found her star once again and cast it a weak smile.

"It didn't quite turn out the way I had hoped but I do appreciate the effort. And I am grateful." The star blurred with her unshed tears. "Regardless of the end, the beginning and very nearly all of it has indeed been a grand adventure. I wouldn't have missed it for all the stars in the heavens."

With that, she descended the steps and allowed her driver to help her into the carriage. Not until he asked where she wished to go did she realize she had no idea where she would go or what she would do now.

And realized as well she didn't care.

Nigel stared at the door in shocked disbelief.

She had walked out on *him*! He was the injured party here. He was the one whose own sister had schemed against him. He was the one who had been manipulated. And Felicity had the nerve to walk out on him?

He paced the floor, his anger propelling every step. How could she? And how could Maddy? This must be how Caesar felt when the knives of those he had trusted sank into him and he'd realized he'd been betrayed. Betrayed, yes that was it. That was exactly how Nigel felt.

Still, a tiny voice of reason sounded in the back of his head, all things considered, the plot against him had been rather feeble. His steps slowed. Maddy and Felicity had done little more than assure that he and Felicity would be in the same places at the same times. Even then, Felicity had done nothing to solicit his attention. He was the one who had approached her. He was the one who had arranged a private dance with her. And he was the one who had climbed uninvited into her room. If Maddy and Felicity had indeed trapped him, from beginning to end, it was with his willing cooperation.

He groaned aloud. What a fool he was. He'd been so angry at this perceived plot against him, he hadn't seen the truth. The fact was, whether he'd realized it or not, he'd been drawn to Felicity from the moment they'd met. Every step he'd taken had brought them inevitably together. No one had truly forced him to do anything. And who could say it was not the hand of fate guiding his actions? Or a force just as power-ful. Instinct? Something inside him, his heart per-haps, recognized that this was the right woman for him even if his head had resisted. Or could it have been, from the very beginning, love? Immediate, ir-resistible, at-first-glance love.

Admittedly it had taken him longer to realize they were meant to be together than it had taken Felicity. But surely that was to be forgiven. After all, he was a man and a foolish one at that. Ask his sister. Maddy never had hidden the fact that when it came to the way Nigel lived his life, she thought he was indeed a fool. In the week of their marriage, Felicity had never once made him feel like a fool.

He strode to the window and gazed up at the stars. Her stars. How could she have walked out on him like that? Certainly he'd been angry. He winced. And indeed he had said some vile things to her, but they were said in the heat of the moment and as such could be forgiven if not forgotten entirely. He would apologize when he saw her. Profusely. Perhaps even grovel. And admit as well his other mistakes.

I shall remove myself from your life.

Surely she hadn't meant it? It was said in the throes of anger. She couldn't possibly have meant that she was leaving him for good. No, of course not. How could she?

At once it struck him with a blinding clarity.

He had given her no reason to stay.

Good God, what had he done? He was angry and justifiably so. But he didn't want her to leave. Still, she had no way of knowing that. In truth, very nearly everything he'd done in these past weeks had been with the express purpose of getting her out of his life. And now, when he had finally realized she was all he'd ever wanted, he had at last succeeded.

He started toward the door, then stopped. No. He had no idea where she'd gone and he very much doubted she would return to his house. To their house. She might have gone to her parents or Lady Kilbourne's house or any number of other places. It was too late in the evening to be chasing after her from one possible refuge to another. Besides, his wife was a clever woman. If she did not wish to be found, he would not find her.

He sank into a worn, overstuffed chair and buried his head in hands. Surely he hadn't lost her just when he'd truly found her. Just when he'd at last come to understand that she'd filled a hole in his life he hadn't known was there. She completed him as he'd never imagined he'd needed completion. How could he possibly let her go?

It would be futile to look for her tonight. Best to wait until morning, until the light of day, when, with any luck, cooler heads would prevail. Besides, he needed time to figure out exactly what he would say to her. Exactly how he would convince her to take him back. It wouldn't be easy. She had been so resolved. Or resigned. He wasn't sure which was worse. He had hurt her; he knew that. What he didn't know was how to make it right.

It was the height of irony. Nigel Cavendish, who had never lacked for female companionship, was now in the position of having the one woman he wanted no longer want him. He'd never been in this spot before. Indeed, he had little experience with apologies at all and none with anything of this magnitude. Regardless, he knew he had to find the right words. It was his only chance.

He raised his head and stared at the stars that twinkled down at him in a silent chastisement. She had wished for him and he had appeared. Now he understood what she'd meant when she'd told him that he had made her believe in magic and fate. It was nonsense, of course. Nothing more than a coincidence, really. Even so, it was odd and enough to make even the most skeptical believe.

He knew it wouldn't be as easy as simply wishing for Felicity to return. There was a penance to be paid for his sins, but perhaps he could ask for a little assistance.

"If you would be so kind . . ." This was absurd. Still, he drew a deep breath. "I have been something of an idiot and I may well have lost the best thing that has ever come into my life. I could use some assistance in this matter. You know her better than anyone." A helpless note crept into his voice. "I don't know what to do."

He had made her believe in fate and magic, and he had to find a way to tell her she had made him believe as well. In fate, in magic, and, more than anything else, in love.

Nigel gazed at her stars and hoped and prayed that somehow they would help him find the answer. He stared until the stars faded in advance of the sunrise, and still he sat unmoving, searching for right words to undo what he had done. He considered and discarded a hundred thoughts, a thousand words; nothing was right. Even when the sun rose and dawn drifted into morning, he still had no idea how to get his wife back. And tried to ignore the thought that occurred sometime before dawn and had grown with the daylight.

Maybe it would be better for her if he didn't attempt to get her back. Maybe she was right about having made a dreadful mistake. As much as he was now convinced she was the right woman for him, maybe he was not the right man for her? She'd said she wanted someone who wanted to make her as happy as she wanted to make him. Nigel had never thought of himself as a selfish man, indeed he'd always considered himself quite generous. But had he ever once considered Felicity's feelings, her wishes, her needs above his own? The more he thought about their time together, the heavier his heart grew. From the start, it had all been about his feelings, his wishes, his needs. Could he indeed make Felicity happy? Did he still have the right to try?

Even when the sun reached the midmorning sky, he had no answers, only an awful ache that radiated from his heart and a nagging thought he could not ignore. If he truly loved her, he should let her go.

Behind him the door opened, and he knew without looking that it was Maddy. He had expected her to make an appearance long before now. Nigel blew a long breath. "I know, Maddy, you needn't say it. I am an idiot. The worst sort of fool."

"Nigel."

"I don't know what to do." He shook his head. "Worse, I don't know what I should do."

"Nigel." There was an odd, strained note in her voice.

He turned in his chair to look at her. "Maddy?" Her face was white; shock glazed her eyes. "What is it?" He jumped to his feet and moved toward her. "Has something happened to Felicity?"

"No." Her voice was barely more than a whisper. "It's not Felicity. It's Father." Her gaze met his, and his heart lodged in his throat. "He's dead."

Fourteen

What a man really wants is to have the woman he loves by his side for the rest of his days. He can only hope he is smart enough to know that.
Nigel, Viscount Cavendish

"Nigel," Maddy said in a no-nonsense manner as she pushed open the library door and stepped into the room. "We need to . . ." She pulled up short and stared.

"What is it?" Nigel looked up from the documents spread before him on his father's—no—his desk.

She stared for a moment longer, then shook her head as if to clear it. "I have never seen you sitting behind Father's desk before."

"As you can see, I have a great deal of work to do. What do you want?"

"You needn't take that tone." Maddy approached the desk and seated herself in the chair Nigel used to sit in when speaking to his father. To the viscount. And now, behind the desk, the very symbol of his father's position, sat Nigel. The new Viscount Cavendish. He brushed the thought away. "It's been ten days, Nigel. We need to talk."

"Do we?" He set his pen down, rested his hands on the desk, and clasped them together. "It seems to me we have spoken any number of times in the past ten days."

"About death and arrangements and the like." She met his gaze firmly. "There are other matters we should discuss."

"Go on."

She studied him for a moment. "First of all, I have not had the opportunity to apologize for what you may have seen as a betrayal—"

"It's not necessary, Madeline. As you pointed out, while you might have set the stage, the actions taken were entirely my own. Besides"—he shrugged—"it's of no consequence now."

"Of course it's of consequence." Her brow furrowed and she leaned forward in her chair. "You do realize Felicity has been here, through the funeral and everything else."

"Of course I realize she's been here," he snapped. "I'm not dead!" She paled and he winced. "I am sorry. I didn't mean . . ."

He was well aware that Felicity had been at Cavendish House, by his side. But then he would have expected no less of her. He had moved back to the house immediately upon his father's death to handle the family's affairs. Felicity had returned to her parents. The house they'd shared stood empty of life. Yet another symbol he didn't wish to dwell on.

"I wasn't entirely sure you had noticed. You have been—I don't know what the right word is, *preoccupied* is as good a word as any, I think." She sighed. "But then I suppose we all have."

"It's been a difficult time." *Difficult* was every bit as insufficient to describe the last ten days as *preoccupied* was to describe Nigel's manner, or anyone else's.

The late Viscount Cavendish had died peacefully in his sleep from what his physician had inadequately termed a stoppage of the heart. Aside from the shocking abruptness of his death, it was odd to think his father had died without fanfare, gently and quietly. It was not at all the way Nigel had imagined Edmund Cavendish would end his days. But then Nigel had long preferred to avoid the inevitable fact that one day his father would be gone.

He spread his hands in a helpless gesture. "I don't know what to do."

"About Father?" She paused. "Or about Felicity?"

"There is nothing I can do about Father except carry on. You see all this." He waved at the papers in front of him. "The details that accompany the passing of a man with varied interests are too numerous to mention. Were it not for these last weeks spent under his tutelage I would be overwhelmed. As it is, I have had no time to indulge in anything other than this."

"No time to make things right with your wife?"

"No."

He had been too consumed with grief over the loss of his father to deal to any great extent with the loss of his wife as well. In many ways, from the moment Maddy had told him the news, he had felt as if he were moving through a fog. Blast it all, he had just gotten to know his father. As a man, not merely as a parent. It was so bloody unfair.

"Did he know, do you think?" The question had haunted him since his father's death. "That his days were nearing an end?"

Maddy shook her head. "I don't—"

"Do you think that's why he wanted to turn all this over to me?" He met his sister's gaze. "Because he knew?"

"I don't know; I wish I did." She picked at a piece of invisible lint on her stark black dress. "I have thought about it; one can't help but wonder. It's the sort of thing he would do, though, isn't it?"

A reluctant smile curved Nigel's lips. "Even in death, Father has made certain the family's interests are run properly."

"He would be pleased with you." She paused. "Although he would not be happy about the rift between you and your wife. He liked her, you know."

"What am I to do, Maddy?" He got to his feet and

strode across the room to the table where Father's brandy was still in place.

"You could try talking to her. Apologizing for being such a fool."

He poured a glass and tossed it back. "She won't speak with me."

"You've tried, then?"

"I have sent a note every day since the funeral. They are returned unopened." He shook his head. "I just want to talk to her."

"She is living up to her vow, all that nonsense about making you happy by getting out of your life."

He narrowed his eyes. "How did you know that?"

She waved away his question. "I might have overheard something."

"Something?" He raised a brow. "Or all of it?"

"Not all of it. I missed a word or two, here and there," she said under her breath. "Damnably solid door on that room."

He should have been annoyed at her eavesdropping but he wasn't. He needed her help now as he had never needed it before. And the more she knew, the greater help she might be.

He refilled his glass. "You should know, I seriously considered not doing anything at all. Letting her go her own way with an eye toward dissolving the marriage eventually."

"Divorce? Are you insane?" Maddy's eyes widened. "Has grief affected your mind? She is the best thing that has ever happened to you."

"I know that, dear sister." He raised his glass to her. "But am I the best thing that has ever happened to her?"

"Of course you are," she said staunchly.

"I appreciate your sense of sisterly loyalty but I have done nothing except think of myself from the moment I first met her. I have been selfish and arrogant and"—he shook his head—"she deserves better."

"Certainly she deserves better. Most women do. Men in general are selfish, arrogant beasts. You are, unfortunately, typical."

"So much for sisterly loyalty," he muttered.

"It has nothing to do with loyalty, it's simply a fact of life."

"That's rather cynical of you."

"Not at all. It's realistic and based on years of marriage to a selfish, arrogant beast." She stared at him. "He has turned out quite nicely now but surely you don't think Gerard was a paragon of masculine virtue when we first met?"

"He always struck me as a decent sort of chap."

"Yes, well, he would because you and he are very much alike, at least when it comes to your behavior toward women." She considered him thoughtfully. "There's only one thing that truly changes a man."

"And that is?"

"Love, Nigel." Her gaze searched his. "You do love her, don't you?"

He blew a long breath. "I'm very much afraid I do.

But if I love her, how can I condemn her to a lifetime with me? With a selfish, arrogant beast?"

"That's my point exactly. You're already thinking of her rather than yourself. It's a very good start."

"It's not enough."

"No, but it is a beginning." Maddy paused. "You do realize she loves you as well?"

He shook his head. "I don't understand how she could."

"Love is not something one understands. It's not supposed to be rational or logical, it simply *is*. You love her and are willing to give her up to make her happy. She loves you and is willing to give you up to make you happy. The end result for both of you is—"

"Happiness?" he said in a dry manner.

"Abject misery." She scoffed. "If you truly love her you can't allow her to be as unhappy as she will inevitably be without you."

He chuckled. "So it's better for her to be unhappy with me than unhappy without me?"

"Most certainly." She nodded firmly. "Let me ask you this. Which would you prefer?"

He met his sister's gaze. "I would prefer to spend the rest of my days in an unending quest to make her life as happy as possible."

"Excellent." Maddy beamed.

"Which leads us back to where we began." He returned to his chair, sat down, and shook his head. "I still don't know what to do."

"Well, you do need to think of something. Some

sort of plan." She pinned him with a firm look. "Do keep in mind, brother dear, that there has never been a divorce in the Cavendish family. Generally we just shoot our spouses."

He grimaced. "You're speaking of Great-aunt Mariah now, aren't you?"

"Among others, although deliberately shooting one's spouse is not to be recommended."

He raised a brow. "I always thought Great-uncle Charles's death was a nasty accident."

"One does prefer to think of such things in the best possible light," she said under her breath. "Now then." Maddy met his gaze directly. "Do promise me you will not give up on Felicity regardless of how long it might take."

"You have my word." He shook his head. "But—"

"Nigel, I do realize you have never had to pursue a woman before, not seriously, that is. Don't let the fact that you are meeting resistance stop you."

He considered his sister for a moment. "I should ask you to help me the way you helped her. It seems only fair."

"My dear Nigel." She smiled in a smug manner. "I just did."

"Were you planning on spending the rest of your life with us, dear?" Felicity's mother said brightly.

Felicity sat beside her mother on the bed in the room she had grown up in, the room where Nigel had first come into her life, and raised a brow. "May I?"

"This will always be your home, of course, for as

long as you require it." Mother paused. "How long will you require it?"

Until this ache in my heart goes away, if it ever does. Felicity shrugged. "I don't know."

"I see." Mother thought for a moment. "Then you have nothing in mind? No plans, as it were?"

"I really don't have any specific plans, no." But then had she ever? "I thought perhaps I would travel, return to the continent. Possibly Italy."

"I daresay your husband can't go at this time. Mourning and all that."

"I hadn't intended for him to accompany me."

Her mother, both her parents really, had been re-markably good about not prying into exactly why their daughter had returned on the night before her father-in-law had died. And why, although Felicity had been beside Nigel during the funeral and burial and all else that accompanied the death of a beloved family member in this day and age, she had not taken up residence at Cavendish House with her husband or returned to the house they had shared. Felicity drew a deep breath. "You should know, Mother, that my marriage was a huge mistake."

"Darling, every marriage is a huge mistake on oc-casion." Mother patted her hand. "Especially in the beginning."

"I loved him for what he was. Exciting and adven-turous and not the least bit dull and respectable. And then I expected him to change. It was terribly unfair of me." She shook her head. "And terribly stupid."

355

"Stupidity is often an element when men are involved. And love."

"I do love him. Desperately." Felicity heaved a heartfelt sigh. "But the only way I can make him happy is to stay far away from him."

"Nonsense. The man can't possibly be happy without you." Mother scoffed. "Why, he has sent you a note every day for a week. And you have yet to open one."

"It doesn't matter. He's just being"—Felicity rolled her gaze toward the ceiling—"honorable. He prides himself on his honor. Obviously he can't simply abandon me."

"Men who are merely being honorable find just one note will suffice." Mother's brow furrowed. "The fact that he managed to write to you at all is significant. He is going through a difficult time, you know."

"Of course I know." Felicity got to her feet and paced the room. "I wish I could help him but I daresay my presence will not make things better. I am a constant reminder of a marriage he did not want. Of decisions regarding his life being taken out of his hands."

"No man truly wants marriage in the beginning. They see it as an end to a carefree life of pleasure and excess." She studied her daughter, then sighed. "Your father had no desire to marry when we met."

Felicity stared at her mother. "I always thought your marriage was a love match."

"It was in the end. But it began more as a match of "—her mother bit back a smile—"scandal. Passion, if you will."

Felicity's eyes widened. "Passion?"

"I never intended to tell you this; it did not seem a good example for a daughter, but your father was quite the rake when we first met, with a reputation every bit as tarnished as your husband's." Mother's eyes twinkled. "Even more so, I would say."

"Father?" Felicity's voice rose. "My father?"

"Well, he wasn't your father then. Then he was . . ." A faraway look shaded her mother's eyes. "Adventurous and exciting and more than a bit dangerous."

"Father?" Felicity could barely choke out the word. "Dangerous?"

"It was in part due to the nature of his work," Mother said in a matter-of-fact manner.

"His work?" Felicity could scarcely believe her ears. Her dull, ordinary father had been involved in something dangerous? "What kind of work?"

Mother waved away the question. "It's of no significance now and not worth mentioning."

"Water under the bridge?"

Mother chuckled. "There does seem to be something of a flood there, doesn't it?"

"More than I have ever imagined," Felicity murmured.

"That spyglass of yours was his, by the way. He's rather pleased that you have found a use for it."

Felicity drew her brows together. "Father was a sailor?"

"Dear Lord, no." Mother laughed. "Your father does not take well to being on board a ship." She shook her head. "He has no stomach for it."

"I didn't know he had ever been on a ship." But then Felicity had had no inkling of her parents' pasts at all until recently.

"Your father was a gambler as well. He lost and won several small fortunes. But then, in those days"— a mischievous smile curved her mother's lips—"so was I."

Felicity stared.

"As I am making confessions of a sort, you should probably know as well our marriage was no more planned than yours, but then I suppose you suspected that when Nigel's father made his comment about history repeating itself."

"I had no idea," Felicity said in a strangled voice.

"It's all rather shocking for you, isn't it, dear? I realize that, and in truth, I had never planned on telling you any of this. You were coming along so nicely too with your study of the stars and your sensible, practical way of looking at life." Mother sighed. "And then we sent you off to see the world."

"And now I have disappointed you, haven't I?" Felicity held her breath.

"Not at all." Her mother met her gaze firmly. "I had long expected that one day you might well burst the bonds of propriety. And frankly, darling, as scandals go, yours was really quite minor, especially when compared to m— Well, never mind. Blood will tell, you know."

"Will it?" Felicity said weakly.

"It always does." Mother paused. "Edmund Cavendish was a fine man and I have no doubt that Nigel is every bit his father's son. You would be a fool to let him get away."

"I don't want to let him get away." Felicity wrapped her arms around herself and stared unseeing into a bleak future without the man she loved. "But I have no choice. It's what he wants."

"I doubt that. The notes, remember? Regardless of what has happened between you, I would wager a great deal that what your husband really wants is you." Mother rose to her feet. "I suggest when his note arrives today, as I have no doubt it will, you read it, respond, and agree to see him."

"I can't." Felicity shook her head. "Not yet. Not until I know what I'm going to do."

"What you're going to do is allow him to apologize and beg your forgiveness."

"He's done nothing to forgive."

Her mother raised a brow.

"Well, he has done a few things." She looked at her mother. "Why are you so certain he wants me back?"

Mother chose her words with care. "Even when he was being something of a boor, I saw the way he looked at you. Only when you weren't looking, of course. I'm not sure if he even realized it then, but a man doesn't look at a woman like that if he truly doesn't want her in his life. If he doesn't love her."

"You think he loves me?" Felicity said slowly.

Madeline had said the same thing. Still, so much had happened since then.

"I am confident of it."

What if her mother was right? Hope surged within her. "Very well, then." She lifted her chin. "When today's note comes, I'll answer it. And if he wishes to see me, I will meet with him."

"Excellent." Mother beamed. "Things always work out the way they're supposed to in the end, you know. That's how fate is."

Felicity blew a long breath. "I do hope so."

She should have taken her mother's wager. As the day wore on and slid into an endless evening, there was no note from Nigel. No communication of any kind from Cavendish House. By the time Felicity retired for the night and fell into her bed with an awful emptiness inside her, she had to face the fact that her mother was wrong. Nigel didn't want her back. In the last moment before she succumbed to what would be yet another restless night, a thought struck her and she bolted upright in bed.

Dear Lord, what had she been thinking? Or indeed, had she been thinking at all? Apparently not. She was making an enormous mistake.

Leaving Nigel to make him happy might well be a noble, selfless gesture on her part but this was her life as well as his. Didn't she deserve to be happy? Now that she thought about it rationally, and she wondered why the thought hadn't occurred to her before now, he had certainly appeared happy in the week of their marriage, even if only in the dark of night. And their last night together, at the Treadwell ball and afterward, he had seemed positively blissful. No man was that good an actor.

She threw off the covers, got to her feet, and paced the floor. Certainly he had been angry when he'd discovered Madeline's role in getting them together, and admittedly that was justifiable to a certain extent, but he had said some vile things. She should be furious with him, and now that she thought about it, she was. Obviously the death of Nigel's father had pushed her own feelings, and everything else, to the back of her mind. And today the blasted man hadn't even sent a note! But perhaps it took that failure on his part to at last bring her to her senses.

Enough was quite enough. The first thing in the morning, she would pack her bags and move to Cavendish House to be with her husband. She loved Nigel, and she was apparently the only one who wasn't sure he loved her in return. If Nigel truly wanted her out of his life, he was going to have to throw her out bodily. But she certainly wasn't going without a fight.

Resolve swept through her, and for the first time since the night in the observatory, she felt like herself.

Things would work in the end. They were indeed fated to be together. And, if necessary, she would spend the rest of her life making him see that.

Whether he liked it or not.

* * *

He didn't like this one bit.

Nigel drew a deep breath and stared up at the trellis that led to Felicity's balcony. Would this be the last time he made this climb, or was he destined to cling to the side of this house periodically for the rest of his days? He could see himself at Lord Fernwood's age, crawling slowly upward toward the balcony, cackling all the way. No, this would be the last time. Unless, of course, he had to. He heaved a resigned sigh. Indeed, if he had to climb this blasted trellis every day for the rest of his life, he would do so. After all, his wife was at the top of it.

He found an all-too-familiar grip on the trellis and started upward. He could have simply pounded on the front door for entry or paid a more civilized call in the light of day, but it seemed to him a grand gesture was needed. Something adventurous and scandalous and completely improper. After his talk with Maddy he'd thought all day about exactly how to get his wife back and had hit upon the idea of a grand gesture. This might not be the smartest grand gesture, but it had a certain symmetry to it. This was how it had all begun, climbing up to her balcony under the stars, her stars, and this was where it would begin anew. Yes, he quite liked that. She would like it as well. Why, she might even be pleased to see him. He refused to consider that the possibility was every bit as great that she might push him off the balcony or threaten to shoot him. Again.

He reached the balcony and pulled himself over the balustrade. He was actually becoming quite skilled at this. The door to her room was again cracked open. He pushed it wider, slipped into her room, and waited for his eyes to adjust to the light. And realized he had no idea what to do now. He certainly didn't want to startle her. She might still sleep with that damn pistol by her bed.

"Felicity," he called softly.

"I thought it was you," Felicity's clear voice rang from the bed. It didn't sound at all as though she'd been asleep. Apparently she'd had little better luck sleeping these days than he'd had. The thought bolstered his courage. A moment later a match flared and she lit the lamp beside her bed. She sat upright in her bed and glared at him. "What are you doing here?"

"You said exactly the same thing the last time I was here." He smiled in as charming a manner as he could muster. Damnation, he was nervous. "You need to think of a new greeting."

"Very well." She narrowed her eyes. "Get out. The way you came, if you please."

He ignored her and stepped toward the bed. "The last time I was here, you asked if I had come to ravish you."

She raised a brow. "Have you?"

"Is it a possibility?" A hopeful note sounded in his voice.

She snorted.

"Apparently not," he said under his breath.

She shoved the covers aside and slid out of bed. Felicity had no idea that her relatively modest sleep clothes clung to her every curve, and when she stood in front of the lamp—

"Why are you here?" She snatched her robe from the foot of the bed and pulled it on. Pity. "Nigel?"

"Why?" He chose his words with care. Obviously, the vague hope he'd had that she would throw herself into his arms was futile. Honesty was apparently his best choice. Yes, that was good, he'd be honest with her. "I wanted to speak with you."

"Go on then." She crossed her arms over her chest. "Speak."

"It sounds like you're talking to a dog."

She raised a brow.

"I've been a beast, Felicity, I admit it. Can you forgive me?"

"Can I forgive you?" She stared in disbelief. "That's it? That's all you have to say?"

He realized at once the only right answer. "No. Absolutely not. Of course not. There's much more." He tried and failed to think of something else. He did think *beast* encompassed all his sins. "An arrogant, thoughtless, selfish beast."

"What else?"

"I'm not very good with words, Felicity."

"The infamous Nigel Cavendish? Who has charmed God knows how many women? Not good with words?" She scoffed. "Hah!"

"Very well, I am good with words. I'm considered quite glib, really." He shrugged. "But apparently I'm not good when the words actually mean something.

I don't know what the right thing is to say at the moment."

"Try." She fairly spit the word.

"You're angry with me, I know, and you should be. I have been—"

"Yes, yes, you've been a beast. An arrogant, thoughtless, selfish beast." She gestured in an angry manner. "Go on."

"You needn't be so emphatic about it," he said under his breath.

"I don't think I'm being emphatic enough!"

"Yes, well, admittedly I do deserve it. More, really. I know that. I just wish I knew as well how to make it all right." He ran his hand through his hair. "You probably should have shot me when you had the chance." He stopped and stared at her. "That's it!"

Her eyes narrowed in suspicion. "What's it?"

He strode to the table beside her bed, jerked open the drawer, extracted her pistol, and held it out to her. "Take this."

Her eyes widened, and she put her hands behind her back. "Why?"

"Just take it."

"This is ridiculous," she muttered but accepted the pistol nonetheless. "You do realize I have reloaded it?"

"I expected no less.

"Now." He stepped back, lifted his chin, and closed his eyes. "Shoot me."

"What?"

He opened one eye. "Go ahead, shoot me."

"You're insane."

"Not at all," he said staunchly. "I'm in love."

She stared at him as though he had indeed lost his mind. "I'm not going to shoot you."

"I deserve to be shot and I have recently discovered that the shooting of a spouse in my family is not unheard of, therefore there is precedent. I do have a request, however."

"I daresay you're in no position to request anything." She waved the pistol aimlessly. "After all, I have the gun."

He eyed it uneasily. He was fairly confident she wouldn't actually shoot him. He wouldn't have given her the pistol in the first place if he'd thought otherwise. Still, it had gone off once before unintentionally. "Do be careful with that. I would hate for you to shoot me accidentally."

"As would I." She smiled in an overly pleasant manner. "Accidentally, that is. Was that your request then? That I be careful?"

"Not entirely." He squared his shoulders. "I would request that you aim for a small, insignificant body part. After all, the purpose isn't to kill me—"

"It's not?" She thought for a moment, then shook her head. "Probably not."

"You just want to make me suffer."

"Yes." She nodded. "That's good, you should suffer."

"So I would suggest that you aim for, oh, I don't

know, a little finger perhaps or a quick little graze on the shoulder."

She stared at him for a long moment, and the tiniest hint of amusement sparked in her eye. That was a good sign. "Perhaps I could simply part your hair with the bullet?"

"You did say you were a good shot."

"Not that good." She was obviously struggling against a smile. It was a very good sign.

"Felicity." He paused in a significant manner. "*Marriage.*"

Her brows drew together in confusion. "What?"

"*Marriage,*" he said again with more emphasis on the word.

"What are you doing?"

"I'm saying *marriage.*" He couldn't resist a smug smile. "I can say it clearly, without choking on it or it catching in my throat or shivers running down my spine. Marriage, marriage, marriage, marriage."

"I'm most impressed, Nigel." The slightest hint of sarcasm sounded in her words. He ignored it. "You have come a long way."

"I had a long way to come." He braced himself and stepped toward her. "Felicity, from very nearly the moment we first met, I have wanted you out of my life because I was terrified of not merely marriage but of what marriage meant. Responsibility and the end of youthful pursuits and everything that I knew would come someday but I had no desire to face, that I was not ready to accept. I'm not sure I ever would have been ready to accept any of it were I not forced to do so."

"Go on."

"I have learned a great deal about myself recently. I am not incapable or incompetent. My father . . ." He paused.

Her voice softened. "Oh, Nigel."

He drew a deep breath. "My father knew that long before I did. I can indeed fill his shoes. Perhaps not as competently as he did at the moment, but I no longer doubt myself and my abilities. And I know now as well"—his gaze locked with hers—"that I can't do anything without you by my side."

"Nigel." Her voice caught.

He moved closer and stared into her eyes. "It's taken me far too long to realize it but I cannot, nor do I wish to, live my life without you in it. Not another hour, not another day. I never imagined when I first climbed over this balcony that it would be the best thing I ever did because I never imagined you. But it was."

She stared at him. "Did you say you loved me?"

He chuckled. "I didn't think you heard me."

"I did. I just . . ." She shook her head. "Now I don't know what to say."

"Say you love me."

She nodded. "I do. I always have."

"As that is the case"—he smiled slowly—"will you marry me?"

"I believe I already have," she said with a weak smile.

"Yes, but I never really asked you, did I? And you

deserve to be asked." He knelt down on one knee and took her free hand. "Felicity Constance Evanston Melville Cavendish, will you be my wife? For now and for the rest of our days? Will you allow me to cherish you and make you happy and try to make every day together an adventure? Will you forgive me my future sins? For surely there will be many."

"Will there?"

"I daresay they will be too numerous to count, but I do promise you women will not be among my sins. I vow to you now, Felicity, there will be no other women in my life. My days of being the infamous Mr. Cavendish are at an end."

"Will you miss them?"

"Not if I have you," he said firmly and realized he had never spoken truer words in his life. He stood and pulled her into his arms. "Well, do I get an answer?"

Her gaze meshed with his, and in her endless brown eyes he saw a love that would last him for the rest of his days. "Do I have a choice?"

"No, Lady Cavendish." He bent his lips to hers. "No choice whatsoever. After all, this is fate." His lips met hers, and the most remarkable feeling washed through him, warm and deep and forever. And he realized this was indeed love and wondered that it had taken him so long to realize it. And thanked the stars above—her stars—for bringing them together.

Felicity had changed his life and, as much as he had fought against it, that was as it should be. And here and now, with her at last in his arms where she belonged and a lifetime together ahead of them, one couldn't help but believe in magic and fate and, most especially, in love.

He pulled her tighter against him, and her one arm wrapped around his neck. And at the very moment he realized he had never known such happiness before, it dawned on him as well that he'd forgotten all about the pistol in her hand and he should grab it before—

The gun slipped from her grasp.

Epilogue

Four days later . . .

"Do you think there's some sort of curse?" Sinclair stared moodily into his glass as if the brandy held the answer.

Oliver raised a brow. "On us?"

"I was thinking more on the bottle of Cognac. It's old and French and who knows where it's been." Sinclair shrugged. "But yes, I suppose it could be on us."

"Don't be absurd." Oliver scoffed. "I don't believe in curses."

"Neither do I," Sinclair said in a firm manner. "Not at all."

"Of course not."

"It's nothing more than coincidence, really."

"Nothing at all."

"The fact that four of us form a tontine and within four months, two of us are married is mere chance," Sinclair said in the manner of a man trying to convince himself as much as anyone listening. "I haven't known Warton and Cavendish very long. Perhaps they were inclined toward marriage."

Oliver grimaced. "I don't know anyone less inclined toward marriage than Warton and Cavendish."

"Even so, it was nothing more than a twist of fate." The American paused. "Agreed?"

"Absolutely." Oliver nodded. "Fate, coincidence, chance, but definitely not a curse."

"Cavendish has certainly been ranting about fate lately." Sinclair paused. "Will he be all right, do you think?"

"I hear the wound is minor." Oliver bit back a grin. "Curious place for a bullet to graze a man, though."

Sinclair nodded. "It certainly could have been worse."

"A few inches in one direction or another and it would have been." Oliver's gaze met the other man's and they laughed.

"One would think, given that the very same circumstances led to his marriage in the first place, that he would have been more cautious."

"I suspect caution is the last thing a man like Cavendish, who abruptly finds himself in love with his own wife, is concerned with." Oliver chuckled. "Today is his birthday, by the way, and as I am certain we won't be seeing him, mourning and all, I suggest we put this evening's libations on his account."

"Excellent idea." Sinclair grinned, then sobered. "Pity about his father."

"Unfortunately, death eventually claims each of us." Oliver blew a long breath. "As apparently does marriage." He rose to his feet. "Come on then, there's no getting around it."

Sinclair stood. "Around what?"

"What is fast becoming a tradition for us, Sinclair, far too quickly, I might add. Let us now toast the happy couples." Oliver raised his glass. "First, to Lord and Lady Warton. May their journeys be filled with adventure and discovery."

"And to Lord and Lady Cavendish." Sinclair paused, then grinned. "May their aim never be better than it is right now."

"Hear, hear." Oliver clinked his glass with Sinclair's and both men took a sip.

"And so," Sinclair said with a wry smile and a lift of his glass, "it comes down to you and me."

"To you and me then. The last men standing." Oliver raised his glass. "God help us both."

In the following pages
you are cordially invited to a tea party
in which the author has invited
some of her favorite characters
to talk about all sort of things.
Join the discussion already in progress . . .

Guests for *afternoon* tea

Name <u>Pandora, Countess of Trent</u>
Address <u>c/o The Wedding Bargain</u>

Name <u>Marianne, Marchioness of</u>
<u>Helmsley</u>
Address <u>c/o The Marriage Lesson</u>

Name <u>Gillian, Countess of Shelbrooke</u>
Address <u>c/o The Husband List</u>

Name <u>Rebecca</u>
Address <u>Undetermined</u>

Name <u>Jocelyn, Viscountess Beaumont</u>
Address <u>c/o The Prince's Bride</u>

Name <u>Elizabeth, Lady Collingsworth</u>
Address <u>c/o A Visit From Sir Nicholas</u>

Continued from A Little Bit Wicked . . .

"Okay then. The topic of discussion," I braced myself, "is men."

This was not my idea, I can't say that often enough. But the small group of heroines I had gathered in my living room: Pandora Effington Wells (Countess of Trent), Gillian Effington Marley Shelton (Countess of Shelbrooke), Marianne Shelton Effington (Marchioness of Helmsley), Jocelyn Shelton Beaumont (Viscountess Beaumont), and Marianne's daughter, Elizabeth Effington Langley (Lady Collingsworth) had minds of their own. Admittedly, that was my fault. I had written them that way.

"Who wants to start," I said brightly, and looked directly at Marianne, who had already appeared to be more or less the leader of the group.

That came as something of a surprise—I thought I'd be in charge—although it probably shouldn't have. After all, Marianne was destined to eventually become a duchess, even if at this particular moment she was not. I had invited these characters to tea at the point in their lives that I had known them best— the end of their own stories. Which was a tiny bit awkward for Elizabeth, because at this gathering she was twenty-nine, whereas most of her aunts were younger and her mother, Marianne, was only twenty-one. Still, Elizabeth was a confident, intelligent woman and shouldn't have a problem with something as insignificant as being older than her own mother. Even so, there was a slight look of unease in her eyes.

"Where to start?" Marianne drew her brows together and thought for a moment. "I suppose we could begin with what we like best in a man."

"A good sense of humor," Pandora said firmly. "I like a man who isn't afraid to laugh at the absurdities of life or at himself. A man who makes me laugh with him."

"I like a man who treats me as if I were the very best thing to ever happen to him. Which of course"— Gillian grinned—"I am."

We all laughed at that. At the smugness of it as well as the truth. The heroes I had paired each of them with did indeed realize how fortunate they were. As well they should. I had created one specifically for the other.

"A handsome face is important, obviously," Jocelyn

said in an offhand manner, and the others stared at her. "Well, it's not on the very top of my list, that would be shallow, but if we wish to be honest—" She met my gaze. "Do we wish to be honest?"

"Sure," I said weakly. Who knew what honesty might lead to?

"Very well then, in the interest of honesty, I dare any of you to deny that one of the first things you noticed about the man you ultimately married was his favorable appearance." She glanced at me. "You did write them that way didn't you?"

"Of course I did." I tried not to sound too defensive. "And I haven't heard any of you complain."

"Nor shall you," Pandora said, and leaned forward to pat my hand. "Certainly it's a superficial sort of thing, appearance that is, but important in its own way at least in terms of initial attraction. I think we can all agree, we like having the man in our lives be an attractive sort."

"I do agree, but one of the first things I noticed about my husband was his overwhelming arrogance." Marianne chuckled. "He really thought he knew what was best for me."

"They all do." Gillian sighed. "Arrogance is as much a part of the male characters she writes as is a finely chiseled derriere or nicely endowed—"

Elizabeth winced. "Aunt Gillian!"

"Don't sound so shocked, Lizzie." Gillian stared at her niece. "I'm quite grateful for the attributes she has bestowed upon Richard—"

"My apologies." Elizabeth nodded in my direction,

then rose to her feet. "I thought I was made of sterner stuff, but I have a difficult time listening to my aunt discuss my uncle's . . . *attributes*. And I'm certain any minute now my mother will join in to express her appreciation for my father's . . ." She closed her eyes for a moment, obviously to pray for strength, squared her shoulders, and smiled politely. "I do so appreciate being invited here today."

Elizabeth glanced around my living room. A nice enough living room, really, but definitely not up to the lofty standards of her mid-nineteenth century world of wealth and elegance. She, as well as my other guests, still could not quite get over the fact that I had no servants. That I actually cleaned and cooked. Okay, not well and not often, but by myself. "It's been most . . . enlightening but I really do think that the presence of a daughter, even one who is at the moment older than her mother, might have something of a dampening effect on the current discussion."

"Not at all, darling," Marianne said. "We love having you here."

"I certainly haven't felt the least bit dampened," Jocelyn said under her breath.

"You never do," Gillian murmured.

"Thank you, Mother, but I believe you all can talk much more freely without me, at least about this particular subject. Victoria." She smiled at me. "Again, my thanks." With that Elizabeth faded away.

Elizabeth was not the first character to have left my little tea party. Her aunt, Rebecca—Becky—had previously vanished because, as the others had pointedly noted, she was lacking in substance, since I had not yet written her story. Still, even though we had already witnessed the departure of a guest, and in spite of the fact that I was the only one here who was not fictitious, watching Elizabeth fade to nothingness was definitely creepy.

"Well, that's that then." Marianne took the teapot and refilled our cups. She had assumed that responsibility when the ladies realized that tea pouring was not a skill I had mastered. "Shall we continue?"

"I don't know." Gillian glanced around the group. "Our numbers have seriously dwindled."

Jocelyn turned toward me. "Could we invite someone else? To liven up the discussion, that is?"

I shrugged. "Why not?"

"For this particular discussion, I think we need someone with more experience with men than we have." Marianne glanced at me. "Who would you suggest?"

"When you say more *experience* with men," I said slowly. "What exactly do you mean?"

Gillian choked on her tea.

Pandora raised a brow. "Come now."

Jocelyn snorted. "I should think you of all people would know exactly what we mean."

"Yeah, well, I just wanted to make sure I didn't misunderstand," I muttered. "It's kind of a problem though. With the exception of a couple of widows, none of my heroines have much more experience than you all do."

"None of your heroines perhaps . . ." Pandora

studied me curiously. "Is this gathering of yours exclusive, then?"

Huh? "Exclusive?"

"Limited to main characters," Pandora said. "To the heroines of your stories, I mean."

"Not really." I thought for a moment. "It just seems to have worked out that way. Probably because I know you all better than other characters."

"So you could invite oh, say, secondary characters if you wished?" Gillian said cautiously.

Jocelyn raised a brow. "Secondary characters? *Minor* characters? Surely not."

Gillian and Marianne traded glances. "Jocelyn," Marianne said in a firm, older sister voice. "There's nothing wrong with secondary characters or even minor characters."

"I suppose not." Jocelyn rolled her gaze toward my less than impressive ceiling. "Still, Becky was a secondary character and in spite of the fact that we all love her dearly and she was in four books, she didn't have sufficient substance to remain—"

"Solid?" Pandora suggested.

"Yes, well, Becky might have been somewhat two-dimensional," Marianne said with a sigh. Obviously no one wanted to admit their own sister was less than fully fleshed out. "Still, most secondary characters are quite delightful."

"Especially the men." Gillian nudged Marianne. "Your husband—my brother—was originally a minor character and he turned out quite well."

"Indeed he did." Marianne nodded and aimed a pointed look at Jocelyn. "As did yours."

"That's an entirely different matter." Jocelyn raised a dismissive shoulder. "Even as a minor character, my husband had a great deal of potential."

"As interesting as those characters may be, this is a female gathering." Pandora looked at me. "Isn't it?"

"Absolutely," Marianne said firmly.

"Without question," Gillian added. "We certainly can't speak freely about them if they're present."

"Good." I breathed a sigh of relief.

I was having enough problems handling my heroines without trying to cope as well with the delicious heroes I create. And when I say delicious, I say it without apology. These guys—these heroes—are very much my fantasy. They're not perfect, of course; even my fantasies don't run to perfection. What would be the fun in that? But they are generally trainable and willing to, eventually, admit when they're wrong. See? Pure fantasy. But as much as I love my heroes, I adore my secondary male characters. They're even more fun because they don't have to be worthy of a heroine. They can be delightfully wicked and thoroughly naughty without being the least bit redeemable or repentant. Ya gotta love that in an imaginary man.

"Why don't you invite that wicked princess of yours?" Gillian said with a casual wave of her hand, as if having wicked princesses to tea was a perfectly ordinary, every day sort of thing to do. Although I suppose it was no more unusual than having imaginary characters for tea in the first place.

"What a wonderful idea." Pandora's eyes glittered with delight. "Now there's a woman who no doubt has had a great deal of experience with men."

Jocelyn gasped. "I can't believe you would suggest such a thing. She is a wicked, wicked person."

"But I believe she has reformed, dear." Marianne turned toward me. "You did reform her, didn't you?"

"More or less," I said, and sounded evasive even to myself.

The reformation of the Princess Valentina Pruzinsky of the fictitious Kingdom of Greater Avalonia had been accomplished somewhat reluctantly on her part when she had lost everything, including her country, and therefore any claim to the throne. When she had nothing left except cousins who neither liked nor trusted her, she'd really had little choice but to change her ways.

"But wicked or not, she is a princess," Gillian said thoughtfully. "Do you think she will come on such short notice?"

"She's rather offended she wasn't included in the first place," an imperious voice rang in the air as the Princess Valentina Pruzinsky snapped into view, seated in the chair vacated by Elizabeth. She appeared instantly, and just like the picture on my aging TV might have looked, a tiny bit blue. "On the other hand"—she glanced around the gathering—"I've never been one for tea with the ladies. And this is such a well behaved little group."

"If by well behaved you mean we've never tried to kill relatives or overthrow a government to seize a throne for ourselves." Jocelyn crossed her arms over her chest. "Then yes, I would say we are."

Valentina sniffed. "And boring as well." She glanced around my living room and raised a haughty brow. "This is where you live?"

"Yep, this is it," I said with a forced smile. "I know it's not up to your standards."

"My dear Victoria, it's not up to anyone's standards. Although, I suppose . . ." Valentina gestured in a casual manner. "Different times and all that. This is quite like visiting a foreign country, so one should make allowances."

Pandora choked back a laugh. "She has reformed."

"Not willingly and with any luck at all"—Valentina's sharp gaze met mine—"not permanently?"

"Permanently," I said firmly.

"Then perhaps I should have my own book." A wicked light gleamed in Valentina's eyes. "I would make an extraordinary heroine."

"Extraordinary isn't the word I would use," I said under my breath.

"You could never be a heroine," Jocelyn said in a lofty manner, and I cringed.

"Because of my past? All that nonsense about murderous tendencies and fomenting revolution?" Valentina accepted a cup of tea from Marianne.

"Not to mention the men," Marianne said with a pleasant smile. "You've been rather busy, you know."

Valentina shrugged. "I like men."

"You've had how many husbands?" Gillian asked casually.

Valentina studied her. "No more than you. Only two."

"Both of whom died suspiciously within a year of their marriage," Jocelyn said darkly.

"Only if you believe gossip born of jealousy. There is nothing at all suspicious in the deaths of men well past their prime. Especially when they have the arrogance to marry a woman less than half their age." Valentina smiled in a deceptively pleasant manner. "They did, however, die happy."

"How many lovers have you had then?" Gillian leaned forward eagerly.

Valentina raised a brow. "For fun or profit?

"Either," Pandora said, then grinned. "Or both."

"And do feel free to be specific as to"—Marianne bit back a smile—"everything?"

I couldn't believe my ears. Here were my heroines, my well behaved, happily married, one-man-per-customer heroines practically drooling at the thought of the amorous exploits of one of my wickedest—if now reformed—secondary characters. Although I suppose, when I thought about it, I had written them this way. Not one of them was the least bit hesitant when it came to sex. In fact, three of them had been what I referred to as eager virgins.

"Marianne!" Shock sounded in Jocelyn's voice. "I can't believe you of all people are encouraging this . . . this creature who, reformation or not, has always used men for her own pleasure or her own nefarious or mercenary purposes without regards to affection or love or even simple courtesy."

"Apparently you are not as well behaved as I thought." Valentina's eyes narrowed and focused on Jocelyn. "Might I point out that for much of your life, you had planned to marry well, for profit as it were. I believe you had your sights set on a prince. That sounds exceptionally mercenary to me."

"One might look at it that way I suppose," Jocelyn muttered.

"And you." Valentina turned toward Gillian. "You needed to marry to gain an inheritance and selected a man based on little more than his need for money. I would call that both mercenary and nefarious."

Gillian winced. "When you put it that way . . . perhaps."

"You." Valentina met Pandora's gaze. "You made a highly improper wager with a man with marriage as the prize—"

"Yes, yes." Pandora waved off Valentina's comments. "I know precisely what I've done, although I would not term it either mercenary or nefarious."

"Perhaps not, but an overabundance of pride certainly entered into it. And pride, I believe, is a sin."

Valentina's gaze met Marianne's. "We all play games with men for one reason or another wouldn't you agree?"

"I daresay I would. I would further say . . ." Marianne smiled slowly. "Each and every one of us quite enjoys it."

"Then we have far more in common than might at first be suspected." Valentina nodded in my direction. "How very clever of you."

"It's nothing," I said modestly. I'd be more than happy to take credit, but the fact was, whatever similarities of nature there were between these determined characters had more to do with their own story evolution than any concerted effort on my part. Still, just like my characters, I do so hate to admit not being entirely in control. Especially of my own creations.

"Now then." Valentina sipped her tea, her gaze sliding around the circle of women as she smiled in a pleasant manner. "What else did you want to know about men?"

To be continued . . .